A HELLION AT THE HIGHLAND COURT

THE HIGHLAND LADIES BOOK NINE

CELESTE BARCLAY

OLIVER
HEBER
BOOKS
GNARLY WOOL PUBLISHING
EST 2011

0 9 8 7 6 5 4 3 2 1

Published by Oliver Heber Books

❀ Created with Vellum

"My tongue will tell the anger of my heart, or else my heart concealing it will break."
~*The Taming of the Shew*, William Shakespeare

As the adage goes, sometimes those least deserving of love are the ones who need it most.

Happy reading, y'all,
Celeste

SUBSCRIBE TO CELESTE'S NEWSLETTER

Subscribe to Celeste's bimonthly newsletter to receive exclusive insider perks.

Have you read *Leif, Viking Glory Book One*? This FREE first in series is available to all new subscribers to Celeste's monthly newsletter. Subscribe on her website.
Subscribe Now

Have you chatted with Celeste's hunky heroes? Are you new to Celeste's books or want insider exclusives before anyone else? Subscribe for free to chat with the men of Celeste's *The Highland Ladies* series.
Chat Now

THE HIGHLAND LADIES

ONE

"That's thievery, my lady!" The irate merchant glared at Lady Laurel Ross as she turned her nose up at a bolt of wool.

"It's thievery to pretend this is your finest Highland wool," Laurel mocked. They stood in the market just outside Stirling Castle. Laurel had experienced the same negotiations countless times over her decade-long tenure as a lady-in-waiting to Queen Elizabeth de Burgh. A daughter of the laird of Clan Ross, Laurel had never been anyone's fool, and she didn't intend to become one now. "You will not convince me that Clan Ross produced such quality, mercer."

"But I swear to you it is," the portly middle-aged man asserted. "Have I not sold you other lengths of the finest-quality fabric?" Laurel watched as beads of sweat dotted the merchant's forehead. She'd haggled with him a few months prior, and she knew he wasn't speaking a falsehood that he'd sold her well-made material in the past. However, what lay before her most certainly hadn't been produced by any spinner on her father's lands.

"So why now do you try to pass this off to me? I paid you well the last time. Yet you still insist this is fine Highland wool.

It is not. And you think me a fool to boot," Laurel argued. "I shall take my business elsewhere, and I shall warn all hither and thither that you are a schemer and a knave, mercer." Laurel narrowed her eyes at the man, irritated that he insisted on an exorbitant price. She wasn't opposed to buying the wool, but she would do so at the price she named. "The price of my silence is five shillings per yard and not a penny more."

"But—but—that's thievery, my lady," the perspiring merchant repeated, stammering.

"So you've said. Make your choice now, or I—" A voice that in equal parts relieved her and made her wary interrupted Laurel.

"What trouble are you causing the mon, sister?" Montgomery Ross asked as he wrapped his arm around his younger sister's shoulders.

"My lord," came the response. The merchant's eyes widened to unbelievable proportions as he took in the Ross plaid wrapped around Monty's waist and pinned over his shoulder.

"Aye. You have the right of it now," Laurel said as she shifted the attention back to her negotiations. She wished to be through with her purchase, so she could speak to her newly arrived brother in private. "What shall it be? Five shillings a yard, or my crowing from the rooftops?"

"How many yards did you say you wanted at five shillings apiece, my lady?" the rotund merchant conceded.

"Eight, if you please," Laurel sniffed. She would make certain the man understood she wouldn't have the wool pulled over her eyes, literally or figuratively.

"As you wish." The wool merchant set about cutting the length Laurel requested while she turned to look at her brother. The man's aggrieved sigh made Laurel's lips twitch. Monty's coppery hair matched her reddish-blonde tresses, but while she considered her features unremarkable, Monty's visage was a work of art. While he had the build and power of any trained warrior, his face was almost too pretty for a man. She supposed it suited his character.

"How did you know it wasn't any of ours? You haven't been home in years," Monty whispered.

Laurel ran her finger along the edge of the freshly sheared wool and turned over a corner. Threads poked through that would soon unravel. While it wasn't well spun, it would serve her purposes. "Shona and her daughters would never make such errors and send this to market."

"That is true, and Mother would have an apoplexy if she knew someone was trying to pass this off as ours. What made the mon think you wouldn't ken?"

"Did you not see his reaction when you walked up? He didn't know I was a Ross. I never wear our colors while I'm at court. The last time I wore one of our plaids was the last time I visited Balnagown three years ago."

"Visited?" Monty cocked an eyebrow.

"You know it hasn't been home since Myrna convinced Mother and Father to send me here." Laurel swallowed a lump in her throat she was certain was easily the size of her fist. She'd arrived in Stirling nearly eleven years earlier as an unwilling lady-in-waiting. Her younger sister had strategically suggested that becoming an attendant at Robert the Bruce's royal court would improve Laurel's chances for finding a husband. The strategy had been to remove Laurel as potential competition to marry Padraig Munro, since both families wished for an alliance. Myrna fancied herself the next Lady Munro and had gone to extreme lengths to enact her plan, making their parents banish Laurel to the depraved wilds of court and attempting to ruin the marriage the king decreed between Padraig and Cairren Kennedy, a former lady-in-waiting.

Arriving alone had terrified Laurel, her father having sent a contingent of warriors with her but no family. She'd felt abandoned, and even though she'd made a home for herself at court, she still felt the same as she had when she was five-and-ten years old. Monty grimaced, then offered Laurel a sheepish frown before lifting the newly cut and rolled wool from the merchant's stall. Laurel paid the man with a self-satisfied smile and a cocked eyebrow. She narrowed her eyes at the smaller man as she leaned forward and whispered, "You'd do well to remember that while I may be a lady, I barter like a Lombard, you crooked-nosed knave."

The merchant could do little more than stand and blink rapidly as Laurel straightened. He wasn't wont to argue with the noblewoman any more than he had, but he chafed at the insult. She might have been right that his claims were ridiculous, and he *was* classless, but the comment smarted. However, he was used to Laurel's ruthless business acumen and viperous tongue. He chided himself for his foolishness, and Laurel cast a smug gaze over the vendor before turning to walk alongside Monty.

"How have you fared since last I was here, Laurel?" Monty asked.

"The same as always," Laurel demurred.

"Miserable," Monty responded.

"Not miserable so much as fed up. But I may as well pick out my burial plot since I shall be here till the end."

"Still prone to exaggeration. The Highlands haven't left you."

"But I've left them far behind," Laurel muttered. She'd had the same internal battle countless times. She longed for the wide open, rugged land where she'd grown up, but she didn't wish to return to a family that rarely thought of her. Her brother was the only member of her clan who she saw with any regularity besides the guards assigned to her detail for years on end and her loyal maid. She sympathized with the men trapped at Stirling Castle, but her arguments that she didn't need her clansmen fell on deaf ears with her father. It was the only condition he set for her while she resided at court. Besides ensuring she was protected when she left the castle, her parents cared not what happened. They'd abandoned their hope of her making a suitable match, just as they'd abandoned her.

"Then why not snag yourself a Highlander at court and return," Monty suggested with a shrug.

"Would that it be so easy to escape Sodom and Gomorrah," Laurel snapped. "Who wants the penniless lady-in-waiting?"

"You are hardly a pauper, Laurel," Monty disagreed.

"Have you brought the chests of coin and silver for my dowry then?" Laurel countered. Her initial excitement at her brother's arrival had rapidly turned into wariness. She turned a withering glare on Monty. "Och, dinna mind me and ma Highland exaggeration, brother. There's nae chests of aught for me." Laurel adopted an accent she'd rarely used in her time at court. She'd lost her brogue within a day of arriving when she realized she faced little but condemnation from the Queen's other ladies, who mostly hailed from the Lowlands.

"That's not true, Laurel," Monty hedged, but Laurel's intensifying glare made him stop. They'd reached the gates of Stirling Castle, so Laurel reached for the fabric Monty still carried. But he refused to relinquish it before he made amends. "Will you dine with me this eve? Will the queen allow it?"

"Aye. I can dine with you," Laurel agreed with a jerky nod. She always longed for the familiarity and comfort of Monty's visits, but it was more a longing for what she wished could be, rather than what existed. She knew she wouldn't be through the first course before she wished to escape. Monty only served as a reminder that she was only a Ross in name since she had so little knowledge of what happened day-to-day at Balnagown. She drew the fabric from Monty's arms and strained to kiss his cheek. "Is Donnan with you?"

Monty recoiled before narrowing his eyes at Laurel. "You know that he is. I never travel without my second."

Laurel shook her head with a resigned frown. "You know I

5

consider him as much my brother as I do you. When will you believe I don't care?" Laurel didn't wait for her brother's response, instead turning toward the keep's entrance and disappearing.

TWO

Laurel hurried through the passageways until she reached her chamber. She kept an eye out for the other ladies, not wanting anyone to see she carried the fabric herself. It wasn't unusual for a lady-in-waiting to order fabric from a vendor, but it wasn't often that they left the market with it themselves. Most women would have their purchases delivered, but Laurel hadn't the coin to offer a page, nor did she want to make her guardsmen carry it. It wasn't often that she purchased goods at the market, but she enjoyed browsing. She'd parted with her hard-earned coins that morning because she needed a hardier gown for the approaching winter months. The one she'd worn for the last five years was nearly threadbare, and she'd repurposed it as many times as she could. Since she shopped that day, she'd foregone the veil and plain kirtle she usually wore when she attempted to blend into the crowd. Her gown that day was hardly up to courtly standards, but it was finer than what she donned when she went to sell her Opus Angelicanum and embroidery. She was one of few Scottish women who knew how to stitch the intricate style so highly sought in England and Europe.

Laurel slipped through the door of her chamber, relieved that once again she didn't have a roommate. She supposed there were a few perks to being one of the most senior ladies-in-waiting in the queen's entourage. The last person to share her chamber had been Madeline MacLeod over the summer. The royal couple had summoned the former nun-in-training to court just before she was to take her final vows. Encountering Madeline in the passageway had been one of the greatest shocks Laurel had ever experienced. They'd once been friends of a sort. Madeline was the former ringleader of Queen Elizabeth's attendants, and she'd risen to that position through manipulation and intimidation. Laurel arrived at court only months after Madeline, and she found a kindred spirit in some ways. Madeline's haughtiness matched Laurel's bitterness. When Laurel let slip a well-guarded secret about Monty, Madeline seized the opportunity to force Laurel's support as Madeline ran roughshod over various members of court, most conspicuously Madeline's future sister-by-marriage, Maude Sutherland.

Laurel opened her chest and lifted several kirtles out of the way before retrieving the Opus Anglicanum collar that was her current project. She hid the just-purchased woolen fabric in her chest and moved to the window seat. She would have a couple of hours to finish the collar's intricate pattern and slip back to the market before the evening meal to sell her own fine embroidery. She considered how many times over the years she'd made this same clandestine dash, and how often she felt the secret satisfaction of seeing women at court wearing her creations, none of them the wiser that Laurel made them. She rued having to be in trade, but with no allowance coming from her father anymore, she had no other coin. Her father had ceased her allowance nearly five years earlier, around the time Madeline first left court, arguing that he was saving the allowance for her dowry. As the fourth of five daughters, and the only unmarried one, there was little left for her dowry.

Laurel's father was the Earl of Ross, so they were hardly a poor clan. Her father had spent an exorbitant amount on the dowries of her first three sisters due to the alliances their marriages made; her younger sister Myrna's dowry had been incentive for the groom to take her. As a result, her father was overly cautious about spending needlessly. He considered the monies he paid for her chamber and the food she ate, along with her maid and guardsmen, to be enough to sustain her. He refused to consider the expenses Laurel faced to be properly attired as a member of the queen's court. Ever resourceful, Laurel had put to good use the hours upon hours of tedious stitching her mother insisted she practice.

Unbeknownst to all but a few, Laurel was her own dressmaker. She cut and sewed every garment she owned, often changing hems, cuffs, and collars, or adding and removing ribbons or other notions to make her older gowns appear brand new. The money she earned from selling her needlework, along with several prête-a-porté gowns. These ready-made kirtles enabled Laurel to clothe herself fashionably and to afford the various extravagances the other ladies indulged in.

Laurel discovered early on that to stand out at court in any way invited ridicule and gossip. Even though she and Madeline had struck up a friendship of sorts, Laurel wasn't free from Madeline's judgement and scathing comments. Madeline learned that Laurel's tongue was just as sharp as her mind, so they rarely crossed swords. But when they did, the other ladies were quick to repeat all that they heard. The price of peace and her family's reputation meant Laurel did what she could to blend in. It only added to the bitterness she clung to as a buoy against the consuming sadness she'd experienced when she left home. The court knew Laurel for her shrewishness; ironically, many considered her shallow for her style and what appeared to be an ever-new rotation of gowns. Only Madeline and Cairren knew the lengths she went to for her clothing.

At five shillings a yard, that was forty shillings, or two pounds. That's a far sight better than spending ten pounds or more on a gown. I have plenty of thread to last me at least three kirtles, nae considering what

I have for the embellishments. If I can have the gown made within the next sennight, then I can cut down ma old one. I can make what's salvageable into smocks for the children at the almshouse, and the rest can be rags for ma courses. I'll need to add fur cuffs and a hem to the new gown to keep the wool from fraying. At least it's sturdy.

Laurel examined her work as the late morning sun flooded her chamber. She sat beside the window embrasure to see her stitches, but she'd sewn the same pattern so many times, she was positive she could do it while she was half asleep. She was fairly certain she had done so more than once. She needed the income she would earn from the three gowns she had stashed away at the bottom of her wardrobe and the embroidery she'd finished the night before. The money would pay for the gowns she needed for Christmas and Hogmanay. She still had several months, but she knew the merchants would increase their prices.

I shall look for Simon to sell the cuffs to this time. Samuel's got a loose tongue that he flaps far too often. He nearly told Sarah Anne that the handkerchief she was buying came from me. The smarmy bitch is worse than Madeline ever was. Who could have known? How am I going to get the three kirtles to the haberdasher without crumpling them horribly? Why do I keep doing this? Two fit in ma satchel without too much concern, but three has it bulging at the seams. After all this time, ye'd think I would learn. That's how Cairren found out in the first place.

Let me finish this before the midday meal, then I'll join the other ladies in the queen's solar until she retires during the prince's midafternoon sleep. I can slip out to the market then and be back before dusk. Monty is likely with the men anyway, so I willna need to avoid ma guards. I can be back in time to dress for the evening meal. Right then, lass.

Laurel may have ridden herself of her Highland burr when she spoke aloud, but in her mind, she would forever be a Highlander.

I'm going to bluidy well murder this wretch. I swear, if he tries to haggle me down one more penny, I shall reach across the counter, snatch him by his scruffy collar, and shake him till his teeth fall loose.

Laurel gritted her teeth as she listened to the condescending prattle the haberdasher spewed as he spoke to Laurel as though she were a peasant. She wore her plainest kirtle and covered her hair as though she were a matron, a veil hanging to her chin to disguise her face. She was careful not to sound like a lady, but not so much that she might accidentally sound like a Highlander. Like courtiers, the residents and merchants of Stirling would perceive being a Highlander as worse than a being Lowland peasant. For all that the non-Highlanders claimed Stirling was the gateway to the Highlands, it was far more like the Lowlands. And that included believing all Highlanders were savages. She knew her brother's arrival that morning had sparked the merchant's acquiescence as much from the plaid he sported as his towering height and brawny arms. The massive two-handed broadsword he carried only fueled the notion that Highlanders were savages bent on running men through.

Drawing herself back to the present, Laurel nodded as the man droned on and on about how he could only accept the best-quality craftsmanship since ladies from court frequented his shop. It was the same monotonous routine each time she came. Drawing herself up to her full height, she raised her hand and shook her head.

"Enough. I haven't the time nor the patience to continue listening to the same prattle you repeat every time I come to sell a gown. You know I am an expert seamstress, and you know the ladies who purchase these gowns pay ridiculous prices for them. You don't need to examine every stitch as though I intend to cheat you. Pay me the fair price, and we can be done." Laurel drew in a breath and looked down, waiting for the real negotiations to begin. The haberdasher would offer an insultingly low price, and she would counter with an absurdly high one. They would go back and forth,

Laurel collecting the gowns and pretending to leave, and finally the man would relent to the price Laurel always wanted.

"I don't think I shall buy any more from you."

Laurel slowly raised her eyes to meet the man's face, completely unprepared for this turn of events. She swallowed as she reined in her temper. Taller than the average woman, Laurel stood nose-to-nose with this merchant, unlike the one she'd towered over that morning. The veil obscured her expression, but her tone was quite clear. "You shall regret that. My sister is a maid to a fine lady at court. I shall tell Mary aboot this, and she shall tell her lady, and her lady will tell everyone. You shall be out of business before the sun sets."

"No, I won't," the man sniffed. "I don't believe you have a sister who is a maid. If you did, then why aren't you employed in the castle as well? Why not be a seamstress for one of those high-and-mighty ladies you boast aboot?"

"Because I don't need to wait on anyone else. I sew and sell as I please. And right now, it pleases me to leave and take my gowns with me." Laurel folded the kirtles and moved to place them in her satchel before she paused. "By the by, my sister's employer is Lady Laurel Ross. Are you familiar with her?"

"The Shrew of Stirling?" The merchant took a step back as he alternated nodding and shaking his head. Laurel stifled her grimace, hating the moniker. She knew she'd earned it, but she'd dulled her sniping and criticizing over the past five years, and she wished she could redeem herself enough that no one continued to call her the Shrew of Stirling. But she wouldn't hold her breath.

"Aye, that be the one," Laurel nodded. If she had to live with the infamy, she would use it to her advantage.

"You wished for sixty pounds." The shop owner nodded several times before pulling forth a chest that rattled with coins inside. "You shall rob me blind, but it's better than Lady Laurel showing up on my stoop or ruining my business."

"That it is, mercer. And it's hardly a plight to cry aboot when you ken you'll make twice, if not thrice, that when you sell them. It is I who should bemoan being swindled. In fact, I think this shall be the last time we do business. I prefer Duncan four shops down. He barely speaks and pays without question. Aye, that is who I shall take my gowns to henceforth."

"Nay!" The man's already-ruddy face turned scarlet, and Laurel knew she was now in the sole position of power to negotiate. No merchant who traded with her could afford to lose her business; all realized that she never tossed out empty threats. "I—I—will give you eighty pounds for the gowns, if you will return."

"One hundred, and I will consider it," Laurel closed the satchel, then crossed her arms. It was an obscene amount for a seamstress, but Laurel knew from experience that the man would sell her gowns for forty pounds apiece. She frequented the stores dressed befitting her status to keep an eye on the patrons and the prices the salesmen requested. This would leave the shop owner with a profit, but it was far less than he desired. But one hundred pounds would ensure Laurel wouldn't have to sew quite so much or quite so quickly to prepare for the upcoming Christmas, Hogmanay, and Epiphany expenses. As the man trembled, she lifted the satchel from the counter, but the haberdasher's hand shot out.

"Very well."

Laurel watched as the man opened the lid of the chest. When he attempted to use the lid to shield the coins he counted, Laurel shifted to see. She kept a running count in her head as the man stacked the coins, having given up trying to hide them from her.

"Ah-ah," Laurel shook her head as he made to close the lid. "You're no dalcop, so don't be an eejit. That's eighty pounds, six shillings that you've counted out." Laurel made a gesture for him to reopen the chest. "I made an offer, and you accepted it. Do you intend to renege? Are you little more than a gillie-wet-foot?"

"I am no swindler!"

"Then pay me the agreed-upon amount," Laurel insisted. The door opened behind her, and several feminine voices carried to her. Laurel's stomach tightened into a knot, recognizing them as belonging to a handful of ladies-in-waiting. She wondered why they were in town so close to the evening meal, when most of the merchants would be packing up their shops in the market. She needed to hurry if she was to make it to the other merchant.

"I have customers," the haberdasher hissed. "Give me the gowns and take what I offer. Then be gone with you."

Laurel didn't budge. She knew the ladies wouldn't recognize her, since they would never imagine Laurel would dress so plainly. Laurel waited, but the man didn't intend to pull out more coins. When he made to step around her, Laurel flipped open her satchel and turned to the young women.

"Ma ladies," Laurel greeted them, infusing her natural burr back into her accent. "Ye must be from the castle," Laurel gushed.

When the women turned toward her, their disgust at the Highlander brogue plain on their faces, she pulled the first gown from her bag. She held it up beside her, twisting it from side to side to catch the sunlight on the embellishments. She took a tentative step forward and lowered her chin.

"I canna say the three kirtles I have are so fine as what ye wear," Laurel demurred, despite recognizing two of her own creations in the group. "But I am newly a widow, and I must sell ma wares to feed ma weans."

Laurel didn't flinch when the haberdasher released a stream of curses that made the young women titter. She felt no remorse for her scheme. If the man hadn't attempted to shortchange her, assuming she didn't know how to count as high as one hundred pounds, she wouldn't have taken such delight in the tale she was spinning.

"The mon here quoted me a price, then tried to fool me by nae paying what we agreed upon. Is that how they be here in Stirling?"

"Nay," Lady Sarah Anne Hay stepped forward, wearing one of Laurel's designs. As the leader of the younger ladies-in-waiting, Laurel had known she would insist upon being the first one to inspect the gown. "The stitching is quite fine."

Laurel bobbed a shallow curtsy, "Thank ye, ma lady."

"Such a gown would easily sell for fifty pounds," Lady Sarah Anne said as she fingered the material. "How many did you say you have?"

"Three, ma lady." Laurel laid the gown over her forearm as she pulled out the next one to several oohs and ahhs. The gown was finer than the first one she'd shown the group. She watched as several women ran their fingers over the velvet and whispered to one another. When she felt the excitement crescendo, she presented her *pièce de résistance*. The satin and velvet gown was a deep amethyst hue with Opus Anglicanum along the hem and train of the skirts, and embroidery covered the bodice. This was the gown that merited the price she'd demanded.

"This is exquisite," Lady Margaret Hay, Sarah Anne's older sister, murmured. "Even Lady Laurel doesn't have something so fine."

Of course she doesnae. She sells any gown this extravagant. To this day, I dinna understand how nay one realizes that they see me in the same five kirtles season after season, year after year. All I do is change out the ribbons and laces. I suppose the different embroidered patterns helps. But still. Daft lot they are.

"I shall take them," Sarah Anne announced.

"Them, ma lady?" Laurel infused surprise and uncertainty into her voice.

"Aye. One hundred and sixty pounds is what I'm willing to pay for the three," Sarah Anne announced. Laurel's stomach flipped in excitement. She knew the amount was more than most serfs saw in a lifetime, and it was more than any of her clansmen were used to seeing. But the Hays had a long-standing reputation at court, and it was rarely for the better. Sarah Anne and Margaret's uncle had once tried to abduct Deirdre Fraser to carry out a proposed betrothal. Deirdre's husband, Magnus Sinclair, had ridden to her rescue, and Archibald Hay died for his scheming. It had been a scandal that rocked the court not long after Laurel arrived.

Sarah Anne loosened a pouch of coins from her girdle and handed it over to Laurel, who shook it and weighed it in her palm. She pulled the strings apart and peered into the small sack. Just as she suspected, there was far more than the amount Sarah Anne offered.

"Are ye certain, ma lady? That is a small fortune ye're offering me," Laurel said.

Ignoring Laurel's questions, Sarah Anne squinted at Laurel, as though she would try to see through Laurel's veil. The material was so thick that it was difficult for Laurel to see through it at times, but it completely obscured her features. "Have you more such as these?" Sarah Anne asked.

"Nae at the moment, ma lady. But I can," Laurel hedged.

Sarah Anne nodded twice before reaching for the gowns, which she dumped in her sister's outstretched arms. Laurel couldn't help but think how similar Sarah Anne and Margaret's relationship was to how Myrna had once treated Laurel herself. But Laurel wasn't interested in observing the sisters or continuing a conversation. She dropped into a deep but purposely wobbly curtsy and slipped from the shop without looking back.

This will last me through autumn. It'll last me through winter and into the new year if I'm frugal.

The relief that washed over Laurel was nearly palpable. She'd been growing desperate as of late. She'd had plenty of trade, but many of the merchants who frequented Stirling only came in the summer months. The leaves were beginning to change, and Laurel feared she wouldn't have enough stashed away before she was forced to rely on merchants such as the haberdasher, a Stirling resident. Just as she had that morning, she hurried back to her chamber where her maid, Ina, helped her prepare for the evening meal. Laurel knew that Ina was aware of Laurel's sewing, since the woman had seen Laurel's handiwork appear on her own gowns countless times, but they agreed via mutual silence never to discuss it.

Ina Ross had known Laurel since she was a babe and chose to remain her maid, even after Laird Ross offered Ina the chance to return to Balnagown. Laurel tried to show Ina her gratitude, but it still surprised Laurel that she had remained after the way Laurel treated everyone upon her arrival at court. While she supposed Ina's loyalty was grounded in pity, Laurel accepted the only reliable link she had to the Highlands. With a last glance in the looking glass, Laurel squeezed Ina's hand before making her way to the Great Hall.

THREE

Laurel smiled warmly at Donnan, the man who sat across from her and beside Monty. Donnan and Monty had been inseparable since they were children, so it surprised no one when Monty named his fellow warrior as his second-in-command. Laurel's gaze shifted to Monty before returning to Donnan, then gave both men a warning glance when their shoulders brushed against one another. As the meal progressed, Laurel enjoyed the banter between Monty and Donnan, and she recognized the ease with which they teased. But when they both reached for the same chalice, and their hands overlapped for a moment too long, Laurel shot them a speaking glare before her eyes darted to the other men at the table.

Laurel had discovered Monty and Donnan together when she was thirteen, and they were eighteen. She'd been out for a ride, telling her guards that she would easily catch up to her brother, who she'd seen leave with Donnan. To this day, she counted her blessings that she'd ridden into the woods on her own. She'd spied them in a passionate kiss that made her yank her horse to a stop. The animal reared and threw her. The couple broke apart and raced to help Laurel, but all she could do was stare at them until air finally filled her lungs again.

They helped her to her feet before exchanging a private glance. Laurel still remembered the conversation they'd had.

"Dinna act surprised," Laurel tsked. *Monty and Donnan stared down at the young Laurel, who shook her head and patted both young men on the chest. "We have three married sisters, Monty. I've walked through the Great Hall at night. I ken what happens between couples."*

"Laurel," Monty gasped.

"Dinna fash, Monty. Though I would recommend ye each pay a little more attention to the lasses if ye wish to keep everyone else fooled. I only reined in Teine *because I thought to leave without interrupting. I suppose he didna appreciate that,"* Laurel said as she patted her chestnut gelding, aptly name Fire for his coat.

"Ye ken?" Donnan asked, his face ashen, and his voice trembling.

"I figured out there was something different between ye years ago, but I didna understand it until Sorcha married. She actually likes her husband, so I've seen how they look at one another. I've seen ye two looking at each other the same way when ye think nay one is watching," Laurel explained. *"This just confirmed it."*

"And ye arenae running for the hills?" Donnan pressed.

Laurel shrugged. "At least two of ma siblings are happy. Morag and Sileas despise their husbands." Laurel shrugged again. *"Mayhap one day I'll be as lucky as ye two."* She nudged her chin in the men's direction.

"But, Laurel, ye canna say aught," Monty pressed.

"Who would I tell? I dinna want either of ye stoned or burned or run through. Monty, I like ye most of the time, but I like Donnan all the time. I'd rather neither of ye die," Laurel said philosophically. *Both men gawked at her, their initial panic over.*

"Do ye think anyone else kens?" Donnan asked.

"Nay. At least nae that I ken. But ye're bluidy lucky I convinced Andrew and Alex nae to ride out with me. Ye canna be doing this so close to the keep. Canna ye go on patrol together?"

Donna and Monty looked at one another again, both releasing deep sighs. Monty pulled his sister into his embrace and kissed her crown. "Can ye truly keep this a secret, Laurel? Can ye truly be all right with this?"

Laurel pulled away from Monty and smiled. "I dinna understand it,

20

and I dinna want to ken how it——" Laurel pursed her lips and furrowed her brow. "Works. But I told ye, I'm glad that ye're happy. If it's with Donnan, then that must be what God planned."

"Most would say we are unnatural," Donnan mused quietly.

"And most are miserable with their husband or wife," Laurel countered. "But Monty, what—what will ye do when ye must marry?"

Laurel watched as both men's faces transformed into matching expressions of despondency. Monty shook his head and closed his eyes. "I have little choice that it will happen one day. But I shall wait as long as I can."

"Just be careful," Laurel warned.

Laurel inhaled deeply as she looked up from the food she'd been picking at while she remembered discovering the secret that could ruin her clan. It was a secret that she'd let slip once in a roundabout way. And it had been to the worst person possible: Madeline MacLeod. It had been the piece of information that Madeline suspended over Laurel's head to coerce her into anything. Madeline threatened to expose Monty, so Laurel felt compelled to do whatever Madeline dictated. She'd never felt more relief than when Madeline's brother, Laird Kieran MacLeod, dragged her out of the Great Hall while she spewed curses at him. When Kieran relegated Madeline to a priory known as the "island of old women," Laurel had finally felt free. She and Madeline never mentioned Monty and Donnan's secret during Madeline's brief return to court that summer.

But as Laurel watched the two warriors, she wondered if anyone else suspected their relationship. They were still breathing, so she assumed they'd learned to be discreet at Balnagown. At court, if they were circumspect and perhaps added a woman into their liaison, few would speak out unless pressed. Still, Laurel could not help worrying about the couple.

"Which tavern are you off to this eve?" Laurel asked softly. She prayed her brother didn't name The Merry Widow, the most notorious alehouse in Stirling, so named for all the women from court who conducted their dalliances there. It was also the one where Monty and Donnan would draw the most attention. Both men were charming and exceedingly handsome, making women flock to them. They avoided committing to any liaisons, often pretending to pass out drunk in the main room rather than retire to a chamber with a woman.

"The Crosspool Tavern," Monty responded. Laurel breathed a silent sigh of relief. Monty named the most respectable inn within the town limits. It was a lively establishment, and while wenches were available to entertain men, they weren't as aggressive as at The Merry Widow, The Picked Over Plum, and The Wolf and Sheep. Monty, Donnan, and the other Ross men could drink in peace. Those who sought company would find it, but when Monty and Donnan didn't, no one would consider it odd.

"Would you care to join us?" Donnan asked with a grin. Just before Laurel left Balnagown for Stirling, the men discovered her in the stables consoling herself with a jug of whisky. They thought to teach her a lesson about the dangers of the potent *uisge beatha*, or water of life, but it had been Laurel who taught her brother and his lover a lesson. She'd been fall-down drunk by that night, but she'd also woken with a clear head and calm stomach, while Monty and Donnan could barely face the day well after the noon meal. The men also discovered she had a ribald sense of humor when intoxicated.

"I shall have to pass," Laurel said with a pretend scowl.

"Then we shall have to have a round or ten on your behalf," Monty chuckled.

"You do that, and I'll look for you in the lists in the morn," Laurel taunted. "Neither sword will be up for much." Snickers from down the table told the trio that the other Ross warriors understood Laurel's innuendo, even if they didn't understand what it meant between Monty and Donnan.

"My wee sister has a devilish tongue," Monty grinned.

"Only a fool makes the same mistake ten times over, and I

believe you're at nine," Laurel said archly. "Then again, you can't teach an auld dog new tricks."

"I have a few tricks that serve me just fine." Monty waggled his eyebrows, to which Laurel rolled her eyes.

"Aye, and they're naught but tuppenny-ha'penny," Laurel snorted. Monty's scowl turned real as the other men howled with laughter. Donnan may have grinned to not stand out, but his eyes darted nervously between Monty and Laurel. She'd insulted Monty's manhood, or at least what he could do with it, in front of a score of Ross warriors.

"You'd do well to learn a trick or two, sister. You might catch a husband," Monty snarled. Laurel's eyes narrowed, knowing she and her brother had both gone too far, but only Monty's barb held truth.

"If it pays well," Laurel mockingly shrugged. "Then neither you nor Father would need to spare me another coin. I could die of the clap before either of you have to pay a dowry." The table sat in stunned silence as Laurel spoke in even tones, no hint of jest in her voice. She locked eyes with Monty and stared.

"That isn't what I meant," Monty muttered.

"Aye. You'd rather I capture a husband by crook or by hook to get a bride price for me. Either way, I wouldn't be a Ross anymore. We all long for the day." Glances darted back and forth between the siblings as the men at the table shifted uncomfortably. Laurel only spoke aloud what had been whispered about her, but it was entirely different for it to come from the lady herself. Laurel glanced down at her trencher and realized they'd made it to the third course before she wished Monty hadn't arrived. They'd remained on civil terms longer than she expected.

"Mother and our sisters would never speak that way," Monty glowered. "You've been at court too long. But I suppose when you lie down with dogs, you get up with fleas."

Laurel's eyes widened as she stood from her seat, casting a glance at Donnan, who sat in shocked silence. "And yet you

23

wish me to be a bitch in heat. There's more than one way to make a scandal in this family," Laurel warned.

"Laurel," Monty rose too. But he was at a loss for words, since he could see his sister no longer threw out an empty threat. He realized, as he saw the depth of pain in Laurel's eyes for the first time, that she hadn't exaggerated how miserable she was at court. She'd been his favorite sister when they were growing up, but he'd scoffed at her bitterness when their parents forced her to live at court. He thought she'd accepted her life, since she'd mellowed over the past few years. But he saw now that Laurel was reaching a point of desperation, and he didn't doubt she would cause a scandal to be sent away. And he suspected she would do it of such epic proportions that their family would never welcome her back at Balnagown either.

"Dinna fash, brother. I'm nay one's problem but ma own," Laurel said as she stepped over the bench. She moved toward the doors of the Great Hall, but a page stopped her.

"Lady Laurel, the king and queen request you join them in their antechamber," the young boy informed Laurel.

"Now?" She glanced over the boy's head to see the royal couple was no longer on the dais.

"Aye, my lady," the page said before turning away. Laurel drew in a deep breath before making her way back across the Great Hall, having no choice but to pass her clansmen. She didn't cast her eyes in their direction, and she ignored Monty as he called out to her.

"Where are you going?" Monty asked as he fell into step alongside her. "Your chamber is in the other direction."

"I told ye, dinna fash, brother," Laurel muttered.

"Laurel, please," Monty begged.

"The king and queen have summoned me. Go away."

"Both of them? Do they do that often?" Monty wondered.

"Do you fear this shall be the scandal? That I'll insult our monarch? Or perhaps you think I should practice those tricks in a *maynage?*" Laurel snapped quietly. "One partner would be enough for me. I'm not the one who needs two."

"That's not fair," Monty whispered.

"Welcome to life at court, Montgomery. None of it is fair. Go away," Laurel ordered. But it was too late. They were already at the doors to the antechamber, and a guard opened it for them. The king and queen looked in their direction.

"Join us, Montgomery," King Robert commanded. The siblings entered and showed their deference to the Bruce and Queen Elizabeth with a curtsy and bow. The tension crackled between them, but they were accustomed to hiding their thoughts and feelings. Their expressions appeared relaxed while neither felt that way.

"It is well timed that your brother attends court, Lady Laurel," King Robert addressed her. "This shall save me sending a messenger. Lady Laurel, how long have you been in service to my wife?"

Laurel swallowed but kept her gaze upon the king. Queen Elizabeth knew exactly how long Laurel had been one of her ladies-in-waiting, as did the king. But he would force her to admit to her prolonged tenure.

"Eleven years, Your Majesty," Laurel spoke clearly.

"That is how long Elizabeth Fraser was at court. Of course, she arrived as a child with her parents. Her service to the queen did not span that entire time," King Robert mused. Laurel didn't need the king's observations to make her feel like a crone. "You are the queen's most senior lady-in-waiting, Lady Laurel."

"Yes, Your Majesty," Laurel responded after there was a lull.

"I shall come to the point, Lady Laurel," King Robert announced. "The time is overdue for you to marry. Your friends have wed, and yet you remain. I understand your unsubstantial dowry is part of the cause." King Robert left unsaid what all four knew—Laurel's temperament and reputation were the other cause. "None of the younger ladies may marry until you do."

"Your Majesty?" Laurel glanced between King Robert and Queen Elizabeth. "I must marry, so the others might, too?"

"Aye. Yours will be the next wedding. Once you are married, the other ladies may move forward with their courtships," Queen Elizabeth spoke up. Laurel felt as though the air that entered her nose lost its way to her lungs. Her heart thudded behind her breastbone and spots danced at the corners of her eyes.

"Who do you wish me to marry, Your Majesty?" Laurel struggled with each word.

"I do not have a groom chosen. Since Montgomery is here, I thought to leave the task to him," King Robert said dismissively.

Queen Elizabeth stepped forward, concerned by Laurel's wan pallor. Laurel's eyes filled with tears, but she blinked them away. When the queen reached for Laurel's hands, Laurel realized they'd gone ice cold. Just like the rest of her, just like her heart. They would marry her off in haste to a man desperate enough to take a bride who came with little invest-ment. She wondered what manner of man he would be. Anger and fear waged a tug-of-war within her chest.

"I will ensure it is a mon who will treat you kindly, Laurel. It won't be a mon who will abuse you or only look upon you to bear him sons," Queen Elizabeth pledged quietly.

"Thank you," Laurel mumbled.

"Perhaps you wish to retire," Queen Elizabeth suggested.

"Yes, please, Your Grace," Laurel whispered. She dipped into another low curtsy before backing away. She didn't look at Monty before turning to the door, but she sensed he followed her again. Once they were in the passageway, Monty grasped her elbow and pulled her to a stop. She swung around, ready to bare her teeth, but when her older brother's arms opened to her, she fell against his chest. She sobbed for every failed dream she'd had over the past decade, for every mistake she'd made along the way, and for the fear that consumed her.

"Laurel, I don't take this duty lightly. I will do my best to find you an honorable mon to marry," Monty said as he held his trembling sister. "If I can't, then I will smuggle you away. I'll take you wherever you wish to go, and I will make sure you are safe."

"There's nowhere to take me, Monty. The king decreed I will marry, so I shall. It matters not to whom, so find someone, and you can leave. Have done with it and return home to inform Mother and Father I am no longer their problem," Laurel said as she pulled away.

"Why do you insist upon saying you're our problem or that we don't want you?" Monty demanded.

"I've been a lady-in-waiting for ten Christmases, Monty. Of those, I've been at Balnagown for two. Besides my guards and Ina, no Ross has ever been here for Christmas. When Father arrives here, it's often days before he seeks me out. He refuses to do more than pay for my chamber and food. What does he think I wear after five years of no allowance? I haven't been to Balnagown in three years, and then the last time was only for a fortnight when Sorcha died." A fresh round of tears began when Laurel thought of the sister who'd been born between Monty and Laurel, who had died giving birth to a stillborn daughter. Laurel had returned to her clan for the impending birth and left in deep mourning.

"How do you have such fine clothes, Laurel?" Monty's brow furrowed. "Are you doing what I suggested? Is that how you have fine clothes? If you're not a maiden, you must tell me."

Laurel jerked away from Monty and crossed her arms. "It's far worse than that, Monty." Her laugh was hollow as she watched her brother's horror. "I'm in trade."

"What?" Monty stammered.

"There are at least a dozen women in the Great Hall at

27

this very moment wearing gowns I made. I'm a seamstress. I sell gowns that I make and embroider, so I have the coin to pay for all the ridiculous and unessential items I'm expected to have here. I wear the same gowns for years on end, changing the embroidery, ribbons, and embellishments. But they're still the same pieces of material, taken apart and refashioned. Who do you think pays for the gifts I give my guards and Ina at Epiphany? Who do you think buys the extra mugs of whisky and ale for the men at Beltane? Who ensures Ina has clothes that aren't threadbare after eleven years of service here? Who pays for my soaps? Who pays for the wool for my stockings or the linen for my chemises? My jewels? All paste. Before I realized I could sell the clothes I made, I sold my jewels."

"But why didn't you ask Father for more, explain to him why you needed an allowance?" Monty asked.

"You really must think I'm addlepated if you think I didn't ask—beg—for at least what I needed for the others. I've asked through missives. I've asked when he's been here. I've asked you to ask him!"

"But I didn't know you were going without proper clothes. Are you making a gown to sell from that wool you bought today?" Monty wondered.

"No. I need that for myself. My sturdiest gown is wearing too thin for another winter. I have fur trim I've been saving that I can use to hide the wool's flaws."

"Why did you go to that vendor? Why not buy better quality?"

"Because I can't afford better, Monty. Do you not understand? I sneaked out of the keep this afternoon and went back into town. I wear my oldest and plainest clothes and cover my hair and face with a veil when I go to sell my wares. I sold three yards of needlework and three gowns today. If I'm careful, the money will last until the new year. I won't have to sell aught else, but I also can't buy aught other than essentials. I must save most of it for Ina and the men."

"Father pays your guards and your maid," Monty reminded her.

"And forces them to remain prisoner here. They are away from their families for all the holidays. The men have no chance to marry while they're assigned to me. Ina has stayed out of pity. What Father pays the men won't even shod a horse."

"I didn't know, Laurel." Monty shook his head and put his hand over his heart when Laurel cast a loathing glare at him. "Truly."

"You see the ledgers. You've been here enough times to understand what life is like here."

"Aye. I have, to both. Father has been very frugal, but Laurel, there is a dowry for you. I promise. I don't know why Father has refused your requests for essentials, but I know he has put aside the allowance he used to send. It's part of the dowry."

"If the dowry is so healthy, then why hasn't he found me a husband? Why hasn't he told me, so I might pursue a marriage in good conscience?" Laurel shook her head. "It matters not. You're stuck with the Shrew of Stirling to marry off in the next fortnight, or however briefly you're here. If anyone wanted me, they would have asked Father already."

"Then what do you want to do, Laurel? Where do you want me to take you?"

"Where is there to go? A convent? I doubt Uncle Hamish and Aunt Amelia will swing the doors open wide for me after the way I treated Maude," Laurel pointed out. Her aunt was her father's sister, but the families hadn't been close while the cousins grew up. And Laurel was already miserable and bitter when Maude and her sister Blair arrived at court. Laurel had begrudged the sisters their relationship and how often their father and their brother Lachlan visited. She'd been just as unkind as Madeline and Cairstine Grant had. But both Madeline and Cairstine had mended their ways and were happily married.

"Do you wish to be a nun?"

"Hardly," Laurel snorted. She'd barely noticed that they'd started walking until they stood outside her chamber door. "I'm sorry this duty has fallen at your feet."

"Laurel, stop." Monty embraced her again. "I don't begrudge the king's decision that I find you a husband. I don't appreciate being rushed, but I would like to see you settled and happy."

"I'm sorry aboot what I said earlier," Laurel confessed.

"I'm sorry too," Monty said with a kiss to his sister's forehead. "Will you be all right?"

"I always am," Laurel shrugged as she opened her chamber door. "Goodnight, Monty."

"Sleep well, Laurel."

She doubted she would, but she appreciated the sentiment. She donned her nightgown and climbed into bed to say her prayers. The day had been too eventful for her, so despite her fears that her mind wouldn't settle, Laurel was soon asleep.

FOUR

The hairs stood up on the back of Laurel's neck the next evening as she entered the Great Hall. Heads swiveled and eyes bore into her as she moved toward the table where she usually sat with Blythe and Emelie Dunbar. Their older sister Isabella had once been a lady-in-waiting, but she'd married a Scottish man raised to be an English knight. They now lived among the Sinclairs, distant relatives to the Rosses through marriage. As she drew closer and more whispers rippled through the diners, she feared Sarah Anne or one of the other ladies from the day before had deduced she was the seamstress who created the gowns Sarah Anne bought.

"None of us will ever marry if we must wait for her. Our wombs will shrivel like prunes, and our hair will turn gray, and our teeth will all fall out before anyone takes her." Laurel heard each word as she drew closer; Sarah Anne did nothing to lower her voice.

So word has already spread. What the hell did Monty do last night?

"Laurel," Blythe waved her over, sliding down the bench from her sister to make room for Laurel. She tried to stifle her bone-weary sigh, already too tired to play along with the courtly intrigue. Neither Dunbar sister nor Laurel spoke until the first course was served. Blythe kept her voice low, "The queen mentioned you would likely marry soon. When Lady Catherine asked when, the queen couldn't give a day. So Lady Margaret asked who you were marrying. The queen admitted that the mon hadn't been chosen, but it would be soon since there would be no other weddings until after yours. Is it true that none of us can marry until you do?"

Laurel flinched, but nodded her head. She looked away in search of her brother. She found Monty watching her, sadness and guilt in his eyes. She wondered what he'd said and to whom while drinking the night before. It was clear the gossip had spread among the women and the men, so her shame was complete.

"My brother will see to a betrothal, but it will be soon," Laurel hedged. Emelie and Blythe sensed they would get no more from Laurel, so their meal continued in awkward silence among the friends. It meant Laurel heard the rumors more clearly. Her head pounded by the time the music began and servants cleared away the tables. She watched as Monty approached, but another man stepped in front of her brother at the last moment.

"Good evening, lass." The man's breath smelled like onions, and Laurel fought not to curl her nose. "I'm Laird Ogilvy's cousin. Shall we dance?" The odiferous man didn't wait for Laurel's answer, pulling her into the crowd that was forming lines for a country reel. Laurel thanked the heavens it was a dance that would make them switch partners often. When they partnered, the man asked her age, how regular her courses were, whether she was a maiden, and asked to see if she had all her teeth.

"I shalln't ask you any questions since I can already smell you're a bilious and gaseous coxcomb. Your mouth is as fusty as your arse. If you wish to examine teeth, bed down with your horse." Laurel pulled away and spun around to find everyone in earshot listening. Heat suffused her cheeks as she looked around, spying hands pressed against mouths in shock while others did so to keep their voices from carrying. Laurel walked toward a set of doors she knew would force people to step aside. Her humiliation was excruciating, but she wouldn't slink away. She held her head up until she entered the passageway. She found Monty and Donnan already waiting for her.

"What did he say to you?" Donnan demanded, looking over her head at the closed door.

"Naught of importance," Laurel dismissed the question.

"Laurel, what did he say?" Monty pressed.

"He asked how old I am, whether I'm soiled, if I bleed regularly, and he asked to see my teeth," Laurel whispered.

"I'll kill him," Monty declared.

"Don't be ridiculous. He asked naught that most prospective grooms wouldn't. I'm six-and-twenty and of middling looks. I may have been taken aback, but I don't have a right to be offended. My future husband will want to ensure there is naught wrong with me since I'm well past my prime. I spoke without thought."

"Laurel, those were not appropriate questions, and he did not have a right to ask them," Monty disagreed. "I'll speak—"

"Nay, you won't," Laurel interrupted. "Maybe you won't consider him, but you have to consider someone. I've made enough of a scene. Making a bigger one will only prolong your search. I'm retiring now, and I shall plead my courses in the morn. It will give me an excuse to remain out of sight and reassure potential suitors that I can breed."

"Laurel?" Donnan spoke up. "I'll marry you."

"What?" Laurel and Monty spluttered.

"I'll marry you. You can come home, and since you already know aboot Monty and me, and since he's your brother, he would be welcome in our home without question," Donnan explained. Laurel stood mute as she considered what her friend offered. She could see the merits of his suggestion, but one thing stood in the way.

"What aboot when I never provide you with children? You will live not only with the shame of having the Shrew of Stirling as your wife, but you'll also live with the pity people will give you for being married to a shew who's barren."

"We—we could—" Donnan stuttered. Laurel shook her head and smiled sadly.

"You shouldn't both have miserable marriages. I would do it if I thought it would make both of your lives easier, but it won't. People will talk more and pay more attention to you, Donnan. Even if we had a cottage where you and Monty could meet, people would still talk aboot us. I thank you for your offer. I know you do it out of kindness." *And pity.*

"Laurel, we'll sort it out. I promise," Monty swore. He hadn't a clue how he would go about it, but he would ensure Laurel married a man he trusted and respected. Unfortunately, he didn't have time to scour the Highlands for a man who would meet his expectations. He would have to settle for a Lowlander, which made his heart ache for his sister even more.

"Thank you both," Laurel mumbled before hurrying to her chamber, only to toss and turn that night.

❦

"What do you think?" Monty asked Donnan over the rim of his mug. They'd returned to the Crosspool Tavern after watching Laurel flee down the passageway.

"I don't ken, to be honest. I still think you both should consider my offer. I can protect her from your family and give her a home where she'll be treated well."

"But can you give her bairns? Do you wish to?" Monty asked.

"You ken the answers to both of those. Aye, I can, but nay, I don't wish to. But if that's what she wishes, if it would make her happy, you ken it doesn't mean aught else changes," Donnan reasoned.

"I ken that, and I ken Laurel would understand too. But she won't agree. She's right that people would talk. You wouldn't be able to protect her from that, and if she doesn't have your bairns, it will only make things worse for her. You'll be pitied, but she'll be scorned."

"And if we said it was my fault?" Donnan pressed.

"Do you love her?" Monty asked, unable to keep the edge from his voice.

"Of course I do. But only the way that you love her. She's as much a sister to me as she is to you. And I fear for her. I fear she will marry a mon she despises, and he'll beat her for her loose tongue. You ken I would never harm Laurel."

"I do. I shalln't say never, but there must be another option before it comes to that."

The men turned as the door swung open, and a contingent of Campbells walked into the inn. The Campbells were one of the most powerful clans in Scotland. The Rosses, Sutherlands, Sinclairs, and Mackays dominated the northern Highlands, but the Campbells claimed much of the southern Highlands as their own. They'd fought alongside the Bruce from early on, and they'd been generously rewarded for their loyalty. In the king's highest favor, the Campbells expanded their territory, bumping the MacGregors off their land and claiming it for themselves. Members of the laird's extended family served among the king's closest advisors, and they held the finest suites at Stirling Castle.

Monty and Donnan exchanged a glance as they waited to see who led the Campbells that night. They both breathed easier when they recognized Laird Brodie Campbell of Glenorchy, leader of the largest cadet branch of the clan. He was a more even-tempered man than his father had been, and while he was as ambitious as the previous laird, he was more diplomatic. He'd come to his position later than many other lairds, already well into his thirties, but he was as active and agile as he'd been when he was a young man. His swordsmanship was renowned, and few who underestimated him on the battlefield lived to tell the tale. He was a few years older than Monty and Donnan, but the three men were well acquainted.

Monty raised his mug in salute when Brodie caught sight of the Rosses.

"Campbell," Monty greeted Brodie.

"Ross, what're you doing in this neck of the woods?" Brodie grasped Monty's forearm in a warrior handshake before doing the same with Donnan.

"We're having another spat with the Mackenzies over land the bluidy bastards keep trying to claim," Monty explained. Seeing Laurel hadn't been his original reason for the journey, but he was glad that he was present, lest the king choose a husband for her.

"Have you been here long?" Brodie wondered as he looked around, accepting a mug of ale from a wench who winked at him. Monty and Donnan watched as he took no notice of the woman, looking weary from his own journey.

"Not even two days," Monty answered.

"Just enough time to get into trouble?" Brodie grinned.

"Not this time," Monty chuckled. The men moved to a table, and another woman brought a bowl of pottage to Brodie. He handed her coins but didn't look at her. Monty observed, curious why a man as attractive and virile as Brodie took no interest in the serving women. He could have gone to court and had food sent to his chamber; instead, the Campbells came to an inn. It struck Monty as odd. He'd known Brodie long enough to have seen the man had a healthy and genuine appetite for the opposite sex. "What have you been up to of late?"

Brodie sat back and looked around. Dark circles cast shadows beneath his eyes, but he was alert to those around them. He leaned forward once more. "There was an incident recently that I need to make the king aware of." Without saying more, Brodie returned to his pottage. When he finished the bowl and the heel of bread that was served with it, he shook his head and sighed. "People will hear of it soon enough. I married Eliza MacMillan a fortnight ago."

"A newlywed!" Monty crowed. "No wonder you look exhausted, mon."

"She's dead."

"What?" Monty stared at Brodie before glancing at Donnan.

"The marriage to Lady Eliza meant my clan would increase our lands along Loch Sween. Since the MacMillans have supported the Bruce since the beginning and the MacMillans' land sits between two parts of Clan Campbell's territory, the marriage made sense." Brodie sighed and ran his hand over his face, closing his eyes for a moment. "We had the wedding, but the lass was very young."

Brodie gave Monty and Donnan a pointed look, and the men knew Brodie meant she was little more than a child compared to Brodie. He hadn't bedded her, so it was little more than a betrothal, but the couple exchanged vows within a kirk.

"We were on our way to Kilchurn when David Lamont attacked. Eliza panicked and tried to ride out of the fray rather than remaining in the circle. She spurred her horse through my men as they fought, and David Lamont took her head from her shoulders before my eyes." Brodie looked down at his empty trencher, reliving the attack for the umpteenth time since it had happened. He could see Eliza's terrified expression, could hear himself yelling to her not to move. He could smell her blood in the air as David held up her head and threw it at Brodie. It had horrified him that David would attack Eliza, who was clearly more of a girl than a woman. But guilt plagued him that he didn't feel guiltier about her death. He regretted it since she'd been a sweet lass, but he didn't feel any significant loss. And he was certain he should have.

"Why did Lamont target you? Are they still bitter that the stand they made with the MacDougalls of Lorne did naught to stop the Bruce becoming king?"

"Aye, there's that. But they also don't want us to increase

our holdings, especially since it will diminish their influence along the Cowal peninsula and the Firth of Clyde. They sought to end the alliance, and they succeeded," Brodie scowled. "I have the MacMillans up my arse, and rightly so. The Lamonts aren't satisfied with killing an innocent girl, and the Bruce expects me to provide more men to fight against the MacDougalls. Bluidy bleeding hell."

"Sounds like you're deep in the shite," Donnan mused.

"Aye. You'd think my eyes were brown for how deep I'm in," Brodie huffed. "Before I go before the Bruce in the morning, I decided a hot meal without prying eyes would put me in a better mood."

"A willing woman helps, too," Monty said before taking a long draw from his ale. He watched Brodie's reaction, but there was none.

"It'll ease your mood," Donnan suggested.

"I'd been prepared to set those days aside when I married. I find I'm not in such a rush to return to them," Brodie frowned.

"How old was Lady Eliza?" Monty wondered.

"Four-and-ten," Brodie answered.

"Plenty of other men would have seen that as a fine age for a bride," Monty pointed out. "Both of my aulder sisters were married close to that age and had their first bairns within a year of their wedding."

Brodie didn't respond. He couldn't admit that bedding any female young enough to be his daughter made him feel ill. And he couldn't admit that Eliza's plain face and grim expression had done nothing to entice him. When he remained quiet, Donnan asked, "How long did you plan to wait?"

"At least two years," Brodie replied.

"Two years of living like a monk?" Monty chortled. "That doesn't sound much like you, Brodie."

"Maybe I grew up. I am nearly forty," Brodie retorted. "Anyway, what brings you to Crosspool? I would think you would prefer a rowdier tavern if wenching is how you pass your time."

"Nay," Monty responded without hesitation. "We're not interested in getting the pox from a Stirling whore."

Brodie glanced between the two men, his eyes narrowing for a flash when Monty answered for himself and Donnan. *He didna say neither of us. He said, "we." Interesting.*

A group of courtiers arrived, already intoxicated, curtailing the three men's conversation. They watched as the men staggered in, waving to Monty when they recognized him.

"Run away from your sister, have you? Tongue like a silver blade, she has," one courtier babbled. "Did she cut off your cods like she did Ogilvy's?"

"Are your bollocks as big as your sister's?" A second drunk man clapped the first one on the shoulder as they both laughed. Brodie looked at Monty and Donnan, waiting for them to defend Monty's sister. Brodie had a vague memory of Laurel, remembering her distinctive hair color more than anything. He leaned forward when neither Monty nor Donnan spoke up.

"Leave it," Monty whispered.

"Looks like Lady Laurel cut off your tongue and your bollocks, Ross," the first man chortled.

"Oliphant, enough. Your breath stinks from here," Monty mused and wafted his hand before his nose. Monty watched Liam Oliphant, cousin to Laird Oliphant, drag a chair over to their table. He wanted to groan when Liam's companion, Nelson MacDougall, joined him. Monty feared a fight might break out between Nelson and Brodie from the sneers and mocking looks Nelson cast Brodie.

"Shouldn't you be searching down every rabbit hole for some unsuspecting sod to marry your sister?" Liam asked. "I'd wager a hundred pounds that you can't find a mon in all of Scotland willing to take on the Shrew of Stirling."

Brodie ignored Nelson and listened as Liam continued to

insult Laurel, with Monty refusing to take the bait. Brodie drained his whisky thrice in the time Nelson and Liam spent antagonizing Monty and Donnan, and neither Ross men became riled. Brodie felt the effects of the whisky despite the pottage, since he'd already had several drams as he and his men approached Stirling. He'd considered it fortification at the time, but now he merely felt sleepy. The droning conversation around him only made him want to seek a bed—alone.

"Sounds to me like the woman needs taming," Brodie mused before hiccupping. Four sets of eyes turned toward him, all with speculative gazes. Brodie shook his head. "I didn't say I was offering. I just made an observation."

"Someone needs to marry the lass. Otherwise, no one else will be married," Liam grumbled.

"What?" Brodie asked in confusion.

"King Robert decided that none of the other ladies can wed until Laurel does," Monty said, keeping his voice low. But he knew there was little point, since plenty of people overheard Liam and Nelson.

"Aye, your bitch of a sister is keeping every woman's dowry hostage, and she doesn't even have one of her own," Nelson spat. Monty and Donnan pushed back their stools, but Brodie—despite being two-and-a-half sheets to the wind—was faster. He grasped Nelson around the neck and shook him.

"The Rosses are more patient and forgiving than I am. I would have beaten you already if you'd been discussing my sister. You go too far, MacDougall," Brodie warned.

"Not so far as to cleave her head from her shoulders," Nelson taunted. "You couldn't protect your bride with your sword. What makes you think your words will do any better?"

Brodie reared back and drove his forehead into Nelson's face, blood spraying from Nelson's nose. "That does," Brodie grunted. He released Nelson with a shove. The man stumbled backward into another table, nearly upending it. Angry shouts followed as Nelson was knocked, unconscious, to the floor.

Liam Oliphant didn't look in his friend's direction, keeping his attention on Brodie instead. "Would that it was so easy to tame Lady Laurel as you did Nelson MacDougall."

"Are you suggesting I should beat a woman?" Brodie asked. His voice was deceptively quiet. Monty and Donnan, along with the Rosses and Campbells, cringed.

"I'm saying, I wager one hundred pounds that you couldn't even get Lady Laurel to marry you, let alone live under the same roof long enough to beat her," Liam said.

"And why on earth would I take such a bet?"

"Because you don't have a wife, but you need one. It saves you having to look, since the last time didn't turn out so well," Liam chuckled. "And you would be doing every lady-in-waiting a good deed to by taking Lady Laurel away."

"No," Monty shook his head. "My sister is not to be wagered over."

Brodie felt the effects of the whisky suddenly slam into him once more. He sank back onto his stool and turned bleary eyes to Donnan. "Why don't you marry the lass?"

"I offered. She wouldn't take me," Donnan responded.

"So she does have good taste," Brodie laughed. He turned his sleepy eyes toward Monty. "Just how bad is she if Oliphant here is certain he won't be parting with a hundred pounds?"

"One moment you defend her, and the next you insult her." Monty stood, Donnan and the Ross guardsmen following suit. "You're no better than these two. I thought more of you, Brodie."

"And are you stuck not marrying either?" Brodie asked.

"What? Laurel marrying has naught to do with when I marry," Monty said with a furrowed brow.

"Your clan needs an heir after you. You have a duty to beget one," Brodie pointed out. Monty sensed Donnan tense, and he fought not to shift his weight.

"I do not need to marry any time soon. It won't be before my sister."

"And at the rate she's going," Liam chimed in. "It'll be

winter in hell before anyone marries."

"I'm not forcing my sister to marry anyone," Monty shook his head as he stepped around the table, prepared to make his way back to the castle. He and his men had overstayed at the Crosspool Tavern.

"What if I could convince her?" Brodie suggested. "What if I could tame the Shrew of Stirling and bring her to heel? I like a challenge. Besides, I need a chatelaine for my keep, and my clan needs a lady."

"No," Monty and Donnan responded together while Liam crowed, "Yes."

"One hundred pounds says you can't make Lady Laurel agree to marry you in the next fortnight," Liam slapped his hand on the table.

"I will not make my sister marry you. She must decide for herself," Monty warned. His conscience nagged that he shouldn't consider trading his sister in a wager, nor agreeing with a drunk man to marry her. But outside of this night, he knew Brodie to be an upstanding man. He knew Laurel would be safe and well cared for–perhaps even loved–if she married Brodie. It would satisfy the king and Laird Ross. "Only if she falls in love with you and agrees on her own."

"Fair enough," Brodie stuck out his arm, and Monty paused for a heartbeat before clasping Brodie's forearm.

"I shall be two hundred pounds richer," Liam remarked. "Neither of you will convince Lady Laurel to accept Campbell's suit. I expect timely payment."

"Nay," Brodie corrected. "I never accepted your wager, and neither did Ross. My agreement is with the lady's brother, not you. You shall be neither richer nor poorer. You have naught to do with this agreement."

"But—" Liam objected.

"I am not doing this for a wager, Oliphant," Brodie interrupted. "I am curious whether I can woo such a woman. But I will not force her to marry me. And I will not bet on her like our courtship is a cockerel fight." *Bluidy bleeding hell.*

FIVE

Brodie woke to a roiling stomach. He rolled onto his back and opened his eyes, vaguely recalling his arrival at Stirling in the middle of the night. Flashes of memories floated through his mind. He recalled meeting and sitting with Montgomery Ross and his second, Donnan, until two other men joined them. Brodie squeezed his eyes shut as he tried to remember who they were.

Shite. Liam Oliphant and his lapdog. Brodie pressed his fingertips to his forehead and yelped. *That's why ma bluidy heid aches. I bashed Nelson MacDougall in his ugly mug. Why did I do that? Och, he insulted Ross's sister. Laurel. Strawberry blonde hair. I remember her from the last time I was at court, and the time before that, and the time before that. But I also recall her reputation. What did I agree to last eve? Something to do with Laurel. I hope whatever it was, wasna an insult to Monty or Laurel.*

Brodie rolled out of bed and swallowed the bile that threatened to come up. He hadn't drunk more than he usually did, but he admitted that he'd been running on far less sleep and food than was his norm. He'd ridden back to Castle Sween with Eliza's body. He'd endured her wailing mother and sister and suffered her father's threats and grief. All the while trying to muster tender feelings, which he believed a

43

husband should feel toward his dead wife. But there were none. It felt as though he'd heard in passing of a stranger's death. He even wondered if drinking enough might make him feel something more than ambivalence. But the guilt that rushed forward when he drank wasn't for Eliza's death or his role in it. It was guilt because he didn't feel guilty about her.

Brodie glanced back at the bed and considered going back to sleep, but he knew he would do better if he got out to the lists and trained with his men. He would sweat the alcohol from his system and clear his mind of his troubles, focusing on keeping his own head on his shoulders. Once he dressed, he made his way to the armory, where he claimed his claymore before going into the lists. Several heads turned in his direction as he spied his men across the field and made his way to them. He eyed them suspiciously as they looked at him uneasily.

"What?"

"Laird, people are talking aboot it already," Graham, his second, spoke up.

"Talking aboot what?" Brodie looked around.

"Aboot how you're going to marry Lady Laurel," Graham answered. Brodie froze. The rest of the events in the tavern flooded his mind. He'd asked Monty how horrible his sister really was and suggested that he could tame her, as though she were a wild animal. He recalled Monty telling him it had to be Laurel's choice, that he wouldn't force her if she didn't love Brodie. He hadn't a clue how to go about making a woman fall in love with him.

"I will offer my suit and see if Lady Laurel will allow me to court her," Brodie corrected. He leaned toward his men. "Does anyone else ken that Oliphant tried to make it a wager?"

"I don't think so, Laird." Graham cast a surreptitious gaze at men from several clans watching them. "I think they're stunned that you are willing to woo her. I don't think anyone

44

has heard that one hundred pounds were offered up against you."

"Ye'd do well to hope Lady Laurel doesnae ken," Michael, a junior guardsman, pointed out. "It'll be more than just her tongue that lashes out at ye." The younger man's grin fell when Brodie cast a dark look at him.

"Let me be clear right now, and you can set straight anyone who wonders. If Lady Laurel becomes Lady Campbell, it's because she wants to of her own free will. I've already had one bride forced to marry me. I won't have another. I won't trick Lady Laurel or deceive her."

"But ye have to make her fall in love with ye," Michael persisted. "I thought ye only wanted a wife to run the keep."

Brodie ground his teeth. Michael wasn't wrong. The only reason he'd agreed to marry Eliza when he did was because his mother had passed three years earlier, and he desperately needed a woman who could be his chatelaine. He would need Laurel to fall in love with him, or at least like him enough to marry him. He thanked the heavens he hadn't been so foolish as to agree that he would love her in return. He'd been honest a moment ago when he said he wouldn't trick or deceive Laurel.

"Enough clishmaclaver," Brodie barked. "I didn't come out here to discuss marriage and wives. I came to train with my men."

Brodie spent the rest of the morning sparring alongside his men, but his mind wandered to what little memory he retained of Laurel. He knew she was beautiful and was intelligent, since her sharp tongue surely reflected her sharp mind, but he knew little else than that. He wondered when he would have a chance to approach her. He needed to meet with the king above all else, and he couldn't dawdle in Stirling. He didn't trust the Lamonts not to attack his clan again. He would have to be efficient in his courtship, and that was only if he decided he wished to pursue Laurel. Brodie retired to his chamber for the afternoon as he considered his potential marriage and waited for the king to summon him.

⚓

"We shall all be dead before anyone wants her," Margaret Hay whined as the women strolled through the queen's gardens during their morning constitutional. Margaret spun around, pointing an accusing finger at Laurel. The lady-in-waiting began her complaints when she was certain Laurel could hear. Any sympathy Laurel experienced for Margaret as the downtrodden sister to Sarah Anne ended with Margaret's tirade. "It's so unfair."

"And it's unfair that God wasted a pretty face on an empty head," Laurel retorted, wishing her excuses had worked with the Mistress of the Bedchamber. She'd listened to several of the ladies complain as they left the keep and made their way to the rosebushes. Queen Elizabeth led her entourage, disinterested in the younger women's conversations. Laurel walked alone, not in the mood for company. But she regretted shooing the Dunbar sisters away, since now she had no way to ignore Margaret.

"At least I am pretty," Margaret sneered.

"And just as empty-headed as I said," Laurel snorted. "A sharp tongue is the tool of a sharp mind, Maggie. Having just a pretty face means the Lord got bored when he made you. He lost interest just like—how many has it been—four men now."

"At least I have suitors," Margaret snapped.

"Suitors wish to marry a woman. Not a one thought aboot marrying you, *Maggie*." Laurel stressed the diminutive that Margaret loathed. She'd claimed only maids were named Maggie.

"What are you saying?" Margaret demanded.

Laurel grinned. "While neither of us has suitors clamoring

at our doors, the difference between us is I haven't lifted my skirts." Laurel snorted again. "Or dropped them."

"You—you— *Tu es une puterelle*," Margaret snarled, switching to French to accuse Laurel of being a woman of ill repute.

"Your French is horrid. '*Tu es*' is you are. You meant '*je suis*.' After all, I'm not the one who keeps buying chicken's blood from the butcher."

"Why you—" Margaret's words died as Queen Elizabeth turned toward them.

"Ladies," Queen Elizabeth's tone stopped the women from continuing their argument. Laurel dipped into a deep curtsy while Margaret wobbled on unsteady legs.

"Your Majesty," Catherine MacFarlane spoke up. "When will Lady Laurel wed? My father wishes me to marry before the first snow. Will my wedding be delayed?"

Laurel sucked in a breath. The ladies had been loudly whispering their accusations since they left the keep, but Catherine voiced the question they all wished to ask, even Laurel.

Queen Elizabeth looked at Laurel as she addressed the women who gathered around her. "Have you ever seen a fox caught in a trap? It hisses and snaps at anyone who comes near, even those who try to help. Why? Because he's ensnared and no longer free, no longer trusts what is around him. The fox will chew his own leg off rather than be a captive. But the fox eventually succumbs whether he remains in the trap or alone in the woods. When a kindly soul comes along, the fox would do well to wait and watch. He might just gain his freedom with far less pain."

Laurel swallowed and gave a single jerky nod. While several other women chatted amongst themselves, trying to sort out the queen's metaphor, Laurel understood its meaning. But she feared she'd been in the snare so long that there were no kindly souls left who would risk her hissing and snapping.

But Sarah Anne's voice pierced any solace Laurel might have found in the queen's words.

"But that still doesn't tell us when Laurel will be gone." Sarah Anne narrowed her eyes and curled her lip in disgust as she looked at Laurel. "After more than half a score of years here, isn't it obvious she'll be a spinster? Why punish us?"

"Lady Sarah Anne, is there someone proposing to you soon?" Laurel asked in a saccharine tone. She held her hands over her chest in mocking delight and excitement.

"Well, no," Sarah Anne confessed. "But it's still not fair."

"On that we agree," Laurel muttered. Queen Elizabeth turned away, and the women continued their promenade through the late summer blooms. As they made their way across the bailey to retire to the queen's solar, Laurel noticed a mountainous man with dark hair watching the ladies. It was clear he was a Highlander from the plaid wrapped around his waist and his billowing leine, but Laurel wasn't close enough to make out the blue-and-green pattern. He could have been from any number of clans, but she thought she recognized him. He walked away before she drew near enough to tell.

"Laird Campbell of Glenorchy," King Robert greeted Brodie. The men had fought alongside one another countless times over nearly two decades, and Brodie had saved the king's life on at least three battlefields. But the king could say the same about Brodie. They'd been friends since their youth, even though the king was a handful of years older than Brodie. The king's younger brothers were closer in age to Brodie. He'd had more than one adventurous night out in Stirling with the Bruce's blood-brother and adopted brother, both named Edward. The latter was married to Elizabeth Fraser and had a passel of children, and the former died only recently, three years after being crowned the High King of Ireland.

"Your Majesty," Brodie responded with a grin. "You're looking younger by the year."

"And you—" King Robert snorted "—don't."

"You wound me, my liege." Brodie took the seat offered to him, and Robert the Bruce settled into the one beside him.

"The queen and I were sorry to hear aboot Eliza." Robert watched Brodie, whose expression barely shifted once the grin slipped away. "I understand why you seek remedy to the harm done to your clan and the MacMillans."

"But?" Brodie didn't care for how noncommittal Robert's tone sounded.

"You've admitted that you never consummated the marriage. You've already returned the dowry. The MacMillan has a stronger leg to stand on than you do, Brodie."

"And the alliance that we were supposed to form? The access and lands I was to receive? I'm not to be aggrieved aboot that?" Brodie demanded.

"You don't need the land," Robert reminded him.

"That doesn't mean it wouldn't have benefitted my people," Brodie countered.

"You sound like your father."

"He was a fine mon," Brodie murmured before looking away. His father died several years ago, but he'd been among the king's closest confidants, and while Brodie hadn't often agreed with his father's policies toward their neighboring clans, there had been respect between them. He'd turned his head not to hide grief, but to hide his annoyance.

"He was. But didn't always know when to accept that he had enough. You have all Glenorchy now. The MacGregors have little left to claim as their own. Must you expand to the south as well?"

Brodie remained quiet, choosing to believe it was a rhetorical question, knowing the king wouldn't appreciate his answer. Robert frowned but nodded.

"The Lamonts will make restitution to you, but you will have to accept the lost dowry and land."

"I can live with that, Robert," Brodie said, keeping his voice low. "What I can't live with is the Lamonts believing they can cross onto my land and attack my people. We were nowhere near their border. They were nearly two days' ride onto my territory. This wasn't some reiving that went badly. They attacked to kill me and Eliza. They won't be satisfied with trying to end my alliance with the MacMillans. If aught, it's strengthened it. But what aboot the next time I try to bring a wife home?"

"Do you have someone in mind?" King Robert asked.

"I'm considering it, but I haven't made any offers," Brodie hedged.

Robert studied Brodie for a moment, and Brodie dreaded what would come of the king's cagey expression. "Do you intend to find a woman here at court?"

"Possibly."

"None may marry until Lady Laurel Ross is wed. Had you heard?" King Robert pressed.

"Someone or other made mention of it," Brodie nodded.

"Someone or other made mention of you marrying the lass." Robert's face split into a grin, his ruddy cheeks pressing deep grooves around his eyes. "I don't ken if you're the lad up to the task. She's a right hellion."

Brodie shrugged. "I like challenges." He forced himself not to look back at where he'd spotted Liam and Nelson pouring over documents when he walked in.

"Ohh-ho-ho. A challenge. That's being kind. Are you aware of what they call her?" Robert laughed.

"Aye. The Shrew of Stirling. I dinna care for it," Brodie snapped, his burr slipping through. He didn't know why the moniker bothered him so much. He wasn't ashamed or even embarrassed that he might marry the woman to whom it belonged. He did find the challenge appealing. He felt sorry for Laurel more than anything else. "You've kenned the Rosses since the very beginning. They're connected to the Sinclairs and Sutherlands like a bluidy spiderweb. You must have met Lady Laurel before she came here."

"Aye," Robert sobered. "She was a sweet lass. She had the bonniest smile and the brightest eyes. But that was a long time ago."

"And why did she change? Did something happen to her?"

"Aye. Court happened to her." At Brodie's look of confusion, the king clarified. "Unlike many women, Laurel didn't want to come to court. The fine gowns and expensive tastes didn't interest her. She wanted to remain in the Highlands, but she had three aulder sisters who married and took princely dowries to their husbands' clans. Her parents thought coming to court would improve her chances of finding a wealthy husband who wouldn't need such a large dowry. The court was rife with speculation about her, but it wasn't long before the Earl of Ross himself confirmed that Laurel's dowry would be a pittance compared to her sisters'. It shrank further a couple of years ago when Ross paid an exorbitant amount to MacGillivray to marry his youngest daughter after she caused an almighty scandal with the Munros. The Kennedys were prepared to ride on the Rosses and bring most of the Lowlands with them."

Brodie knew much of the story, having heard about how King Robert arranged a marriage between Cairren Kennedy and Padraig Munro. He recalled that there had been talk for years that Padraig would marry Myrna Ross. As best Brodie could remember, Myrna didn't accept the change of plans and did everything she could to keep Padraig from Cairren. In the end, her ploys hadn't mattered. Padraig loved his wife, and she—for reasons Brodie couldn't fathom after what she endured—loved her husband.

"You should ken that Laurel won't come with a large dowry. It's unlikely that it'll be as large as Eliza's," Robert warned.

"The Rosses are not a poor clan," Brodie pointed out.

"Nay, they are not. But any laird who has to pay five dowries is a mon who will worry himself into an early grave."

"Then he should make Montgomery marry and use his bride's dowry to replenish their coffers," Brodie suggested.

"I've said the same more than once," Robert shrugged. "Are you serious aboot considering Lady Laurel?"

"Besides her acerbic tongue, is there any other reason not to?" Brodie wondered.

"None. Like I said, she was a sweet lass before she came here but never wanted to come. Unlike her cousins, Maude and Blair, her family did not help her settle here. Unlike Hamish, Tormud rarely comes to court, and it's not to visit Laurel. Hamish and Lachlan took turns coming to check on Maude and Blair, even traveling together with Amelia. Monty comes from time to time, but they aren't close like they were as children. All the women she once knew have married, but no mon wishes to make a harpy his wife if she doesn't come with a healthy dowry. It's a vicious circle: she didn't want to be here, knowing she had little dowry to offer. It made her bitter and scornful, so no men approach, leaving her even more bitter because she's alone."

Brodie listened in silence as he considered what he learned from the Bruce. He'd suspected much of it from knowing Tormud Ross most of his life. The man was angry with the world for giving him five daughters and one son instead of the other way around. It didn't surprise Brodie to learn that the laird never visited his daughter. He pitied Laurel and made a silent pledge to be patient with her. He would return each jab or taunt with a compliment, and perhaps she would learn that not everyone would disappoint her.

"Brodie?"

"Huh? I beg your pardon, Robert. Woolgathering."

"Aboot Laurel? Have you spoken to her?"

"Mayhap once or twice, but it would have been several years ago. My tastes ran toward a different type of woman— an experienced woman," Brodie clarified lest the king think it was a comment about Laurel's character, "—when I came here more frequently."

Robert nodded. "You have my blessing to pursue her. I'd rather she marries a mon like you than someone else. But I can only give you a fortnight. If she doesn't come around to you by then, I will choose. And I won't promise that it'll be you."

"Aye, Your Majesty," Brodie said as he rose and bowed. He cast his gaze around the chamber and wanted to groan when he spied Liam and Nelson still watching him. Liam's gloating mien and Nelson's smirk made him wonder what they might have overheard. The two meddlers reached the door before he did.

"Does the king wish to enter the wager, too?" Nelson asked.

"There is no wager," Brodie growled.

"But you still intend to subdue your shrew, make your hellion heel?" Liam guffawed.

"Enough," Brodie warned. "You may wish to make a jest of this, but I do not. Do not think to interfere."

"We shall just wait in the stands and watch the tourney begin," Liam taunted.

"Leave Lady Laurel alone. Regardless of whether we suit, regardless of whether we marry, she has my protection. Harm her with word and deed, and you will find the might of the Campbells at your door." Brodie didn't wait for a response, pulling the door open and marching through.

"Poor sod doesn't know what he's in for with her," Nelson mused.

"He'll be ruing the day soon enough. Then he'll be begging us to get him free of her hooks," Liam shook his head before both men turned back to the correspondence they'd been sorting. A missive from Laird Lamont caught their eyes.

SIX

Nay, nay, nay! This canna be happening. Shite.

Laurel looked at the rent fabric of her sapphire-colored satin skirts and wished to cry. She had attempted to remove an embroidered panel from her finest gown, but the material was old and worn. She tugged a mite too hard and done more than split the seam, she'd torn the satin.

Now what? I canna go to the feast in aught less than a gown like this. Today would have to be the Lady Day in Harvest. Why did I join the others for the morning walk? I should have stayed here and worked on the gown despite being told otherwise. Mayhap this wouldnae have happened, or if it did, I would have more time to fix this.

Laurel hurried to her chest and kneeled beside it. She sorted through the various swaths of loose fabric and trim, but she had nothing that would both match and hide the tear.

There's naught for it. I must go into town again. But I didna want to spend the coin. Ye dinna have much choice though, do ye? If ye dinna want Monty or the king picking yer husband, ye'd do well to show yer face and make nice. And ye canna show yer face with yer arse blowing in the breeze.

Laurel stripped out of her day gown and hurried to change into one of her plain kirtles. She poured a few coins into a small pouch, fastening it to the girdle around her waist before she snagged her veil as she shut the lid of her chest. Easing open the door, she peered down the passageway in both directions. With no one in sight, she hurried to the servants' stairs and wound her way through the keep until she reached a door leading to the postern gate. She put her veil on and slipped outside, hurrying across the narrow stretch of the bailey before ducking through the portal. She didn't stop to look around, making her way to Simon, the merchant to whom she'd recently sold her needlework.

As Laurel approached the shop, she glanced up at the sky and estimated that it was just past midafternoon. She would have three hours to make her purchase and repair her gown. The torn satin would be hard to make inconspicuous without several alterations. She wished she had the time to pull it apart and start fresh, but there was no way—even with the amount of sewing she'd done in her lifetime—that she could sew a new dress in a few hours. She breathed easier when she realized she was the only person in the shop.

"Goody Smyth, I didn't expect you back so soon," the shop owner greeted Laurel as she hurried to the counter. She'd chosen a generic name and proclaimed herself a widow years ago to ensure her anonymity.

"I'd like to buy a couple of yards of garnet satin, if you have any," Laurel requested. She forced herself to speak evenly and to take deep breaths. If the shopkeeper, Simon, realized her desperation, he would gouge her.

"I have three yards of this bolt right here," Samuel pointed to the end of the counter. "Would this work?"

Laurel examined the satin, impressed with the quality and the color. Only minutes ago, she'd been panicking that she wouldn't be able to salvage the gown well enough to hide her blunder. Now she grew excited at the prospect of redesigning the kirtle that awaited her.

"This is very nice, Simon. But it might be a bit dear for what I can afford. I only have what you paid me earlier," Laurel said innocently.

"That isn't enough, Goodwife," Simon grew serious, all pretense of charm gone now that he no longer saw a potential sale.

"Have you sold my work already?" Laurel asked as she looked around.

"Aye. You weren't gone five minutes before a lady bought all of it," Samuel grinned, unaware that he'd just fallen into Laurel's trap.

"Then you already have the profit you made from my labors, and I'm repaying you what you paid me. That more than covers the cost of the satin."

"That isn't how it works," Simon argued.

"It is if you'd like to keep making the tidy sum you do from my embroidery. If not, I shall go to Samuel down the way."

The wizened old man glared at Laurel, trying to make eye contract through her thick veil. He threw up his hands and abandoned his attempt. "Very well. It isn't worth arguing with you since you'll outsmart me one way or another. It's best to give in now and have you on your way before you rob me blind."

"I'm glad we could come to an agreement," Laurel chirped. She poured the coins onto the counter as the shop-keeper measured and cut the fabric. Laurel pushed the coins toward him as soon as he finished folding the satin. "Thank you," she called over her shoulder

Laurel stepped into the street and turned back to the castle. She hadn't taken more than three steps when a woman's voice called out before a chamber pot emptied just in front of Laurel. She had the wherewithal to push the brand-new material behind her back, but malodorous sludge splashed down the front of Laurel's kirtle. She released a slew of curses in Gaelic, including one about the woman's grand-mother, that she knew no one understood.

"Cursing the woman's *seanmhair* willna do ye much good since she's likely been dead a score-and-ten years." A baritone voice wrapped around Laurel, the brogue comforting and familiar even if she didn't know who it belonged to.

"Mayhap her grandmother should have taught her to wait a moment before tossing turds at people," Laurel grumbled. She looked up as the woman above stood gawking at her. "In case you didn't understand since you're daft as a brush, I'm 'avin a right cob on. Aye, stand there gormless, having just chucked shite on me."

"I thought no one was below," the woman called down.

"Aye, and do you ken what thought did? He followed a muck cart and thought it was a wedding." Laurel stepped around the fresh pile of refuse, ignoring the deep laughter coming from behind her left shoulder. Laurel huffed and nearly pulled her arms back in front of her until she remembered her gown would ruin the satin. With another aggrieved sigh, Laurel began walking back to the castle. She had no idea how she would sneak back into the keep without leaving a trail of foul odors behind her.

"Lady Laurel?"

Laurel missed a step and pitched forward. With her hands behind her back, she stumbled. Strong hands grasped her shoulders and helped right her. "Thank you," she mumbled before trying to hurry on.

"Lady Laurel," the man repeated. "We both ken I know who you are."

"I'd rather you didn't," Laurel muttered as she continued toward the keep.

"And how do you expect to get back inside looking like you've had a roll in the stables, and not the fun kind?"

Laurel spun around and finally looked at her annoying shadow. Her eyes widened as she took in the dark-haired man from that morning. He was even more colossal than he'd appeared from a distance. She also noticed that he was older than she expected, touches of gray at his temples and flecks of it in his stubble. His dark gray eyes were the shade of pewter.

"Buggering hell," Laurel muttered.

"You have quite a collection of words to describe the situation."

Laurel looked around before turning back toward the keep again, but she waited for the man who was both her rescuer and tormenter to step beside her. She glanced at his plaid and cringed.

"Laird Campbell, I presume," Laurel said.

"In the flesh, lass," Brodie grinned as Laurel's head jerked up. He couldn't see her face clearly, but he could picture her expression. He'd glimpsed her as he left the lists that morning, and he'd found himself wondering what she would look like up close. Now she had the hideous veil obscuring her looks. "Are you not going to ask how I kenned it was you? I suppose you believe no one else recognizes you in that ensemble."

"It's worked for five years," Laurel blurted. "I'm guessing my reputation precedes me, and you can think of few other women who'd be carrying fine satin and cursing a blue streak. Have I entertained you, my laird?"

"Not entertained so much as intrigued," Brodie confessed. "You don't sound like a Highlander except for when you speak Gaelic; then I would never guess you spoke anything else."

"I'm not a Highlander anymore," Laurel whispered. She didn't know why the man caused a gaping chasm to open in her chest, since he wasn't the first Highlander she'd encountered while in Stirling. But despite his ferocious appearance, she'd caught the humor in his voice and seen the crinkle around his eyes when he smiled. The melding of fierce and friendly was how she thought of Highlanders, both men and women, and something about Brodie Campbell made her homesick in a way that her brother and father's visits never had.

"I dinna believe that for a moment," Brodie said, switching to Gaelic. "Ye can never stop being a Highlander. It's in our blood, lass. In our bones. It's the first breath of air we breathe as we come squalling and fighting into the world.

Ye can speak like a Lowlander, and ye can dress like them, too. But ye will never cease being a Highlander, Lady Laurel."

Laurel's throat tightened, listening to Brodie describe just how she felt about her home and the way of life she'd been forced to give up. There'd been other ladies-in-waiting from the Highlands, but like Laurel, they'd all assimilated into courtly life. There were few times that she spoke about what her home among the rugged landscape had been or how much she longed to return.

"Ye dinna need a plaid to tell ye're a Highlander," Laurel smiled. "Ye have the gift of the gab."

"Mayhap, but ye dinna disagree with me," Brodie's grin broadened.

"There'd be nae point, since we ken I'd be lying. There are few places created by God that can be finer than the Highlands."

"Dinna let a Hebridean hear ye," Brodie chortled.

"Or the Irish," Laurel giggled. She caught herself, unfamiliar with the light-hearted sound coming from herself. She couldn't remember the last time she'd sounded so young. But her humor died when she spotted the postern gate. Brodie sensed her discomfort and slipped her arm through his. When she tried to pull away, he patted her hand and shook his head.

"Dinna fash, Lady Laurel. Let me speak. Hand me the fabric, lass." Laurel did as Brodie instructed, and she breathed easier when he tucked it under his opposite arm, keeping it well away from her soiled gown. As they approached the postern gate, Laurel recognized the guards and was mortified. They didn't know who she was beneath her veil, but they certainly recognized her from her countless trips in and out of the keep over the years. "Shh," Brodie soothed.

Laurel expected comments about the stench that clung to her or about her wretched appearance, but with Brodie beside her, the guard at the gate and the ones they passed within the bailey said nothing. Laurel led them to the side door she used and along the passageway to a stairwell. Their booted steps echoed against the bricks, so neither spoke until they reached the floor with Laurel's chamber.

"Thank you, my laird," Laurel said, dipping into a shallow curtsy, all traces of her Gaelic accent gone.

"Back to sounding like Scots, are we?" Brodie whispered conspiratorially as he handed the fabric to Laurel. "Lady Laurel, before you go, I have a question that I've wanted answered since I first saw you."

"Aye?" Laurel said, not bothering to hide her dread.

"Where were your guards?"

Laurel looked around, praying no one heard Brodie say her name. She gasped when he reached toward her face, but he eased the veil back so they could see one another clearly. "I didn't ask any of them to come with me."

"And why do I get the impression that's not unusual for you? Does your brother ken you sneak out of the keep?" When Brodie watched Laurel's gaze shutter, he wanted to kick himself for pressing too soon.

"My brother is rarely here. He knows little of what I do or where I go. Since he doesn't ask, and I don't offer, we're both content," Laurel said archly. "Thank you once more, Laird Campbell."

"Laurel," Brodie reached out but didn't touch her arm when she cast a scathing glare at him.

"You may be a laird, but I didn't give you leave to use my given name. I will scream the bricks down around your ears if you think to do more just because I let you walk with me," Laurel warned.

"I apologize, Lady Laurel. And I didn't mean to be rude or distress you," Brodie replied.

"Distress me? You would have to matter enough for me to care aboot what you say or do for me to become distressed. Good day, my laird." Laurel pulled away.

Brodie groaned inwardly. He didn't want to part with Laurel while she was aggravated with him. It would only make approaching her that evening more difficult. He stepped forward as she took a step back. He held up both hands, nearly touching her arms, which held her new fabric away from her soiled gown.

"Lady Laurel, I seem to be blundering through this," Brodie said sheepishly. "I don't mean offense. I simply wondered because I saw your guards training today. They are diligent and attentive to their surroundings. I don't understand why you wouldn't have them accompany you while you shop."

Laurel stood silently.

"Lady Laurel?"

"Aye?"

"Have you naught to say to that?"

"You hadn't asked a question," Laurel answered archly. "I have plenty to say, but for once, I'm keeping my own counsel."

"Do you not fear moving around the town unac-companied?"

"Clearly I do not."

"You should."

"Dressed as little more than a peasant widow?"

"Why do you dress that way?" Brodie pressed.

"I prefer it."

Brodie scowled, his expression hardening. He knew it was generally intimidating, and it caused people to jump when he wore it at home. But Laurel grinned, then laughed. She shook her head and turned toward her chamber.

"Lady Laurel, must you always be so difficult?"

Laurel looked back over her shoulder. "Aye. But at least I respect you." She didn't wait for his response before she continued down the passageway. She glanced back when she reached her door and found Brodie standing with his arms akimbo, watching her. She giggled and shook her head. On a whim, she waved before she ducked into her chamber.

Laurel glanced out of her window embrasure and realized she'd dawdled far longer than she realized, but she'd enjoyed her banter with Brodie. But it had cost her time she needed to work on her gown. She rang for Ina while she stripped off her ruined kirtle. When her maid arrived, the woman took one sniff of Laurel and rushed to order a bath. With as much care as she could, she laid out her evening gown and unfolded the new garnet fabric. She knew the easiest solution would be to cut a seam where the material tore and make the garnet satin into a decorative panel. While she waited for Ina, Laurel gathered her needles and threads. She dug out her shears and held her breath as she cut her gown. She'd reconstructed enough gowns that she knew she shouldn't feel nervous when she took the scissors to a kirtle, but she always did, especially when time was not on her side.

Ina returned with servants carrying the tub and buckets of hot water just as Laurel finished cutting the garnet satin to fit the panel she would make. Sensing her anxiety, Ina silently scrubbed Laurel's hair while Laurel ran the sudsy linen cloth over herself. She would have preferred to soak until the water chilled, but she didn't have that luxury. She was in and out of the tub in less than five minutes. She sat before the fire to dry her hair, her back to the flames while she worked on the gown. Her nimble fingers quickly added the yards of fabric, making it appear as though the blue and deep red materials were seamless. Glancing once more at the window, she sighed as church bells rang in the town. She had an hour before she would need to dress for the evening meal. Feeling calmer, Laurel pulled embroidery thread from her basket and set about stitching.

An hour later, Laurel straightened her back and looked at her work. A smile tugged at the corner of her mouth as she considered the scene she'd stitched. While she usually sold embroidery that included complicated patterns and designs, she tended toward flowers and birds on her own gowns. It ensured no one connected the goods she sold to what she wore.

When Ina returned to fashion Laurel's hair, she glanced at the gown she'd just finished, and her heart felt lighter than it had in years. She almost felt like she had before she arrived at court. She opted to wear her hair down, a rarity these days. Laurel felt that despite her maiden status, she was too old to wear her hair down like most unmarried women. But her carefree mood railed against having pins pushed into her scalp from every direction to hold her thick locks in place. Ina wove a ribbon into Laurel's hair, framing her face, but otherwise, Laurel's hair was unadorned. With a warm smile and a pat on Ina's shoulder, Laurel donned her gown and headed to the Great Hall.

SEVEN

B rodie knew the moment Laurel arrived in the Great Hall. It wasn't that heads turned in her direction because he didn't notice. He sensed it. Some silent force drove him to look toward the doors the moment she entered. Her hair hung in long waves over her shoulders and down her back, far longer than he'd imagined earlier that day. And he had imagined it. As sparks flew from her blue-hazel eyes, he'd wondered what she would look like with her hair unbound and spread across their bed. He'd startled himself when he realized that he'd thought of any bed as theirs, a shared destination rather than just a piece of furniture.

After parting with Laurel, Brodie had returned to his chamber for a rest before dinner. He'd closed his eyes, not to doze, but to relive his walk with Laurel. He'd enjoyed their repartee as he accompanied her back to the castle, but he'd been awed by her beauty when he lifted back her veil. He hadn't anticipated her clear alabaster skin and dazzling hazel eyes. Standing within arms' reach, he realized that Laurel's hair held a deeper tint of red than Monty's, whose hair tended more toward blond. The fiery strands woven among the blond —seemingly matching her temper—peeked through when she moved in a particular way. Having his sporran covering the front of his plaid avoided Brodie embarrassing himself when his body once again took notice of Laurel's elegant feature; despite her muck-covered kirtle, he'd recognized a fine figure beneath the gown.

But it had been her giggle that made his cock twitch. It was infectious and, he suspected, rare. As he reclined on his bed, he discovered he longed to run his fingers along her body, exploring where she might be ticklish. Once more, the image of her laying beneath him materialized before his eyes. But this time she giggled and kissed him while he tickled her. His imagination was so vivid it made him want to bang on her chamber door and make it real.

Now, as he stood watching her enter the enormous gathering hall, the sound of her teasing voice echoed in his head. Even her scathing rebuke about not being distressed made him smile. Catching himself lest he look like a loon, he pushed away from the wall. He observed as Laurel's eyes widened a fraction when she spotted him. She glanced around, and Brodie wondered if she looked for her brother or a means to escape, perhaps both. But his long strides carried him toward her, people moving aside to avoid his broad shoulders from bumping into them.

"Lady Laurel," Brodie said softly, his naturally deep voice huskier than usual. "You look lovely."

"Thank you, Laird Campbell," Laurel spoke equally quietly. She felt the heat entering her cheeks as Brodie's eyes locked with hers, unrelenting, as though they looked into her soul. She feared all he would find was a black abyss. She swallowed, unsure what else to say and not understanding why he didn't let her pass. Brodie's hand moved of its own volition to reach for hers, but he caught himself before he embarrassed them both. He couldn't be sure she wouldn't spurn him and ridicule him, but part of him looked forward to the possibility. He was curious as to what she might say, even if it would put him on the receiving end of her barbs.

"Is that the fabric you purchased today?" Brodie

wondered. He'd recognized it and knew the answer, but he thought it might encourage conversation. But he watched as Laurel withdrew, even though she didn't move.

"Yes, my laird."

"Your maid must be an excellent seamstress to finish your gown so quickly. And the embroidery. Well, I'd be cack-handed if I were to try such. I can stitch a wound but never aught so fine," Brodie grinned. But he snapped his mouth shut when he realized Laurel looked markedly uncomfortable. "The gown is as lovely as you are."

Laurel blinked, then smiled shyly. Brodie detected she was uncomfortable each time he paid her a compliment, but there was also something about discussing sewing that made her uneasy.

Mayhap I insulted her if she thought I meant her maid did the embroidery. That skill could only come from a lady.

"Did you stitch the Highland scene?" Brodie tried again. He'd recognized the small red birds as crossbills, a breed of finch indigenous to the Caledonian Forests.

"I did," Laurel admitted.

"It must remind you of home," Brodie grinned again, but Laurel looked away, finally breaking the connection.

"Stirling is my home. It doesn't remind me of here." Laurel wanted to flee. Standing before Brodie made her realize that a particular Highlander inspired the flora and fauna she'd created. Her heart sped.

"Back to claiming you're not a Highlander, lass?" Brodie chuckled, struggling to lighten the mood once more.

"Excuse me please," Laurel said, but she didn't wait for a reply. She stepped past Brodie and wound through the crowd until she reached her table. She sat, taking a deep breath. She felt more unsettled than was reasonable for such a benign conversation. She struggled not to let tears slip from her eyes. She tried to reason through her reaction to Brodie's comments. As she thought about everything they'd said to one another, she understood why she was on edge.

Brodie wasn't the first man she found attractive, but he was one of the few who had more than handsome features to draw her attention. While she wondered what it would feel like to have his brawny arms wrapped around her, to feel his stubble abrade her cheeks and chin while they kissed, to have her breasts caught between them as she pressed herself against his muscled chest, she also wondered what it would be like to share a lifetime of banter with him. An emptiness that threatened to swallow her whole encircled her as she chided herself for being foolish. She couldn't fathom a man such as Brodie wishing to spend a lifetime with her.

Mayhap he's friendly merely because he and Monty are well acquainted. Or mayhap I'm too daft to realize he's mocking me after this afternoon's spectacle. He's likely forgotten aboot me already.

Laurel shifted her gaze to find Monty, needing to speak to him after the meal. But when she found her brother, she also found Brodie staring back at her. A bolt of electricity seemed to crackle between them, and as his penetrating gaze locked once more with hers, it was a jolt that made her heart skip. There was interest in Brodie's gaze; Laurel recognized it as such, but it had never been directed toward her before. She'd seen it as, one after another, her friends and fellow ladies-in-waiting met their soulmates and paired off. She worried that she would draw attention, but she couldn't disengage. Eventually, someone spoke to Brodie, pulling his focus from her, but she caught him glancing at her several times throughout the rest of the meal.

Brodie spent the following three days finding reasons to encounter Laurel in the bailey and around the keep. The morning after their encounters in Stirling and at the evening meal, Brodie maneuvered himself into a seat behind Laurel for Mass. When the Pax Board reached Laurel, and she had to turn around to pass it to the pew behind her, she found Brodie standing behind her.

"Peace be with you," Brodie murmured.

"And also with you," Laurel replied, whipping back around as soon as the blessed piece of wood left her hands.

He timed his arrival and exit from the lists to coincide with when the ladies came and went from the flower gardens during the queen's morning stroll. While he noticed other young women attempting to gain his attention, his greeting was only for Laurel. They danced twice each night, but Brodie found Laurel grew more subdued with each set. He wondered why, but he feared the answer if he asked. Instead, he delighted in the time spent with her, even if there was little more than small talk about the weather.

Laurel spent the fourth hiding in her chamber. She'd battled a nearly constant headache for three days, confused by Brodie's persistent interest while the ladies continued their snide attacks about being forced to wait for Laurel to marry. She chided herself for thinking Brodie might consider her an eligible bride. He'd been pleasant, but he'd made no overtures toward her. But she couldn't fathom why he would show interest in her without a purpose.

After a day of rest, Laurel emerged feeling more herself, but it all came crashing down during the morning meal. She arrived to break her fast later than she normally did, having gone back to her chamber to replace a bootlace. When she arrived at the Great Hall, she found the other ladies huddled together, laughing uproariously. She approached, curious about what had happened in the short time she was away. But her world came crashing down in the matter of a handful of words.

"Liam Oliphant and Nelson MacDougall wagered Laird Campbell one hundred pounds that he couldn't woo the shrew," Catherine MacFarlane announced. "Why else would he pay attention to her? He doesn't want to be out one hundred pounds. He must make her fall in love with him and agree to marry him. I'd make my own wager that he doesn't show up to his own wedding."

"That explains why he's paid attention to her," Emelie Dunbar mused. "We've all wondered why."

Laurel trembled as she listened, no one yet aware that she'd arrived. She swallowed the sour bile that burned her throat. The weight that took root in her chest pressed every organ, threatening to make her knees buckle as she continued to listen.

"I heard even her brother agreed to the wager," Emelie's sister Blythe said. "I can't believe that. For all Lady Laurel's faults, her brother is fond of her."

"Fond of the notion that he can rid himself of her," Sarah Anne snorted. It was at that moment that Emelie looked up and caught sight of Laurel. Emelie elbowed Blythe, who looked in Laurel's direction. Mortified, Laurel turned on her heel and ran into a glowering Brodie Campbell. When he moved to help her as she teetered backward, she slapped at his hands.

"Don't touch me," Laurel hissed.

"Laurel," Brodie whispered. Laurel's eyes narrowed as her nose flared, and Brodie waited with bated breath. If he didn't feel hideous for what he overheard—and knew Laurel had, too—he would have thought her magnificent. He wondered what was wrong with him that he waited to see what Laurel had to say.

"Dinna speak to me, dinna touch me, dinna come near me," Laurel spat, uncaring that her brogue had returned with such force that she doubted any Lowlander could understand her. "I didna think the almighty Laird Campbell of Glenorchy would be a roiderbanks, but I should have kenned all along that there is a reason why yer people must grab everything within reach. Ye're someone living beyond yer means. Why else would ye stoop to such lows as to consider me—the Shrew of Stirling—for a bride? Why pursue me if ye ken that everyone thinks I'm a triptaker? That all I do is find fault with everyone. Ye are naught more than a churlish mumblecrust." Laurel snapped her mouth shut, having hurled enough insults at Brodie and finishing by calling him a toothless beggar.

"Laurel, I didn't accept the wager," Brodie explained.

"But ye kenned of it. And now everyone else does, too. And ye didna try vera hard to disabuse people of the notion that ye refused it. Ye heard them. I'll give ye the bluidy hundred pounds to be done with ye." Laurel spoke in anger, but she would part with the hard-earned coin if it meant she never had to look at Brodie Campbell again.

"I dinna want yer coin, Laurel," Brodie kept his voice low, his own burr slipping back into his words. "That isnae why I've paid attention to ye."

"Och aye. I suppose it was to see what ye could get for free. Ye thought to make a fool of me just as everyone else. I suppose ma brother kens aboot this too." Laurel feared the rising gorge she fought would soon strangle her.

"Monty and Donnan were there when the wager was suggested. Monty refused to even consider it," Brodie explained.

"He refused to consider it. Nae ye. Him." Laurel stepped around Brodie, but his arm swung out and blocked her way. Without thought Laurel spat at his boot. "Ye want something from me. There ye have it. That's all I'll ever give ye."

"And if I wish to give ye ma name, a home in the Highlands where ye didna feel alone, the respect and appreciation ye havenae had?" Brodie asked as his hand settled on Laurel's waist, holding her place with little pressure.

"I thought ye were different. But ye're naught. Ye're worse. Ye're cruel," Laurel hissed as the first tears fell.

"Why do ye assume I'm lying?" Brodie asked.

Laurel looked back over her shoulder at the crowd of people watching her argue with Brodie. There wasn't one look of sympathy directed at her. Those who cast a pitying gaze directed it at Brodie, not her. Most watched with morbid fascination. She wished she could slink away, never showing her face again. Laurel turned back to Brodie and shook her head. If she attempted to speak, she would sob instead. She pushed his arm away and mustered as much dignity as she could, holding her head up as she walked toward the doors. She found Monty and Donnan standing there, matching expressions of shock on their faces.

"Fine choice ye've made for me," Laurel snarled as she pushed past her brother and friend. Once in the passageway, she lifted her skirts nearly to her knees and bolted.

EIGHT

"I never accepted a wager," Brodie growled at those watching the disaster unfold. He spun on his heels and stormed after Laurel. When he reached Monty and Donnan, he halted. "She's yer sister. When are ye going to protect her like ye should?"

"She's a woman full-grown," Monty corrected.

"Aye. But she was dumped in the woods and left for the wolves when she was a lass. Now everyone faults her for learning to protect herself," Brodie argued.

"She's not the first woman to come to court unwillingly. But she's the only one who can't fit in," Monty stated.

"When will ye realize she isnae like other women? And that isnae for the worse," Brodie barked. He left Monty and Donnan staring after him as he ran after Laurel. He chased her until he spotted her rose-hued skirts in the distance. His longer legs soon covered the distance that separated him. He called out to her, "Laurel."

Without looking back, Laurel pushed herself to run faster, but she knew the battle was lost when she reached stairs she could never climb faster than Brodie. She slid down the wall until she sat on a step, her shoulders shaking from the power of her sobs. Brodie sank down beside her and pulled her against his chest.

"Dinna," Laurel choked, but she didn't push Brodie away. She curled into herself and sagged against his powerful frame. Neither spoke, but Brodie held her as she cried. She'd thought she'd been upset when she sobbed against Monty's shoulder only days earlier, but it failed to compare to the gut-wrenching torrent of tears and emotions that engulfed her. The only thing that kept her anchored to earth was Brodie's solid presence, his silent strength.

Brodie's heart ached for the woman in his arms. Her ire hadn't surprised him, and he'd welcomed it directed at him rather than anyone else. He understood others would ridicule her for her diatribe toward him, but he had skin thick enough to weather it. Any man maligned as Laurel had been would have struck out with his fists. A physical fight wasn't an option for Laurel, so she defended herself with what she had. He could see a wildness to her that was never meant for the confines of court. If others had recognized it, too, and perhaps offered her compassion and warmth when she arrived, her time at Stirling Castle would have been different. But Laurel wasn't meek. Her family may have profoundly wounded her, but she was resilient in her own way. Brodie intuited that when Laurel least deserved love and kindness, she needed it the most.

Laurel inhaled the pine and sandalwood scent from the skin that peeked through the laces of Brodie's leine. The heat he generated soothed her much like a hot bath helped ease tension. His calloused palm ran over her back as he comforted her with his presence rather than with platitudes. As her tears slowed, and she no longer scrunched her eyes closed, she listened to the steady rhythm of Brodie's heart. It was predictable and even, a point to focus upon as she tried to calm herself. The tension slipped from her shoulders and back, leaving her pliable and relaxed against Brodie's chest.

"How can ye care?" Laurel whispered. Brodie considered

her words. She hadn't asked for the reason he did care. Rather, she didn't understand his ability to. Brodie's heart tugged even more as it dawned on him that Laurel felt entirely unlovable. He considered that Laurel had spent nearly as many years at Stirling as she did at Balnagown. But she wouldn't have remembered much of her first four or five years among her clan in any case. It must have felt like she'd spent more time at court than with her family. It was more time spent feeling left out than included.

"Because I understand ye, or at least I believe I do."

"What is there to understand? I'm spiteful and hateful, and probably the most unladylike woman of yer acquaintance."

"Ye're a thistle," Brodie responded. When he said no more, she leaned back. Her watery eyes showed her confusion. "Ye're beautiful from near and far, but ye're prickly when someone comes too close. But ye're also as hearty as the Highland flower. Nay matter the strength of the gale, ye and the thistle survive. For those brave enough to face the spiny leaves, they discover the flower smells sweet. The thistle is a solitary plant, easily overlooked compared to roses and heather. That doesnae mean that it isnae worthy of admiration. The thistle is the symbol our Scottish pride for a reason. It's like our people, indomitable and proud. Ye're a thistle, Laurel. Indomitable, and ye should be proud."

"Brodie," Laurel shuddered as she burrowed back against his chest. Brodie tipped her chin up and brushed away the last tears with his thumb.

"Shh, Laurie. It tears at ma heart to see ye so wounded." Brodie saw the spark in Laurel's eyes when he used the diminutive. "Do ye like me to call ye Laurie?"

"Aye," Laurel breathed. "I've never thought of maself as a flower. But if I ever had, I suppose I would consider maself a bush of nettles." Laurel offered Brodie a watery smile, and he returned it with a grin.

"As prickly and itchy as the nettle might be, even its tea is good for the body," Brodie pointed out.

"Do ye intend to boil me alive to find ma softer side?" Laurel gazed up at Brodie, but a shiver coursed along her spine when she caught the spark of desire in Brodie's eyes.

"Laurie, I've already found it," Brodie whispered before he lowered his mouth toward hers, giving her a chance to push him away. Laurel slid her hand up Brodie's chest and over his shoulder until her fingers tangled in the hair at the base of his skull.

"I think I've found yers," Laurel murmured before their lips pressed together. The spark of desire turned into a raging fire as Brodie fought the urge to crush Laurel against him. He flicked his tongue against her lips twice before growing bolder and pressing it against the seam of hers. Guessing what he wanted, she opened to him. Her gasp of surprise when his tongue entered her mouth made Brodie wonder what else he could do to elicit such a sound. Laurel shifted restlessly against him, twisting her body closer to him. Brodie's hand slid down to cup her backside. When she gasped again, Brodie fisted his other hand in her hair, steeling himself against the temptation to press her beneath him on the stairs and hike up her skirts before thrusting into her.

A sound in the stairwell a flight below them made them jerk apart. Laurel turned a terrified expression toward Brodie, who was already pushing to his feet. He helped Laurel to hers, but neither moved beyond that. They waited to determine if the sound drew nearer. When it receded instead, Brodie wrapped his arm around Laurel's waist and pulled her against him. She put up no fight, her hands pressing high upon his chest.

"We canna stay here, Laurie. There's more to say to one another, but I willna have ye forced into marrying me because someone finds us like this."

Laurel nodded as she looked around them. Brodie was right; if anyone found them, even if they weren't kissing, she would have no choice but to marry Brodie. He might have shown an interest in her—he might even desire her—but Laurel was unconvinced that he wanted to marry her. She stepped back and lifted her skirts, prepared to finish climbing the stairs, but Brodie blocked her route.

"Are ye all right to make it to yer chamber?" Brodie asked.

Laurel cocked an eyebrow and fell back into her courtly speech. "Do you believe your kisses sufficient to keep me so weak kneed that I can't walk to my door?"

"Keep you weak kneed?" Brodie smirked. "Then they have done a fine job to start."

Laurel rolled her eyes. "If anyone is in need, it is you." Her gaze flickered downward for a moment. "Of having your sporran remain in place."

"Saucy as ever," Brodie laughed, his hand darting out to cup her backside as he took two steps down, bringing them eye-to-eye.

"Do you wish me to be otherwise?" Laurel quipped, but Brodie felt her anxiety as her body tensed.

"Not in the least."

"Brodie?" Laurel waited until he nodded. "I truly am sorry for what I said and did earlier. What possessed me to spit at your boots is beyond me. That went much too far, even for me."

"You were justly upset," Brodie placated, but Laurel shook her head.

"Please don't make excuses for me. I'm ashamed of how I acted. I—I—I don't want you to think that's how I would treat you normally. I spoke the truth the other day. I respect you, and I—I—would like you to respect me, too."

"Laurie, I already do. If I didn't, would I have come after you? Would I have stayed with you?"

"That's just pity," Laurel said dismissively.

"It is not," Brodie corrected.

Laurel's lips thinned before she nodded. "My point is, I don't want you to think—fear—that I will treat you like that again, especially not in public. I humiliated myself, but I embarrassed you in the process. I'm sorry."

"I ken, my wee *cluaran*," Brodie murmured before he brushed a kiss against Laurel's lip. *Clu-air-an. She is ma wee thistle.*

Laurel's face softened as she nodded. "Thank you, Brodie."

"Will you join the other ladies?" Brodie asked tentatively, but Laurel shook her head.

"I think I should let the fire run its course and not add fuel to it."

"Laurie, will you let me accompany you to the evening meal? My men and I have sat with Monty and his men since we arrived. You haven't eaten with us once. Do you not wish to see them?"

Laurel gritted her teeth, and Brodie frowned. In two questions it seemed he'd lost any ground he'd gained. He wondered which one ruined his progress. He had his answer to his surprise.

"I would appreciate you walking me the Great Hall, but I will not sit with my brother."

"Would you sit with me?"

"Do you intend to sit with him?"

"I had."

"Then I won't." Laurel crossed her arms and shook her head. She could only imagine how petulant she appeared. "You said we shouldn't linger here."

"And I also said there is more to be said," Brodie reminded her. "Laurel, we can't sit together at the evening meal without your brother as a chaperone. We both know that."

"And I cannot sit with him at the evening meal without stabbing him."

"Bloodthirsty and tart," Brodie mused.

"He knew aboot the wager, Brodie. You both did. Neither of you tried to ensure people wouldn't believe Liam and

Nelson." Laurel sighed and shook her head again. "I don't think sitting with you would be wise. None of this was wise."

Laurel's eyes widened, and her mouth dropped open. She spun on her heel and took the steps two at a time. "You did this, all of this, to win." Brodie seized her around the waist and hoisted her off her feet, tired of worrying she would fall down the stairs each time she moved. "Put me down!"

Once on the landing, Brodie put Laurel back on her feet and reared away from her scornful expression. The loathing that poured from her eyes was enough to make Brodie doubt why he was pursuing the woman. But behind the anger, he saw the hurt and fear.

"This has naught to do with a bet. If it were only aboot a bet, could I feel this way?" Brodie backed Laurel against the wall and swooped in for a kiss that made the previous one seem like an innocent peck. He was persistent and aggressive, but Laurel opened to him without hesitation. Her hands fisted in his leine, tugging him toward her, told him she was a willing participant. He was certain he would devour her, his hunger to touch and taste her verging on the irrational.

Laurel Ross sparked something within Brodie that he never suspected he'd feel. He'd lusted for women in the past, but he'd rarely taken more than a passing interest in anything beyond the physical. He'd pleasured his lovers, but he had never envisioned those women as equal partners; mostly he had performed to ensure the satisfied woman returned the favor. With Laurel, he wanted to watch her come alive, to give her passionate nature an avenue that wasn't so self-destructive.

Laurel was certain she would float away on a cloud if Brodie's body weren't pressing her against the brick wall. She returned his kiss with abandon, the excitement of their touch surpassing even the wildest ride across the rolling hills of Ross territory. Brodie's hands roaming over her body caused her skin to prickle as the nerves over-fired, and a throbbing ache settled low in her belly. She'd seen more than one couple locked in amorous embraces while living in Stirling Castle, but never had she dreamed she might experience it herself. Brodie's allure tempted her toward all the hedonistic sins she could imagine but given up years earlier, and she hoped there were ones he could introduce that were well beyond her knowledge. When he pushed his sporran aside, and his length rested against her mons, her moan was foreign to her ears, but the vibration in her chest told her where it originated.

"If this were aboot a mere bet, would I want to rip every thread from ye, and sink into ye until I bellowed ye name in delight?" Brodie panted. "Would I be tempted to ride off with ye, uncaring if anyone kenned where we went or what became of us?"

"I dinna ken," Laurel confessed, barely able to follow Brodie's logic since she cared about little beyond the next kiss. Brodie rocked his hips against her, and a whimper escaped Laurel's lips as she nudged his head toward hers, bringing their mouths together again.

"Lady Laurel!"

Laurel and Brodie turned toward the shocked voice, finding a group of stunned, openmouthed ladies-in-waiting, staring at them. It had been Sarah Anne who screeched her name. Brodie twisted, pushing his sporran back into place, shielding Laurel from the prying eyes of the courtiers. But he and Laurel knew it mattered little. All the damage had already been done.

NINE

Laurel stepped out of Brodie's shadow, determined to accept the fallout of her actions, both in the Great Hall and in the passageway. She notched up her chin and cast her gaze down at Sarah Anne, who stood nearly a head shorter than Laurel. She flicked her gaze to the other women, daring any of them to speak aloud their accusations and questions. A malicious gleam came into Sarah Anne's gaze as she accepted Laurel's challenge.

"I see Laird Campbell found a way to occupy your tongue that doesn't involve you talking," Sarah Anne proclaimed.

"Aye. Shame you can only speculate on how enjoyable it is," Laurel sniffed.

Sarah Anne gasped, unprepared for Laurel to accept the accusation even if it came with a jibe. "Only a trollop would say such a thing."

"Just as a prude would say such a thing."

"Lady Laurel," Emelie stepped forward. "Are you all right?" Emelie didn't look as convinced as everyone else that Laurel welcomed Brodie's attention.

"Quite. Laird Campbell and I resolved our disagreement and made amends," Laurel said offhandedly. She glanced up at Brodie and nodded. "Thank you. I bid you good day."

Brodie stood in stunned silence, unsure what to make of Laurel's calm acceptance of being caught. She neither railed at him for the inevitable outcome, nor did she attempt to make excuses to avoid it. He wondered if she might wish to marry him as much as he was finding he wished to marry her. She said no more as she walked past the women and entered her chamber without looking back, leaving Brodie with a gaggle of tittering ladies.

Brodie adopted his most menacing glare, and the women scattered. When no one remained in sight, he stalked to Laurel's door, knocked once, and pushed it open. He found Laurel sitting in the window embrasure, with her embroidery in her hands. If he hadn't known she'd been locked in the most erotic interlude of his life and then stared down the accusatory looks from her fellow ladies, he wouldn't have been able to tell it from the look of serenity on her face.

"Laurie," Brodie started, but he didn't know what to say next.

"I meant what I said, Brodie. Thank you." Laurel spared him a glance before she continued her stitching. Brodie hadn't a clue what she was thankful for, since her reputation as a maiden now laid in tatters. He closed the door and crossed the chamber. With an aggrieved sigh, Laurel lifted her legs from the window seat and made room for Brodie, but he opted to stand. When he didn't move, she shrugged, and extended her legs once more, crossing them at the ankles.

"What are you thanking me for exactly?" Brodie wondered.

"For accepting my apology. For understanding me. For not blaming me. And most of all, for giving me my freedom."

"Your freedom?" Brodie understood each sentiment but that.

"Aye. With my reputation now completely obliterated, I am free. Whether I remain here or go where I please, I owe no one aught anymore," Laurel said with a shrug.

"Go where you please? Owe no one?" Brodie was baffled

by what she meant. She would go to Kilchurn with him, and she would owe him—or rather, they would owe one another—the customs of marriage.

"Aye. I'll likely be sent down from court since the queen won't countenance the scandal, but I won't be welcome at Balnagown either. Monty might suggest a convent, but he said he wouldn't force me. I shall find a village somewhere in the hills and say I'm a widow. I've done it before. I can be a seamstress for real and do as I please. Any way I look at it, I'm free, so thank you."

"You cannot be serious, Laurel."

"And why not? It won't matter to you or your clan that they found you kissing a lady-in-waiting." Laurel assessed him as she looked into his storm-gray eyes. Her lips thinned. "If your indignation is aboot not winning the hundred pounds, or rather having to pay it to Liam Oliphant, fear not. I will ensure you aren't out a penny of your own money. Besides, I'm saving you a bride price that my dowry likely wouldn't repay. You'll fare better than even me."

"You cannot think it's that simple," Brodie said, aghast. The woman he'd considered marrying earlier that morning and he would now be required to marry sat before him as though she were describing plans for a summer picnic. But his temper flared when she returned to thinking what he felt had anything to do with a nonexistent wager. "Put your sewing aside, Laurel, and look at me."

Brodie's tone rankled, and he knew he'd made a mistake when she not only tossed it aside but stood up. "Save that tone for a wife. One that is your own. Since I am not she, do not think to command me. However, this is my chamber, and I command you to leave."

"We are as good as betrothed, and you are not so daft that you don't know that. I am driven to make you my wife," Brodie barked.

"Driven? Hardly," Laurel scoffed. "Whatever drove you here may drive you away."

"It might very well, since it's your shrewish tongue, but it won't be enough to convince the king and queen that I shouldn't take you as my wife."

"Mayhap, but perhaps I shall leave you as not my husband." Laurel tapped her toes as she looked over Brodie's shoulder at the door. "I believe I told you to leave."

"And I believe I'd still be kissing you senseless if we hadn't been interrupted."

"While that's quite likely," Laurel huffed. "We aren't kissing now, so go."

"There's an easy remedy to that." Brodie cocked an eyebrow.

"Perhaps you should bed me while you're here. Make my fall from grace a *fait accompli*."

"Are you offering, Laurie? Because I won't turn you down." Brodie snapped his mouth shut, not having intended to admit such.

"I suppose you assume every woman who kisses you intends upon falling into bed with you. Arrogant mon." Laurel reached for her sewing and sat down once more. Brodie remained glowering at her. "You may remain there until you become part of the furniture if you wish, but it won't change aught."

"If I am but a piece of furniture, then perhaps you should sit on me," Brodie taunted, his smirk and cocked eyebrow confirmed the innuendo.

"I can think of more comfortable places upon which to rest my arse," Laurel didn't shift her attention from her embroidery. "And you hardly look up to the task."

"I assure you I am vera much up to the task."

"So you say. Furniture is meant to carry weight, so must you."

"Women are meant to carry, so must you."

Laurel's laugh was hollow. "Not by you, if that's what you mean."

"Since I will be your husband, there is no one else I could

mean." Brodie crossed his bulging arms over his expansive chest, continuing to glower at Laurel. If he'd thought his expression would change her mind, he'd foolishly underestimated her mettle. But he didn't miss the lust that returned to her eyes when she glanced up and noticed his taut muscles bunching beneath his leine. He reached out a gentle hand to her, his fingers resting on her pulse point and his thumb settling into the hollow at the base of her neck. When Laurel's eyes met his and she set aside her embroidery, he pulled lightly with his fingers. She rose and stepped toward him. "I tire of arguing with you, Laurie. I never wanted to in the first place. I enjoy the banter, but not when we are at odds with one another."

"You've known me a sennight. Why does it matter? Why do you bother if not for the bet or your pride?"

"I took your memory to be better than that," Brodie softened his tone. "Can you have already forgotten what I said in the stairwell?"

"But why do you think you understand me?"

"Because I do." There was no arrogance in his tone. It was merely matter of fact.

"Then how do you understand me?" Laurel pressed.

"Because in each situation, you say just what I would have. Why do you think our rapport is so easy? How it came to us so smoothly?"

"We are rather alike. I can usually anticipate how others will respond because they are predictable. You are hardly that. However, our minds run along the same path, and I'm unaccustomed to it. It's a wee disconcerting." Laurel grinned. The light-hearted expression lit up her face, and Brodie found himself dazzled. She lifted her chin, and he accepted the offer, pressing a soft kiss to her pliant lips. Unlike the previous two, there was no frenzy in this one. Passion, yes, but affection too.

The episode was brief—and over before Laurel wanted—but church bells chiming interrupted the moment. Laurel bit her bottom lip as she gazed up at Brodie, unsure of what would come next. She hadn't lied when she said she appreciated her freedom, and she hadn't lied when she said she intended to find a cottage where she could make a life on her own. Her budding interest in Brodie warred with her everlong wish to escape. She wondered if Brodie was her means of escape. But she feared she would only place herself in another cage, one where she was locked with someone else. She didn't know if there was any that could accommodate them both.

"Laurie, you're still thinking aboot striking out on your own," Brodie whispered. "I see the doubt and the contemplation in your eyes. You have to know that would never be possible, if for no other reason than you're a laird's daughter."

"Soon to be disowned," Laurel corrected.

"Soon to wed," Brodie challenged.

"I doubt you are as certain aboot marrying me as I am aboot my freedom. You have not spent years wishing for me as I have spent wishing to be on my own."

"Would that our world worked that way, one where a woman can determine her future for herself. But that is not where we are." Brodie shook his head. "Hear me out, please. I don't doubt that you could keep hearth and home within a cottage or that you would work to earn your keep. But you would never to be safe."

"I would if people thought I was a widow," Laurel countered. "And you've met me. No mon but you has braved my temper."

"And many men wouldn't care what your temper is while they've got you pinned on you back or over a table."

Laurel's eyes narrowed at Brodie's warning. She would never admit out loud that what he said was her singular fear about striking out on her own. "I will note your concern and ensure I am tucked away in my cottage before nightfall."

Brodie's chin jerked forward before he glanced at the bed and then out Laurel's window. "You think a mon would only force you when it's dark? Laurel, it's not even mid-morn, and I was ready to have you against the wall or toss you on that bed.

Daylight or dark, morn or eve. People couple at all hours of the day and night. It would take but one mon dragging you behind a building or into a copse of trees."

"Why do you care? I wouldn't be a noose around your neck."

"Because it would break you, Laurie. You might survive an attack. You might go on living your life. But it would break your spirit. You wish for control over your life, and that is the one thing they would take from you," Brodie explained.

"You underestimate me," Laurel hissed, her arms crossed. But Brodie saw what the movement was. She hugged herself as if to ward away the threat he described.

"No, I don't by a long shot. But I would hate to think of the fire dimming from your eyes. That someone took that from you," Brodie said as he brushed the back of his fingers against her cheek. He saw how her blink lasted a moment too long, knew that she savored his touch. He eased his other hand to her waist but did nothing else.

"I might have a completely content life with no harm coming to me," Laurel whispered.

"You might. But you're not a fool, Laurie. You know the risk outweighs that possibility."

"Then what am I to do? Marry you and become your property?"

"When have I given you the impression that I would treat you as such?" Brodie tensed.

"How can I know you won't?" Laurel countered.

"Because every time your temper flares, I want you more," Brodie admitted.

"Aye. The challenge of taming the shrewish Laurel Ross must be tempting indeed."

"You assume the worst of yourself, and in turn, you assume the worst of me. I will not set out to break your spirit."

"Why does that matter so much to you? Why are you so bent on what happens to me or my spirit?"

"You remind me of my mother. She—" Brodie frowned as

Laurel pushed him away.

"What woman wants to marry the mon who claims she reminds him of his mother?" Laurel curled her nose and lip in disgust.

"I didn't say everything aboot you reminds me of her. I can say plenty of things I'd like to do with and to you that have never crossed my mind aboot her," Brodie finished with a grin. His hands came to rest on her waist again. "What I was going to say was, she had a tenacity and willfulness that made her a force to be reckoned with when I was a child. But year by year, my father chipped away at it. He forced her to become someone she wasn't. By the time my father died, she was nearly a shell of herself. She kept to herself when she could, and she rarely spoke to my father for fear of angering him. When he passed, she came back to us. She found her freedom. She passed a few years ago from the ague. But until she fell ill, she rode across hill and dale every day. She challenged me to become a better laird. She returned to the woman I remembered. But for more years than not, my ambitious and unrelenting father browbeat her."

"And you think the same would happen to me if I lived on my own?" Laurel's tone held an edge, but she kept her voice low. As much as she disliked the comparison to a man's mother, she had to admit that the woman sounded like her. It surprised her that Brodie would share something so intimate with her. She found it warmed her heart that he trusted her and understood her.

"You know, despite how you argue against it, that you won't have that life. What you are likely to have is a marriage to a mon like my father. Laurie, don't you see?"

Laurel shook her head, tears filling her eyes. She didn't understand, but she knew there was something she should grasp before the opportunity was gone.

"I want to give you the very freedom you crave."

"But I would be your wife. You would control me."

Brodie dropped his hands and turned away, his patience

fraying. He turned back around. "No. I have no interest in controlling you. I believe you are precisely the woman my clan needs. We are large and influential throughout Scotland. It means that many people envy us and wish to see us fall. There is a never-ending array of plots against us by those who wish to have our land and our standing. I need—want—a wife who will stand beside me. Whose council I can trust. One who will fight to keep our home and our clan safe. A woman who few would think to cross, and fewer who would survive if they did. Eliza never would have done that."

"Eliza?" Laurel's heart pounded in her chest at the mention of a faceless woman, a woman that perhaps Brodie loved.

"Aye. The woman I married," Brodie replied with a frown. At Laurel's astonished expression, Brodie realized how his words sounded. He ran a hand over his face before he took the seat she'd originally offered on the window embrasure. He held out his hand to her and prayed Laurel would take it. She hesitated, then slid her hand into his. He drew her to sit next to him. The tight fit meant Brodie's shoulder rested against the back of hers when he twisted to make room.

"How can you marry me if you're already married? Or rather, are you widowed?" Laurel whispered.

"Of a sort." Brodie's smile was regretful as he gazed into hazel eyes that held nothing but doubt and questions. "I wedded Eliza MacMillan a fortnight or so ago. It was purely for the alliance it would bring my clan. She was barely four-and-ten. I loathe saying that since I could be the lass's father."

"How auld are you?" Laurel interrupted.

"Eight-and-thirty."

Laurel mulled over Brodie's response. She supposed his age brought maturity and perhaps an understanding of human nature that a younger man might not possess. She wondered if it was also why he had such patience with her. But then an idea that made her queasy flashed through her mind.

"Are you so patient with me because you see me as a wayward wean who needs minding?" Laurel blurted.

Brodie chuckled. "Lass, there is naught aboot you—your sharp tongue or the delicious mouth in which it lies—that makes me think of you as a wean. And what I wish for us is decidedly not what I would do with a girl."

Laurel nodded, but her brow furrowed. "Why would you marry someone so young? Do you wish for a young bride?"

"Hardly. What I needed was a chatelaine since my mother passed. What my clan needs is the access to the waterways the MacMillans would have given us."

"You say was. Did your wife pass?"

Brodie sighed. "I struggle to think of her as such. I couldn't imagine consummating the marriage, let alone bringing myself to do it. I intended to wait at least two years. Saying our vows in a kirk was the only thing that made it a marriage rather than a betrothal. We were on our way to Kilchurn when our party was attacked, and they murdered Eliza."

"Oh! Brodie, I'm so sorry for your loss," Laurel said as she squeezed his hand. Perhaps he hadn't married the girl out of love, but he'd intended to spend his life with her. When she caught his pained expression, she wrapped her arm as best she could around his shoulders. Brodie inhaled Laurel's lavender scent and nearly licked her neck. His hand rested on her ribs as he turned his head for a kiss, but she reeled back.

"You tell me your wife died a fortnight ago, you clearly still grieve her, and yet you would kiss me again. Ugh," Laurel tried to pull away, and Brodie let her. She stood and moved beyond his reach. She watched as Brodie closed his eyes, and she assumed he didn't wish for her to see his guilty eyes.

"I don't grieve her, Laurel. Not even the moment it happened. And it makes me a wretched, heartless bastard."

"What?"

Laurel didn't realize she drifted forward until she cupped his jaw in her hands. She caught the relief in his expression.

When he opened his legs, she stepped between them. The gentleness of her touch was a balm to Brodie's troubled mind. Neither moved for a long moment before Laurel reached out her hand and caressed Brodie's chestnut-brown hair. She kept the movement light, but she felt as much as heard his shuddering sigh. Laurel realized it was a moment when she could offer him comfort, just as he had done for her earlier. She draped her other arm over his shoulders, and with a tiny nudge, Brodie laid his head against her middle. He wrapped his arms around her, and they merely held one another.

With a long sigh, Brodie resumed his story. "I know I should, but I didn't know the lass. She barely spoke enough to say her vows. I'm certain I terrified her despite me reassuring her several times before the wedding and during the journey that I would leave her untouched for years. I wish she wasn't dead. But that's only because she was innocent, not because I long for her to still be my wife. I just can't muster any grief over her death. The guilt I feel is for not feeling enough aboot her. I ken I should, but I don't."

"Och, Brodie. If she were but a stranger to you, then how can you blame yourself? You didn't know her well enough to have aught to miss or regret losing. You can grieve that they killed an innocent woman, but you can't grieve for something —or someone—you never had. You are not a bad mon for this. That you feel remorse at all tells me more than you or anyone else could put into words. And before you fash, it tells me what I already kenned. You are not a bad mon." She repeated her final words, praying the emphasis would get through Brodie's guilt.

"What aboot how I am drawn to you in an inexplicable way, and I have no wish to stop? Not even knowing that I should be in mourning. What aboot how I haven't thought of Eliza since I last spoke to the king? That was before we even met."

"Brodie, she wasn't part of your life. She didn't have time to be. I have family who I rarely think aboot. I think aboot

Balnagown and the Highlands. But I don't miss my family, and I've kenned them my entire life. They're not part of the life I have now, so there is naught for me to miss. I confess I cannot let go of my anger, but I don't miss them."

"But did you grieve their loss when you moved here?"

Laurel paused as she thought back to when she arrived at Stirling eleven years earlier. She'd cried countless times, but it was never for her family specifically. It was for her clan and her life among them. Bitterness and anger filled the hole she supposed should have been gaping from leaving them behind. "No. Mayhap I wouldn't still be so angry if I had. Mayhap if I'd admitted to myself just how much it hurt me, rather than hiding behind my anger, I would have let it all go."

"Laurie, I was already forced upon one bride. I don't wish to do that to another woman. I don't ken that we can avoid marrying. But if you don't wish to, and we can avoid it, I will take you to Campbell territory, to Kilchurn, and make sure you have the cottage you want. I can ensure your safety there, and you can have your freedom," Brodie offered.

Laurel looked down at the head that rested against her belly. She closed her eyes as she imagined what life would be. Her heart was filled with pain rather than hope. Living among the Campbells, right outside Brodie's gate, would mean watching him marry another. As his cheek pressed against her, she realized the life she thought she wished for meant never having a family of her own. She'd sworn to herself countless times that she would never abandon her children. But she wouldn't have children without a husband. However, in Campbell territory she would be forced to watch Brodie's children with his future wife grow up. She couldn't conjure a reasonable explanation for her visceral reaction against that, but she knew she couldn't do that.

"Laurie?"

"Aye, Brodie. I was just thinking aboot what you offered. I can't do it," Laurel whispered the last four words.

"But I could protect you. You could be a seamstress as you

said. Mayhap one day you might fall in love and wish to marry." Brodie didn't know how he voiced the last idea without choking on the words. He didn't want to see Laurel marry someone else, find happiness with someone else. While he thought he could endure the agony of her living within reach but not having her, the notion that someone else would share her life, tore at him.

"Mayhap this is but a passing infatuation between us. But I can't—" Laurel drew her lips in, unable to admit her feelings, unable to leave herself that vulnerable. Brodie looked up at her before he stood. They fell against one another, their mouths fusing as need clawed at them both. Brody lifted Laurel, and she bent her knees as he moved her over the window seat. Kneeling on it, they were at eye level, making the kiss easier. When they drew apart, both gasping for air, they leaned their foreheads together. Brodie kept his arms wrapped around her narrow waist, while Laurel cupped his jaw and nape.

"I dinna want ye to fall in love with someone else, Laurie," Brodie murmured. "I will do aught I can to help ye, but I confess I dinna want to spend ma life watching ye with someone else."

"Neither do I. That's why I canna." They both fell back into their brogues, and Laurel realized how much she missed the lilting tones. "I dinna want to wish any mon I married was someone else, and I dinna want to watch ye with bairns that arenae mine. Mayhap this is naught more than lust, but it pains me to think aboot that. I would rather be across the world from ye than to spend the rest of ma days seeing that."

"It doesnae have to be that way," Brodie reminded her.

"Brodie, I want to trust ye. I do. But I'm scared to. I'm scared because it would hurt so much more than it did when I left Balnagown or when ma father cut me off."

"Cut ye off?"

Laurel didn't have a chance to answer before a forceful rap sounded at her door.

TEN

"Laurel?" Monty's voice floated through from the other side. Laurel's eyes widened as she looked at Brodie. The most notorious gossips among her peers had already caught them, but even that was less scandalous than anyone finding Brodie in her chamber.

"A moment, Monty," Laurel called back. She turned horrified eyes to Brodie, who didn't look perturbed in the lease.

"Are we in agreement to wed?" Brodie whispered.

"I—I think so. But that doesnae mean I wish for it to be entirely in shame," Laurel hissed. Brodie sighed but dropped a peck on her nose. He pointed toward her armoire, and Laurel gave a doubtful nod. She watched as the giant forced himself into what looked like a pea. Her gowns peaked out the door that didn't shut all the way. She hurried to the door and opened it to find Monty alone in the passageway. "I'm sorry, I had to make myself presentable."

Monty narrowed his eyes at her before they swept her chamber, coming to rest on the armoire. "Get out, Campbell. My sister's chin looks like you tried to swallow her alive. Next time, shave first."

Laurel's hands flew to her face before her shoulders slumped when she realized she confirmed Monty's suspicions.

The wardrobe door swung open, and Brodie climbed out, narrowly missing his head on the frame.

"Hiding? I cannot believe you're such a coward," Monty said in disgust.

"Get out," Laurel said.

"We must talk," Monty argued.

"No. Not if you're going to insult Brodie." Laurel narrowed her eyes as she leaned forward and lowered her voice. "We all have secrets we wish to keep and will go to quite long lengths to protect."

Monty's gaze hardened as he looked from his sister to Brodie, who came to stand behind Laurel with his arms crossed. "It wasn't enough that you compromised my sister in a passageway where half the ladies-in-waiting saw you. Everyone is abuzz aboot it. Now, I find you in Laurel's chamber. Bluidy hell, Brodie. I wished for you to take her off my hands, not destroy our family's reputation. You may like a challenge, but it wasn't to bed her. It was to make her love you enough to marry."

Laurel froze. She feared if she moved, even twitched a muscle, she would vomit down the front of her brother. Everything she and Brodie shared that morning felt like a sham with Monty's careless words.

He didna mean what he said. He already committed to marrying me. He just wanted me to go along without a fuss. But why? He doesnae need to strengthen an alliance with us. And ma dowry isnae worth even looking at. Likes a challenge? Was this just aboot his pride?

Brodie spun Laurel around and pulled her against himself, but she didn't move. She didn't pull away, but neither did she return the embrace. Despite the numbness that spread to each pore, Laurel needed the solidity of Brodie's body and arms to keep her on her feet and, ridiculous as she found it, his presence offered her comfort.

"You are an arse, Montgomery," Brodie seethed. "You may have said it where no one but us can hear, but you've humiliated your sister."

Brodie made as if to pull away, but Laurel's hands shot up and tugged on his leine, urging him not to let go. He pressed Laurel's head to his chest, shooting Monty a thunderous glare. "Wheest, thistle," Brodie whispered. "I will tell you everything I remember of that night. But it had naught to do with today. Today happened because it was meant to. We're two peas in a pod, and everything I said today was the truth. All of it, Laurie."

Laurel still couldn't move. She closed her eyes as tears seeped from beneath her lids. Brodie held her as he ran his hand over her back. Never had she appreciated her height until that moment when Brodie cooed in her ear endearments and promises that Monty couldn't hear. He promised to take her away from court, to take her riding every day that he could once they were at Kilchurn, to take her to the sea or to the mountains, or to do whatever she wanted once they married. Eventually, Laurel nodded and released him. She turned to look at Monty, her eyes still burning from her tears. Brodie's arm around her middle kept her from lunging at Monty and tearing at his face, but it also made her feel protected unlike she ever had before.

"I told you to get out already, Montgomery. Go away," Laurel commanded.

"So you can finish your romp?" Monty stomped to the bed and ripped back the covers.

"There's naught to find, Monty, because naught happened," Laurel stated. "We talked. Aye, there were kisses, but I am in the same condition as I was when I entered my chamber."

"And what, pray, is that? You allowed him to maul you where anyone could see. Word is he was humping you right there."

"Montgomery," Brodie's voice was enough to make Monty snap his mouth shut. "Cease, or there will be no heir to Clan Ross. Whether you made up the last part or that is the gossip, it isn't true. I kissed your sister. More than once, in fact. But

97

only that. And I trust that Lady Laurel is a maiden, but even if she weren't, I still wish to marry her."

"Wish to?" Monty snorted. "You haven't a choice."

"That is neither here nor there when it comes to whether I run you through. Montgomery, I shall relish the day I take Laurel from here, and I swear to her—" Brodie turned Laurel to look at him. He tipped her chin up. "—I will never force her to lay eyes on you or any member of your family if she doesn't wish to." Laurel shivered at the certainty in Brodie's voice and eyes. She nodded, tipping her head back further. She cared little that Monty watched. Brodie brushed his lips against hers, ignoring Monty clearing his throat.

"You goad me," Monty accused. "You stand here compromising my sister right before me and think I will do naught."

Brodie opened his mouth, but Laurel spoke first. She didn't peer back at Monty, fusing her gaze with Brodie instead. "You are but an earl's son. He is Laird Campbell." Laurel spoke with such surety that she may as well have been proclaiming Brodie king.

"Perhaps it would be best if you continued kissing her. Then her viperous tongue would be better occupied," Monty snarled.

"I warned you once, now I warn you a second time. There will be no third. Don't speak to your sister like that," Brodie ordered.

"Or what? You wouldn't run me through any more than you would marry my sister if you weren't caught with your hand up her skirts. Your bravado is for show. You know it's what a groom is expected to do, but I doubt you're as eager as you would have others believe. But a challenge is what you wanted, and a challenge is what you shall have. She'll likely drive you to an early grave, so it shouldn't last too long."

"Why are you being so cruel, Monty?" Laurel whispered. She and her brother had exchanged various tart and belittling comments, but none had ever been to this degree.

"Because it was one thing when everyone thought you a bitch. Now you're a bitch and a whore."

Brodie lunged past Laurel, who whimpered, then shrieked as Monty's words pierced her heart, and Brodie terrified her. He wrapped his hand around Monty's throat and squeezed. But the men were close in size and equal in strength. Monty swung, but Brodie lifted his arm to shield his face. However, Monty slammed his other fist into Brodie's jaw. Brodie couldn't block that blow since his hand was still strangling Monty.

"Stop!" Laurel screamed, unsure of who would be the victor. She may not have wanted to see Monty again, but she didn't wish her brother dead. But her word fell on deaf ears as the men tumbled to the ground. Brodie lost his grip on Monty's throat as they landed with a bang. They rolled around, one gaining an advantage only to lose it the next moment. Laurel looked around her chamber for anything she could use to break them apart. She glanced at the ewer of water on her washstand, but there wasn't nearly enough to even faze them. She searched for something that might make a loud noise, but she could think of nothing. She looked back and spied her sewing basket. With a glance at the brawling men, she dashed to the basket and fished out two long pins. Daring to draw close to the flailing arms and legs, she stabbed one into Monty's waist, just below his ribs. She pressed the other equally hard into Brodie's backside. She was quick to withdraw them as the men roared and broke apart. Both men lithely came to their feet, ready to attack whoever interrupted. Laurel stood wide-eyed with a sewing pin in each hand.

"You wouldn't stop," Laurel said lamely.

"So you stabbed me?" Brodie said incredulously.

"Och, it didn't go in very far. It was like pushing a pin into stone," Laurel scowled.

"Where did she get you?" Monty asked as he pulled up his already untucked leine and found the prick where a dot of blood bubbled.

"In the arse. At least she got you in a respectable place like your side," Brodie grumbled.

"It was what I could reach," Laurel snapped. "If you want to duel, take it to the lists. Not in my chamber, where you're likely to tear it apart. Monty, you should leave. I won't say it again, and I don't believe Brodie wishes to hear it again."

"Naught is resolved," Monty argued. "You still disgraced yourself, and he compromised you."

"So you've said," Laurel said as she cast Monty a withering stare. "Sort out the contracts and inform Father that whatever pittance he calls my dowry needs to be delivered to the Campbells. For all my faults and sins, I just allied the Rosses with the most powerful clan in Scotland. If the next words out of your mouth, Monty, aren't thank you, I'll run you through myself."

Monty shifted his gaze to the resolute expression on Brodie's face, and his defensive posture near Laurel. He shook his head but smiled. "I sense you deserve one another. If you are so quick to defend my sister, I believe you carry genuine sentiment toward her. And I suspect she ended our fight out of pity and fear for my life more than worry for your safety. Laurel, I will send a missive to Father to inform him of these good tidings. And despite the words—and blows—exchanged here, I will stand beside you no matter what anyone says. And I do not doubt Father and our clan council will be, dare I say, jubilant to learn that you're marrying into the Campbells.

"I shall sleep well kenning I've made Father and the clan council happy," Laurel said snidely. "And you're welcome, Monty."

"Och, thank you, Laurel," Monty stepped forward to kiss his sister on the cheek, but her pinched look and her eye that twitched made him pull back. "We should see the king as soon as we can gain an audience."

ELEVEN

Laurel was sandwiched in a chair between Brodie on her left and Monty on her right. The trio sat across from an aggrieved King Robert. They hadn't been made to wait when they requested an audience. The sneer the chamberlain cast her said more than his haughty greeting. Word had clearly spread to nearly every echelon within the court, and she could only imagine what awaited her on the other side of the portal to the Privy Council chamber. What she discovered was a very irritated monarch.

"Your Majesty," Brodie said. "Lady Laurel consented to be my wife."

"Before or after you nearly sucked her face from her head?" King Robert snapped.

Brodie ignored the Bruce's comment. "I did not intend to remain at court overly long, but I wish to remain and properly court Lady Laurel."

"You seem confused, Campbell. The courtship occurs before the marriage proposal and generally before you compromise the chit," King Robert grumbled.

"Be that as it may, Lady Laurel and I seem well suited to one another, but I will not have her forced. I wish for Lady

Laurel to have time for us to come to know one another, and then decide if she still wishes to proceed."

"That is not how things work, Campbell. And well you know it. You both made the decision that you knew one another well enough when you trysted on the landing of the ladies' floor. Unless you forced her," King Robert glowered. "And now you wish to excuse yourself."

"Laird Campbell did not force me," Laurel said evenly, her head held high, and her spine rigid. "I was an equal participant."

"Your honesty and courage are commendable, but your common sense is deplorable," King Robert stated. "You have caused a scandal of proportions I cannot last recall. At least your peers usually cause their scandals far away from court. And how am I to believe that you or Laird Campbell came willingly to this agreement, when the men who sit beside your sport cuts and bruises?"

"That was my fault, Your Majesty," Monty spoke up. "I had unkind words and less-than-brotherly comments for Lady Laurel. I justly received my comeuppance."

"And Laird Campbell's swollen nose and split lip?" King Robert pointed out.

"Proof that I defend Lady Laurel by choice, not merely out of duty." Brodie didn't look at Laurel, but he reached for her hand. She jumped, unprepared for the contact, but quickly splayed her fingers for Brodie to intertwine with his.

Robert cocked an eyebrow at the gesture and scowled. "That is still not how courtship works. And it certainly isn't how a scandal works. There is no taking one's time to become better acquainted—though the nature of the scandal is that you are already too well acquainted. I have already decreed that there will be no weddings until after Lady Laurel's." Robert turned his attention toward Monty. "I've also read your father's missive. I reasonably suspect you aren't aware of its contents."

"I am not," Monty admitted. "My father directed me to

deliver it to you with haste, but I wasn't made aware of its subject."

"You won't be sitting so comfortably when you are," Robert mumbled. He looked at the couple, then Monty. "Lady Laurel, I received a missive recently from your father, which prompted me to order you to find a groom with haste. Your father offered me a choice, one which I was not pleased to receive. His last missive stated that either you wed before the new year and keep your dowry, or you remain here as an attendant to my wife with your dowry to pay for your upkeep."

Laurel swallowed. She'd known the day would eventually come, so the king's words hardly surprised her. She was a spinster, and her father had given up hope five years earlier. But she couldn't imagine what the newest missive could contain if her father had already provided an ultimatum. King Robert sighed and pinched the bridge of his nose.

"I'd rather be crawling on my belly in a bog facing the English right now." King Robert scowled. "Your father decided on another alternative, retracting part of his previous offer. You are to wed and receive your dowry, or you may remain here either at the queen's behest and expense, or you may find a protector to pay for your upkeep."

Laurel gasped. The protector her father intended wasn't a man willing to defend her honor like Brodie. Just the opposite. Her father intended her to become a man's mistress, so she might have a roof over her head and food in her belly. As she saw it, her father intended to make her little more than an expensive prostitute.

"Then I am fortunate that it was God's will to bring me to court," Brodie responded. "And His will that I should meet Lady Laurel."

Laurel cast a dumbstruck look at Brodie as though she heard his voice but didn't understand his words. She shifted to look at the king, but she refused to look at her brother. She believed he didn't know what the missive held, but she couldn't bear to look at him since he bore a striking resemblance to their father. She feared she would lash out with wishful thinking that it was Laird Ross rather than Monty.

"Ross and I will sign the contracts this afternoon, and Lady Laurel will remain here as she has, but as my betrothed. I accept responsibility for aught that my lady needs or wants," Brodie announced.

"Are you amenable to that, Montgomery?" King Robert asked quietly, unprepared for the turn of events.

"Quite," Monty said tightly. He leaned toward Laurel, but her gaze made him pull back. He looked at a shell of the woman he'd known and knew her expression would haunt him for the rest of his life. He was certain their father had finally struck the blow that broke his sister. "Laurel?" he whispered.

But Laurel looked at him as though she saw nothing. It was unnerving to Monty, who shot a panicked look at Brodie. Easing Laurel from her seat as he rose from his, Brodie guided her around the table before he swept her into his arms. He didn't wait for the king to dismiss them, nor did he ask permission to go. He carried Laurel to her chamber in silence because she fell asleep before they reached her floor. He laid her on her bed and covered her with a blanket after removing her satin slippers. He noticed for the first time how they were threadbare around the sides. He pulled a chair to the head of the bed and sank into it, his body as weary as his mind. But he refused to leave Laurel to wake alone. She was already isolated enough in her own mind without feeling abandoned by Brodie.

Laurel was in the Highlands, but she didn't recognize the hills surrounding her. But the swaying wildflowers, bright cerulean skies, and crisp air told her that she was home. Her horse, Teine, nickered beneath her as she galloped across the meadow, and the breeze lifted her hair from her shoulders. It streamed out behind like a shimmering golden banner as she and her steed charged ahead. She knew not where she was going, only that she was free. Laughter burbled from her lips as she tilted her face to the sun before drawing her attention back to her mount. She heard nothing but birdsong and the tall grass rippling beneath Teine's pounding hooves.

When a keep came into sight, Laurel slowed her mount, cautious for a moment. But she caught sight of a dark-haired man riding toward her, and while she couldn't make out his face, she didn't fear him. Just the opposite. She relaxed and grinned before kneeing Teine forward.

"I thought you would wait for me, thistle," Brodie said by way of greeting.

"You snored so loudly. Who could sleep? But I feared I exhausted you last eve, so I thought to let you sleep," Laurel grinned as they sat, alongside each other, atop prancing horses, facing one another. Brodie swooped in for a searing kiss that left Laurel breathless, but hungry for more.

"Indeed you did. You ken I'm normally a light sleeper."

"Aye. But in truth, I was up with the bairn, so once he slept again, I slipped out. I hoped you would join me." Laurel gazed at Brodie and noticed the gray hairs at his temples now wove through more of his chestnut mane, and his beard was more salt-and-pepper than it had been when they met. She glanced down at herself, noting her bust was larger than it had once been, and her belly was no longer flat. She looked at Brodie, a smile reflecting happiness that came only from living a life filled with love spread across her face.

"Fear not, Laurie. I will join you, but it shall be in our bed. Ride back with me?" Brodie asked. Laurel sensed it wouldn't anger him if she refused, but she wanted to return home with her husband.

"Don't you have duties to tend to?" Laurel asked.

"There is always time to love my wife," Brodie grinned.

TWELVE

Laurel's eyes fluttered open, but her mind was still groggy. She clung to the last moments of her dream, wishing she could fall back to sleep and see what would happen next. She rarely remembered her dreams, but this one had been so vivid that it felt more like a memory than the product of her imagination. She'd been somewhere she loved with someone she loved, and she sensed he reciprocated her feelings.

As her vision cleared, and she opened her eyes wider, Laurel found Brodie watching her. Pushing up on her elbow, she looked around her chamber, but nothing was amiss except for the mountainous man in the chair beside her bed. She closed her eyes once more, but the memory that surfaced stole her breath. She placed her fist over her chest, pressing as though it could ease the knot that formed.

"Laurie?" Brodie's soft whisper brought her back to the present. When she looked at him again, he was leaning forward. Worry etched deeply into the grooves upon his forehead and around his eyes.

"I'm all right," Laurel rasped, but she doubted she ever would be. "How did I end up here? What are you doing in my chamber again?"

"Do you remember me carrying you out of the Privy Council chamber?"

"Sort of."

"You were asleep before I made it to the stairs, so I brought you here to rest."

Laurel spotted her shoes beside the bed, and her face heated. If Brodie had removed them, he likely noticed their tattered condition. She wondered if he'd noticed how many times her stockings had clearly been darned. "Why did you stay?"

"Because I didn't want you to awake alone. I didn't want you to be by yourself when you remembered what happened," Brodie explained.

"You mean when I learned my father would rather I be a whore than pay another penny to keep a roof over my head or bread in my belly?" Laurel rolled over and sat up, bringing her knees under her chin. She wrapped her arms around her legs and rested her cheek on her knees as she looked at Brodie. She didn't know what to say. She still felt numb. She was too far beyond hurt to feel pain, but she couldn't drum up the energy to be angry because she wasn't entirely surprised anymore.

"Laurel, what do you want? Do you wish to remain here, so I can court you? My offer remains in place, both to give you time to decide how we proceed—if we do, and to ensure you have what you need while you are here. Do you wish to go to Kilchurn, whether it's as my wife or a new villager?"

"I don't know, Brodie. My mind feels fuzzy when I try to think aboot it. What I do know is that I'm grateful for you. You could be on a horse halfway home after what you learned aboot my family and what you've learned aboot me. But rather than leave, you remained here," Laurel looked around the chamber. "Beside me, so I wouldn't wake alone. No one else would ever think to do that, to understand what it would have meant for me to be here by myself after what I heard."

"I'm not going anywhere. Not without you unless you say otherwise," Brodie promised. He moved to sit beside Laurel.

His heavy arm wrapped around her caused her to topple against his chest. She sighed as she closed her eyes again. The sense of peace and security she felt in her dream swept over her as she leaned against Brodie.

"Do you think that sometimes one part of our mind can know more than another?" Laurel asked.

"Aye. I think parts of our mind can sense things or deduce them before the part that forms our thoughts does. It's how men stay alive in battle when they have no reason to suspect an attack, but they move away in time. It's how a bairn learns to walk and talk, I suppose. It's how I know I don't want to leave your side."

"I worry aboot what you will see if you sign a betrothal contract," Laurel admitted.

"Not if, when. And Laurel, quite honestly, I don't give a shite what your father does or doesn't offer. My clan doesn't need your dowry, and any lands you might have are too far from Campbell territory to be of benefit. I can ensure I set aside dower lands for you and any daughters we might have. I can and will provide for you."

"You may say that, but your clan council likely will not agree," Laurel countered.

"As you said earlier, you bring the Ross name to our marriage. That will suffice."

"How can it? I bring naught else. No plates, no silver or gold, no linens. Naught."

"You don't know that," Brodie soothed. "And don't you see? I want you, Laurel. I want you as you are and who you are. I don't want what your father does or doesn't offer."

"Are you this wise because you're auld?" Laurel said playfully as she brushed her fingertips through a streak of graying hair.

"Mayhap, but I'm not so auld that I won't chase you around our chamber and into our bed," Brodie said before kissing Laurel. Before the fire turned into an inferno, Brodie pulled away with a groan. "Waiting for you may very well be the death of me."

"Our?" Laurel asked timidly.

"Yours and mine," Brodie nodded.

Laurel swallowed. "Would it have been yours and Eliza's?"

"Not anytime soon. Mayhap one day, but I honestly doubt it," Brodie admitted. "I never thought of sharing my chamber with her or anyone else before you."

"Despite what the king relayed from my father, and despite my years here, I've never—I haven't—I don't know how…" Laurel stumbled over her words before shaking her head and twisting to bury her face against her bent legs. She was humiliated all over again. She squeaked when Brodie lifted her into his lap and leaned back against the headboard.

"And I told the truth. It doesn't matter to me if you have or you haven't. But I know you're a maiden."

"How can you possibly know? You haven't touched me —there."

"It's how you react to each of our kisses or when I touch you. It how you touch me. You're tentative at first, but your natural courage and curiosity pushes through. You're not a liar, so I don't think you're pretending," Brodie answered. Laurel flinched, then winced.

"Brodie, I have lied, and you know that. I've lied countless times since I've been here. White lies to flatter other ladies, nasty half-truths to be mean. Full-fledged lies to get what I need since I don't receive pin money."

"Have you lied to me?" Brodie asked.

"No. I—I could have. More than once, but I haven't. I don't want to."

"Do you think you will continue to lie if your circumstances changed?" Brodie prodded.

"Only if it protected you or someone I care aboot, if it kept our clan safe."

"Those are understandable reasons. Laurie, I don't fear you lying to me. You enjoy telling me the blunt and painful truth far too much," Brodie chuckled, and it rumbled against Laurel. She closed her eyes and sighed. "Are you comfortable?"

"Immensely," Laurel yawned.

"Do wish to sleep more?" Brodie stroked her hair.

"I'm tired, but no, I don't want to sleep. I'd rather spend time with you," Laurel admitted shyly. "Would you tell me more aboot your mother?"

"Och, naught would make me happier than to stay here and tell you stories," Brodie grinned. "My mother had hair as dark as a raven's wing and eyes the color of the most aged whisky. She was a wee thing. Barely came to my chest by the time I was three-and-ten."

"I suspect you were not a wee lad at three-and-ten," Laurel pointed out.

"Mayhap not, but she could still skelp me even at the size I am now," Brodie chortled. "When I was a wee bairn, she used to take me riding with her. I would sit before her on her gelding. I would beg her to go faster and faster. She indulged me to a point, reminding me that what I want and what I can do isn't always the right thing to do. She refused to gallop with me, insisting she wouldn't risk me falling. She reminded me that we might want to, and her horse could, but it wouldn't be right. It was one of the most valuable lessons either of my parents taught me. But I loved those rides. She would laugh and make up stories aboot the fae she swore lived in the forest and our loch. She laughed a great deal back then."

"She sounds wonderful," Laurel said wistfully.

"She was. I wish she were alive for you to meet her. I think you would have found a kindred spirit," Brodie mused.

"Will you tell me more?"

Brodie and Laurel settled onto her bed, lying beside one another as Brodie told her one story after another about his childhood. He told her aboot his cousin Kennan who married Laird Grant's younger daughter. And Laurel mentioned she knew the laird's other daughter Cairstine well, and that her friend Madeline recently married Fingal Grant, the laird's heir. Brodie regaled her with tales of the mischief he and his younger brother Dominic got into when they were children. Laurel learned about Dominic and his wife, who awaited them at Kilchurn.

As the afternoon progressed, they moved onto stories about Laurel's childhood. Brodie was wary to ask, unsure of what he would learn. But he discovered Laurel had a happy childhood until her parents sent her to court. He understood why leaving her idyllic life had been so traumatic once he learned about how involved she'd been with her clan and even how close she and Monty had once been. The more Brodie learned about the life Laurel had, the more resolved he was to offer her what she missed. He knew she was no longer a child, and she couldn't have all the whimsy and carefree days she'd once had, but he could offer her the respect that she'd earned among her people. And he could offer her the chance to be at peace with herself. It was late afternoon when they sighed in unison before smiling. They could no longer avoid returning to the Privy Council chamber if Brodie were to review and sign the betrothal contracts.

THIRTEEN

Laurel's toes curled within her boots as she sat among the other ladies-in-waiting. She'd been refused entry into the Privy Council chamber when she arrived on Brodie's arm. Brodie had insisted that the chamberlain permit her to enter, and the pugnacious man nearly wet himself when Brodie leaned so far forward that their noses nearly met. But it had done neither of them any good when the chamberlain let them pass. King Robert shook his head and dismissed Laurel, phrasing his order as a suggestion that she join the queen. Brodie only conceded after he insisted either Laurel remained or that he be allowed to accompany her to the queen's solar.

Brodie walked her to the door. When a guard pushed it open to a group of staring facing, Brodie kissed Laurel on the temple and gave her hand a squeeze. She'd squared her shoulders and took a step forward, but Brodie didn't release her arm. She looked up at him, and he mouthed, "I'm proud of you. Be brave." It was the infusion of courage Laurel needed to face the queen and her entourage. She'd crossed the chamber and found a seat in the center where she opened the book she'd been reading the day before. As the group tittered around her, she steeled herself for what would inevitably come. Her toes ached as she waited.

"Lady Laurel," Queen Elizabeth addressed her. Laurel rose and approached the older woman, dropping into a deep curtsy until she noticed the queen's fingers flicked the signal for her to rise. "Please keep me company."

Laurel lowered herself onto the overstuffed pillow that laid beside the queen's feet. Sitting there always reminded her of being a loyal hound. She understands that was precisely why the queen positioned as it was. It gave Queen Elizabeth a position of superiority, and it humbled whoever sat upon it. Laurel remained silent, awaiting whatever the queen would say about the scandal Laurel caused.

Keeping her voice exceptionally low, Queen Elizabeth said, "While I wouldn't have advocated making such a public declaration, I am gladdened to know your future is with Laird Campbell. He will be a good husband to you, Lady Laurel. The two of you are well matched. You will challenge him to no end, I'm sure, but he will not begrudge you it. In fact, I suspect he rather enjoys it. He might have spent his life with a quite different woman than you, and I don't think it would have been a happy match."

"Do you mean Lady Eliza?" Laurel asked softly.

"You know of her?" Queen Elizabeth asked in surprise.

"Aye. Laird Campbell told me he'd exchanged vows with her, but she'd died before they made it a true marriage. He mentioned we were not much alike," Laurel hedged.

Queen Elizabeth snickered. "Not much alike indeed. She was a nice lass, but mousy. I doubt that would have changed, no matter how long she lived or how long she served as Lady Campbell. The alliance would have been advantageous to the Campbells, but I fear the laird was shortsighted in his choice. His clan will not live and die by access to Loch Sween. They may live and die by who stands beside their laird. They are a powerful clan, and they need a lady with the gumption to stand beside her husband and against those who would threaten the clan. There are many who would."

Laurel remained quiet, surprised to hear some of what

Brodie shared with her being articulated by Queen Elizabeth. She wondered if the queen would say more, but when the conversation lulled, or rather the queen said nothing, Laurel wondered if she was dismissed. She didn't dare stand, but she wasn't certain what to do. She jumped when the queen spoke again.

"Lady Laurel, I anticipate your life being even more trying over the next several days. But it was easy enough to read Laird Campbell's lips and the look in his eyes. You won't avoid the rumors or the scornful looks, but I believe Laird Campbell will do what he can to shield you. But if you would heed my council, you'd do well to curb your tongue."

"Aye, Your Grace," Laurel replied.

"I'm certain the ladies will goad you. But remember, in the end, you are the one Laird Campbell chose. They may have caught you in...a delicate moment, but anyone with eyes will see soon enough that it is not just lust that lies between you two. Bear that in mind when they test you."

Laurel looked up at the queen, shocked by the maternal and sage advice the older woman offered. Laurel recalled the queen had suffered great public scrutiny when she married King Robert, especially when she returned after eight years of imprisonment by the English King Edward Longshanks.

"Thank you, Your Grace." With a nod, Queen Elizabeth dismissed Laurel, who stood then dipped into a low curtsy. As she made her way back to her stool and her book, she took in the faces that watched her suspiciously, those who gloated, and those who turned their noses up at her. She noticed Emelie and Blythe watching her, but neither woman had defended her that morning. Emelie had been less convinced than the others, but she'd hadn't spoken on Laurel's behalf. The sisters' ease with which they turned from her hurt more than any rumor Sarah Anne or the others spread. She'd considered Emelie and Blythe her friends, and she'd defended them and their sister Isabella when people cast barbs at the younger women about Isa marrying a man who once served King

Edward. With a sigh, she returned to her seat and returned to her book, but her attention wouldn't settle on the words before her. Her mind conjured various scenarios that might be occurring in the Privy Council chamber as she pretended to read. Her belly ached as it clenched over and over. She practically threw the book aside when it was time for the ladies to dress for the evening meal.

"You have made sure you will marry in haste." Laurel disregarded Sarah Anne's taunt, pretending to be set on her course to her chamber. But Sarah Anne refused to be ignored. "You had best pray Laird Campbell doesn't delay having the banns read, lest you deliver an eight moon bairn."

Laurel ground her teeth, repeating the queen's advice that she curb her tongue. Sarah Anne's accusation that she might be pregnant made many of the ladies gasp, and Laurel heard a fresh wave of whispers follow in her wake.

"Liam and Nelson will have their noses out of joint since they have lost their wager," Margaret mused.

"They have not. Laird Campbell must show up to his wedding. He might still run all the way back to the Highlands before he shackles himself to the Shrew of Stirling," Sarah Anne corrected.

"Do you think he would really jilt her?" Emelie asked.

"Wouldn't you?" Sarah Anne asked.

"Lady Laurel," Brodie's masculine voice made the women jump. He stepped away from the wall against which he leaned just beside Laurel's door. "I've come to escort you to the evening meal."

Laurel's smile was tight as she nodded. "Thank you. I will only be a moment. My maid Ina should already have my gown ready."

"No need to hurry," Brodie assured her, bringing her hand to his lips when she stopped in front of him.

Laurel told herself to relax when Brodie smiled, but the other women's presence put her nerves on edge. She nodded and slipped into her chamber, relieved to find Ina awaiting her. Laurel considered the gown Ina had selected, wishing she hadn't worn her newly reconstructed gown so recently. She twisted her lips from side to side, knowing the king would announce their betrothal that night. While Ina chose one of Laurel's more favorite gowns, it was rather subdued. Narrowing her eyes as she considered what hung in her armoire, Laurel's lips twitched before she drew them in to keep from grinning. She crossed the chamber and flung open the doors, pulling out the one she desired.

Sensing her lady's impatience, Ina worked quickly to lace Laurel into the dress she selected before her deft fingers created an intricate coiffure of braids and ribbons. When Ina finished, Laurel beamed at her maid. What Ina accomplished in a hurry impressed her.

"You've done a wonderful job, Ina. I don't thank you nearly enough for all that you do for me. Please know that I appreciate it all," Laurel said as she stooped to kiss the older woman's cheek. "Thank you for staying with me."

"Och, ma lady, wheest. Ye'll have me blubbering into ma hanky," Ina chuckled. "Go to yer mon. He's been pacing in yon passageway for at least the last half hour."

"He has?" Laurel asked as she glanced at the door.

"Aye. Gave me a right fright, he did, when I came around the corner with the pitcher of warm water. Nearly sloshed the entire thing down the front of me." Ina grinned. "I nearly forgot! The laird asked me to give ye this." The maid moved to the window embrasure and lifted something Laurel hadn't noticed. She sucked in a whistling breath when she recognized the swath of Campbell plaid. She took it from Ina and held it up to her face. She could smell a trace of Brodie's scent on the wool. He'd worn his own *breacan feile* the entire time he'd been at court, which many Highlanders abandoned in favor of breeks and a doublet. Brodie would have draped the plaid she held over his shoulder if he opted for the Lowland attire. Instead, it now draped over Laurel's. She moved to her jewelry box, a moment of regret that none of her jewels were real or fine enough to compliment the Campbell plaid, but she selected a brooch and clasped the sash as her waist on the opposite side from where it covered her shoulder.

"I wish ye happy, ma lady," Ina said as she opened the door for Laurel.

"Laurie," Brodie breathed as he turned to watch Laurel enter the passageway. She took his breath away. Her cream gown made her alabaster skin glow, while it made her hair shimmer like flames beside snow. She was the image of fire and ice, innocence and passion. The stitching along the top of her skirts just below her waist was exquisite. But it was his plaid resting over her heart that made him smile with happiness. She fingered the hem of the plaid with unease, and Brodie realized she wasn't certain how to interpret his greeting. "You look beautiful. Thank you for wearing my colors."

"Does it mean you've signed the contracts?" Laurel asked tentatively.

"Aye, Laurie. We are betrothed now." Brodie watched to see if Laurel gave any sign of regret. What he spied was excitement and relief. "Are you happy, thistle?"

"I didn't imagine I would be, at least not this much, but I am, Brodie. I really am," Laurel admitted. "I wish I had something to give to you."

"I don't expect aught," Brodie slid his arms around her, holding her in place. "And don't think I said that because I believe you haven't aught to give. I didn't give you the plaid because I wanted aught in return. I gave it to you because I want you to ken I'm proud to call you my bride. I want you to ken I welcome you into my clan and my family."

"Why are you so wonderful?"

"Och, we shall see how wonderful you think I am when you discover I snore. And when I track mud into your Great Hall," Brodie grinned, then lowered his voice. "Or when I make love you in our bed throughout the night and well into the morn."

Laurel's cheeks blazed scarlet, but she didn't shy away

from Brodie. "When?"

"Three sennights. The time it takes to post the banns," Brodie informed her.

"I thought you only intended to stay a fortnight. That would mean only a sennight longer. Don't you need to return to Kilchurn?" Laurel bit her lower lip. "Are you going home then coming back to claim me?"

"Kilchurn needs its laird, but right now, I need to be here more," Brodie answered.

"I shouldn't be what keeps you from your duties, Brodie. That's not a good impression to make with your people."

"Laurie, I told you I wish to court you. I signed the contracts, but I was clear to King Robert and Monty that you may refuse me without penalty. We have three sennights. It's not long, but I hope it is time enough for you to ken if you wish to come back to Kilchurn with me, whether it's as my wife or a villager."

"I already told ye, I canna live there as just another member of the village," Laurel said as a lump formed in her throat. Her emotions pushed her burr back into her accent.

"And I dinna want ye to, but I will do what ye wish. If ye dinna wish to marry me, I willna leave ye here, and I willna let Monty take ye to Balnagown or somewhere ye'd be miserable." Brodie's brogue came back when he heard the familiar rolling sounds of Laurel's Highland speech.

"Thank ye, *mo dhìonadair*," Laurel said as she leaned into Brodie's chest, and he drew her into his tight embrace.

"I will always be yer protector, thistle." Brodie pressed his lips to Laurel's in an achingly tender moment that was shattered by a slamming door. The word "strumpet" floated to them, but when Brodie and Laurel looked around, there were too many shocked faces to know who'd uttered the accusation. Laurel sighed before she glanced up at Brodie.

"Mayhap one of these days we'll learn."

"Keep kissing me like that, and the only thing I will learn is to find more ways to keep kissing ye."

FOURTEEN

Laurel steeled herself for entering the Great Hall with Brodie. It felt like a lifetime ago, but it had only been that morning when she'd spat on his boots in front of half the court. She'd insulted him and been more disrespectful than she had ever been on her worst day in the past. They'd argued in the stairwell, then kissed. They'd argued in her chamber, then kissed. They'd met with the king, and Laurel faced the most debilitating news she'd ever received. Rather than abandon her, Brodie had remained with her while she slept for several hours. Then they'd kissed.

Now she walked beside him as they approached the table where the Ross and Campbell men sat together. Laurel couldn't help but overhear the whispers about Brodie being forced to marry her, that he'd only kissed her to silence her. She heard more than one man whisper suggestions about how to keep her from talking. She swallowed her rising gorge, forcing herself to breathe lest she cry or her cheeks go up in flames. Despite her fair complexion, she wasn't prone to flushing.

Brodie adjusted their arms, so they held hands rather than Laurel's arm looping through his. That set off another tsunami of gossip, but Brodie merely squeezed her hand.

Monty and the other men rose when she approached the table, showing her deference that normally didn't exist. She supposed it came from her soon-to-be position as Lady Campbell, assuming she did nothing to ruin her buddy relationship with Brodie. She tensed when King Robert and Queen Elizabeth entered the gathering hall, knowing the announcement was imminent. The queen seated herself, but the king remained standing.

"We toast today to the upcoming nuptials of Laird Brodie Campbell and Lady Laurel Ross. As of this afternoon, they are betrothed to wed within a moon. May they be blessed with a prosperous marriage," King Robert cheered as he raised his chalice.

Laurel plastered a serene expression on her face. She hadn't missed that King Robert hadn't wished them a long or happy marriage, merely a prosperous one. She couldn't imagine how that was possible since she was the pauper she'd feared. Before arriving at the evening meal, Brodie and Laurel met with King Robert and Monty in the Privy Council chamber. She discovered her father included land along the coast in her dowry. Had it been on the western side of the country, it might have benefited Brodie. But on the east coast, there were few trading routes that would help his clan since they lived diagonally across the country. There was a paltry sum of coins and the wardrobe which Laurel currently owned. There were no household items, but her father's mother bequeathed her a handful of jewels. The woman died after Laurel arrived at court, so she had no knowledge that she'd inherited them. Since nothing else would be sent from Balnagown, she didn't hold her breath that the jewels would arrive.

Monty appeared shaken when he heard the king read her dowry, confusion flashing across his face more than once despite having read it himself earlier. Laurel watched him the entire time. She knew her brother's expressions, so she knew he'd believed there was more. She'd wanted to tell him smugly, "I told you so," but it would have gained her nothing, and she knew there would be little vindication in it. She wondered what their father told Monty before he departed. When the king finished reading the brief list, Laurel turned her gaze to Brodie, who'd been observing her. Shame washed over her. It had been one thing to know, in theory, that there was an insufficient dowry, but it was entirely another for her groom to hear it proven.

Brodie had leaned to whisper in Laurel's ear, "I've told you I'm not marrying you for the dowry."

"I ken. You're marry me because the king is making you."

"Laurie," Brodie didn't hide the exasperation from his voice. But he said no more, knowing Laurel struggled with the vast changes laid out before her. He would return home with a wife on his arm, but little else would change. Laurel faced meeting a new clan and a new home. She would once again have her world turned upside down. She would leave behind the life she knew, even if she didn't like it. She would assume the duties of chatelaine for the first time in her life. And she would do all of that knowing her new clan would realize she brought little but the clothes on her back.

As they sat together in the Great Hall, Brodie slipped his hand onto Laurel's leg, stopping it from bouncing with nervous energy. He encouraged her to eat by moving the most select cuts of meat onto her half of the trencher they now shared. But Laurel could do little but pick at it. Her stomach ached, and she felt people watching. Despite her feigned bravado, she feared she would be ill if she ate. The only time she relaxed was when she danced with Brodie and Donnan. She accepted two dances with Monty, and it wasn't as uncomfortable as she thought. Her brother was kind to her, not mentioning anything about that day or what was to come. Instead, he offered to take her riding the next day. She accepted, eager to escape the castle, even if only for an hour. Donnan told her off-color jokes, much as he had when they were younger. She couldn't help but giggle at several, especially the one that involved a goose's bill and a sheep's back end. But it was the dances with Brodie that strengthened her resolve to muster through the coming weeks. He held her closer than propriety dictated. She supposed it was a combination of lust and his intention to prove to the crowd that he wished to be with Laurel. She didn't question it, instead, drawing strength from his silent encouragement.

Laurel's feet ached by the time the queen signaled the ladies-in-waiting may retire. Even though she sat with the men, the queen's expectations still bound her. Brodie walked her to the door of the Great Hall, but Laurel declined his offer to escort her to her chamber. People had witnessed him on the ladies' floor far too many times that day.

"Monty told me he offered to take you riding tomorrow," Brodie said as they came to a stop before the stairs. "Is that what you would like?"

"I wish to escape the keep for as long as I can," Laurel smiled ruefully, but then pulled her lips in and looked at the floor. Brodie sensed what she wished but was too afraid of his rejection to ask.

"May I join you?" Brodie asked. He wanted to cringe when his tone sounded needier than he intended, but he wished to spend the day with Laurel. He wanted to see her on horseback, free of the courtly trappings.

"Yes," Laurel blurted. With a plan set for the morning, Laurel retired to her chamber. Despite the long nap, the day's events exhausted her. She barely undressed before she collapsed into bed. Brodie considered finding his men and venturing out to a tavern, relishing several drams of whisky after the unpredictability of the day, but he decided to pass. He may have wanted the relaxing sensation whisky would bring, but he was in no mood to face anyone from court. He settled for a swig from his own flask before he fell into a sound sleep.

FIFTEEN

Monty and Donnan nursed their mugs of ale at the Fox and Hound. Neither felt talkative after Monty relayed the day's events. Discovering Laurel's scant dowry was a shock. He'd been certain her dowry was less than their sisters', but he couldn't conceive of how meager it was. He was certain his clan's finances were strong enough to weather more generosity. But he considered how his mother bemoaned Laurel's reputation, harping on her unmarried status. It only irritated his father, who grumbled that the money spent on her lodging at court would have been better spent on a dowry. But often, Monty wondered—even asked—why his father didn't choose someone who wanted the dowry more than he cared about Laurel's reputation or personality. It wouldn't be the first arranged marriage where the couple couldn't tolerate one another. He'd given up suggesting she come home to Balnagown. At first, he'd noticed interest in his father's eyes. But it dulled over the years as his mother continued to complain about her daughters who moved away and the one who was a failure.

As the two men sat mulling over life in silence, Monty wondered if his mother had more influence than he realized. He considered whether she could be the reason for Laurel's mockery of a dowry. While it might have sufficed for a lesser laird's daughter or a chieftain's, it was insulting for an earl's child.

"Do you think your father made that hideous ultimatum to actually force Laurel home?" Donnan spoke up.

Monty considered Donnan's question, replaying various conversations with Laird Ross and then factoring in what he now suspected about Lady Ross. "He might have. He wouldn't be asking her to come back, but he would be duty bound to accept her. It would put the shame on Laurel's shoulders, but it would bring her home. It would likely give him a reprieve from Mother's nagging."

"Does no one realize how similar Laurel and Lady Ross are?" Donnan mused. "For quite different reasons, mind you. But the outcome is the same. They're both harpies." Donnan had no love lost for Lady Ross, but he rarely spoke against his lover's mother.

"I think that's why Father hasn't wanted her to come home enough to make it happen. I think he fears having them both under the same roof."

"Doesn't he remember how she used to be? Does he believe it's impossible that she might sweeten if she were away from a place she loathes and people she detests?"

"I've suggested as much, but I don't think he does. I think he believes she's unredeemable," Monty confessed.

"What do you think? You know my opinion."

"I believe she is. I think that's what Brodie sees in her. Despite their scene this morning, have you not noticed how she's calmer when she's with him? I mean, she's still a spitfire —her glares threatened to make me go up in flames—but she's not as on edge, as defensive as she used to be."

"I noticed at the evening meal," Donnan shared. "I even sensed it while we danced. She's always grinned at my jokes when we've danced in the past, but this eve, she fully laughed —even giggled. She'd danced with Brodie the set before each of ours."

"He said he liked a challenge. Mayhap his goal isn't so much to tame her as it is to enjoy her fire."

"From how you described her face when you discovered him in her chamber, I would assume he's enjoyed it already," Donnan grinned, and Monty grimaced. The door to the inn swung open, and a rowdy group of courtiers entered. Both Donnan and Monty groaned. "Why are they choosing respectable places? I can think of three taverns they're better suited to."

"They can't afford the whores there," Monty muttered. The couple lowered their heads, hoping not to draw attention to themselves, but Monty's hair was unmistakable.

"Ross!" Andrew MacFarlane, Lady Catherine's cousin, bellowed. The man swiped a mug from a passing serving wench's tray and dropped a coin down her cleavage with a wink. He and half a dozen men made their way to Monty and Donnan's table. Monty flashed Donnan a wary gaze before they smiled at the newcomers. Monty recognized only half. "I'd introduce you to Montgomery Ross and his second, Donnan Ross," Andrew chirped.

"Good eve, I'm Seamus Mackenzie. I represent my laird at court," a blond man nodded.

"I'm Stephen MacBain," the man who sat down beside Daniel said.

"Matthew MacDougall," the last unfamiliar man grunted at Monty. "Nelson's brother."

"Speaking of the arse," Andrew turned to Matthew. "Where is he?"

"The Merry Widow as far as I know. With bluidy Oliphant up his arse. Likely buggering him."

Monty and Donnan knew better than to look at one another, but their grips tightened on their mugs. "Gunn, Mackay, MacKinnon," Monty greeted the three he knew. He was indirectly related to the Mackay representative through marriage. He was on friendly terms with him since he was Laird Tristan Mackay's cousin.

127

"What brings you here?" Magnus Mackay asked.

"The lack of a crowd," Monty said pointedly, to which Andrew guffawed.

"More likely escaping your wee sister. I was surprised she wasn't breathing fire at you. She's a dragon if ever there was one," Andrew laughed.

"She's my sister," Monty warned.

"If anyone should fear for his arse, it's Campbell," Matthew MacDougall sniped. "I don't even like the mon, but I'd rather he roast in hell than from Lady Laurel."

Donnan nudged Monty under the table before placing coins on the table. Because of Donnan's position as Monty's second, he was able to share a chamber with Monty, rather than sleep in the barracks. The arrangement suited them well. The Rosses made to rise, signaling their men, but Laird Edgar Gunn placed a pouch of coins on the table.

"I didn't have an opportunity to enter the wager Oliphant placed. But I offer a new one. I wager fifty pounds Campbell doesn't show up to his wedding," Edgar announced.

"I shall up that ante," Daniel said. "To one hundred pounds, just as Oliphant offered."

"I bet he will," Magnus replied. "She doesn't need to speak if he keeps her occupied enough, and she has a fine figure to distract him if she does."

"You will not wager on my sister," Monty snapped. "Put your money away, Gunn."

"Join the wager or not, but you cannot stop me," Edgar taunted. "Aye, throw your fist at me. I shall just arrange the bet elsewhere."

"I wager you're likelier to marry before she does," Stephen suggested.

"I'm not here to see to my own wedding. I'm here to arrange my sister's, which I've done. It will happen as soon as the banns have been read," Monty insisted.

"That gives the poor bastard three sennights to get lost

among the hills," Andrew snorted. "He'd do well to ride off tonight."

"Leave off," Monty threatened, rising to his feet with his hand raised toward the claymore strapped to his back. At his movement, all the Ross men rose. The newcomers foolishly arrived without guards, presumedly believing they could defend themselves and one another. The Rosses outnumbered them.

"Bah. Dinna get in a twitch, Ross," Andrew waved at his seat. "I say, rather than betting whether Campbell marries, we save the poor bastard."

"Have him compromise some other lady?" Edgar snickered.

"Doesn't he know Lady Laurel is a pauper compared to your other sisters?" Matthew asked. "He must have read the contracts."

"He's not interested in her dowry," Monty stated, his chin raised.

"Then she must be good for a tumble," Magnus said, and the men roared with laughter.

"Cease," Monty slammed his hand on the table, making it wobble. "My men and I leave now before there is bloodshed. But I promise you I will kill each of you in your sleep if you continue to disparage my sister. She's always been my favorite, and I shall always be her brother. Attack her character again, and I will watch you laid in the ground." Monty didn't wait for any of the men to respond. Monty, Donnan, and the Ross guards left the tavern with haste.

"His favorite?" Edgar sniffed. "How bad are the rest?" The men roared at the snide comment.

"You heard aboot Lady Myrna and her antics with Padraig Munro. And his brother," Stephen reminded them. "MacGillivray is miserable, and she still hasn't bore him a son."

"Pitiful sod," Matthew said as he raised his mug in Chieftain MacGillivray's honor. "I say Andrew has the right of it.

Campbell needs rescuing, and since ours isn't the only wager we've each entered, we'd do well to see their marriage doesn't last."

The six men raised their mugs and grinned before each of them drained it and bellowed for more.

SIXTEEN

It had been twelve days since King Robert announced Laurel and Brodie's betrothal. She'd expected doubt and regret to fill her during the ensuing days, but she'd become spoiled by Brodie's attentiveness and the taste of freedom he offered her each day. Depending on her commitments, Brodie took Laurel riding every morning or afternoon. Monty joined them the first five days under the auspices of being her chaperone, but he soon tired of watching the couple when he preferred being in the lists. Ross and Campbell guards accompanied them, and Laurel figured with her reputation in shambles, it mattered little if anyone chaperoned them. She understood that even without the banns posted, they could make their betrothal into a binding marriage by coupling.

Laurel and Brodie fought the temptation to do just that, since neither wanted to begin their marriage under a darker cloud than they already would. The rides offered them an opportunity to become better acquainted, and Laurel discovered Brodie had been correct from the beginning. Their minds worked in remarkably similar ways. When he told her about his clan, he often asked what she would do if she was laird and faced the challenges he did. He chided himself for ever being surprised at her astute observations and sound solutions, but she impressed him over and over. In turn, Laurel felt validated, her self-confidence genuine rather than feigned.

Their time together wasn't entirely without disagreement, most often about Laurel's penchant for speed and jumps Brodie was certain would break her neck. It wasn't until he articulated his fears that she ceased goading and rebuking him for being old and staid. Laurel balked when Brodie insisted she ride within the center of the men the first few days. She kept her most scathing comments for when they rested their horses, and Brodie dragged her out of earshot. But each of their spats ended with compromises they were both willing to accept. And a kiss. A passionate, explosive, earth-shaking kiss that would leave them clinging to one another as they tested their resolve to do nothing more than that.

Laurel sat beside Brodie each morning and at each midday meal, but the queen refused to allow Laurel to join Brodie for every evening meal. Laurel understood the queen was already indulging her by allowing her to ride out with Brodie every day. But the two days that filled her with the most satisfaction were the Sundays they sat together as the priest read the banns, then posted it on the kirk door. Brodie held her hand beneath the folds of her skirts. He'd gifted her a bolt of honey-colored satin after the first week's Mass. Laurel had been speechless, and tears brimmed at her eyes when he presented matching slippers. He'd grown self-conscious when she said nothing at first. He assured her that if she didn't care for the color or if it didn't suit her, he would take her to exchange it. She launched herself at him and nearly knocked them both over with the force of her exuberant thanks.

Brodie's chest felt as though it would burst when he saw the excitement and gratitude on Laurel's face. While it was costly fabric, the gesture hadn't seemed as significant to him as it was to her. He'd wanted to give her something as a token of their engagement that she would appreciate. But he realized after years of receiving so little from her family, the mere fact that it was a gift overwhelmed her. When they rode out that afternoon, she'd confided in him the extent to which she'd gone to hide her dire financial circumstances. She told him of how she'd pawned her jewelry, hoping to earn enough sewing to buy her jewelry back and still have enough coin for what she needed. But she explained that the window of time she had expired before she could claim her finery. She shared the nights she'd stayed awake to remake her gowns, and how her disdain grew for the people not astute enough to realize that it was the same kirtle over and over but merely with different embellishments. She admitted the pleasure she derived from seeing so many women wearing her creations, none the wiser that the woman they disdained provided the couture in which they preened.

Brodie had listened with alternating waves of amazement, sadness, and anger as she described how life changed over the eleven years she lived at court. She held little back from Brodie as she admitted her sins like he was her confessor. The Laurel he'd witnessed in the brief time he knew her only lashed out when she felt cornered. Her tongue was sharp, but he didn't understand how she'd earned her reputation until she admitted how she'd behaved when she was more newly arrived.

"I was horrible to many of the other ladies. I was so angry all the time. I didn't want to see others happy around me when I believed I could never feel that way again. It was easy to follow the others' lead. When I think back to what I said to and aboot Maude, I make myself sick. I remember one evening in particular. Maude stood beside Arabella Johnstone, the most beautiful lady-in-waiting in decades. They were friends, but I said Maude looked like a sow standing next to a dove. I claimed that her endowments made her look more like a tavern wench than a lady. The worst part is I leaned she overheard everything Cairstine, Madeline, and I said, and I didn't feel a moment's remorse."

The only time she grew evasive was when she mentioned Madeline MacLeod—now Madeline Grant—discovered something she wished she hadn't let slip, and that was how her former companion manipulated her. Brodie attempted to glean more from her, but she was too astute to give away more. She'd cast him a warning glance before moving onto another story. But Brodie already suspected what the secret was.

He noticed slight gestures and mannerisms between Monty and Donnan that struck him as odd. As he watched the pair more and more, he noticed they were in sync with one another like an old married couple. He and his second had been friends since they were weans, and he was close with his brother Dominic, but the dynamic between Monty and Donnan was notably different. It reminded him more of Dominic and his wife Colina or his cousin Kennon and his wife Fenella. He'd puzzled over why the men's relationship didn't bother him more. He knew he should have recoiled in disgust, thought it unnatural and against God's will, even named them as sodomites. But he found he cared little once he noticed how much Donnan cared for Laurel. And Monty even redeemed himself when Brodie learned there'd been a disagreement the night of his betrothal, and Monty defended Laurel against a group of men. Monty and Donnan avoided explaining what caused the argument, and Brodie decided it was for the best he didn't know, or he would have sought the men himself.

As the couple charged across a meadow that twelfth day, Laurel inhaled the unfettered air that only came from riding an hour north of Stirling. She looked at the mountains in the distance, seeing the Highlands nearly within reach. She laid low over Teine's back as she raced Brodie toward the foothills. The ground had few obstacles, so she allowed her steed to have his head as they charged on. The couple raced across the field many times during their outings, and both were competitive, just like their mounts. Neither consistently won, taking turns in victory and challenging the other to a rematch.

Laurel's tinkling laughter filled Brodie's ears as they

galloped neck and neck. He glanced at her, caught speechless once more by her beauty and the happiness that radiated from her. He'd assumed she exaggerated the significance of the rides. He thought it would be a nice outing, but she'd blossomed with fresh air and exhilaration.

"Yer wee beastie shall be embarrassed once more when Teine thrashes him," Laurel teased as she spurred her chestnut gelding to go faster. She'd surprised all the Campbell men when her horse soon outpaced half of them. He was faster than every gelding Brodie's men rode and at least half of the stallions. Riding at the front of their group, Brodie's horse was the best within the pack, but Laurel's expertise as a jockey ensured she won their races as often as he did. She and Teine won that day by a nostril. The climate had shifted in the fortnight and a half Brodie was at court, and the early autumn air pinkened Laurel's cheeks and ears.

"You look like you belong among the fae," Brodie mused. "You charm the animals into doing your bidding, for surely you must have tricked *Lann* into letting you win."

"Letting me win? If your steed were as sharp as the blade he's named for, perhaps he would cut through the wind faster," Laurel teased as Brodie helped her from her horse. After nearly two weeks of riding out with the couple, the guards knew to look away. Brodie cupped Laurel's backside as she rose onto her toes to meet his lips halfway. Their rides were the only time they dared indulge except for a brief kiss before they retired alone each night. Laurel reached between them and pushed Brodie's sporran away, sighing as she felt his length rest against her mons.

"You shred my resolve, Laurie. I watch the joy you get from riding your horse and wish you were riding me," Brodie murmured beside her ear. His provocative words made the ache between Laurel's thighs become a low burn. She shifted restlessly as she looked into his soulful gray eyes. Kisses alone hadn't nearly satisfied her curiosity. The first time she grasped his backside, Brodie had lifted her off her feet and nearly ran into the nearby woods with her. He'd growled as he kissed a blazing trail along her neck to behind her ear, making her shiver with arousal and the unknown. Her knees had buckled when his hand slid beneath her skirts, and his fingers slid along her seam. When his pressed his finger into her entrance, she'd gripped his leine and rested her head against his shoulders. But when a second finger entered her, and he worked the satiny skin within her sheath, she'd fought and failed to stifle her moans. Her hips rocked against his hand as he brought her to the brink and then pushed her over. The passion that simmered between them was rivaled by the affection they shared in the aftermath.

"And if no one were to know?" Laurel whispered. Brodie groaned as he fought against considering Laurel's implications. He struggled each night that he left her on the landing to her floor, finding relief alone in his chamber. His men playfully jested that he should ease his bollocks at a tavern, but he'd pummeled one after another in the lists that day. His men discovered he found nothing humorous about their suggestion, nor would he entertain it. Instead, he remained in lust-filled longing, knowing Laurel suffered as he did. But he suspected she didn't know how to ease the torment like he did. He eagerly anticipated teaching her, knowing there would be nights when duty forced him away from their home and their bed.

"Laurie, we have five days until they post the banns for the third time. We could marry that Monday," Brodie suggested, then held his breath. They'd spoken of their desire for one another and how they might relieve it, but Laurel had yet to assure Brodie that she wished to marry him once they could. He hadn't pressed her, standing by his pledge to give her time for him to court her. He was more convinced than ever that he'd been blessed with the right woman, but he wasn't certain that she felt he was the right man for her. He would be heartbroken if she rejected him, but he would see her to wherever she wanted to make her life and check on her regularly once she was there.

Laurel glanced down at the Campbell plaids that draped over both of their shoulders. She'd taken to wearing Brodie's clan pattern, even though she was yet to become Lady Campbell. From the uncertainty in Brodie's voice, she realized he didn't understand that the reason she wore it was because she'd already decided she would marry him.

"You sound worried that I won't agree," Laurel said as she ran her hand over the wool across his chest.

"I haven't wanted to press you," Brodie admitted.

"Brodie, I'm sorry I wasn't clearer." Laurel offered an encouraging smile when Brodie's face fell. She cupped his jaw. "I've worn your plaid since the day you gave it to me. I thought you understood that meant I'd already agreed. Why would I dress like Lady Campbell if I never intended to be her? Why would I suggest we couple if I didn't want our betrothal to be a binding marriage?"

Laurel sucked in a deep breath that made her ribs expand as she watched Brodie's handsome face turn into the most attractive sight she'd ever beheld. She was awestruck once again that he'd chosen her as his wife. He was both braw and kind, and she marveled that a man so wonderful accepted a risk like her. It made her want to try harder to be gracious and kind in return. She squeaked when he picked her up and twirled her around, his booming laughter eliciting another giggle from her. She'd laughed more in the days she'd known Brodie than all the years at Stirling Castle. When he lowered Laurel so that her arms could wrap around his neck rather than her hands resting on his shoulders, she snagged his mouth in a kiss that made Brodie groan.

She'd grown more confident and more eager to lead their exchanges as she grew more comfortable with Brodie. She pressed her tongue against his lips and sighed when it slid past his teeth. She twirled hers against his, before luring his tongue into her mouth. The first time she'd lightly sucked on it had been a kiss goodnight. It was the one time Brodie returned to her chamber. He'd nearly torn her arm from her shoulder as he dragged her into the room, then kicked the door shut, and came within a hair's breadth of ravaging her.

As Laurel tempted him this time, Brodie maintained control by his fingernails. He wanted to sink to the ground and lay with Laurel beneath him. He'd encouraged her to speak aloud what she wished to know, what she wished to try, and after a few prompts, she'd whispered the things she imagined doing with Brodie. He wanted to fulfill each of those dreams in the very meadow where they stood. Eventually, the kiss calmed to soft pecks until Laurel rested her head against Brodie's chest.

"I never imagined I would find a happier place than being outside in the Highlands, but I have," Laurel said as she leaned back. "Can you guess where it is?"

"Is it with me?" Brodie smiled wolfishly.

"*You* were supposed to say you couldn't," Laurel huffed as she playfully tapped his chest. "*I* was supposed to tell you."

"I'll happily listen if you did." Brodie cocked a teasing eyebrow before waggling both of them.

Laurel fingered the hem of Brodie's plaid as an idea stuck her. "Brodie, being out here with you is the happiest I've ever been. I know there is still much for us to learn aboot one another, and I hope it brings us closer together. I also know that most people would say six days is but a moment in time to wait. But I really don't want to." Laurel reached down to where the two ends of her plaid overlapped with a brooch pinning them together. "We're in the Highlands now, even if it's not Campbell territory and still dreadfully close to Stirling. But we are both Highlanders." Laurel paused to look up at Brodie, praying he wouldn't reject her idea or her. "We could handfast. I want to handfast."

Too choked up to speak, Brodie twisted Laurel's sash until he could unpin it. He released a whistle that sounded like a birdcall, and Laurel watched the guards materialize after virtually disappearing in the tall grass. Brodie wrapped the wool around their wrists and cleared his throat.

"I want that too, thistle," Brodie said solemnly.

"Is this instead of the kirk? Will it be a year and a day?" Laurel needed to know if Brodie saw this moment the same way she did.

"Nay, Laurie. This is but a prelude to our many years together. I will never repudiate you."

"Nor will I you, *mo dhìonadair*."

"By the power that Christ brought from heaven," Brodie began. "Mayst thou love me. As the sun follows its course, mayst thou follow me. As light to the eye, as bread to the hungry, as joy to the heart, may thy presence be with me, oh one that I love, till death comes to part us asunder."

Brodie made his solemn vow, and he knew within the depths of his heart that he meant each word. They had made no declarations of love, and they both knew the word was part of the ancient vows, but he fervently hoped that one day Laurel would reciprocate his feelings.

Laurel gazed into Brodie's eyes and saw nothing but earnestness. She smiled shyly as she composed herself. "I promise to trust you and to be honest with you. I promise to listen to you, respect you, and support you. I promise to laugh and play with you and grow and bend with you. I promise to cherish every day we have together. I promise to do all of this through whatever life brings us until the end of my days."

With their hands still joined beneath the plaid, they stepped together and covered one another's heart as their kiss sealed their timeless pledge. Laurel infused all the love and devotion she could into her kiss, wishing Brodie might one day feel for her what she was certain she felt for him. She longed for him to love her as much as she knew she loved him.

"*Mo bhean*," Brodie whispered. My wife.

"*An duine agam*," Laurel said with pride. My husband.

The couple stood together as the Campbell and Ross men cheered and applauded, barely aware that anything existed besides them. The men scattered as the couple returned to kissing. Brodie made her shiver when he whispered what he intended to do to make her his wife in word and deed. The sun was setting by the time they returned to the keep. Laurel led Brodie through a servants' side door and along a servants' passageway until they reached Brodie's chamber. There would be another round of scandal by morning, but Brodie taking Laurel to his chamber would be better than anyone finding Brodie in Laurel's room again. When they entered Brodie's chamber, he locked the door and watched his bride look around.

SEVENTEEN

As Brodie turned the key in the lock, some of Laurel's confidence faded as she looked at the bed where they would consummate their marriage. She shivered when his hands rested lightly on her shoulders. He stepped forward, engulfing her in his embrace, cocooning her in comfort. She leaned back against Brodie and closed her eyes.

"I know we've both been eager, but I also understand this must be intimidating for you. We have all night and beyond to explore. There is no need to rush the moment," Brodie reassured. Laurel nodded, her hands coming to rest on the forearms wrapped around her chest. Not having to look at Brodie made it easier for Laurel to share her feelings.

"I know what's supposed to happen. But I don't know how to do it. I don't know how to—a woman should make sure—is a wife supposed to?" Laurel felt like a fool. She couldn't form a complete sentence, too nervous and embarrassed to admit her uncertainty, even though she feared Brodie would think her hen-wit.

"I know you don't know how, Laurel. I don't expect you to. You aren't a tavern wench whose next meal depends on her making sure her customer is pleased. And plenty of people believe a wife shouldn't enjoy being bedded. None of that matters. The only thing that matters is what we choose to do together. I told you, there is no hurry."

Laurel released a choked laugh. "That's part of the problem." She drew in a shaky breath and turned toward Brodie. "I don't want to wait. I want everything—all of it—now, but I don't know what that is or how to do it."

Brodie tugged at the laces of Laurel's gown, the gleam in his eyes seductive and predatory. "Patience is a virtue, Laurie. But that is not what I intend to teach you tonight."

As Brodie continued to unfasten her gown, Laurel removed Brodie's brooch at his shoulder, catching the yards of wool. With one hand easing a sleeve from her shoulder, Brodie removed his belt with the other. Removing his scabbard forced him to release Laurel, but she used the opportunity to kick off her riding boots and roll down her stockings from beneath her skirts and chemise.

Brodie tugged off his boots and hose until they stood barefoot before one another. He uncharacteristically tossed his plaid on the nearby chair, not usually so careless with it. In just his leine, which hung to his mid-thigh, Brodie eased Laurel's sleeves from her arms, dropping petal-soft kisses on her neck and shoulders. Her head lolled from side to side as she reveled in the exquisite sensations Brodie created from his kisses and the knowledge that he was stripping her bare. She caught his mouth as Brodie pushed her skirts down over her hips. Left in only her chemise, Brodie lifted Laurel until her legs came around his waist, her chemise and his leine the only barrier to their bodies joining.

Laurel knew Brodie carried her toward the fireplace, but she felt as though she floated. His powerful hands gripped her thighs as she locked her ankles behind his back. Kneeling with ease, Brodie lowered Laurel to the floor and kissed the tip of her nose.

"Wait here," he whispered before gathering the pillows from the bed, the cushions from the two chairs, and his plaid. Laurel smiled and reached for the items, setting about making them a nest while Brodie lit a fire. When it roared in the fire-place, Brodie turned back to Laurel. He fought the urge to maul her. Laurel lay bare against the pillow, Brodie's plaid spread beneath her. Brodie stood staring a moment too long because Laurel shifted nervously. It spurred him into action, reminding himself to be gentle. Brodie whipped his leine over his head and tossed it aside as carelessly as he had his plaid. He came to lie beside Laurel, his hand cupping her jaw before sliding along her neck, then trailing his fingertips over her chest, her tightening nipple, along her belly, and to her waist. He continued his lazy exploration as his hand swept over her hip and thigh before the back of his hand brushed against the thatch of strawberry curls at the juncture of her thighs. His palm slid up her belly until he scooped her breast and brought his head to her nipple. His tongue swirled the peak as he observed Laurel. She watched him with heavy-lidded eyes, her breaths coming in short, deep pants.

"Touch me, Laurie," Brodie instructed. He witnessed the relief on Laurel's face as she lifted one hand to his shoulder while the other ran over his other shoulder and upper back before drifting over his chest. Her warm palm rested over his defined pectoral, feeling the thud of Brodie's racing heartbeat, letting her know that he, too, was excited. She drew her nails over his ribs, making him squirm for a moment. She raised an eyebrow and smiled mischievously, storing that revelation for another time.

As Laurel's hand rested on his chiseled backside, taut muscles bunched beneath her palm, Brodie drew Laurel closer. He lifted her leg over his hip, bringing his cock to her seam. Laurel didn't know how to describe the sound she made. It was part whimper, part moan, a bit of a sigh, and most definitely a gasp. Whatever it was, Brodie understood it. Sensing her need, he rocked his hips against her as his fingers skimmed the inside of her thighs.

Laurel shivered, wishing she could climb inside Brodie, where the furnace that was his body would surely keep her warm. But her core ached for Brodie to slide inside her. She moved her hips in unison to Brodie's, his groan telling her he wanted to join their bodies as much as she did.

"Laurel, do ye ken what will happen? Can ye tell?" Brodie was too intent upon pleasing Laurel to consider his courtly accent.

"Aye, Brodie. Yer cock will go inside ma sheath. Can ye soon?" Laurel closed her eyes as she asked her question.

"Look at me, Laurie." Brodie waited until her blue hazel eyes met his gray ones. They reminded him of the glassy waters of Loch Awe, the body of water his home overlooked. "Do ye ken it might nae feel vera good at first?"

"I ken. But if I lie still it will pass, and ye will be done," Laurel answered.

"Och, it will pass, but I dinna want ye to lie still, and I have nay intention of being done that soon," Brodie grinned as his fingertips dipped within her seam. Laurel's hips bucked forward at the familiar sensation. Her fingers bit into his shoulder and bicep as she moaned. "Do ye like that?"

"Ye ken I do," Laurel panted.

"Laurie, what we do together is as much aboot yer pleasure as it is mine. If there's aught ye dinna like, that doesnae feel good after the first few moments, promise me ye'll tell me. I dinna want to do aught that will hurt ye if I can help it."

"I ken, Brodie. Ye've protected me since the beginning. I ken I'm safe with ye."

Brodie's heart pounded against his ribs. Laurel's trust meant more to him than that of his entire clan or the king. He knew it didn't come easily, and he wanted to remain worthy of it always. "If there is aught ye wish me to do, that ye like, ye need only tell me, Laurie. Dinna let what ye enjoy embarrass ye. I want ye to enjoy our coupling."

Laurel nodded and bit her lip. "Can we start?"

Brodie chuckled at her impatience. He growled and pounced when she gasped as he flipped her onto her back. His tongue traversed the length of her body from her neck to her sheath. Laurel watched, stunned by what she anticipated would happen, as Brodie kissed the creases of where her thighs and hips met. He slipped one finger into Laurel, easing her into the intimacy. As it had when they slipped away from the guards when they rode out, for only a moment, his broad finger felt large and intrusive, but soon it wasn't nearly enough. Laurel shifted her hips, trying to find the satisfaction Brodie had taught her about. Brodie eased a second finger into her channel, careful not to be rough when all he wanted was to thrust his cock into her over and over until she screamed.

Laurel wasn't able to reach much more than Brodie's hair. She tunneled the fingers of one hand into his hair, unintentionally tugging while the other fisted his plaid when he blew cool air onto her eager flesh before his tongue rasped along her nub. Like a flower in bloom, Brodie peeled away the petals until his tongue dipped into her core. His masculine hum of pleasure made Laurel's hips buck off the floor. He captured her hips and pinned her entrance to his mouth as he feasted. His teeth grazed the bundle of nerves as his tongue worked her slick flesh. He knew Laurel struggled for release, unaware of how to ease her need. He would teach her that night and every other for a lifetime.

Laurel arched her back, longing for Brodie's ministrations, enjoying every touch, but impatient for more. Her breasts felt heavy and ached. She wished he had at least two mouths that could work her core and her breasts in unison. Instead, she kneaded the mounds as Brodie watched her. Her head fell back and eyes shut against anything that might distract her from Brodie. She moaned as a familiar tingle began low in her belly. Her sheath tightened, and the nub Brodie sucked throbbed. Unprepared for the pleasure that surged through her, wave after wave, Laurel cried out and reached for Brodie. His powerful body hovered over her until she pulled him down to press against her. She held him as he nudged the tip of his rod into her, tensing and waiting for the pain.

"Laurie, ye must relax, or I willna be able to enter ye. I dinna want to hurt ye by being too forceful," Brodie explained as he stroked her temple, noticing how her hair was strewn across their pillows just as he'd envisioned the first day he met Laurel. His cock pulsed with need of its own, impatient to be buried with Laurel. She sighed and nodded as she made her body go lax. Brodie surged into her, her tight channel becoming a vice as she tensed around him. "Wheest, thistle. I ken it hurts. I'm so vera sorry. So, so sorry. But I promise I can give ye that pleasure ye just had. I willna move until ye're ready." *Though I may die in the process.*

Laurel gasped lungfuls of air as the burning pain made her squeeze her eyes shut. But when she inhaled Brodie's masculine scent—pine and sandalwood now mixed with the musk of sex—she realized the pain was more a memory than acute. "Brodie," she moaned as she shifted restlessly.

"Aye, lass."

"I—God, I need ye."

It was all the encouragement Brodie needed before he nudged his hips against Laurel's, moving slowly as she adjusted to each sensation. When her knees squeezed his thighs, and she raised her hips to meet his shallow thrusts, he dared to move a little faster and a little harder. He watched in awe as he finally unleashed the passion he'd been certain was laying dormant within Laurel. Her eyes sparkled as she moved her body, a natural seductress, a siren drawing him to the edge of the world. Their kisses grew wild as their hands explored all that they could reach.

"More," Laurel panted, squeezing Brodie's backside, trying to press him harder against her mons.

"Hurt ye—" Brodie panted. Laurel shook her head, strands of her fiery hair brushing over his hands.

"More."

Brodie clung to his conscience that warned him to be gentle with his maiden bride, but savage need to possess and be possessed howled within his breast. He increased the force with which he surged into her core, keeping the pace deliciously and frustratingly slow. Laurel clawed at his back, urging him to move faster, but he refused to spend yet. Their eyes locked as Laurel moaned, tugging him down to kiss her once more. Without the same slowly increasing tightness as the first time, Laurel's body exploded with wave after pounding wave of pleasure. Brodie watched as her neck strained, her head titled back, and her mouth opened in a silent scream. Unable to wait, he dipped his head to her breast, suckling and nipping as his hips finally led the charge until his release flowed through him in pulsating jets.

Brodie rolled over, pulling Laurel with him. Her hair cascaded over her back and his chest as her forehead rested against his neck, and she dropped light kisses where his throat met his shoulder. Brodie snagged the edge of the plaid and drew it over them. His brawny arms held Laurel in place, but they both knew neither intended to move beyond sucking in quivering breaths as their hearts pounded in unison. When he could breathe again with some ease, Brodie stroked Laurel's hair while his other hand cupped one globe of her buttocks. When his body withdrew from hers, Laurel whimpered.

"Wheest, thistle. I dinna like it either." Brodie tried to peer at her, but the position was too awkward. "Are ye all right, Laurie?"

"Aye, vera," Laurel replied as she shifted and nuzzled closer, her body draped over his. "I ken now why they dinna tell virgins what that's like. There wouldnae be any left."

Brodie chuckled, shifting so he could kiss Laurel. He wished he could tell her it wasn't always like that, or it had never been so passionate for him before, but he didn't dare bring up his past liaisons as he laid in his bride's arms. But he should have known what she was thinking.

"I dinna have aught to compare, but was that good? I mean, did I do it right?" Laurel asked.

"Dear merciful God and all the angels, if ye did it any

better, ye'd stop ma heart," Brodie grinned. "Aye, ye did it right, Laurie. Vera, vera right."

"So ye'll want to do that again with me?"

Brodie rolled them back onto their sides, so he could see Laurel's face. He heard what she said and what she left unsaid. He brushed hair over her shoulder before sliding his hand down her arm until he could bring her hand to his heart. He covered her much smaller one with his.

"I want to be inside ye every minute of every day if I could. I have never felt so connected with someone, nae physically or any other way. Laurel, I dinna ken what—or rather how ye think a husband will act, but I will only share ma body with ye."

Laurel nodded, but Brodie knew there was a niggling question in Laurel's mind, his expression asking her to speak. She stared at him a long time, and Brodie wasn't sure if she was mustering her courage or deciding if she dare ask. Perhaps both.

"Do ye have a leman?"

"Nay, Laurie. I never have. Ye ken I wasna a virgin, but I dinna have a mistress, or even someone I visited regularly."

"But ye werenae going to bed Eliza for at least two years. There must be someone—" Brodie placed his finger of her lips and shook his head.

"I'm as healthy as the next mon, but I'm also auld enough to ken that there is more to life than bedding a woman—or bedding a woman that ye dinna care aboot, dinna want to pledge yer life to. I would have lasted the two years or until Eliza was ready. I may nae have enjoyed it," Brodie grinned ruefully. "But the vows a couple recites before God and a priest say to forsake all others. If I canna honor that, how can ma people believe me honorable enough to lead?"

"Brodie, we both ken clan members dinna care if the laird has a leman. Too many of them do. People dinna consider it dishonorable despite what the mon pledges," Laurel pointed out.

"I consider it dishonorable," Brodie stressed. "I will nae betray ye, and I will nae forsake ye. If I didna think—nay, ken —I could keep maself only unto ye, I wouldnae have hand-fasted with ye. If I'm honest with us both, I wouldnae have kissed ye the first time. Part of me kenned the risk we took of being found, and I disregarded it. I wasna displeased or regretful when we were discovered. It was a relief."

"A relief?" Laurel's brow furrowed.

"Aye. It meant I didna have to hide from ye or anyone else that I want ye as ma wife."

"But ye ken that everyone says ye kissed me to make me quiet, and that now ye regret it."

"Would I have spent each day with ye, mournful when we each had other duties to attend to? Would I have agreed to exchange our own vows today, if I regretted having ma future linked to yers? Would I have needed ye with the consuming passion that I just did, that I still do? Laurel, nay one forced me to pursue ye, and nay one forced me to marry ye."

"But the wager," Laurel whispered. While they'd settled the disagreement they'd had the morning Laurel overhead the ladies talking in the Great Hall, Brodie hadn't explained how the rumors came about.

"When I arrived in Stirling," Brodie began. His chest tightening as he prepared to tell Laurel why he'd initially sought her out. He prayed she didn't gather her clothes and run from the chamber by the time he was through. "I didna come straight here. I wanted a hot meal and a few drams of whisky before finding ma bed." Brodie nudged his chin in the bed's direction.

Laurel listened and watched, noticing that Brodie had grown uncomfortable. She fought back tears that threatened merely from her anxiousness.

"I found yer brother and Donnan at the Crosspool Tavern. I'd already had more than a little whisky as I rode. When Oliphant and MacDougall began talking aboot ye, I was curious. I was nae even close to sober at that point and jested that I liked a challenge. When Oliphant suggested a wager, Monty refused. I confess I considered it for a moment," Brodie looked at Laurel shamefully. She nodded and offered him a tight smile. "I said I liked a challenge, and I was curious aboot ye. I hadnae even met ye, but ye intrigued me. It was happenstance that I stumbled upon ye in town the next day. If ye hadn't rattled off all those curses in Gaelic, I wouldnae have kenned it was ye."

"But ye did because I am the Shrew of Stirling," Laurel said bitterly.

"I did because ye are quick-witted and have a way with words. Yer tart comments come sooner and faster than others can manage. Ye've moved onto the next idea before they've understood yer first one. Ye fascinated me as we walked together. But yer lack of guards deeply concerned me. Laurel, ye may have been oblivious, or mayhap ye purposely ignore them, but men watched ye. They didna ken who ye were under that ugly veil. But they kenned they liked what they saw of yer figure. It scared me that ye—or any woman—would so brazenly tempt fate."

"I told ye why I did it," Laurel whispered.

"I ken, and I dinna fault ye for what ye thought ye should do. But ye scare me with yer disregard for yer own safety." Brodie's shoulders slumped as he took a deep breath. "I ken ye dinna think anyone would care if harm befell ye, but I would. I would care to ma core. I dinna want to lose ye when I've just found ye."

There was sadness in Laurel's eyes as she nodded. He'd spoken aloud what she'd believed for years, what she'd had proven true too many times. But she no longer wanted to take reckless risks. She didn't want to torment Brodie by making him scared to trust her or for her safety. And she didn't want to lose the tenderness she received from him.

"I dinna want to lose ye either, Brodie." Laurel kissed him softly before nuzzling closer to him. They laid together for a long moment before Brody eased himself away and went to the washstand. He filled the basin and dipped a linen square into it, preparing to take it to Laurel. He returned and kneeled beside her. Despite her deep flush, he eased her hands away and tended to her. His brow twitched when he noticed Laurel's chemise folded beneath her. He hadn't noticed it before. Closing her eyes against her embarrassment, she pulled it from beneath her and held it up.

The streak of red on the white linen explained what Laurel was too uncomfortable to admit. Brodie realized she'd had the forethought to know it wouldn't have shown up on his deep blue and green hunting plaid. They would have had no proof that they'd consummated their handfast or that she'd been a virgin. He assumed she'd retrieved it while he built the fire. He kissed her forehead before taking the damp cloth back to the washstand. Laurel rolled onto her belly and watched the flames dance in the hearth. Brodie slipped beneath the plaid beside her, his arm across her back. His dormant cock stirred as soon as it touched her silky skin. He feared Laurel was too exhausted or too sore for more, but he craved the feeling of sliding into her. He nudged her right leg up, giving him room to place his thigh between hers. Laurel's breath hitched as she shifted to brush her slit against his leg.

Brodie felt Laurel's breathing change, her arousal obvious. He massaged the tense muscles of her back, ringing a moan of pleasure and pain from her. She reached back and clasped his thigh as she clamped her thighs around his. Careful not to crush her, Brodie shifted his body over hers, pressing against her back. Brodie groaned when Laurel instinctively raised her hips.

"Ye'll be sore if ye arenae already," Brodie whispered beside Laurel's ear.

"Didna ye promise me an entire night?" Laurel countered.

"That doesnae mean every five minutes," Brodie chuckled.

"Nae up to the task," Laurel taunted, humor in her voice. Brodie pressed his hardened length along the crevice between the halves of her backside.

"Ye ken nae only am I up to the task, but I shall relish every moment." Brodie kissed her shoulder before growing serious once more. "It's ye who I fear willna relish it. I dinna want to harm ye."

Laurel twisted to look back over her shoulder, seeing the concern in Brodie's expression. "Then will ye at least hold me like this?"

"I'm too heavy. It willna be comfortable," Brodie worried.

"Please. I promise to tell ye if it's uncomfortable. But I like it," Laurel shrugged. "I dinna ken why. I just feel vera protected with the floor beneath me, and ye at ma back. It's as though naught can reach me without having to go through ye first. It's like ye're an enormous *mathan*. And I ken ye wouldnae let aught happen to me."

"I wouldnae," Brodie kissed her shoulder once more, settling over her. But temptation proved too powerful. They shifted restlessly against one another until they disregarded caution, and Brodie slipped inside Laurel. Neither moved, just enjoying the sensations that came with the new position until their need dominated their actions. Long, slow thrusts grew into a maelstrom of pounding surges when Brodie drew Laurel onto her hands and knees. She arched her back, pressing her hips to meet his, naturally seeking a position and rhythm that enthralled them both. Brodie reached around Laurel, circling her button until he sensed she was closer. He increased the pressure until she shuddered, then pinched the tiny sack of nerves. Laurel cried out as Brodie roared, "Laurie!" He sounded like the bear she'd called him earlier.

They collapsed together, a tangle of sweaty limbs, falling asleep for a few hours before waking to couple again. And so went their night of brief hours of respite before hours of all-consuming passion. They ignored the sun that rose outside Brodie's window, the sounds of men passing outside the door, and even their hunger for food—more interested in their hunger for one another. But they couldn't ignore the door slamming into the wall.

EIGHTEEN

Brody leapt to his feet in one fluid motion, despite his nakedness. He snatched his sword, which always laid within reach, while Laurel scrambled to cover herself. She watched in horror as the king's men swarmed the chamber, followed by Monty, Donnan, and King Robert himself. She heard voices in the passageway and could envision the scene as people rushed to discover what was happening in Laird Campbell's chamber.

"I see you couldn't wait a sennight," King Robert mused.

"I see you've corrupted my sister," Monty bellowed as he pushed forward. He spared a glance at a mortified Laurel, who Brodie attempted to shield as she reached for his discarded leine and struggled into it while showing no more skin. She couldn't don her own chemise, which had the proof of her maidenhood on it. That would be too much to bear, and she suspected she would soon be compelled to hand it over to King Robert.

"I spent the night with my wife," Brodie snapped. "Out. Every single one of you until my wife is dressed."

"You think to command me," King Robert's voice chilled Laurel, despite the nervous perspiration at her brow.

"Yes," Brodie said, sword still in hand. "My wife has a

153

right to make herself decent without a horde of men staring at her. That includes you, Your Majesty."

"I wouldn't make a habit of this," King Robert warned.

"As long as no one makes a habit of intruding upon my wife's privacy," Brodie countered. Laurel was growing fearful for Brodie's life, but she wouldn't dare contradict him. Instead, she sat wide eyed and trembling.

"I am not going anywhere until you explain why you claim she's your wife," Monty snarled before turning a wagging finger at Laurel. "Don't you dare tell me you handfasted. You claim not to be a Highlander anymore."

"I will always be one, Montgomery. I just blessedly am no longer a Ross," Laurel quipped. "Have an ounce of Highland honor and get out."

"You heard Lady Campbell's wishes. Out," Brodie barked. King Robert sighed and turned to the door, the others following him.

"Five minutes, then I return," the Bruce insisted.

Brodie gave a jerky nod as the chamber emptied. He spun around, dropping his sword as he went to Laurel. He helped her to her feet and engulfed her in his embrace. He grew concerned when her trembling didn't stop. She didn't feel chilled, but she clung to him, her fingertips digging into his shoulder blades.

"What scares you most, thistle?" Brody stroked her back as she lessened her grip on him.

"I may like you being *mo mathan* when you hold me, but roaring at the king is likely to land you in the dungeon, or worse, dead." Laurel's arms tightened as she spoke aloud the consuming fear that wouldn't release her.

"Wheest. The Bruce needs me and the Campbells too much to do more than scold me. I suspect he will levy a hefty bride price." Brodie smirked, "Payable to the crown. And then he will suggest we depart with haste. The entire Campbell clan has been loyal to the king from the beginning. Each sept has sent men to fight alongside him, and I lead the largest one.

Now that he is on the throne, he relies on us to help keep him there. I think I made it clear who I will defend."

"Aye, and it'll likely get you accused and found guilty of treason," Laurel shuddered.

"Dinna fash. Let's dress, and then we will deal with the outside world."

"We don't need him barging in again."

"I promise you he wouldn't dare."

Laurel gave him a halfhearted nod as she let go and searched for her stockings. While she slipped into her gown, Brody folded his plaid and retrieved a fresh leine from a satchel. When he stepped behind Laurel to help her with her laces, he kissed the bare skin on her shoulders and the base of her neck, brushing the back of his fingers along her spine. "I won't be able to think of aught but kenning you are bare beneath this gown. If you must wear something, I wish it could be my leine. You looked quite fetching in it, wife."

Laurel shivered as Brodie's warm breath caressed her skin as he spoke. She felt goosebumps on her arms and legs, and her breasts ached for his touch. Brodie mentioning that she wore nothing below her gown made her more aware of the sensual feeling of the fabric and the memory of Brodie's touch. It was a drug, and she was already an addict. Brodie cupped her breasts as she leaned back against him, her eyes drifting closed as she sighed. He kneaded the flesh as he kissed the silky skin behind her ear.

"We will resolve this, then we will return here." Brodie's declaration was seductive, his tone pure honey.

"I'll race you," Laurel murmured.

"Only if you will ride me." Brodie nipped her earlobe.

"I shall need many lessons to become an expert rider." Laurel turned in his arms and licked her lips. Brodie guided her backward until her legs brushed the back of the bed. She was ready to fall back upon it and bring Brodie with her when someone pounded on the door. They sighed wistfully as Laurel smoothed her hand over her hair. It was tangled, and there

155

was little she could do with it, but she attempted to make it presentable. Brodie quickly finished her laces.

"Enter," Brodie called as he wrapped his arm around Laurel's waist but angled himself as a shield should he perceive a threat. Laurel sagged against him for a moment, and he kissed the top of her head. But as the door opened, she straightened and raised her chin imperiously. Brodie glanced down and noticed she stood with the haughtiness that surely contributed to her title. He was proud of his wife.

"You can let go of the lass," King Robert said. "No one is taking her from you."

"No."

"Campbell, let go of Lady Laurel," King Robert ordered. Brodie narrowed his eyes but released Laurel, only to entwine their fingers together.

"Lady Campbell," Brodie corrected.

"That's to be determined," Robert snapped.

"There is naught to determine, Your Majesty. As least not now. Mayhap ten hours ago," Laurel stated as she released Brodie's hand. She moved swiftly to the spot where the pillows and her folded chemise still laid. She picked up the under-gown and shook it out. "You can see from the creases that this has been folded and crushed beneath our weight." Laurel didn't flinch as she confessed that they'd coupled before the fireplace. "You can also see it's dried. Neither of us could have done this before you returned. It happened well before you barged in. Your Majesty," Laurel added the honorific as an afterthought. She walked back to Brodie's side but thrust her chemise at King Robert, even shaking it when he didn't immediately accept.

"Campbell and Ross guards witnessed the handfast," Brodie said.

"Aye. When no one could find Lady Lau—Lady Campbell —" King Robert glared at Brodie. "—Montgomery thought she might have gone for an early morning ride. The Ross guards said she was last seen with you. Her husband."

Laurel seethed as she looked at her brother. "You knew before you entered that we handfasted. You led the king here with a contingent of men to humiliate me, to punish me. You could have come by yourself. You could have knocked and been admitted. Bully for you. You solved the great mystery of where I went. You also ran to tattle like a wean." Laurel stepped back to be behind Brodie's shoulder. "Do not think for a moment that I fear you, Montgomery. I'm making sure you are out of reach, lest I claw your eyes out and spit in their sockets."

"She's your wife now." Monty pointed at Brodie. "You said you would tame her."

"I've discovered I prefer my wife as a hellion. Makes me confident my clan won't fall to ruin when I must ride out."

"She has your bollocks in her fist. She'd likely drag you into battle by them," Monty sneered.

"If it means she's touching them," Brodie grinned and winked.

"Enough," King Robert barked. "You did not have my permission to handfast, Laird Campbell."

"Neither did you deny me the right to. Whether we handfasted or merely consummated the betrothal, we are married."

"The church wasn't done reading the banns," Robert pointed out.

"I can name several couples who weren't made to wait for them to be read even once," Laurel mused. "Something aboot you having the right to decide without Rome." Laurel threw down a dangerous gambit. Pope Clement V excommunicated King Robert early in the monarch's fight for the throne. They remained at odds, but Robert used it as an excuse to allow more than one lady-in-waiting to marry with haste. Laurel banked on the reminder being enough to goad the king into relenting.

"Lady Campbell." King Robert gazed at Laurel, something akin to respect in his tone and his gaze. "You are a formidable woman. I praise the saints that the Campbells are ever loyal. I would not want to run afoul of you." Neither Laurel nor Brodie missed the subtle reminder that the Campbells served the king and not the other way around.

"We depart for Kilchurn in two days," Brodie announced, wrapping his arm around Laurel's waist once more. "We will be sure to say our farewells."

"What aboot the bride price?"

"Montgomery, inform your father that the bride price was paid the moment he withheld an appropriate dowry," King Robert snapped. "What he saves is his payment."

"But—"

"Ross, pipe down and don't sound like the wean your sister accused you of being." King Robert didn't wait for a response before he turned to the door. "You're leaving, too."

Monty cast a withering glare at the couple, but he was forced to follow the king's order. King Robert, Monty, and two royal guards left Brodie's chamber. The couple stared at the closed door for a long moment before they fell into one another's arms.

"That went far better than I expected," Laurel confessed. "I regret speaking out of turn, Brodie. I should have remained quiet. You should have been the only one to speak."

"And miss you calling Monty a bairn?" Brodie shook his head with a grin.

"A wean. Bairns don't have tantrums," Laurel corrected.

"Laurel, I'm proud that you stood up for us. It means you want our marriage—will defend our marriage—just like I do. You're intelligent and beautiful, a formidable combination. Men may underestimate you because of your beauty, but once they realize your intelligence, just like the king said, they will not want to run afoul of you. That's why I'm proud of you."

"No one has ever told me they're proud of me. Not when I lived among my clan, and certainly never here. Granted, the latter was for good reason."

"You may not be what every mon envisions as the perfect bride, but I am grateful for that. It means I am the lucky mon

158

to call you wife. You are the perfect wife for me." Brodie pulled the laces loose from Laurel's gown. He stood back as she inched the fabric down her arms, then her ribs and hips until it pooled on the floor. He knew she'd purposely gone tantalizingly slow. But seeing her bare form in front of him left him with no patience. He tore his clothes off before lifting Laurel and carrying her to the bed. He laid her down, and she hurried to pull back the covers. They'd explored one another throughout the night, discovering sensitive and erotic places on each other's bodies. The bunch and pull of Brodie's muscular frame fascinated Laurel, who was previously unaware of the extent to which their bodies differed. Brodie reveled in Laurel's responsiveness to his touch, and how her hands roamed over his body.

Laurel reached between them, braver than she had been early on, grasping Brodie's length. The night before, she'd stroked as he'd shown her before his eyes rolled back, and he'd had to grip her wrist to pry her hand away. As they laid together on the bed, once more bringing him to the brink, Brodie captured both wrists in one hand and raised her arms over her head as he lowered his mouth to her breast, swirling his tongue over her nipple. His other hand lazily meandered to the thatch of curls at the apex of her legs. Laurel writhed in anticipation as his roving fingers made the hair on her arms rise. She splayed her legs wide as Brodie's questing digits finally eased into her sheath. With each moan, they plunged into her, stroking and probing as she labored to breathe.

"I want to touch you, too," Laurel whispered. Brodie grinned at her with a wink before he shook his head.

"I shall torment you just a while longer before I give you what you want."

Laurel twisted, bringing her mons against Brodie's length. She slid her toes along the length of his calf as her thigh rubbed his. She arched her back, thrusting her breast against his lips. Brodie tightened his grip on her wrists, but Laurel continued to twist and rub her body against his.

"You are not the only one who can tease," Laurel purred.

"But I am the only one who can do this." Brodie lifted her leg to his hip and thrust into her. Her carnal moan spurred Brodie on as he surged into her over and over. She winced once, and he froze. He'd forgotten that Laurel would be sore after so many rounds of lovemaking. She'd assured him over and over that she was well, but the moment of discomfort made him feel contrite.

"That wasn't pain, Brodie. Or least not in a bad way. I ache for you to keep going. I was trying to ease it." Laurel tugged her arms again, and Brodie released her immediately. Her hands flew to his backside, pressing his hips, urging him on. "It'll only be painful if you stop."

"I will call for a hot bath as soon as we're done," Brodie promised.

"It won't be until this eve," Laurel grinned. Their kiss signaled the end of any conversation, their only communication their moans. They moved like they'd been lovers for years rather than mere hours. Their climaxes washed over them in unison, leaving them boneless and weary. They curled close together and fell back to sleep. Brodie made good on his promise of a bath, and Laurel learned couples didn't have to lie down to make love.

NINETEEN

"You will not leave this castle without a proper marriage," King Robert decreed.

"We have the contracts signed and a handfast in place. Lady Campbell and I can exchange our vows at Kilchurn in front of our clan," Brodie argued. King Robert summoned Brodie to the Privy Council chamber the morning Brodie intended to depart Stirling with Laurel. A less demanding, but nonetheless persistent, knock interrupted their respite from court life. Now he stood before an aggrieved monarch while attempting to keep his temper in check.

"None of the other ladies may marry until after Lady Laurel's wedding," King Robert said for at least the third time, to which Brodie gave the same response.

"She had her wedding in a meadow when we exchanged vows. Lady Campbell is married. The others can go on aboot their lives without any more fuss. And I intend to leave with my wife." Brodie crossed his arms. "Today."

"You shall find that hard to do when the gates are locked to Lady Laurel, and you find yourself in a cell within my dungeon," King Robert threatened. Brodie bit his tongue, knowing he'd finally pushed too far. Even if the king was goading him and bluffing, he wouldn't risk Laurel being left alone so soon after they married.

"Very well," Brodie relented. "But we're not waiting until Monday. We can have the wedding this eve."

"You are waiting until Monday, and you will have the ceremony at sunset," King Robert insisted. Brodie pressed his lips together and swallowed the angry retort, but he nodded. "And in the meantime, you will leave Lady Laurel alone. She will return to her chamber and her duties to the queen."

"You go too far," Brodie hissed, keeping his voice low so only Robert heard. "You've seen the proof that we're married. You will not keep me from my wife. I do not trust for a moment that she's safe here."

"She has been for eleven years."

"She hasn't been an impediment to anyone else's marriage until now. There are many angry courtiers here, and I don't trust them not to do something."

"Very well. She may return to your chamber, but her days are to be spent as the queen demands."

"Aye, Your Majesty." Brodie bowed before taking his leave. He entered the passageway to find Graham, his second, rushing toward him with a piece of parchment in his hand. Brodie hurried to meet his most trusted guardsman.

"This just arrived from Dominic," Graham announced. "Danny said it was urgent."

Brodie nodded, knowing it wouldn't be good news if his brother sent their fastest messenger and Graham was nearly running to find him. He slid the wax seal from the parchment and scanned the missive. Brodie clenched his jaw as he reread it. Not only had the Lamonts led another raid well across their border, the MacDougalls joined them by raiding several other villages. Brodie looked up at Graham.

"The Lamonts are harrying our villages, and the bluidy MacDougalls are in on it too," Brodie explained. "I must find Lady Campbell, but first I must return to the king and share this turn of events." Brodie wanted to groan at the prospect of dealing with the Bruce, but he had no choice. While Graham waited in the passageway, Brodie went back to stand before the king. He handed the missive over and waited for King Robert's reaction.

"The Lamonts ended your alliance with the MacMillans, so why are they still harassing you?"

"I would like an answer to that too. Your Majesty, you must see that I cannot remain here. Lady Campbell and I need to return to Kilchurn, and I need to sort this mess out with both the Lamonts and the MacDougalls."

"Absolutely not. You are not riding with another bride only to have the Lamonts attack again. Lady Campbell remains here until you return. She may be a nuisance, and she may be your wife, but she's still the Earl of Ross's daughter. An earl whose sister married the Earl of Sutherland, who is the brother-by-marriage to the Earl of Sinclair, who is the bluidy father-by-marriage of Laird Mackay!" King Robert was practically yelling by the time he rattled off the complicated family into which Brodie married. "She isn't leaving this bluidy keep until you can promise me that whatever this is—" King Robert shook the parchment. "—is resolved."

Brodie scowled, but he knew the Bruce was right. He wasn't eager to travel with Laurel while bands of Lamonts and MacDougalls rained havoc on his clan. But he wasn't eager to leave Laurel alone either. He'd just argued against doing that very thing. "If this weren't so urgent, I would insist on the wedding today, but I must find my wife, then ride out."

"Aye. She'll be in the queen's solar at this hour. They will have just returned from their walk," King Robert offered, and Brodie bowed once more.

Brodie hurried through the castle's passageway, with Graham his silent shadow. When the two Highlanders reached the doors to the queen's solar, Graham stopped short and stepped aside. A royal guard opened the door only to reveal Laurel standing toe-to-toe with Sarah Anne. The queen wasn't in sight, and the other ladies encircled the arguing pair.

Laurel turned to look at the newcomer, her eyes widening when she recognized Brodie. She muttered something to Sarah Anne before swishing her skirts and making her way to Brodie.

Brodie could only imagine what made the color rise in Laurel's cheeks, but he doubted he would have any sympathy for Sarah Anne when he learned. He brought Laurel's hands to his lips, an appropriate greeting. But when he noticed Graham shift from the corner of his eye, he recalled he would soon leave Laurel. He pulled her toward him and brushed a soft kiss against her lips. Shocked, it took Laurel a moment to reciprocate. She kept it just as brief, but Brodie welcomed the touch.

"Something has come up, and I need to speak to you," Brodie whispered. Laurel nodded as Brodie offered his arm. Graham trailed behind them until they reached their chamber, where the three entered. Laurel sat in a chair near the hearth and looked back and forth between the two warriors. "The Lamonts and MacDougalls led raids on our land."

Laurel was on her feet and across the chamber in four strides. "What do you need me to do?"

Brodie thought his chest would explode. Pride and love filled his heart as he looked at the woman before him. He cupped her jaw and smiled. "Och, lass. I am a lucky mon." The couple gazed at one another before Brodie sighed. "There is naught for you to do just yet. I thought to take you home, but King Robert pointed out how unwise it would be to travel with you until this is resolved."

"You want me to stay here," Laurel stated.

"It's not what I want, but it's the right choice. I won't risk your life, Laurie. Here you are protected by Ross and royal guards. On the road it would only be my small contingent of men."

"That's not what I wanted to hear, but I know you're right."

"Graham and I need to ride out this morn, Laurie. I'm

sorry to leave you behind, especially since we haven't had the wedding yet."

"We're already married as far as we're concerned. It doesn't matter if the wedding takes place in six days, six moons, or six years. Seeing to our clan is more important. King Robert is only insisting upon it so he can have the last word."

"You are a wise woman, Laurel Campbell." Brodie bent to whisper in Laurel's ear. "I would make love to you one more time if I had the time. Know that I will return as soon as I can. Know that I will miss you. Be well, thistle."

"I will miss you, too, bear," Laurel said as she pressed her cheek to Brodie's chest. "And please, for the love of the Lord, be careful. I don't want to be your widow before I have a chance to be your wife."

Brodie and Laurel's kiss blended passion and tenderness, a fitting symbol of their burgeoning relationship. All too soon, they drew apart. While Brodie fetched his satchel from beside the wall, Laurel was already folding his spare leines and stockings. He held the bag open for her, and she dropped the clothing inside. With another searing kiss that was over much too soon, Brodie departed.

Laurel avoided her brother as much as she could for the next eight days. She was hurt and angry with him, and she didn't trust herself not to cause a scene if they were in one another's company. She also avoided the ladies-in-waiting when she could. She'd thought to go riding with her guards, but she recalled what Brodie said about not wanting to travel with her because of the murder of Eliza MacMillan. Laurel didn't trust the Lamonts and MacDougalls not to set their sights on her. She opted to remain at the castle, spending as much time as she could in her old chamber. She and Ina packed most of Laurel's belongings, but she spent much of her time creating a beautiful gown from the fabric Brodie gave her. She embellished the new slippers with intricate embroidery, and her project gave her a sense of purpose. The nights were painfully lonely; she laid in her bed wondering where Brodie was and if he was safe. She remembered when her father and Monty rode out and the uncertainty of whether they would return. But the aching pain her fear created was far greater now that she'd fallen in love.

The only time she couldn't wholly avoid people was at the evening meal. Whispers went around when people noticed Brodie was no longer at court. As the days dragged on, and the Monday of their wedding came and went, Laurel struggled to ignore the speculation that Brodie wouldn't return. Doubt wormed its way into her mind as she waited for his return, but there was no sign of when—or rather if—Brodie would come back for her. While the comments and barbs annoyed her, Nelson MacDougall was the only man to make her uncomfortable. He watched her like a hawk whenever she was in the Great Hall, and she noticed him turning up whenever she joined the ladies. She reminded herself that he was courting Margaret Hay, but he seemed less interested in Margaret and more interested in taunting Laurel.

"Lady Campbell!"

Laurel turned to find a man in a Campbell plaid hurrying toward her. She recalled the man's name was Michael, and he'd ridden out with Brodie. She looked past Michael's shoulders, then looked at him as he drew near.

"Ma laird sent me ahead to tell ye that he will be here within the hour. He wishes ye to meet him at the kirk. He—uh—" Michael glanced away nervously. "He—uh—said that ye are to be there, or he will drag ye to yer wedding in naught but yer chemise if he must."

"An hour? Laird Campbell will be here within the hour?"

"Aye, ma lady," Michael nodded. Laurel looked in the castle chapel's direction and was ready to run there now. But she forced herself to be reasonable. She was going to stand before the entire court and pledge herself to Brodie just as he would to her. She wore one of her plainer gowns, and her hair hung in a loose braid down her back. She had time to make herself more presentable, and she wanted to look her best for Brodie.

"Does the king ken yet?"

"Nay. I was on ma way to the Privy Council when I spotted ye, ma lady."

"Thank you, Michael. Inform the king and assure him that I will be there, ready for Laird Campbell to join me." The two parted ways, and Laurel dashed to her chamber. There wasn't time to bathe and dry her hair, so she washed with the basin and ewer, rubbing lavender oil into her skin when she finished. She sat before Ina as the maid created an exquisite coiffure while Laurel tried to relax. Her emotions were a jumble, vacillating from joy and relief that Brodie was safe and on his way to nervousness and excitement to see him, impatience to touch him, and trepidation about standing before the entire court to say their vows. She would have rather avoided the public scrutiny, but she'd known it was coming.

"Which gown will ye wear, ma lady?" Ina broke into her thoughts.

"The new one. I'm glad that I finished it last eve."

"Laird Campbell will be reight chuffed with himself for having chosen such a bonnie bride. Nay one will be saying ye're livin' tally again," Ina beamed.

"People don't believe we handfasted?" Laurel gasped. "They think we were living in sin for two days?"

"Och, people blather aboot aught. But dinna take it to heart, ma lady. They will all see when Laird Campbell kisses ye. And I ken he will. And likely before the end of the ceremony."

Laurel appreciated Ina trying to lift her spirits, but it wasn't working. She remained quiet while Ina wove the ribbons through the eyelets, then cinched the gown closed.

When her maid finished, she peered into the looking glass. She thought she looked attractive, but she prayed Brodie would think so too.

"Will ye walk with me to the kirk?" Laurel asked absent-mindedly as she swept her gaze over the chamber. She prayed it was the last time she would see the inside of it.

"Of course, ma lady," Ina nodded. Laurel returned the older woman's smile before they left the chamber and made their way to the kirk.

TWENTY

"He's not coming."

Laurel heard the stage whisper and the ensuing laughter. She'd been standing on the kirk steps for twenty minutes. She'd expected Brodie fifteen minutes ago, but she reminded herself that there were plenty of reasons why he hadn't arrived yet. Michael, the Campbell guard, could only estimate how long it would take, but he couldn't guarantee it. Laurel kept her chin high as she ignored the mocking stares.

But when another thirty minutes passed, Laurel couldn't keep the unease from taking hold. Brodie was nearly an hour late, and she feared he wasn't coming. She glanced around for Michael, but he wasn't among the crowd. She wondered why her husband's warrior wouldn't be at the kirk to attend his laird's wedding. The guard's absence sent Laurel's mind into a tailspin of why Brodie wasn't there and how he wouldn't arrive for the wedding.

"This is pointless. It grows cold and dark. The mon grew some sense and is likely tucked away with a willing and welcoming woman at Kilchurn."

Laurel struggled not to cry, hearing her exact fear voiced aloud. A handfast wasn't binding like a marriage performed in a church. Either party could repudiate it, and it would end after a year and a day if the couple didn't marry before a priest by then. Brodie could leave her at court and find another woman to marry, and there was nothing Laurel could do.

"Leave her here just like he has," a woman's voice floated to Laurel.

"Nay. I wish to see how long she waits before she realizes he isn't coming," another woman responded.

Monty and Donnan, along with the Ross guards, stood behind her, but neither had spoken to her when they arrived. She didn't know if she was further humiliated by having her clansmen with her or if they gave her courage. She couldn't make heads nor tails of her wildly fluctuating emotions as the minutes dragged on. She didn't want to accept that Brodie wasn't coming. She was more inclined to send men out to search for him, but she wouldn't make a fool of herself by suggesting such a thing, at least not where others could hear. She would ask Monty if she had to.

The last rays of sunlight disappeared as dusk drew to an end. Laurel noticed people drifting away from the kirk, and she didn't blame them. They'd been congregating outside the kirk for nearly two hours, and all she could do was stand looking toward the portcullis. The crowd abandoned any discretion and spoke as though she could neither see nor hear them. Her resilience faded as it grew dark. She no longer had the strength to stand proudly, ignoring the constant insults. The king and queen had already abandoned the crowd. The king promised Laurel that they would return "if" Brodie appeared. When she flinched, King Robert realized how he misspoke and apologized. But now Laurel believed the man was wiser than she.

"Monty, will you walk me back to my chamber?" Laurel admitted defeat to her brother. She didn't want to spend time with him, but she didn't trust herself not to fall apart somewhere and dissolve into a puddle of tears before she made it to her chamber.

"Aye, Laurel," Monty whispered as he stepped forward. Laurel gathered her skirts and walked down the steps just as the clatter of pounding hooves entered the bailey. Laurel knew it was Brodie before she saw his face. She sensed it as much as she recognized his horse, Lann. She watched as Brodie swung down from his horse, tossing the reins toward the stable boys running to greet the arriving warriors. A buzz swept through the crowd as Brodie pushed his way through.

When Laurel finally saw Brodie clearly, she gasped. His leine was filthy and torn, his plaid had fabric ripped and trailing behind him. His boots were encrusted in mud, and Laurel realized blood was splattered across Brodie's face. His hair and beard were matted. He looked like he'd rolled around in a pigsty before arriving. But Laurel didn't care. He was alive, and he was barreling through the crowd to reach her. When he was within reach, she moved toward him, but he caught her arms and kept her away.

"Thistle," Brodie whispered, his voice noticeably hoarse. "I want naught more than to hold ye, devour ye, but ye are too beautiful in yer new gown. I dinna want to ruin it. I would remember ye and this eve as both being perfect." Brodie smiled, and Laurel's world lit up as though it were the middle of the sunniest day in Scotland.

"It's only a gown," Laurel responded.

"One I ken ye made, and one I wish to see ye in many more times," Brodie said before dropping a kiss on her cheek.

"Do ye have a clean plaid?"

"I dinna," Brodie admitted. "But mayhap one of ma men does." He looked at her in confusion but called out to his men just as King Robert and Queen Elizabeth returned.

"Dear God, mon!" King Robert exclaimed, as he wafted his hand before his face. "Ye smell worse than ye did after Bannockburn, and I thought ye were a wild beast then." In his surprise, King Robert didn't notice that his own burr slid into his voice. It was a rare occasion for the man to be caught so off-guard that he dropped his refined speech.

"I'm late."

"We ken. You may as well get cleaned up since you're already late," King Robert said as his surprise wore off and his courtly speech returned.

"Is a wedding aboot what a mon wears or aboot the words he speaks?" Brodie asked.

"Would you accept a bride who appeared as you do now? King Robert asked.

"A bride? Nay. Ma wife, Lady Campbell? Aye. I would welcome Laurel if she came to me in rags because I would still be richer for having her as ma wife."

"He couldn't bother wiping the muck from his face. He's in such a rush to have it done with," a man called out. "Show him some mercy, Your Majesty."

"Show us all some mercy," another voice demanded.

"I think he looks fitting for a marriage to a harping fish-wife," Sarah Anne announced.

Brodie gazed down at Laurel, horrified by what he heard. He wondered what they'd said when he wasn't there; if they were brazen enough to say such damning things within his earshot. He worried that he'd erred by not stopping at an inn to bathe like he considered. But he'd been too impatient to reach Laurel to delay any longer. But now he feared Laurel would be hurt not only by what she heard but by his lack of consideration.

"It was more important to me to reach ma wife's side than to worry aboot ma appearance. I've kept Laurie waiting long enough," Brodie explained, not realizing he'd used the diminutive. His gaze locked with hers, his expression questioning.

"I dinna care what ye wear," Laurel whispered. She looked around and spotted a Campbell guard with the extra plaid she asked about. She reached out her hand "May I have that?"

The guard handed her the folded Campbell plaid, which she opened and shook out. She wrapped it around herself, covering her gown. Understanding her intention, Brodie engulfed her in his embrace, her arms pinned beneath the yards of wool.

"Kiss," Laurel mumbled. Brodie's mouth crushed hers as he pressed his tongue against her lips. She opened to him as though she was starving, and his kiss was her only succor. Brodie felt light-headed as all the blood drained from everywhere but his groin. It pooled there, making his cock stand at attention.

"Do ye wish me to change?"

"Nae one bit," Laurel answered with a broad smile. "Can we just get married?"

"Ye heard the lass," Brodie said as he turned toward the bemused priest who stood silently watching the couple.

"We hear the shrew giving you orders, Campbell. And we see you are quick to follow!" Nelson called out.

"I wonder which one has the bigger bollocks," Liam snickered.

"Enough prattle," King Robert commanded. "Campbell, you have kept us waiting for hours. Let's have the wedding. My stomach grows tired of wondering if my neck's been cut off. We have a feast to attend."

Brodie guided Laurel up the steps of the kirk to stand before its doors, where she unwrapped herself from the plaid but kept it draped over shoulders and back. Laurel thrust out her hand, and Brodie grasped it. He couldn't overlook the contrast between his grimy hand and her clean, well-manicured one. But Laurel didn't seem to notice, or at least it didn't seem to bother her. She wove her fingers around his as the priest bound their wrists with the end of the plaid Laurel wore.

"Wait," Laurel said. "I ken this is a Campbell plaid, but it isn't yours. I want it to be your plaid that binds us."

"Even I ken it's too filthy for that, Laurie."

"I dinna care if it's dripping with shite if it's yers."

Brodie nodded before he slipped the brooch from his shoulder. The priest warily took the edge of the wool Brodie offered and wrapped it around the couple's joined hands. After waiting for what felt like years, the brevity of the ceremony disconcerted Laurel. She blinked several times before shuffling to wrap the yards of material around her again. Brodie helped her cover her gown, then once more kissed her until she feared her knees could no longer bear her weight. The crowd called out randy comments and wagers on how long it would be before Brodie came to his senses. There were suggestions that he send her to a convent. Others argued he had to at least wait until she bore him a son.

Brodie's temper was pushed to the limits as he heard the hideous comments, knowing Laurel heard them, too. He couldn't force any of them to stop other than by running his sword through all of them. He wrapped his arm around Laurel and guided her down the kirk's steps.

"Bathe and change, then meet your wife on the dais." King Robert stood at the bottom of the steps, blocking the couple's way. Brodie looked down at Laurel, seeing the fine skin pulled taut over her cheeks and the pinched look around her eyes. She appeared exhausted, and he couldn't blame her. He knew she'd been standing for hours, waiting for him, not knowing whether he would arrive. He could imagine what she'd thought as she faced the crowd without him at her side.

"Ma wife and I are retiring," Brodie spoke quietly, but there was steel in his voice. "Ye wanted the ceremony, so ye had it. But I didna agree to a feast. Ma wife doesnae need to be on display to these people, and I have important clan matters to discuss with Lady Campbell."

"If you were so worried aboot people staring at Lady Campbell, you shouldn't have sent word you would arrive within an hour, then take nearly three."

Brodie gritted his teeth and seethed. "I stopped to bury two of ma men. Ma apologies to ye and ma wife that I couldnae rush ensuring their eternal souls went to heaven."

"Brodie," Laurel gasped. She looked at the weary Campbell warriors who stood silently while she and Brodie exchanged their vows. The men looked like they could barely remain on their feet, some leaning against one another. She glanced around for her maid. She left Brodie's side and hurried to the woman. "Ina, fetch the healer and send a tub and hot water for each of the Campbells. If they dinna wish to join the feast, have trays brought to them. Have a Ross mon sent to our chamber if any of the wounds are serious. Please hurry."

"Aye, ma lady." Ina spun on her heels and pushed through the crowd, lifting her skirts once she broke free and ran into the keep. Laurel had never seen the woman move so fast. She walked over to the men who'd ridden with her husband.

"I dinna ken what happened, but I can easily guess," Laurel said softly. "I dinna doubt ye each played a part in ensuring yer laird returned here—returned to me. Thank ye. I —" Laurel caught herself. "I thank ye."

Brodie came to stand behind her. His men looked to him, wide-eyed. They'd gotten to know Laurel while they accompanied the couple on their daily rides, but none had expected her to thank them personally or to call for the healer and baths.

"Ye're welcome, Lady Campbell," Graham spoke up. "We welcome ye to Clan Campbell." Laurel's smile shone in the early night's darkness.

***

"Laurie, I canna tell ye how sorry I am to have kept ye waiting. I can imagine what ye must have thought, and it pains me to ken I caused ye any anguish," Brodie said as he stripped off his soiled clothes and stepped into the tub Ina had waiting. He dunked his head beneath the water, shaking the dirt loose. When he emerged, he found Laurel standing with a sudsy linen in hand. Working on his back while Brodie scrubbed his front, the couple remained quiet. Laurel was too grateful to see and touch Brodie, knowing he'd survived whatever danger he'd found. Once Brodie's hair was clean and he had a drying linen wrapped around his waist, he guided her to sit on his lap before the fire. Laurel finally felt the gorge in her throat drop, and she could speak.

"I feared ye were dead, that Michael hadna told me aboot some grievous injury," Laurel whispered.

"But ye also feared that the crowd was right, that I left ye at the altar."

"Aye. I'm sorry I doubted ye."

"I dinna blame ye, thistle. It must have been agonizing, wondering if they spoke the truth. I need ye to ken that I will always come for ye. Till ma vera last breath. It may nae be as soon as I wish or in a manner," Brodie nudged his chin toward the pile of discarded clothes, "I wish. But I willna forsake ye, Laurie."

Laurel thought Brodie might say more. She prayed for a declaration of his feelings. She'd nearly admitted hers when she stood before his men. But neither broached the topic, and Laurel already felt vulnerable to having Brodie turn a blank face to her if he didn't reciprocate those feelings.

"Will ye tell me what happened?"

"I will. All of it. But I wish to hold ye for a little while, *mo ghràidh*." My darling.

Laurel supposed it was a start, and she clung to the endearment as she clung to him, resting her head against his broad chest. She supposed he bore the weight of the world on his shoulders, so she wouldn't push him to speak before he was ready. She trusted he would share when he felt it was right. One hand ran over his hair while the other caressed his chest. It wasn't long before need overtook affection. Brodie carried his bride to their bed, where they spent the night reassuring one another that there was no place they would rather be.

TWENTY-ONE

"Laurel," Monty said as he stepped beside his sister, who held the reins to Teine. The siblings hadn't spoken in two days, largely in part because Laurel and Brodie didn't leave their chamber during that time, and Monty didn't dare show his face again. "At least say goodbye to Donnan," Monty whispered.

Laurel looked at her brother for a long moment, then nodded. She handed the reins back to a groom and made her way to where her brother's partner stood watching the Campbells prepare to depart. She didn't hesitate to return her friend's embrace.

"Lass, I'm pleased for you. I couldn't have guessed it, but you and Brodie appear in love," Donnan whispered.

"I don't know that it's love, Donnan," Laurel said cautiously. Neither the bride nor the groom had articulated their feelings, and Laurel was wary to believe Brodie's ran deeper than lust and affection. She'd promised herself that she could live with that, even though she prayed one day he would reciprocate her feelings. She was certain she both loved and was in love with her husband. They'd spent long hours talking during their two days in seclusion, sharing their ideas for their clan's future and what they hoped their life would be together.

He'd recounted his days of tracking the Lamonts and MacDougalls, the skirmishes they fought, and how things were still unresolved.

"I pray that one day it is. For all your brother's faults, and you and I know there are plenty, I couldn't imagine my life without him," Donnan confessed. "I hope you find the love we have."

"I hope so, too. Monty's words have hurt me, but I'm not angry."

"Will you tell him that?"

"I don't know how," Laurel admitted.

"Och, just say to him what you said to me. It doesn't need to be harder than that."

Laurel looked at her friend and smiled sadly. She wasn't sure if Donnan was right, but she supposed she faced her last opportunity to find out. She embraced Donnan once more before she pulled away, but Donnan caught her hand.

"Send word, and we will come for you," Donnan promised. Laurel heard the sincerity in his voice and knew that for once someone other than Brodie was offering their protection. It came from Donnan's free will, not duty. Laurel glanced at Monty and found him watching the pair. She smiled and waved him over. Laurel looked back at Donnan before she wrapped her arms around Monty's waist. Her brother hesitated for a heartbeat, then hugged her so tightly she had to tap on his back lest he suffocate her.

"Monty, I'm hurt, but I'm not angry. Mayhap you were angry with me or with Brodie when you couldn't find me, or mayhap you were worried. Mayhap it was discovering I'd married without telling you, including you. I didn't give you a chance to explain. I was embarrassed, so I lashed out. Your words only made me feel worse. But I don't want to be angry all the time. Bitterness has made me an ugly person, but I have a chance to start fresh. I don't want to begin my new life with the trappings of my auld one. I'm sorry I've been difficult to tolerate."

"Laurel, it's never been aboot tolerating you. You've not been easy to like since you left Balnagown, but I was the one who refused to consider how unhappy you've been. You've tried to tell me each time I've seen you. But I refused to listen, telling myself that you were just being awkward. It was easier than admitting that I can't help you. And each time I can't, I lash out just as you do when you don't get the love you deserve. I'm sorry, Laurel. I don't want you to ride away hating me."

"I don't hate you, Monty. That's why it hurts." Laurel rested her head against her brother's chest, finding comfort there but wishing Brodie was closer. She felt the tears threatening, and it was Brodie who she wished to turn to.

"Laurel, send word if ever you need me," Monty murmured beside her ear. "I don't care what anyone else thinks. I will never leave you to fend for yourself again. Ask, and I will come."

Laurel looked up at the older brother she'd adored as a child. She watched the breeze rustle hair that was so like hers before she gazed into eyes a reflection of her own. She nodded and strained to kiss his cheek. She knew when Brodie came to stand behind her, sensing his presence. With a nod to Monty and a smile to Donnan and him, she turned to accept Brodie's proffered hand. Her husband drew her into his embrace, and Laurel felt like she could once more face the world.

Once Laurel mounted, she turned back and waved at the Ross men gathered in the Stirling Castle bailey. She'd prayed for when she could ride away from everything that tied her to the clan of her birth. She thought she'd feel elation. But it was a sense of peace that wrapped around her. She looked at Brodie, who rode beside her as they clattered under the portcullis and onto the road.

"Are you ready for the Highlands, thistle?" Brodie smiled.

"I canna wait, bear," Laurel grinned. She'd taken to calling Brodie bear, and she thought it fit him as well as his pet name thistle fit her. She enjoyed having a special endearment for him. He'd told her how much it pleased him to hear it, then he'd shown her. They had a three-day ride ahead of them, with nights under the stars instead of in a private chamber. The couple made the most of the early morning hours to tide them over. When they were clear of the town, Brodie encouraged Laurel to race. It was her first day of real freedom, and he wanted her to enjoy every minute of it.

"If we're going to do aught, it must before they reach Kilchurn. Once she's behind the gates, there'll be no way to reach her." Nelson looked at Liam and the men who sat with him at The Merry Widow. He'd watched Laurel, Brodie, and the Campbell men ride out that morning with the Ross entourage leaving within an hour of the Campbells. "The eejit doesn't realize what he's done. He's too enamored with what's under her skirts to realize the mistake he's made."

"But he defended her before he bedded her," Stephen pointed out.

"You really believe he didn't tup her before they handfasted? You're just as much an eejit as he. We all heard what Lady Sarah Anne and Lady Margaret saw. Half the ladies-in-waiting watched him pawing her in the passageway. Why else did they ride out every day for hours on end? Even her brother stopped chaperoning them. Campbell's blind to her ways. He hasn't known her for years like we have."

"MacDougall, why do you, of all people, care? Your clan's been raiding the Campbells," Stephen pressed.

Nelson sat back and looked at the surrounding men. He'd thought he would have less trouble convincing them to support his plan to end Brodie Campbell's marriage. He'd thought it a stroke of brilliant luck when Liam offered the wager that Brodie couldn't tame Laurel. He'd assumed Brodie would fail. Even when Brodie and Monty refused the bet, he still believed Brodie would fail. He'd eagerly awaited his enemy's humiliation before the entire court. Instead, he'd made Lady Laurel into the image of a doting wife. He wanted to be ill.

"And how many years have I been at court? I may as well be a MacDougall by name only. I don't dislike Brodie Campbell, even if my clan hates his." Nelson hoped his shrug and his attempt at nonchalance would convince the others. "Besides, after the wake of unhappiness Lady Laurel left behind, why does she deserve a happy life?"

"Does it matter? She's gone, and I can get on with courting Lady Catherine," Edgar stated. "Andrew and I are nearly done with the contracts, and we'll send them to her father within a sennight. I need her dowry to repair the clan's accounts after my ne'er-do-well relatives practically ran us into the ground. If anyone were eejits it was my uncles James and Tomas who started trouble with the Sinclairs, then my own bluidy father and brothers who nearly ruined us by taking on the Sutherlands and Gordons. I have much to make up for since Arlan and Beathan's deaths."

"Aren't you sniffing around Lady Margaret's skirts, MacDougall?" Magnus asked. "Why leave court when you could woo the woman and secure her dowry? I say the lot of us move forward and not look back."

Nelson clenched his jaw and darted a glance at his brother Matthew, who feigned disinterest. They'd formed a strategy years ago of pretending to dislike one another. It meant they learned twice as much at court. But regardless of their act, both men were loyal to the bone, and they would do anything to advance their clan's wealth and standing. If that meant making Brodie Campbell's life miserable, then it was a sweet reward. "And why do you think I wish Lady Laurel ill will? In defense of my Lady Margaret. The hellion made Lady Margaret unhappy. I do it as a wedding gift."

"I didn't take Lady Margaret for being so bloodthirsty, but the Hays have brought aboot their share of bloodshed with poor allies. They shouldn't have taken on the Sinclairs over

Lady Deirdre or Lady Brighde." Matthew raised his mug to his brother and sneered. "You pick the worst bedfellows."

"Anyone ever notice how the Sinclairs are at the center of most Highland conflicts?" Edgar mused. He threw his hands up when Magnus and Seamus reached for their blades. Magnus was Laird Tristan Mackay's cousin, and the laird married Mairghread Sinclair, the only daughter to Laird Liam Sinclair and younger sister to Callum, Alexander, Tavish, and Magnus. Seamus's older half-sister Siùsan married Callum, heir to the Sinclair lairdship. Seamus fostered with the Sinclairs, and Magnus cared for his cousin-by-marriage.

"Don't forget that they are also the center of the most powerful alliance in the Highlands," Magnus pointed out.

"Do you ride with me or not?" Nelson grew tired of the conversation drifting from his goal.

"What do you intend to do? Kidnap the woman right from under Campbell's nose? She won't be out of arms' reach of the mon." Seamus shook his head. "I'm out. I'm not dying over Laurel Ross, or rather Laurel Campbell. Like it or not, she's still Lady Sutherland's niece. I'm not bringing the Sutherlands down on my clan's head. I know the Sinclairs will side with them before they do the Mackenzies, even if I grew up there. And that's not to mention the trouble we're already having with the Rosses."

"You wagered a small fortune on them, but you're willing to walk away." Matthew smirked before he raised his mug in salute. "Wise mon."

"And the rest of you?" Nelson locked eyes with each man.

"I'm out." Magnus rose from the table. "Even if I cared enough to get involved, my laird would kill me. Besides, he expects me back at Varrich, not wondering aboot the Highlands."

Nelson to stared at Stephen, Edgar, Andrew, and Matthew. He knew his brother would ride with him, along with Liam. But the other three could pose a risk if they disagreed. They could warn the king or Brodie. Nelson and Matthew wouldn't take that chance. Edgar was the only laird in the bunch. Stephen and Andrew were only representatives. The Gunns and Oliphants were at each other's throats, so Nelson would consider Edgar's death as a gift to Liam and his clan. Money and women were what kept them civil to one another at court.

"Aye, I'll ride with you. The Gunns have no love lost with the Rosses." Edgar raised his mug and toasted his pledge.

"MacBain?" Matthew looked at the last man to speak.

"I'm in." Stephen sounded the least confident, but he'd placed one of the highest wagers.

"Then we ride out before dawn. Campbell will have stuck to the roads for her sake. We ride over land to catch them." Nelson was pleased by the sound of authority in his voice.

"You still haven't told us what you plan to do once we catch them." Stephen narrowed his eyes, doubt niggling at him. His clan had barely recovered from their encounter with the Camerons. Lady Cameron was Lady Sutherland's daughter, which made her Laurel's cousin. The women were hardly close, but they shared blood. The last thing the MacBains needed were the four strongest clans in the northern Highlands descending upon them, and Magnus's glare reminded him that his own clan would be forced to face the Rosses, Sutherlands, Camerons, Sinclairs, and Mackays.

"Don't forget she's Lady MacLeod's cousin too," Magnus whispered to Stephen. "Do you want them on your doorstep too?"

Stephen considered his options. He'd committed to Nelson, and he didn't trust the man not to stab him in his sleep. But he didn't need to start a feud on behalf of his clan, nor did he think he'd survive his uncle if he turned up at home to announce the six mighty clans were chasing him. He nodded to Magnus. He would ride with Nelson, but the first opportunity he had to leave the group, he would.

"Be ready to leave an hour before sunrise." Nelson put coins on the table and rose. Matthew followed him, grinning at Edgar and Stephen before he and his brother left.

"We're deep in the shite now," Stephen muttered.

"Nay. But we will be deep in the coin," Edgar countered.

"But everyone wagered Campbell would fail. How can you think that you'll win aught?" Magnus knew he would lose money since he'd betted that Brodie wouldn't woo Laurel.

"Because we adjusted the wager to how long their marriage would last. We never stipulated how it would end," Edgar reminded the men who remained.

"You're a fool, Gunn." Magnus rose. He only tolerated Laird Gunn at court to keep up appearances that their truce held. If they'd been in the true Highlands, they would have already drawn swords days earlier. Magnus would ride for Varrich and warn his cousin, but he knew he would reach home days after whatever happened. He walked out of the tavern with Seamus. "My men and I leave as soon as I return to the keep. You'd do well to leave too, lest you wish to die in your sleep tonight. MacDougall won't risk us informing the Bruce or Campbell."

"Aye. That's why I head to the keep now. We'd be safer if we rode together until I turn west."

"Aye." Both men hurried back to Stirling Castle, not casting a backwards glance at the town. The Mackenzie and Mackay contingencies rode out within fifteen minutes, putting as much distance between them and Stirling as they could despite the dark.

TWENTY-TWO

L aurel gazed at the stars as Brodie snored softly beside
her. She knew she should be asleep, but it was her first
night sleeping in the open in months. She'd traveled with the
royal couple on summer progress each year the journey
happened, but she'd always slept in a tent with at least four
other ladies. This was the first time since her last trip to
Balnagown that she lay out in the open. She imagined how
the stars came to be, God placing each one. She picked out
shapes by connecting the pinpricks of light. They'd made
camp near a pine forest, and the heavy scent filled the air. It
reminded her of how Brodie smelled after he bathed. She
nestled closer to him, and he tightened his arm around her.

"Cold?" Brodie whispered.

"It's all right." Laurel patted the muscular arm around her
waist.

"Can ye nae sleep?"

"I'm enjoying the stars too much."

"Ye ken they'll be there in four more nights when ye can
watch them from our bed." Brodie yawned as he drew Laurel
as close as he could, his heat almost stifling her. He'd opted for
taking a longer route back to Kilchurn, but it would keep

Laurel far away from Lamont territory and allow them to travel on roads rather than overland.

"I ken. But I havenae seen them this bright in years."

"Are ye happy, Laurie?"

"More than I could have ever imagined."

"All it took was the stars?"

Laurel rolled over to look at Brodie, careful not to disturb the men sleeping around them. "It's nae the stars that make me happy."

"Could it be me?" Brodie's grin made his teeth flash white in the dark.

"Arrogant mon." Laurel tickled the spot she'd discovered their first night together. "Ye ken it is. Ye ken what it means to me to be away from Stirling and to be outdoors. I wouldnae have this without ye."

"I would do aught to keep ye as carefree as ye've been today. Ye are the thistle I've always said ye are. Ye kept apace with ma men despite the arduous ride. Ye've weathered the storm that was yer life at court. And ye've blossomed being in the wild."

"Then ye are the sunshine, rain, and rich soil I needed."

"Nay, Laurie. Ye've always found those on yer own. But I am the lucky mon who watches ye bloom."

Laurel's fingers trailed over Brodie's temple to his cheek bones before brushing his stubble. She longed to tell him how she felt, but she didn't want to ruin the moment. She recalled Brodie's handfast vows, and the ones said outside the kirk. She prayed one day he would feel the love he pledged. She never imagined it would mean so much to her. She certainly hadn't when she met him. But now, she hoped to inspire it.

"What're ye thinking aboot?" Brodie's voice broke into her thoughts.

"That I couldnae conceive that we'd marry when I met ye. I didna believe I could be this happy. I nay longer fear that ye married me because of a wager or because ye were forced. I dinna even care how it came aboot."

"It came aboot because ye were meant to be ma wife. I ken I should feel guilty that I dinna grieve Eliza, but I canna when I'm so happy to have found ye. I ken I should feel guilty for that too, but I canna muster aught but happiness."

"I may never understand how ye knew me so well from the start. I ken now that we think much the same, but that didna guarantee ye would know me as I really am, or that ye would even like who I am. I still think it's because ye're auld." Laurel stifled a giggle when Brodie tickled her. At twelve years her senior, she'd questioned what their life would be like as he aged sooner than she did. She feared being left a widow all too soon and the years she would be left on her own. But Laurel would seize every moment, every month and year she had with Brodie, and cherish all of them.

"Dinna question ma wisdom, lass," Brodie chortled before he kissed her. "We have another long day tomorrow. Ye should sleep while ye can."

"I ken. I'm ready to now." As if on cue, Laurel yawned. "With the stars overhead, and ye beside me, I suspect it will be the best night's sleep I've gotten in ages." They shifted to be more comfortable, and by morning, Laurel knew she'd been right. She woke refreshed, ready to face another day that brought her closer to her new home.

Laurel rode in the middle of the party as they approached the village of Locherhead, which lay at the foot of Loch Earn. She'd never heard of the village, but it reminded her of all the other Highland ones she'd passed through over the years. People moved about the village square as women fetched buckets of water and men herded animals toward the ferry that would take them to St. Fillans at the other end of the waterway.

It was nearly midday, and Laurel's belly rumbled. She was glad the ding of animals and people kept anyone from hearing it. She discovered that the fresh air did wonders for her appetite. It was also likely because the kirtle she wore was older and material had given. Coupled with Brodie loosening the laces, Laurel breathed easier and could eat more comfortably. She gazed at an enormous castle at the far end of the road they traveled. She also breathed easier knowing that they were nearing Campbell territory, and even members from a lesser sept lived in the area.

"Lass, we'll stop for the midday meal and to let the animals rest." Brodie broke into her musings as the group neared an inn. They'd traveled along the foothills to the Trossachs. She'd seen the peak of Ben Vorlich an hour earlier as they passed through a glen. The route had been rocky and uneven, so she was glad to let Teine rest before they carried on. She also looked forward to stretching her legs and giving her backside a reprieve after the jarring ride.

"Thank you. I'm quite hungry."

"I ken. Your belly signaled it was time to eat nearly a half hour ago." Brodie's grin made Laurel scowl, but it was in jest. He helped her from the saddle and grasped her upper arms as she steadied herself. "Let's feed you."

"Yes, please." The couple moved toward the door of the inn, but movement to their left made Laurel peer behind Brodie. She thought she'd seen Stephen MacBain, but she reminded herself that was impossible since the man was likely still at Stirling Castle. And even if he headed home, he wouldn't be on the same route as the Campbells, and Laurel reasoned he couldn't have arrived ahead of them unless he'd ridden through the night and for two days straight. She pushed aside the notion and entered the inn with Brodie.

She took a seat on a bench between Brodie and Graham, who she'd immediately liked when she met him. He reminded her of Donnan, and he'd put her at ease. She didn't doubt that he wondered why his laird married Laurel, but he'd been polite every time she encountered him. She hadn't determined where Michael disappeared to the day Brodie returned. She was certain he hadn't been in the bailey when she went to the kirk, nor was he there while she waited. But she recalled finding him with the other Campbell men when she went to thank them. She supposed he'd sought rest while he could. All the men appeared to be on their last leg by the end of the ceremony. There was something about Michael that put her on edge, so she avoided him when she could.

"Rest for a while, Laurie." Brodie kissed her forehead when they finished eating. "I'm going to check the horses and add to our provisions. I fear we may encounter foul weather as we climb higher. If we're delayed, I would prefer more food with us in case there isn't much to hunt."

Laurel was eager to arrive at Kilchurn, but she wasn't in a rush to get back onto Teine. She loved her steed, and she loved riding, but she could admit—at least to herself—that the journey was not the same as a jaunt across a meadow. She watched as Brody and Graham left the tavern. Two men remained, and one was Michael. She pretended to be interested in her mug of ale to avoid having to make conversation with the man who made her uneasy.

"Too high and mighty for the likes of us." Laurel heard Michael, even though he kept his voice low. She wished she didn't have better-than-average hearing. It meant she caught conversations not intended for her. "Can't even bother to look in our direction."

Laurel wanted to prove she didn't consider herself superior to either of the men, but to look in their direction now meant admitting she heard them. She opted for another tack. Grabbing her mug, she moved toward the counter but stopped before the men. "Would you like another pint?"

Both men narrowed their eyes at her as if they could determine an ulterior motive. Michael nodded. Laurel took that as progress. She moved toward the counter where the tavern keeper stood. The inn was more crowded than she'd expected, but the crowd was respectful. She didn't fear moving around, and Brodie hadn't warned against it.

"May I have another pint of watered ale for me, and two pints of ale for my husband's men?" The barkeep nodded, but he didn't refill Laurel's mug before Michael stepped next to her.

"The laird is ready to leave, ma lady." Laurel looked back at the door, but Brodie wasn't there. "He sent Danny to fetch us." Laurel looked again, but the man Brodie introduced as his best rider wasn't in sight. "He went back to the horses. The laird took several to the farrier to have their shoes checked. We're to meet him there."

Laurel paused for a long moment before she agreed. She followed Michael, and the guard whose name she couldn't remember followed her. When they left the dim tavern, the early afternoon sun blinded Laurel. She tried to shield her eyes, but they watered, nonetheless. She relied on Michael to lead the way while she tried to adjust. She thought she'd seen the horseshoe fitter's workshop from atop Teine, so she wondered why they moved in the opposite direction. She heard the noise coming from the ferry landing and was certain they headed in the wrong direction. They entered a crowded portion of the village, and Laurel realized it was market day. She reached out to tap Michael's shoulder to ask if they were going the right way, but he slipped between men standing ahead of them. Laurel turned back to look for the other guard, but he was nowhere in sight.

Laurel had been to enough markets not to fear being lost. She would find a merchant and ask where she could find the farrier. She spotted a woman selling apples that she thought might help her. She was within earshot when Edgar Gunn stepped in front of her. She reared back, surprised to find him in the village. She discovered Stephen standing beside him. It hadn't been her imagination. But just as she knew Stephen shouldn't be in Locherhead if he was bound for home, she knew Edgar shouldn't be either. He would have taken the same route as she if Laurel was returning to Balnagown.

"Lady Campbell," Edgar extended his hand for hers. She

looked at his upturned palm before placing hers above his. She nearly snatched it back when his fingers wrapped around the sides of her hand and lifted it to his lips. They skimmed her skin, and she wished to wipe her hand against her skirts.

"Laird Gunn." Laurel was eager to find Brodie. "MacBain."

"What are you doing alone, Lady Campbell?" Stephen looked over her head.

"I became separated from my guards, but I'm on my way to the farrier where my husband awaits. Good day."

"We will walk you there." Edgar's tone was adamant, and his expression matched it. Laurel didn't want to make a scene, but she intended to do just as Michael had—slip away in the crowd. She would find her own way to the farrier's or return to the inn and await Brodie there. But her intentions slipped away when Edgar pulled her arm around his. "I wouldn't want you to get separated from us either."

Laurel glanced at Stephen, who studiously avoided looking at her once they began walking. Edgar steered them from where Laurel thought she saw Michael headed. In the short time she'd stood talking to the two men, more people arrived at the market. It dawned on Laurel that this might be the only market in several miles. What appeared like a sleepy hamlet when they arrived was now a bustling village with vendors calling out and pushing their way in front of passersby. Forced toward the water when a herd of cattle blocked the way, Laurel strained to pull free of Edgar's grip. He released her so suddenly that she stumbled. Catching herself before she fell, Laurel tried to walk against the tide of people headed to the ferry. They pushed her along as she fought to make her way free. When the crush of people arrived at the dock, Laurel couldn't fathom how so many could fit on the boat without it capsizing or sinking.

"I have no coin," Laurel said to the ferry master. "I don't intend to board."

"I'm paying for her." Laurel's head whipped around when

she heard Nelson MacDougall. Her heart raced as she looked at him and his brother. Stephen was already aboard, and a shove from behind with a snicker told her Edgar intended to make her get on the boat. She tried harder to break free, but the crowd and Edgar were too much to fight against. She found herself caught in the center of the two MacDougall brothers, Stephen MacBain, Andrew MacFarlane, and Liam Oliphant. Despite being tall for a woman, the five Highlanders hid her from view.

"You're allies," she hissed at Andrew.

"But we're not allies with the Rosses." With that, Andrew crossed his arms and looked down his nose at her. She glanced at Liam and knew she would be at their mercy until Brodie found her, or they killed her. She'd burned every bridge, so she had no way off the ferry.

TWENTY-THREE

"What do you mean you lost her?" Brodie roared as Michael stood before him. The younger man didn't cower; he didn't even look remorseful.

"She wandered off, ma laird."

"There is no wandering off when you're her detail. You go where she goes."

"Some bright little bauble likely caught her eye. She's probably spending yer coin on a new hair ribbon or to get more expensive fabric that she likes."

"Shut yer gob afore I knock every bluidy tooth from yer flapping gums. Dinna think I will forgive and forget because I dinna deal with ye now. Once Lady Campbell is with us, I shall beat ye within a hair's breadth of yer life." Brodie shoved Michael away, furious at the news that Laurel wasn't with them. But he trusted she could manage the market on her own. It was Michael's flippancy that angered him. He'd known the man since Michael was a child and had never liked him. But Michael entered the lists because his father and uncles were warriors for Brodie's father. There was little thought given whether he would remain among Brodie's forces when Brodie inherited the lairdship. But now Brodie wondered if he'd erred in assuming Michael would mature.

193

He'd brought him on the journey to give him that opportunity. Not only had the man disappointed him, Brodie no longer trusted him.

"Lead the way," Graham barked as he shoved Michael's shoulder from behind. Brodie ordered one man to remain behind with the horses, then followed Michael and Wallace, the other man he'd tasked with Laurel's safety. They worked their way through the market, but Brodie couldn't spot Laurel, and his two derelict guards were no help. Brodie grew alarmed when he realized how busy the market had grown as they moved toward the waterfront. He scanned the crowd, praying he would spy a head of reddish-blonde locks, but he found nothing.

"Naught but trouble." Brodie heard the grumble from one of his men. The man muttered it under his breath, so Brodie couldn't tell who said it.

"Should have kenned. Michael's likely right. She's gotten herself lost after buying some do-dad or another. Ay up!" Brodie looked back to find Graham's hand moving away from Walter's head. The man was Wallace's uncle. Brodie wondered what else his men thought. He'd believed they'd accepted Laurel after spending so many hours with her, but now he feared they'd already closed their minds to her despite the kindness she'd shown them on their wedding day.

"She's still your lady," Graham snapped.

"Pair up and ask around. We meet here in twenty minutes," Brodie ordered. He looked at Graham, but his second looked as perplexed as he felt. "Where could she have gone? Laurel would not wonder off. If she wanted something from the market, she would have told me. If she was upset aboot something she would have most definitely told me."

"I ken, Brodie," Graham kept his voice low, abandoning formality. "Something is very wrong with this."

"Do you think she went back to the tavern?"

"That would be my guess."

The pair turned toward where they'd had lunch, struggling to make their way along the busy lanes. When the tavern keeper told them what he'd heard, Brodie was certain he would tear Michael apart. He'd never sent a message that he was ready for Laurel to join him. One horse needed a new shoe, so they would have been delayed an hour. He wanted Laurel to rest for as long as she could. Between their lack of sleep as newlyweds and the rigors of traveling on horseback, Brodie knew the journey exhausted her.

"I need to find her. Then I will kill Michael and Wallace. Whatever's befallen my wife, they were a part of it."

"But why?" Graham looked as baffled as Brodie felt— when his anger wasn't about to boil over.

"You heard what they said. They think she's frivolous and selfish. They know aboot the wagers and aboot me compromising Laurel. Do you think they believe I didn't marry her by choice?"

"That's my thought. If they think she trapped you, they might think you don't want to be married. How far do you think they would go to free you, so to speak?

"They're men trained to fight and kill. I wouldn't put aught past them," Brodie growled. Then shook his head. "Nay. They may not like her, but not every one of them is dishonorable. I don't think it involves all of them."

"I pray that's the case, or we have another disaster on our hands."

"Aye. Treason."

Graham watched the resolve settle across Brodie's features, and he caught himself shivering. He didn't expect Michael or Wallace to return to Kilchurn with them, but he wondered what fate awaited anyone else involved. He couldn't be the only one to see his laird loved his lady. They returned to where they left the men. Each pair reported the same thing: they hadn't seen Laurel, and neither had anyone they asked. Brodie noticed a shift in the men's demeanor. Most looked worried, and a few ever looked fearful.

"Laird?" Brodie looked at Walter, who shifted nervously

before looking at Wallace. "Ma nephew or Michael must have led Lady Campbell to someone. If they'd just left her alone, one of us would have found her."

Michael glared mutinously, but Wallace looked conflicted. "If you ken aught, Wallace, speak up," Walter pleaded. "Think what will happen when yer ma and da learn ye were a part of this. Yer da will nae forgive ye."

"Aye, so what's the point in speaking up?" Michael snapped. "He doesnae ken aught, anyway."

Brodie stepped in front of Michael. "As much I wish to kill you where you stand, I won't until you tell me who you handed Lady Campbell over to." Michael looked unimpressed. "I said I wouldn't kill you. I didn't say I wouldn't torture you."

"Laird!" Graham ran toward Brodie, who hadn't seen Graham walk to the ferry landing. "The dockmaster saw Lady Campbell board on the arm of a mon. He said she tried to get out of the crowd, telling him she had no coin to pay her fare, but another mon already on board said he would pay. He said she looked surprised but didn't try to get away. But he also admitted that they were already underway, and a group of men in different plaids surrounded her."

"Lamonts?" Brodie demanded.

"Nay, but two MacDougalls."

"Bluidy fucking hell. Nelson and Matthew." Brodie plowed his fist into Michael's face. "Why?"

"What does it matter? Ye're free of the bitch now."

"What did you call my wife?" Brodie's deadly quiet voice made the others take a step back.

"Ye heard me," Michael smirked, and with added sarcasm, "ma laird."

"Och, I shall enjoy making your death the slowest, most painful torture I can imagine." Brodie looked at Graham. "When's the next ferry?"

"Not until tomorrow morn," Graham said.

"Then we ride. Bind and gag him." Brodie didn't look

back as he marched to the stables. He trusted his men would follow his orders. He'd seen how aghast they were when they learned other Highlanders had taken Laurel and heard Michael's death wish. They were mounted and riding along Loch Earn's coast within a quarter hour.

TWENTY-FOUR

Laurel drew the Campbell plaid she wore as an arisaid over her hair. She looked over the side of the ferry into the depths of the deep blue water. It was clear the loch was a deep body of water. While she'd learned to swim in the North Sea, she'd done so in a chemise that she would tuck into the neckline. She would sink with the layers of velvet and wool she wore now. She wouldn't free herself. She would drown herself. She would go from little likelihood of seeing Brodie again to no likelihood.

"He must have noticed," Nelson laughed. "Probably thinks she ran off."

"You don't think Michael will cave?" Stephen asked. He'd been the only one to handle her kindly. He'd ensured the waves didn't knock Laurel off her feet until she found a spot where she could huddle against the wind and fear.

"He'll die before he tells," Matthew grinned. "He's been tupping our cousin for years. She's borne him two bastards. The poor sod's in love with her."

"Don't you think Campbell loves her?" Stephen pressed. "You saw him at their wedding. He was eager to be there. He didn't look like a mon trapped."

"Hurried to get it over with," Edgar chuckled. "Mayhap we'll discover if she's as good as the Campbell makes it seem. Spread your legs for us, will you, lass?"

Laurel didn't look in his direction as her stomach tightened into a knot yet again. She watched Stephen shift his weight, so he hid her from Edgar's sight. He made it look like the roll and pitch of the ferry caused him to move to remain on his feet. Laurel couldn't understand why Stephen was shielding her from anything if he was part of her kidnapping.

"The more I think on it, the more I think we've underestimated the mon's feelings. And even if he doesn't love her, he'll still search for her. He'll demand justice," Stephen insisted.

"Like he did for the MacMillan chit? He gave that up as soon as the wind changed, and he got a whiff of her." Liam jutted his chin in Laurel's direction. "He'll be glad to have her off his hands. He'll move on."

We're married, not handfasted. The only way Brodie could move on without being a bigamist is if they kill me.

"What're we going to do with her?" Andrew finally broke his silence after two hours of watching and listening. Laurel hadn't perceived a moment of remorse or doubt from Andrew. He'd simply remained quiet and alert. "Whatever it is, my name can't be linked. The MacFarlanes are allied with the Campbells."

"Then mayhap you should have considered that before you wagered against your friend," Nelson snapped.

"I thought you intended to return her to court or to her clan. I didn't think you intended to kill her," Andrew insisted.

"Did I ever say that?" Nelson narrowed his eyes.

"You didn't have to. But none of us are fools. There can be no annulment, so the only way for Campbell to marry again is if he's a widower. That mean she's," Andrew pointed at Laurel, "got to die."

"Cheaper than losing the wagers. I wagered it wouldn't last a sennight. They married four days ago." Liam patted his sporran.

"But they handfasted nearly a fortnight ago," Stephen pointed out.

"Nay one is counting that." Nelson waved away Stephen's comment.

"But if he'd intended to set her aside, that would have been when he would do it," Stephen insisted. "He wouldn't have shown up at his wedding looking like he'd just walked off the battlefield if he hadn't been in a hurry to reach her, to get to their wedding."

"You sound like you're having second thoughts," Liam accused. "You don't have to be involved."

Stephen looked at the men standing before him. He didn't dare look back at Laurel. If he wasn't careful, they'd both wind up dead. "Just not looking a for clan war. I told you that already."

"What's done is done. She's with us now, and we each wagered less than a moon. Those who wagered he wouldn't show up have already lost, and those who wagered longer than a moon lost as well. We keep the kitty and split it among us, Matthew and I being closest to the date get the bigger shares." Nelson looked at the barge tethered to the stern of the ferry. It carried the livestock, including the men's horses. "We'll be on shore in an hour. They won't catch us even if they figure out how we traveled. Don't buy trouble, MacBain. You'll earn your portion if you just go along to get along."

The men fell silent, and Laurel let herself doze. She felt fairly safe among the passengers, so she capitalized on the chance to sleep. She wouldn't let herself sleep when she was alone with the men, so she needed what rest she could catch. But the ferry's sudden lurch jolted Laurel awake. She looked around and realized they'd reached their destination, and people were disembarking. She struggled to her feet before falling into step behind Nelson and Matthew. She'd had time to consider why Nelson watched her so often while Brody was away. He'd been plotting all along. She even wondered if he had something to do with the MacDougall and Lamont attacks on the Campbells that drew Brodie away.

The more Laurel thought about it, the more she wondered if Nelson had hoped to get her separated and alone while Brodie was gone. He'd trailed her more than once, so she'd been more cautious. She'd stayed with the ladies or asked her guards to accompany her, even when she moved about the keep. She hadn't shared her fears with the Ross warriors, but she'd sensed they perceived a lurking threat too. She knew she'd chosen wisely to remain in her chamber as much as she could. Now she was on her own with no one to protect her but herself. However, she knew her usual tactics to keep people at a distance wouldn't work now. Using her viperous tongue was more likely to get her assaulted, then killed. She would watch and bide her time.

"Up you go, my lady," Nelson said as he grabbed her arm and pulled her in front of him. He didn't wait for her to respond before he lifted her into a saddle and mounted behind her. She wanted to retch at the feel of his arms around her. He lowered his voice. "I shall enjoy this."

Laurel kept her back ramrod straight as she attempted to maintain some distance between her body and Nelson's, but he pulled her back hard. She was grateful his sporran rested between them because she suspected what she would have felt otherwise. They rode through the evening until darkness forced them to make camp. Matthew bound her wrists after she ate, but he didn't bind her ankles or tie her to a tree. She could have gotten up, even tried to run. But she knew she wouldn't outrun any of the men, especially if they were on horseback. She didn't want to die. She wanted her husband. She would wait until she could find a safer alternative.

When the sun rose, Matthew tossed a waterskin at her. She pulled the stopper and sniffed.

"Just drink it." The barked command resulted in her casting a scathing glare at Matthew, but she put the waterskin to her lips. She was thirsty, and she doubted they would give her another chance to drink for several hours. She hesitated when the water had a bitter taste to it. She sniffed it, but there was no scent. "Drink it or go without. But don't ask for aught if you don't drink this first."

Laurel closed one eye and looked down the neck of the waterskin, spying some sediment at the bottom. She assumed it was from the river they'd camped near. She prayed it wouldn't make her ill. Using her teeth to strain the water, she kept whatever had settled at the bottom from entering her mouth, but the water still tasted off. When she finished, she handed the container back to Matthew. He watched her as she slipped behind a bush for a moment of privacy. With no more reason to dawdle, she joined the men and found herself in front of Nelson once more.

The sun wasn't high in the sky, but Laurel was sweating profusely. Her stomach churned as she considered what she might have ingested. She no longer assumed what she'd tasted in the water was there when it was drawn from the river. She was convinced she'd been drugged. She felt light-headed, and she struggled to keep her eyes open. Her lids were heavy, and she caught herself dozing off more than once. She thanked God for small mercies since Nelson left her alone, his hold around her waist light as he steered his horse with his other hand. Whatever tincture they added to the water, Laurel doubted any of the men knew how to brew it. Someone— some woman, more likely—brewed a tea or made a tincture that Matthew or one of the others later added to the water. They wanted her to sleep, but she couldn't understand why she was sweating so horribly.

As Laurel's head finally became too heavy for her neck to support, she considered how she must look. She was certain she looked ill, her pallor ashen. She suspected the MacDougall brothers drugged her to keep her complacent and to make it look as though she ailed in case they ran across anyone who wondered why they traveled with a slumbering woman.

"She's finally asleep," Nelson stated when they stopped to rest the horses. "Hopefully, she remains asleep while I give her another dose of the catnip tea Margaret gave me."

"Won't she choke?" Andrew wondered.

"We shall see," Nelson said with a shrug. He handed Laurel down to Andrew before he dismounted. Andrew propped Laurel against a tree and supported her head when it lolled from side to side. "She's sleeping more deeply than I expected."

Nelson put a waterskin to Laurel's lips and eased the contents into Laurel's mouth. The natural response to swallow kept her from choking, but a small rivulet trailed from her lip to her jaw. The men waited with bated breath to see if she would wake. But when her body went lax and slumped, Nelson smiled.

"Better than sleep. She's unconscious. Now to just keep her that way." It wasn't long before Nelson ordered the men to mount. Riding without Laurel pitching to one side or another proved more challenging that Nelson expected. His frustration with the unconscious woman grew when she continued to sweat, and it poured off her forehead onto his forearm. He called for them to make camp early.

"Riders approach," Andrew called out.

"Campbells?" Nelson asked.

"Nay. Looks like Rosses. Her brother."

"Perfect!"

The men turned to look at Nelson, who left Laurel to slump to the ground. He scooped dirt into his hand and forced Laurel's fingers to scrape through it, leaving her nails encrusted with it. He grasped a nearby twig and ran it over Laurel's cheeks and forehead, leaving scratches but no significant wounds. Her hair was still mostly neat. Nelson tugged at it, eliciting a moan from Laurel, but she didn't move. He pulled strands loose and made her look unkempt. He threw dirt onto her gown and around her neck. By the time he'd finished, Laurel looked as though she'd been crawling through the woods on her belly.

"Ross!" Matthew called out when the party was within earshot. He waved to Monty and signaled for him to stop in the clearing where he and the others rested with Laurel. "Bluidy good we found you. We have your sister."

"What?" Monty jumped from his horse and spotted Laurel. He ran to her side, looking suspiciously at Nelson, who appeared to be cradling her. "What happened?"

"We found her yesterday near Loch Earn," Nelson said.

"Loch Earn? What was she going there? What were you doing there?" Donnan asked as he came to kneel beside Monty.

"Look at her. She's obviously been mistreated. She must have used the ferry to get away from Campbell, or mayhap he dumped her there. We hoped we would catch you or we would have taken her to Balnagown," Edgar spoke up. He and Stephen were the only ones who lived near the Rosses. Both the Gunns and MacBains lived further north. The Oliphants lived east of where they were now, and the MacDougalls lived to the west. They were the only ones who had any plausible reason to be near Loch Earn, but even then, it was out of the MacDougalls' way. The MacFarlanes lived closer to the Campbells. Monty wondered why Andrew was with the party when he could have parted with them near Ben Vorlich and never gotten near Loch Earn. But seeing the men all together, with his unconscious sister among them, made him wary. None seemed so honorable that they would help Laurel merely because she was a woman on her own.

"Did you look for Campbell?" Monty inquired.

"We thought to, but when we tried to move her, she screamed and thrashed as though she fought someone off. She kept saying his name and trying to defend herself. We figured he was the one who did this to her," Edgar explained. Monty nodded and glanced at Donnan. His partner looked as convinced as he felt. But until he was certain, he would take Laurel to Balnagown and not Kilchurn.

"Thank you," Monty said as he scooped Laurel into his arms. "You have my gratitude." He handed Laurel to Donnan while he mounted, then cradled his sister against his chest.

"We passed through a village this morning, and the healer gave us this. She said it should help ease Lady Campbell's discomfort and mayhap even rouse her," Nelson said as he handed a pouch to Donnan. "She said to brew it in a tea for her."

Donnan nodded and tucked it into his sporran. He knew Monty had as little intention of giving it to Laurel as he did. The guardsman mounted but cast a long speculative look at the men in the clearing before he looked at Monty. The Ross party spurred their horses and left Nelson and his friends behind.

"Do you think they'll give her the medicinals?" Stephen asked.

"Not bluidy likely. But she's apt to sleep until they arrive at Balnagown." Nelson curled his lip. "We follow at a distance and make sure the Campbells don't catch up to them because they're surely headed this way if they discovered she was on the ferry. Mayhap she'll be a widow rather than Campbell becoming a widower." Too proud of his scheme, Nelson didn't notice the look Stephen and Andrew exchanged. Edgar and Liam stood with Nelson and Matthew, looking thick as thieves. Nelson's plot had evolved into something far more dangerous than Andrew and Stephen expected. It had always seemed like Liam was the instigator, and Nelson was a hanger-on. But Nelson had shown his true self, and he worried Andrew and Stephen far more than Liam. Both men were torn between breaking away from the group and riding for their homes or riding with their co-conspirators and hoping they could keep anyone from dying.

"Do you stay or do you go?" Andrew asked under his breath.

"Stay for now. First chance, I tell Campbell or Ross. I didn't agree to kill her." Stephen murmured as they reached their horses. They waited for the other three to mount before the five men trotted a safe distance behind the Rosses.

TWENTY-FIVE

Brodie ran his hand over the smaller boot print, confident that it was Laurel's. But the five pairs scattered around it made him wonder who had her. He knew for certain Nelson and Matthew were there, and he now suspected they'd orchestrated it. However, he didn't know who the other men were. He'd questioned the dock master, but the man didn't know the plaid patterns well enough to identify any of them. Brodie had swallowed his anger, instead ordering his men to ride east along Loch Earn's northern shore. It was away from MacDougall land, but it would take them toward the Rosses. When he considered who he'd seen Liam and Nelson associating with, he told Graham that they could take her to Edgar's home at Clyth Castle along the north-eastern coast. He doubted that Andrew MacFarlane would invite them home to hide the kidnapped wife of an ally. If they'd injured Laurel even in the slightest, he would sever his ties to the MacFarlanes and support the Colquhouns, who were the MacFarlanes' rivals.

"We track them and ride hard. They can't be that far ahead of us. It's obvious they made camp here last night since the ground is still warm from their fire, and they only set off an hour before us. The ferry might have made the journey faster than by land, but not by much since we're riding light. It's barely two hours past dawn, and we've already found where they spent the night." Brodie looked at Michael once more. He'd ordered the man kept away from him. He didn't trust himself not to stab Michael if he was within reach. Some Campbell warriors tried to coax Michael to speak, but he'd given nothing away. Brodie learned Wallace was just a lemming who'd followed Michael when he said they could help their laird.

Brodie chided himself for not starting earlier that morning. He might have caught them before they were underway. He was angry and frustrated to discover Laurel had been within two hours' ride of him. If he'd pushed the men longer the night before or made them rise earlier, he could have found her. But his common sense told him they couldn't have done either of those things safely. He didn't have enough men to risk losing more. He'd arrived at Stirling with two score men. He'd lost nearly a dozen fighting the MacDougalls. He couldn't afford to lose more since he didn't know how many men his nemeses rode with.

If Edgar was leading Laurel's captors to Clyth Castle, they had a ten-day ride ahead of them. Brodie told himself that gave him plenty of time to catch them. He gritted his teeth when he acknowledged to himself that he would pass near Balnagown on the way. It would still be a sennight's ride, but he could seek the help of his father-by-marriage if he didn't find Laurel first.

Brodie looked north and considered how to implement his plan. He needed a strategy, and he needed to consider logistics. Chasing after Laurel wouldn't guarantee that he ever caught up to them, even if he wanted to believe he could. He couldn't count on Nelson not to harm her before he reached her. And while he believed Monty would help him, he couldn't be sure Laird Ross would. He picked up a twig and squatted beside the footprints. He drew the topography that he faced between where they'd stopped and Balnagown, then added the route to Clyth. He studied his map as he pictured the landscape, judging where he and his men could gain speed and ground over Laurel's captors. His goal was now to get ahead of them, taking a stand where he chose.

"We abandon the road for the open land. I plan to be waiting for them at Dalwhinnie. If not there, then before they reach Inverness. They'll likely follow the road and skirt the Cairngorms, but may sail up Loch Tay. If they do, we can catch them at Kenmore. Regardless of whether we find Lady Campbell there, we don't linger. It's bluidy Gordon land, and the last thing I need is them involved. We sail from Inverness to Balnagown if we must." Brodie drew the twig through the dirt to show the route he and his men would travel. It would be even more arduous than the one they'd been on to Kilchurn, but he trusted the Campbell horseflesh. With his resolve to find his wife, he'd seen a shift in his men. He believed they finally understood it wasn't duty that drove him to find Laurel. It was love.

"Mount!" Graham called out. The Campbell men rode north, remaining on the northeastern side of Loch Tay. He suspected the MacDougalls would attempt to hire birlinns to get them up the loch, but he and his men could still make better time. He had a day's ride ahead of him. He prayed that he would have Laurel in his arms by nightfall.

Laurel was going to be ill. She felt the bile rising in her throat, and the horse's gait beneath her was only making it worse. She struggled to open her eyes, but she was still so sleepy. She thought it would be fitting punishment if she vomited all over Nelson's leg and boot. Despite her foggy mind, she could no longer hold back the need to cast up her accounts. She pitched to the side and heaved over and over.

"Laurel?"

Laurel's brow furrowed. She recognized the voice, but she

couldn't understand how her brother sat behind her on the horse. She'd been riding with Nelson the last she recalled. She squeezed her eyes closed against the sunlight, fearing she would be sick all over again. Her arms felt too leaden to wipe her mouth, and her hair was plastered to her neck and forehead as she continued to sweat.

"Mayhap she needs another dose if she's coming around."

Laurel was certain she heard Donnan. But what could they be talking about? A dose of what? With horrifying certainty, she recalled drinking the water Matthew gave her. She'd grown too hot and then too sleepy. She didn't remember meeting her brother, but if Donnan intended to drug her, then Monty was in league with Nelson. Laurel wanted to cry out, thrash against Monty. Anything to break free if her brother colluded to keep her from Brodie. But her body still felt sluggish and out of her control.

The horse drew to a stop, and Laurel fought once more to open her eyes, but it was too hard. Her mind was slowly clearing enough to be aware of what she heard. But it wasn't sharp enough to understand what it meant. She tried to break free when someone tilted her head back and pressed a waterskin to her mouth. Her instinct to swallow allowed some liquid down her throat, but she recognized the taste. She fought against her captor.

"It's working. Give her more," Donnan encouraged.

Working? I'm struggling to wake. I'm not falling back to sleep. At least not yet. If they want me asleep, then why would he think it's working? I need to tell them. Tell them what? What was I just thinking aboot? Brodie. Tell them.

"Want Brodie," Laurel mumbled. "Want Brodie."

"What did she say?" Monty asked. "It sounded like she wants Brodie."

"Ye—" Laurel was battling the need to sleep as she forced each sound from between her lips. "Bro—"

"It sounds like she's asking for him not trying to get away," Monty said, skepticism lacing his tone.

"Stay Bro—" Laurel's mind went blank as she sagged back into unconsciousness.

"She wants to be with Brodie. That doesn't fit with what Nelson told us," Donnan said.

"It doesn't. I knew it was too much of a coincidence that they'd found Laurel. But I was more relieved to get her away from them."

"Aye. Whatever we gave her made her worse."

"I was desperate to rouse her. I took the chance because I feared how deeply she slept. I think the last dose only pushed her mind deeper into blackness." Monty gazed down at his slumbering sister. He'd been hesitant to trust that the herbs they gave him would help Laurel, but he'd grown desperate. "If she wishes to rejoin Brodie, then we ride in the wrong direction. We double back. It's two days' ride to Kilchurn."

"Hopefully, she rouses if we don't give her anymore of the water. Then she can tell us what happened." Donnan frowned as he looked at the woman he'd considered a sister rather than a friend. He hadn't agreed with Monty many times about how he treated Laurel, and they'd argued in private each time. But he recognized the genuine discomfort Monty experienced. He recognized the guilt. "Make it up to her by getting her back to her husband."

"That won't be nearly enough, but it's a place to start from."

Laurel shivered, finally feeling cold rather than overheated. Someone pulled her arisaid tighter around her and held her against a broad chest. For a moment, she thought it was Brodie. But the man's scent wasn't right. She recognized it, though. Her eyes didn't want to open, but her mind was clearer than it had been. She fought the haze and tried to speak.

"Monty?"

"Aye, Laurel. It's me. Do you want a drink?" When Laurel struggled to break free, Monty cooed at her. "It's fresh water, I swear. I didn't ken what was in it before. I need you to wake up, Laurel. I need to ken what happened."

Laurel offered a weak nod as she opened her lips to the waterskin. The fresh, cool water slithered down her throat. When she drank her fill, she sagged back against Monty. Her thoughts were coherent once more, but her body still felt heavy.

"How did ye find me?"

"We came across Nelson and the others on the road," Monty explained. "He claimed he found you near Loch Earn. You looked worse for wear. Your gown is filthy, but we washed away the dirt from your face, hands, and neck. You still have the scratches. I'm guessing they came from branches while you ran."

"I never ran." Laurel shook her head and regretted it. She put her fingertips to her forehead, shocked to find the skin roughened. "I would have, had I the opportunity. I didna leave Brodie. Edgar and Stephen pushed me onto the ferry in Locherhead. Once we reached St. Fillans, they started drugging me to make me sleep."

"And they must have prayed we would believe their story and continue drugging you. They said they'd found a healer in a village, and the woman gave you medicinals to rouse you and give you back your strength. We'd just ridden through a village an hour earlier, so it seemed plausible to me."

"How'd you get separated from Brodie long enough to end up in their company?" Donnan cut in.

"I was following one of Brodie's guards. He led me into the most crowded part of the market, then left me. The other guard disappeared, too. Before I could do aught, the crowd was pushing me toward the docks. I tried to tell the ferry mon that I had nay coin, but that's when Nelson spoke up and said he would pay. I found maself on the packed boat with Stephen MacBain, Andrew MacFarlane, Nelson and Matthew

MacDougall, Liam Oliphant, and Edgar Gunn. I never left Brodie."

"But the scratches and dirt?" Monty asked.

"One of them did that. Probably when they spotted ye to make their story sound real. I was on horseback with Nelson or sitting on the ground the entire time. There were nay bushes or branches."

"Laurel, we're riding west now. We're taking you to Kilchurn." Monty adjusted Laurel's plaid again. "You're freezing."

"I was too hot before. I thought I would sweat off ma own skin." Laurel couldn't muster the effort to sound like a courtly lady. She no longer cared either. "Brodie must be beside himself. He wouldnae have let me go. After what happened to Eliza MacMillan, he must be worried Nelson and Matthew intend to do the same to me. Where are we?"

"We're close to Morenish, along Loch Tay. We found you near Kinnell, at the base of the loch." Monty pointed to the shimmering water a few yards away.

"Do ye think the men scattered now that I'm with ye? Stephen and Edgar might still travel our route, but Andrew never should have traveled so far north."

"Nay. They're following us."

"Monty, what?" Laurel exclaimed.

"Aye. Donnan's been keeping an eye on them. They think they're following far enough behind. Daft bastards. They're downwind of us. We've caught whiffs of their horses. They're just out of sight but not out of sniff."

"Then how do we double back?"

"We're approaching the next fishing village, Milton Morenish. We'll see if we can hire birlinns to take us across. We ride back toward Kinnell and then onto Kilchurn."

"And if they cross too?" Laurel worried her bottom lip.

"It still puts us ahead of them and back in the right direc- tion," her brother reassured. "And in the right direction to find Brodie. He'll be tracking you."

Laurel nodded. She believed they would follow the route Monty described; she even prayed that they would find Brodie. But she was unconvinced that they would outwit Nelson MacDougall. He wanted her dead too much to have given up. She'd puzzled out the reason for her captivity during her brief moments of lucidity. The MacDougalls, nor any other rival clan for that matter, could afford the Campbells doubling their strength by allying with the Rosses. The Campbells were already more powerful than any singular clan in the Highlands. While Laurel and Monty weren't close to their cousins, it didn't negate that their father and the Earl of Sutherland were brothers-by-marriage, and the Earl of Sutherland was brothers-by-marriage to the Earl of Sinclair. Rarely did she think of the three men by their official titles because they were family. But no one else would underestimate the forces each man commanded. Should they call upon the tangled web of familial connections, the Campbells and Rosses would be unstoppable.

"I'm sending Martin back to Balnagown," Monty said, naming their best rider. "Father needs to ken what's happened. All of what's happened." Monty's pointed look made Laurel purse her lips.

"Vera well. He'll ken one way or another. Hopefully, he realizes patience is a virtue. His least favorite child has made the best match in the bunch."

"Laurel," Monty glanced over her head at Donnan as they continued to ride. "We don't think it was Father's doing so much as Mother's insistence. She's always been the first to insist on her title as the Countess of Ross. It's always been obvious that's the only reason she married Father. You going to court but not marrying aggravated Mother. We think she's the one who refused to let you come home. She would have considered it her own failure. Father gave in to keep the peace."

"He feared having two carping women was more than he could tolerate," Laurel surmised. She'd long suspected the same, but it hadn't mattered where the lack of parental support stemmed. Her father could have, and should have, done more for her.

"Aye. But he'd still our father. He won't stand for what's happened. Affection or not, his pride won't allow such an affront."

"Thank heavens for small mercies," Laurel muttered.

The fishing boats bobbing high in the water came into view, and the Rosses spurred their horses forward. When they arrived at the docks, Laurel remained with Donnan and the men while Monty negotiated their passage. She no longer felt comfortable around any of the men. The men who rotated through her detail were always civil to her because it was their duty. But she knew none of them liked her. As a direct link to the life she lost, her bitterness kept her from being kind to them for years. It was only the men who'd been assigned to her over the past five years who had seen a softer side to her, who had received thoughtful gifts rather than perfunctory ones at Hogmanay and Epiphany. As she sat upon Monty's horse, she knew none—not even the men who had served her at Stirling—were happy about the delay she caused. They wished to be at Balnagown, not chasing across the Highlands to return a wayward bride to her addlepated husband. She'd heard their grumbles while they waited.

"I paid extra to ensure they don't give passage to the others once they discover we've crossed over." Monty said as he reached for his horse's bridle and led them to the birlinns. "We'll be across in less than a half hour."

It was Laurel's second boat ride, but at least this time she didn't fear winding up in the water and dying. Besides the handful of fishermen on the two birlinns, there was no one else in sight. She preferred it that way.

TWENTY-SIX

"Riders approaching from the hill, my laird," Graham called out. Brodie had spotted them too. Whoever they were, they were galloping toward the Campbells and had clearly already caught sight of them from the higher elevation. It was too late for the Campbells to move off the road to avoid whoever approached. Instead, the men drew their weapons and prepared to stand their ground.

"Brodie! Brodie!"

Brodie heard the voice at the same moment he recognized the two heads of flame-orange hair racing toward him. He spurred his horse, sword still in hand. When he drew close enough to see Monty and Donnan's smiles, he didn't fear an attack. He sheathed his sword as his horse came abreast Monty's. Laurel launched herself into his arms and nearly slipped between the horses. Brodie caught her, and Monty untangled her skirts. He crushed her against his chest, and she collapsed into his embrace.

"Laurie," Brodie's voice rasped. They turned their faces to one another, their elated expressions matching before they came together in a passionate kiss. The rest of the world—their witnesses and their woes—ceased to exist for the couple. Their lips mashed together as their tongues tangled. Need and fear melded into joy and relief. It made for a conflagration of emotions. Those who watched could never deny that the couple's feelings were mutual, and there was no hesitation on either's part.

As their kisses calmed and became shorter and less intense, Laurel allowed herself to believe she was truly reunited with her husband. Brodie had never experienced a feeling more consuming than the power of having Laurel in his arms once more. While he never could have imagined it, it surpassed even their most tender or their wildest lovemaking. They rested their foreheads together as Brodie stroked Laurel's hair back from her face and shoulders. She wrapped one arm around his waist and the cool fingers of her other hand pressed against his neck.

"I will always come for you, thistle," Brodie whispered.

"I ken, bear. I didn't doubt that."

"I can't express how sorry I am that my men—that I— failed you."

Laurel pulled back, her brow furrowed. She glanced at the Campbells; her face morphing into a visage of pure hatred as her gaze fell on Michael. "You are alive and breathe this very moment because my husband has me in his arms, you stinking pile of dung. If my husband doesn't kill you, I will find you while you sleep. I will geld you and send your wee, shriveled bollocks to that MacDougall bitch you've been tupping for years. Then I will have you hanged from the gallows, so all may see how the Shrew of Stirling had you by the cods. Believe you me, my reputation doesn't even touch on how merciless I can be. You've plotted against your laird, my husband. I will see you dead for that. You, I will never forgive."

"What're you talking aboot?" Brodie asked as he looked between Laurel and Michael. He'd been unable to reason why Michael betrayed him. Michael's mutinous demeanor had gone far beyond claiming he'd led Laurel astray for Brodie's or the clan's sake.

"He's in bed with the MacDougalls. Literally. He's been bedding Nelson and Matthew's cousin for years. He has two bastards with the woman. The MacDougalls don't want an alliance between the Campbells and Rosses. With me out of the way, there would be no ties to bind you. How Michael came to be involved with the woman, I don't ken. But he's obviously been disloyal for years. Lord only knows what he's told them during that time."

Brodie signaled to the man riding beside Michael, who'd been tied to his saddle. The man removed Michael's gag, and the traitor spat in Laurel and Brodie's direction. Laurel cocked an eyebrow at him. With Brodie cocooning her, she didn't fear Michael any longer. She wouldn't cower as he returned her loathing. She hadn't exaggerated the malice she felt toward the conniving guard.

"Have you aught to say?" Brodie demanded.

"Ye are a fool, and every mon here kens it. It's nae ma bollocks that'll go missing. Hellfire, she's already taken yers. Ye're weak. Ye're nae fit to lead our clan. I've hated ye since I was auld enough to swing a sword. Smug bastard, just because ye were the laird's son and tánaiste. Ye've always been a fool. Do ye ken how I know? Because ye never once figured out that I was the once who told the MacDougalls the route ye were taking with the MacMillan bitch. They told the Lamonts."

"You caused the most recent raids," Graham accused.

"Ye mean the ones that drew our laird away from his slut. But ye should ken that the most recent ones are happening while the great Laird Brodie Campbell chases after a quim."

Laurel looked at Brodie, and everything fell into place. "While you were gone, Nelson was always watching me. He hoped to get me alone, either to kill me or abduct me. He knew you'd look for me as soon as you knew I was gone. It would have kept you away even longer. When he couldn't do that, he had to get me away from you once we set off. This was all a distraction."

"So were the wagers. I don't doubt he hoped you would humiliate me, and that I would fail to earn your hand. When he realized that he would lose a small fortune, he couldn't let it go."

"He changed the wagers." Laurel looked at Monty, then back to Brodie. "He wagered against how long we would remain married. You found us by accident. He likely intended to kill both of us, hoping it would cause conflict between the Campbells and Rosses. He couldn't stand the idea that our clans would ally.

"He claimed that while the MacDougalls and Campbells might be feuding, he didn't dislike you." Andrew MacFarlane walked out of the trees, leading his horse's bridle. "He claimed you would regret your decision, and that you deserved your freedom."

"You were in on it!" Laurel pointed an accusing finger at Andrew. "You knew he intended to kill me."

Campbells surrounded Andrew, but MacFarlane men and MacBains emerged from the woods. The MacFarlanes and MacBains rivaled the Campbells and Rosses in numbers.

"I bet far too much on your courtship failing and then your marriage being a disaster. I believed we were taking Lady Campbell back to court or Balnagown. It wasn't until after we had her that I realized the MacDougalls wouldn't settle for that. I should have known, and I'm a fool not to. You married, ending your handfast. There could be no repudiation or annulment. The only way to sever the Campbell and Ross alliance was to make Brodie a widower."

"MacFarlane and I led our men from camp last night," Stephen said as he stepped forward.

"Last night?" Laurel said in confusion. "You rode with us this morning. I'm sure of it."

"Laurel, you slept through all of yesterday and half of today," Monty said quietly. She turned a confused mien to Monty and Donnan, then Stephen and Andrew.

"Let me see what you gave me." Laurel held out her hand,

and Donnan maneuvered his horse closer. She opened the pouch and poured the remaining herbs into her hand. She poked it with her finger, spreading the tiny pieces before bringing it to her nose. She pinched a few, rolling them between her finger and thumb before bringing it back to her nose. "Catnip. No wonder I couldn't stop sweating, and I couldn't stay awake."

"Catnip?" Brodie asked in confusion.

"Aye. It's a remedy for the ague. It causes a person to sweat heavily, releasing whatever bad humors cause the illness. It helps the ailing person to sleep and recover. But I wasn't sick, just sedated."

"We didn't know why she wouldn't wake," Monty interjected. "When we found her with them——" he nodded toward Stephen and Andrew "——she looked like she'd been dragged through a hedge backwards. They said she'd been trying to escape you. Nelson claimed the herbs were to rouse her, that they'd gotten them from a healer at a village they passed. I doubted them, but when Laurel wouldn't wake, I grew desperate enough to try it. Little did I ken it only made it worse."

"That bitch Margaret," Laurel muttered then looked up at Brodie when she sensed he stared at her. "To think I ever felt sorry for her because she reminded me of me." Laurel pointed at her chest. "And Sarah Anne reminded me of Myrna. I should have kenned better. She's the one who would have given Nelson the catnip and told him what to do."

"How would she have known?" Donnan asked.

"For the same reason I ken. She and I were both trained to be chatelaines, and catnip isn't an uncommon remedy. A healer would do better, but most ladies raised to run a keep know the basics aboot medicinals. Nelson's supposedly courting her. She would have given it to him if he asked."

"Aye. She has the right of it," Andrew confirmed. "Campbell, MacBain and I kenned there was nay choice but to leave when we overheard the brothers speculating how much longer it would take before their clan and the Lamonts attacked. MacBain and I believed this was aboot a bet and helping you out. That you were too besotted to ken what ye were doing. They always intended it to be a distraction."

"Fuck," Brodie breathed. He needed to get to his land, but he had Laurel to consider, too.

"We ride back to Kilchurn," Laurel whispered. "Whether or not I'm with you, you must get back to our people. You need my brother and his men, and neither of us would be wise to trust MacFarlane or MacBain to take me back to court. There's no other choice. I ride with you, and we ride to Kilchurn."

"I ken. But it doesnae mean I must like it," Brodie said. He was weary from chasing Laurel and the ongoing conflict with his neighbors. Now he had to consider whether to end his alliance with the MacFarlanes. The one thing he wanted most —a happy welcome home with his bride—was the furthest thing from his reach.

"We ken the attacks are coming," Laurel said. "It won't be a surprise. I can hide somewhere before you ride into battle."

Brodie gazed into Laurel's earnest expression. He wished it would be as simple as finding trees for Laurel to hide among, but he knew it wouldn't be. He was certain he knew which villages the Lamonts and MacDougalls would target. Neither clan would come within spitting distance of Kilchurn alone because they'd know they couldn't defeat Brodie's full army of men. They would fan out and raid the outlying settlements. He would send Danny to Kilchurn to summon more men to fight alongside him and demand Monty take Laurel there too. He wouldn't ride into battle with his wife. Not again.

"MacBain, you've done enough." Brodie turned his disdainful glare at Stephen. "Do not presume this is over just because you live. You'd do well to warn your uncle. There will be reprisal. You're just not important enough to deal with now."

Wisely, Stephen MacBain nodded and mounted. He and his men rode out without a word or a second glance. Brodie turned his attention to Andrew. "You have one chance to redeem yourself. I will let you live, so you can ride home and call your clan to arms. I expect you to show yourself, ready to fight on my side, within three days. If you don't appear—with or without men—I will end our alliance and allow the Colquhouns to tear you apart. I will send them coin and weapons to do it. You sentenced yourself to death the day you thought to harm my wife. I will decide whether you have a reprieve. Go."

Laurel listened as Brodie commanded Stephen and Andrew to do his bidding. Both men owed no allegiance to Brodie, and he held no authority over them. But both men knew he'd spared them. The man who sat atop the horse with Laurel was the man who'd earned his reputation on the battlefield, and the man who ensured his clan dominated those who crossed his path. She shivered as she considered the fate that awaited the Lamonts and MacDougalls. She feared it would be years before either clan recovered. While her heart ached for the innocent, just as it did when her family feuded with others, she felt no sympathy for those who cast their lot against the Campbells, against Brodie.

"Laurie, are you cold?"

"Nay, Brodie. I just thought aboot the grievous error the Lamonts and MacDougalls made when they took you on. Naught bodes well for them. That made me shiver."

Brodie kissed her temple before he nodded. He didn't relish his bride seeing this side of him, the ruthless warrior. However, he had no choice. While we would have preferred to be a husband first and a warrior second in front of Laurel, he would always be a laird first.

"Dinna fash. I ken what must be done. I was five-and-ten when I left Balnagown. Auld enough to remember my father and Monty riding out. Auld enough to understand what they did. I arrived at court only a few years after Queen Elizabeth returned and the wars ended. I heard the stories aboot the Bruce. I heard the stories aboot you. I didn't know who you were at the time, but now I recall. You're the 'Black Campbell.'"

"Nay, Laurie. That was my father. But my reputation isn't any different from his. This isn't what I want for you."

"But this is what we have." Laurel gave Brodie a quick, hard kiss before she released him and slid from his lap. She darted to where Teine stood watching her. The horse nodded his giant head and pawed at the ground. When Laurel took his reins and stroked his nose, he released a loud whinny, his rump dancing from side to side. Laurel grinned and looked back at Brodie, giving him a saucy wink. "Nay the only male happy to see me. But alas, the only one I'm riding."

As if Teine agreed, the horse nickered before Laurel kneed him, and the horse surged forward. The band of riders settled into formation with Laurel riding in the middle of the pack, Monty and Donnan on each side. When Brodie looked back at her from the lead, she gave him an encouraging nod. Laird Campbell led the charge to defend his land and his people.

TWENTY-SEVEN

I t was an unrelentingly hard two-day ride to Campbell territory. Rather than continue west when they reached the border, they swung south. They'd seen the charred shells of two villages and stopped to search for survivors. But they found nothing more than remains. The violence with which the attackers killed their victims made Brodie uneasy about separating Laurel from the larger group and sending her to Kilchurn with the Rosses. There were only two score of them, including Monty, Donnan, and the men who'd been at Stirling with Laurel. But neither did he relish bringing her near the inevitable battle.

Ultimately, the choice was taken from him. Before dawn on the third day, Brodie sent Graham and three men to scout from Crianlarich, or Ben More mountain. The path was steep, rising over a thousand feet in less than three miles, so the men went on foot. He was certain they would summit just as the sun rose, and they would have an unobstructed view in all directions. It was the highest point in the southern Highlands. They'd made camp at the base of the mountain, but they'd only kept a fire going long enough to cook what they'd hunted. Brodie didn't want the plume of smoke against the clear autumn sky to signal their location. He'd held Laurel close the entire night, barely sleeping because he was unable to relax. He remained vigilant now that Laurel was back where she belonged—in his arms. Now, she huddled against him as they stood together, his broad back shielding her from the wind whipping down the mountain face.

"I see them." Donnan pointed toward four shadowy figures moving down the path. It was only a few minutes before Graham and the others returned to camp, winded and flushed.

"It's nay good," Graham warned. "There's a camp to the other side of Ben More. It looked like Lamonts, but mayhap a score or two. There's another northwest. Lady Campbell and the Rosses would have to ride through the hills to Ben Lui to avoid them."

Brodie shook his head. The mountain didn't have a clear pass for riders. It had five ridges with four corries, or deep valleys, between them. Even though it was early autumn, it wasn't unheard of for there to be snow already.

"What else?" Laurel asked quietly. She shifted nervously, not yet convinced that any of the men besides Brodie welcomed her voice. But he'd encouraged her to contribute to the conversation the night before, and it had been her idea to send scouts up Ben More.

"We saw smoke toward Inverarnan. That's where they last attacked," one scout added.

"Damn it," Brodie hissed. When Laurel turned questioning eyes to him, he explained. "If we pursue them, we have to contend with the Falls of Falloch." At Laurel's blank gaze, he continued. "They're a few miles from here. The land is hard for men to traverse, but it's not ideal for horses. We face losing at least one mount or leaving them behind and approaching on foot. The latter isn't worth considering now that the sun is rising. Without darkness to hide us, they'll spot us before we can surprise them." Brodie scrubbed his hands over his face. He looked at Monty, who's grim expression matched his own. He shifted his eyes to the top of Ben More, and Monty nodded.

"Donnan, take Laurel up," Monty instructed his partner.

Laurel looked between Brodie and Monty, then Monty and Donnan. Her eyes widened, but she nodded. She stepped forward and embraced Monty. She knew he would lead the Ross warriors while Donnan took her to safety. She didn't relish watching her husband or her brother ride into battle. When Monty released her, she stepped in front of Brodie. His brawny arms lifted her off the ground, bringing them to eye level.

"Be careful," Laurel choked. She still couldn't bring herself to confess her feelings, partly because they were too raw to express. She kissed him, hoping he would understand. When his deep gray eyes looked into hers, he nodded. It was the closest either came to professing their love, but they understood one another.

"I trust Donnan. Stay with him no matter what happens."

"I ken, *mo chridhe*." My heart. Laurel kissed him once more.

"I will return to you," Brodie stated emphatically. He cast a long, wistful look at Laurel's upturned face. He held her chin between his finger and thumb. Brushing his lips against hers in the barest hint of a kiss, he whispered, "*mo chluaran, mo ghaol*." My thistle, my love. Laurel nodded her head as she swallowed. Then he was gone. Laurel watched as his plaid swished against the back of his muscular thighs before he mounted and rode east.

"Laurel, we need to start the hike. It will be harder for you because of your skirts. I want you out of sight and out of reach before the sun casts enough light for anyone to see us." Donnan led the way. Four Ross men surrounded Michael and prodded him up the mountain. Laurel caught herself praying there would be a reason to push him to his death.

Brodie looked back once, but he couldn't spot Laurel or the men tasked with guarding her. He trusted Donnan, and he trusted the Ross men. Michael, he would relish punishing. But he didn't fear Michael harming Laurel as long as he remained bound and gagged. He'd given his men quiet instructions the night before that if the traitor made any move to endanger Laurel, they were to kill him without fear of reprisal.

Facing forwards once more, Brodie led the Campbell and Ross warriors north to the encampment that barred Laurel and the Rosses from continuing to Kilchurn. He'd decided that attempting to make it to Inverarnan wasn't a wise use of their time. There would be little he could do for the village, and the risk to the horses wasn't worth traversing the Falls of Falloch. Whoever led the raid there would have moved on by then. So they rode toward the first impediment to getting Laurel to safety. If she remained at Ben More's summit, he didn't fear the Lamonts finding her.

It was an hour's hard ride before they saw signs of the camp. Graham once more scouted, creeping through the conifers as he counted the MacDougalls who were breaking camp. He returned to Brodie, grateful that he could inform his laird that their party outnumbered the MacDougalls. With their war cry, "*Cruachan!*" bursting forth, the Campbells charged into the camp, catching the MacDougalls off guard. The Rosses had circled around the camp, and with their clan motto "*spem successus alit*"—success nourishes hope—on the breeze, they roared into their attack. Outnumbered and unprepared, the MacDougalls fell in quick succession. Brodie recognized Devlin MacDougall, the laird's youngest brother, among the men. With a bird call, the men closest to him surrounded Devlin. By the time he was subdued, the battle was over.

"Fancy meeting you here," Brodie said as he stalked toward Devlin. He suspected it was Devlin's daughter with whom Michael was having an affair.

"Go to hell," Devlin barked.

"Undoubtedly. Just not today." Brodie walked around Devlin, as if he were considering the man from every angle. "I hear your grandbairns are half Campbell." Brodie hit the mark when Devlin sneered but said nothing. "How fitting that you named your daughter Eve. You must have known she'd be a whore."

"Bastard."

"I'm not, but those grandbairns of yours are. Bastards in the laird's own family. Tsk, tsk. And not only were they born on the wrong side of the blanket, their father is a traitor and a Campbell. Och, they shall have a fine life among your people." Brodie antagonized the man, watching each reaction. "But then again, is Michael really a traitor? You were lured onto my land, and I've found you. How could that be?"

Brodie watched the doubt flash across Devlin's face before his bravado returned. He raised his chin and glowered at Brodie. "If he were loyal to you, then why would he have told us where you rode with the first Lady Campbell? Why would he tell Nelson the route you would ride home from Stirling?"

"You're here, aren't you?"

"I do not believe for a moment that you sacrificed Eliza MacMillan to trick us. And from what I hear aboot you and your newest Lady Campbell, you wouldn't risk her life for aught. Unfortunate that she's dead."

Brodie laughed, and his men followed. "My wife is alive and well. She was spewing curses at Michael just this morn. She has a way with words."

"Aye, a right skilled mouth from what I hear," Devlin taunted.

Brodie shook his head. "You really must not care for your wife and daughter. Insulting my wife, endangering her—not a wise choice. You have harmed two women in my life. Now I shall do the same to you." Brodie watched as fear entered Devlin's eyes. Brodie had guessed that the man would care about his womenfolk, but he hadn't known for sure. He'd taken a chance and come out the better. "I think I shall give your wife to one of my men. Your daughter—ha-ha—there's a busy tavern in Kilchurn. I'm certain she can find work there."

"You would make my wife and daughter whores," Devlin accused.

"I'm not making them aught. They did that themselves." Brodie squinted at Devlin, then put his hands on his hips and leaned back. He laughed again, but there was still no mirth. "You don't ken, do you? Arnold's been tossing your wife's skirts for years." Brodie named Nelson and Matthew's father, Laird MacDougall, as Devlin's wife's lover. Brodie caught wind of the rumor years earlier, but the rage that washed over Devlin confirmed it.

"You did know! You're naught but a cuckold. Should we check to see if you still have any bollocks, or did your wife give them to your brother?"

"Bugger off, Campbell."

"Where to? I'm on my land." Brodie raised his hands in question. "Speaking of land. You're on mine too. Do you think anyone will come looking for you and your men?"

"You know they will," Devlin seethed. "And they will burn every village in their wake."

"Haven't you done that already? What's left?" Brodie hissed, pretending to lose his temper.

"We haven't razed your lands west of Kilchurn. That's next," Devlin smirked until he realized what he'd done.

"Kill him." Brodie turned back to his horse.

"Wait!"

Brodie prolonged the man's agony by taking his time to turn around. He looked over his shoulder before twisting his body, then finally turning to face Devlin. He raised an eyebrow and crossed his arms, boredom clear on his face.

"I ken you're going to kill me. But I will tell you what you need to know if you spare my wife and daughter."

"Mayhap. Depends on what you tell me." Brodie had no intention of going after either woman. He didn't fight his battles by harming those who couldn't fight him fairly. But he would use them as bait.

"Arnold wants to marry the Lamont's daughter. He wants to bind our clans by blood, but the Lamont won't consent. Lamont insists we need to prove we're worth the alliance. Arnold already has sons, so he doesn't need a wife. But he caught sight of the chit and decided he fancied her. He wants her in his bed, and he wants the Lamonts as his bedfellows. He thinks our two clans can weaken yours. His plan is to marry Matthew to Brenna MacArthur."

Brodie's lips thinned as he considered what Devlin told him. The Campbells and MacArthurs descended from the same lineage, and they'd been rivals since before the days of King Alexander. They'd once been the dominant clan, especially with their ties to the Lord of the Isles, John of Islay. They were the famed pipers of Islay's clan, the MacDonalds of Sleat. But the Campbells loyalty to Robert the Bruce increased their power throughout Argyll and Lorne. The increase in wealth and status had rubbed the MacArthurs the wrong way. Brodie could guess what he would hear next.

"And I suppose the MacArthurs are all too happy to court the MacGregors to their side, riding campaigns against us. You think to surround us and squeeze."

"Aye. That's just what Arnold plans." Devlin nodded his head. "Will you spare my wife and daughter?"

"One or the other. Choose."

"My daughter." Devlin didn't think twice.

"Choose between your daughter and your grandbairns."

"I—I can't," Devlin stammered. Brodie enjoyed the stricken look on Devlin's face. It was what he hoped for.

"Then tell me where the Lamonts attack next and where your brothers have their men." There were three MacDougall brothers. Arnold was the eldest and laird. Devlin was the youngest. Martin was in the middle. Arnold was too ambitious for his own good, and Devlin was a milksop. But Martin was the one who gave Brodie the most concern. He had no conscience and reveled in causing others pain. Brodie had been certain Martin led the raids on the villages they'd passed through. He was the only one perverse enough for the level of carnage they encountered. He'd tried to spare Laurel, but she'd caught sight of too much before Brodie could shield her.

"The Lamonts are south of Ben More. Arnold led the attack on Invararnan, while Martin brings his men west from your border. We're to meet at Inverchorachan tonight and ride for Kilchurn tomorrow. The MacArthurs and MacGregors camp near Edenonich. They will attack from the north and the east while we come from the south."

Brodie nodded and turned away again. "Kill him." When he heard Devlin thrash and try to break free, he knew two men restrained him and a third approached. He tossed over his shoulder just before the Campbell warrior's sword speared him, "By the by. I never intended to touch your family. I'm not you. I don't target the innocent."

Brodie heard the strangled gasp as Devlin MacDougall breathed his last. The Campbells and Rosses retreated from the camp, leaving the MacDougalls' bodies in their wake. Away from the clearing, Brodie and Monty stood together.

"The route is clear for Laurel to go to Kilchurn. You and your men take her there, while my men and I ride for Dallmally. Neither the MacArthurs nor the MacGregors can reach Kilchurn from Edenonich without crossing the River Orchy. There's only one place for them to cross, and it's downstream from a dam. I have patrols that ride that area to protect it. If we time it right and release the dam, the flood will wash away the MacArthurs and MacGregors. Any who survive will wind up in the estuary to Loch Awe—just in front of Kilchurn village."

"Do you think the MacFarlanes will rally?" Monty asked doubtfully.

"Mayhap. If they do, it will be the Lamonts and MacDougalls sandwiched between us and the MacFarlanes. If Laurel is behind the walls, then I don't care whether the

MacFarlanes show their faces. I have enough men to obliterate both the Lamonts and MacDougalls. My guess is they think Michael will be there to let them in. Or mayhap they even have someone else within my clan. At this point, naught would surprise me. The MacFarlanes would do well to lend their arm, but I don't need them."

Monty nodded as he looked in the direction from which they rode. The peak of Ben More was visible as a hazy outline. Both men mounted and led their men back toward Laurel and Donnan.

"I can summon men from Innes Chonnel, Inishail, and Fraoch Eilean, Monty. She will be safe once she's home." Brodie prayed he could get Laurel to Kilchurn before anything more happened. He regretted that his clan's new lady would arrive without him and that her introduction to her clan and castle would be hide within the keep. But there were few choices left for him. If all went to plan, there would be little more than a skirmish with the Lamonts and MacDougalls. If it didn't, his clan faced a mighty battle against four enemies. All of whom wanted nothing more than to see the Campbells' demise. He'd fought too many battles alongside his father to see his people lose even an acre of land. He would fight to the end to defend Laurel, his people, and his home. God help anyone who thought he wouldn't.

TWENTY-EIGHT

L aurel watched in horror as the Lamonts seemed to
multiply before her eyes. She crouched beside Donnan
as men arrived from the south and joined those camped at the
southern base of the mountain. They fanned out like ants as
they moved to encircle the mountain.

"They've seen us," Donnan whispered.

"Likely seen my bluidy hair," Laurel muttered. She'd
grown warm and allowed her arisaid to slip off her head until
Donnan pointed out that her hair would be noticeable to
those at the foot of the southern trail. She'd hurried to cover
herself, but she feared it was too late.

"We need to get back to the horses and ride before they
converge on us," Donnan explained as he motioned to the
four Ross men. Laurel looked at Michael and stopped short,
Donnan bumping into her.

"He signaled them." Laurel pointed to a coin in Michael's
hand that glimmered in the sunlight. "He drew their
attention."

Donnan lunged at Michael, jabbing his fist into the man's
face. When Michael stumbled backwards, his ankles now
bound along with his hands, he had no way to keep his
balance. He pitched toward the edge of the path. Donnan

shoved his chest, pushing him over the ledge where they rested. Laurel watched as Michael appeared to soar through the air before his body crashed into the rock face. He rolled and bumped from one crag to another. There was no chance that he survived by the time he reached the ground. The Rosses didn't wait to see. Laurel had already lifted her skirts and was flying down the path between Donnan and one of the guards, the other two at her back. She skidded along the shale and pebbles, reaching out to Donnan's shoulder more than once.

When they reached the base near where they'd camped, Donnan whistled. A Ross appeared with their mounts. Laurel didn't stop to think when Donnan tossed her into the saddle. She slipped her feet into the stirrups and gathered the reins.

"We need to get closer to Kilchurn," Donnan called as they charged away from Ben More. "There's no avoiding them. We have to outrun them."

Laurel knew he spoke the truth. She had a greater chance of surviving if they could reach Brodie and Monty and if they could gain ground toward the keep. She didn't doubt that Nelson, Matthew, and Edgar led their men toward them. Between following their trail and knowing of the MacDougalls' plans, they would ride in this direction. They couldn't go back the way they came without facing her captors.

The seven riders laid low over their horses' withers, making it easier to gallop and to make them less of a target for the arrows that flew toward them. Laurel watched as Lamonts rode toward them, swarming like an angry hive of hornets. Seeing their direction, men rode to intercept them while others came from their left and behind. Laurel squeezed Teine's flanks, encouraging him to continue galloping. She gave him his head while grasping hanks of his mane along with the reins. She'd only encouraged him to run like this a handful of times when he was a colt, and she was still a young girl at Balnagown. She'd grown fearful that she would harm him if she was so reckless. But now, she let him run. He sensed the danger and the race. It was as though her gelding knew he raced against stallions and sought to prove himself. She knew he could outrun most horses, even when she restrained him. She prayed now that he had the stamina of the warhorses and more speed.

The Lamonts arrows were within striking distance as the Rosses barreled across the open grassland. The arrows imbedded in the ground around the horses' hooves as they churned up the soil beneath them. A battle cry made her look toward her attackers. A man on an enormous pure white stallion charged toward her, his sword pointing at her. She recognized David Lamont in an instant. She also recognized that she was his sole target. She had no weapons, and even if she had, she still would have been no match for David. Donnan and the Ross guards noticed him at the same time, shifting their formation to shield Laurel. Rather than surrounding her, they rode two-wide on her left.

Laurel turned her attention back to where they headed. Her eyes swept the landscape, scanning for anywhere that offered them protection. But there was nothing. Her head whipped around when a pained whinny came from beside her. The horse had an arrow protruding from its neck, and a matching one stuck out from its rider's neck. The horse and man fell away, but she and the other Rosses continued their mad dash as they tried to put distance between them and their pursuers. It felt like only a heartbeat later that another Ross fell. Laurel looked at Donnan, noticing for the first time that a splintered arrow stuck out from his bicep. She hadn't seen it strike him, nor seen him snap it off.

"Donnan!" Laurel cried over the sound of the horses' pounding hooves.

"Ride!" Donnan didn't look at her, his attention focused on the men drawing closer. Laurel looked ahead once more and witnessed a band of riders approaching.

"Donnan! Ahead of us!" Laurel couldn't tell who the men

were, but they were riding as swiftly toward them as the Lamonts were.

"Monty," Donnan barked. Laurel strained to see, unsure how Donnan had already noticed her brother's hair. But as their horses ate up the distance that separated them, Laurel knew Donnan was right. Beside Monty rode her husband. She kept her eyes on Brodie, praying over and over that she could just reach him. Her attention was so singular that she didn't see David Lamont until his sword flashed in her peripheral vision. She looked at him, shocked to find him so close. David felled the third Ross when he impaled him. He withdrew his sword, locked eyes with Laurel, and grinned.

Laurel knew how Eliza died. Brodie had finally admitted it, and she saw her life pass before her eyes. But instead of seeing her own face, she saw a faceless dark-haired girl. Laurel was certain David intended for her to have the same fate as Eliza. Laurel refused to consider it. The only fate she accepted was growing old with Brodie. Lamont men drew alongside David, their attention on Donnan and her last guard. The Lamonts engaged Donnan and the other Ross, forcing them away from Laurel.

"Come on, Teine. Just like it used to be," Laurel said to her horse. The gelding's ear twitched as though he understood her. She'd spent hours riding her horse once Teine was old enough to take a rider. They'd raced across Ross land, her guards charging along with her. But her best rides were with Monty and Donnan. They encouraged her daredevil nature, but they drew the line at some of her more reckless stunts. But it hadn't stopped Laurel from trying them. She'd fallen from Teine more than once, but she blamed only herself. She kicked her left foot free of the stirrup as David came closer. When he swung in a wide arch, she leaned away, bringing her left leg onto the seat of her saddle while holding tight to the reins. Her body pressed along her horse's flank. Teine whinnied when the tip of David's sword slashed his ear. But Laurel trusted her mount. Teine didn't slow. Laurel was certain he moved faster. Glancing over the top of Teine's neck, she saw David watch her in shock. Pushing with all the strength she could muster in her right leg, she righted herself.

Laurel saw Brodie and Monty drawing closer, but they still weren't near enough to protect her. Donnan was free of his attacker and racing after David and her. Teine wasn't a trained warhorse, but he had a foul temper to match Laurel's when he felt others encroached. Laurel whipped her steed around, and Teine barred his teeth at David's horse. Despite clearly being an experienced warhorse, the Lamont's horse was unprepared to come face-to-face with Teine. Laurel loosened the reins, pulling back as she leaned back. Teine followed the command. He reared, his front hooves striking out at David's horse. She'd practiced the move with Teine countless times, but he'd always pawed the air, making him look like he danced on his hind legs. Now he fought with the valiance of a trained destrier.

Teine's right hoof struck David's horse in the face. The Lamont struggled to maintain control, unprepared for the attack. It was obvious to Laurel that David and his mount were used to David controlling the beast with only one hand, but she'd caught them both unaware. She slackened the reins, and Teine chomped toward David's horse. His teeth clamped the end of the other animal's nose. Laurel saw the blood before Teine pulled away. She steered him right as David swung his sword again. Laurel pushed herself forward, out of the saddle and over Teine's neck. David's sword struck her saddle where she'd sat a moment ago. She slid back into her seat as Teine kicked out his back legs. They struck David's mount in the face. Still angry, Teine bucked again, striking the other horse in the neck and pushing it sideways. Laurel swung Teine around once more, intending to ride past David and out of his reach, but Teine disagreed. The Lamont's horse had nipped his arse. Laurel squeezed her legs and clung to the reins, unprepared for Teine to rear again. But she swore she would give her steed every carrot and apple she could find, and all the hay the horse could manage when he unseated David. Teine barreled forward, and to avoid another ferocious attack, the other horse sidestepped. He knocked David to the ground and shied away.

"*Clì.*" Laurel commanded Teine to the left then to go. "*Ir.*" Teine lurched forward until he stood over David. She commanded him to step. "*Ceum.*"

Teine stomped down each time Laurel gave the command. By the fifth time, David's face was mangled, and Laurel was certain he was dead. She reined Teine in, waiting to see if David moved or made a sound. She noticed Donnan fought another man, and she couldn't see the last Ross guard. Sound coming from her right made her look up. Brodie's hair flew behind him, his sword in one hand, the reins in the other. He looked like an avenging angel. He also looked enraged. She wondered if her husband would send her to heaven or hell.

Brodie entered the meadow to the horror of the Lamonts' attack on Laurel and her guards. He watched as his wife charged toward him as she sought to flee her pursuers. His mind absorbed the scene, taking in the sounds of the Lamonts' battle cry, the swish of arrows flying toward him, and the clatter of horses' hooves as he and his men, along with the Rosses, charged toward Laurel. He scanned the battlefield, noticing the Lamonts were far greater in number than Graham saw from Ben More. He watched in horror as they drew closer to Laurel from three sides.

Fear had never driven him in battle before that day. He'd always had a healthy respect for the fragility of life. Trepidation came to every warrior, and it kept them vigilant. Duty spurred Brodie to act when the Lamonts attacked the last time and took his first wife's life. As he watched David Lamont draw closer to Laurel, terror unlike he'd ever imagined possessed him. He would later understand it came from love, but as he fought to make his way to Laurel, it was heart-pounding, lung-crushing fear. He swung his sword indiscriminately at any man or beast who thought to keep him from his wife.

As he charged forward, the scene before his eyes flashed to the one where David Lamont rode for Eliza, and he watched his first bride cut down. He was certain he was about to witness the same scene played out but with Laurel this time. His chest would surely explode as he witnessed Laurel pitch sideways from her saddle. Brodie called her name, convinced her horse's hooves would pummel and kill her.

"She did it!" Monty cried. Brodie spared Monty a glance and saw the determination that formed when they entered the glen be replaced by beaming pride. He couldn't process what he saw, so he turned back to Laurel. He watched in horror as her steed reared, convinced the gelding would throw her. Fear took a moment's reprieve as astonishment took hold. He'd never imagined Teine would be so ferocious as he witnessed the animal attack David Lamont's mount. Teine's stamina and speed had impressed him, but he hadn't foreseen the animal's strength and tenacity. It matched his owner. Brodie swore he would give Teine the best stall in his stables and the choicest treats.

Laurel's name died on his lips as he watched David fall from his horse. He heard Laurel's commands as he drew nearer. She ordered the horse to step over and over as her billowing copper mane gave her the appearance of a warrior goddess. No other moment in their courtship had ever given him the surety that he'd chosen the right woman to lead his clan alongside him. He would forsake his lairdship, his clan, and his life if there was a better way to protect Laurel as he battled to reach her. But rather than panic and attempt to flee, she defended herself without a weapon. He chided himself. Teine was the most powerful weapon she could wield. As he called out Laurel's name, he had a moment of clarity. Deeming her the warrior goddess he saw wasn't a mere similarity. It was in truth. His hellion had been born of the Highlands and drew her strength from the earth that surrounded her, just like the thistle. This was where she was meant to be. This was her home. Not the rigidity and insincerity of court. It was the wildness that set her free.

"Laurel!" Brodie bellowed again as her head whipped toward him. She turned Teine toward her husband and brother, spurring the horse again. His men and the Rosses had remained together despite how the Lamonts fought to break through their ranks. He looked at Monty. "Lead."

Laurel fell into place at Brodie's right, away from the oncoming Lamonts. The Ross and Campbell warriors surrounded Brodie and her. She kept low over Teine's withers as arrows continued to fly toward them. She heard more men cry out, but she didn't dare shift her attention as she rode in the pack. She'd breathed a moment's ease when she watched Donnan fall into the lead alongside Monty. Blood soaked his sleeve, but he appeared to maintain his strength as that arm controlled his horse while the other was ready to slash and stab with his sword.

"We lose them at Ben Lui!" Monty called back. Brodie shared the same thought, even though hours earlier they'd decided to avoid the mountain. But it would offer them safety that the flat land would not. It would be dangerous traveling along the ridges and over the peaks, but he and the others would fan out and evade the Lamonts. His men knew the mountain, climbing it in spring and summer for training and hunting. Brodie prayed there was no early autumn snow and that none would come. He would order no one into the hills during winter because of the precariousness.

Laurel watched her brother and friend as they guided them toward the mountain. She'd never had reason to witness them lead as they did now. She'd never seen them fight outside the lists. She'd never caught sight of the resolve that turned their features brutal. They'd entered a fight that wasn't their own because of her. They'd drawn her clansmen along with them. But as the men surrounded her and positioned themselves to be the targets rather than her, she realized she would never not be a Ross. She'd just become a Campbell, too. She owed her life to these men who defended her. But more than that, she owed them her respect and loyalty. There might never be an amicable relationship between her parents and her, but she wouldn't forsake the Rosses because they hadn't forsaken her.

TWENTY-NINE

The climb up Ben Lui forced Laurel's heart into her throat, and there it remained. Brodie barked orders that the Campbells would partner with Rosses and lead them toward different peaks, taking shelter where they could. Just before they'd reached the gritty path that began the ascent, Brodie shifted position to lead while Donnan and Monty bracketed her. She didn't dare look back to see how their persecutors fared. She watched as the men broke off and nudged their horses off the trail and over the loose rocks and shale. It wasn't long before Brodie signaled with his hand that they would veer left. Laurel set her heels back in her stirrups, gathered handfuls of Teine's mane along with the reins, and kept her body parallel to her horse's.

It was here that the difference in training for her gelding and the warhorses showed. He shook his head and neighed, but Laurel cooed and encouraged him. She even pointed to how the other horses progressed without complaint, playing to her horse's masculine ego. It shocked her when it worked. She knew it was a coincidence, but a grin tugged at her mouth before she reminded herself of the gravity of their predicament. Their sudden shift in direction and the added height gave her a moment to spy the Lamonts. They were far closer than she realized, and panic finally threatened to get the better of her.

"Don't look, Laurel," Monty said. "They are where they are, and it can't be helped. Focus on your own progress."

"Watch Brodie's elbows. Know how he steers his mount, so you can do the same as you cross over the same spot. Watch how he shifts his weight, so you can follow," Donnan pointed out. Laurel never would have thought of such.

"Thank you," she stated as she studied her husband's movements, adopting them as her own, and finding it easier to handle Teine. She sensed her mount calm, and it added to her reassurance that they would weather this passage. As they rounded a hairpin, Laurel's stomach lurched at the steep drop off into a corrie. There was no easy descent into the valley, only plummeting to one's death. She looked back at Brodie and noticed the remaining men were disappearing into the surrounding crags. That left her with Brodie, Monty, and Donnan. She couldn't think of any men she trusted more than the ones with her.

Brodie's eyes swept the mountainside as he led Laurel and the two men over ground he'd explored as a child. He'd spent over three decades traversing these peaks and valleys. He and his men climbed the trails as conditioning. Shepherds came into the hills to gather their flocks twice a year for their shearing. Brodie and Dominic had hunted among the peaks since they were old enough to carrying their own bow and supplies. He'd slept beneath the stars and daydreamed under the sun as a young man. He hoped one day he could bring Laurel back under better circumstances, so she could enjoy the breathtaking vistas.

But his greatest concern that day was leading Laurel to a cave he was certain the Lamonts wouldn't detect. He needed to put a greater distance between his party and those following them. He no longer dared speak, knowing his voice would echo and carry his instructions to their enemy. He'd heard Donnan's advice to Laurel, and it eased some of his apprehension. He suspected the three riders following him wondered why he'd doubled back and descended several yards before climbing once more. His father had trained him and Dominic to use such tactics to lose anyone who tracked them into the hills. He watched the shadows the Lamonts cast over the lower ridges, knowing the sun worked in his favor.

The four riders summited the first peak after nearly two hours of riding. Brodie knew they all needed to rest, but he feared most for Laurel. Donnan and Monty would endure longer than Laurel, and he couldn't risk having to take her onto Lann's back or leaving Teine behind. He wouldn't allow himself to consider anything worse. As they came over the crest, he turned them back in the direction they'd come on the other side. He found the sheep trail he wanted and reined Lann in. In silence, the four riders dismounted and led their horses along the path. Brodie feared Laurel wouldn't manage with her horse and long skirts. He looked back and found Laurel had Teine's reins in her mouth as she tucked her skirts into her belt making culottes. He couldn't resist the grin that spread across his face. He should have known his wife would have a solution.

It was another half an hour of silently leading their horses before they entered one of the valleys among the mountains. It was narrow, but grass grew tall, and Laurel spotted ewes with their summer lambs. She startled when Brodie pushed aside a bush, stepping over it and disappearing. Lann followed his master, so Laurel followed too. She discovered she was in a cave that she never would have spotted. It was large enough for at least ten men and their mounts. There was plenty of space for the four of them and their horses. Brodie led them to the back of the cave. Laurel suddenly found herself engulfed in a plaid she hadn't seen Brodie retrieve. She looked around and the few stray sunbeams that breached the bush illuminated the cave to show Laurel the stack of supplies against the wall.

Brodie could wait no longer. He needed to feel Laurel in his arms. He needed the touch to believe she was unharmed. He'd worried the damp cavernous air would chill her, so he'd made it a priority to add another layer over her arisaid. He pulled her as much as she leaned into his embrace. They held each other, too relieved to do more. Laurel closed her eyes as she inhaled Brodie's woodsy and musky scent. It was familiarity and security, reassuring and soothing.

"Laurie," Brodie breathed against her hair. He knew Monty saw to Donnan's wound, but he had no interest in anyone but the woman he clung to, whose arms squeezed around his waist. His need to taste superseded his need for touch. As Laurel's head tilted back, Brodie knew their needs coincided. Their mouths fused together as they drank in the restorative powers of coming together. Brodie angled Laurel to press her backwards into the darkest corner of the cave, but he paused to look at Monty and Donnan. He knew Laurel did too. The men stared at one another, Donnan's arm bandaged.

"I don't care," Brodie called out with a nod.

"You know?" Laurel gasped.

"I wasn't certain until now." Brodie looked back at the two men. "If you feel as I do aboot my wife, then do as you please. I'm more interested in her than either of you." Monty and Donnan stared at Brodie as he and Laurel disappeared into the shadows. They found their own dark recess to share their reunion.

"Brodie, I don't understand," Laurel said, her voice tinged with fear.

"I noticed little things aboot them, and it struck me more like an auld married couple than friends or brothers. I thought it would bother me. I suppose it should. But I decided before we even left Stirling that if they protected you before they did themselves, I couldn't care less what they do in private. You will always be more important. Let God and St. Peter decide their fate. That isn't time I want wasted when it can be spent on you."

Laurel swallowed as she nodded. "You're very sage. It must be your auld age."

"I shall show you just what an auld mon can do with a lively young lass." Brodie swept in for another kiss, but this one was passionate and lusty rather than passionate and tender. Laurel moaned softly against his mouth as her hands roamed over his back and down to his buttocks. She pressed his hips to hers, glad he'd pushed his sporran out of the way. She felt her skirts fall loose from her belt, and a breeze soon brushed the back of her legs.

"I ken it's only been a few days, bear. But it's felt like a lifetime."

"I ken, thistle. I would sink into you and remain there. It is the closest to heaven on Earth that I shall find."

"Do we dare?"

"The Lamonts will not find us here. I noticed Monty and Donnan already found the healing supplies and the barrel of oats for the horses. If the horses remain quiet, and none of us are too loud, we remain safe. Can you keep from screaming my name this time?"

Laurel gasped and playfully slapped Brodie's chest. "You shall have to test me to see." She squeaked when Brodie's hands slid along her bare legs before he lifted her off her feet. She snatched the front of his plaid and drew it up before wrapping her legs around Brodie's waist.

"I ken there will be nay finesse."

"I don't need it. Just you. Now." Laurel's forehead fell against Brodie's shoulder as he thrust into her. His cheek rested against her shoulder, and neither moved as the sensation of joining was their first wave of bliss. Soon desire took control as they moved together. Laurel pressed Brodie's mouth to hers as she tipped over the precipice. He swallowed her silent scream before kissing along her jaw and throat, while his fingers bit into her backside. He wouldn't have lasted any longer, even if they'd had true privacy and no unrelenting threat. His release crashed over him as he grunted with two more thrusts. He felt depleted as the euphoria waned, but despite the wave of fatigue, he wasn't ready to release Laurel. He turned them so his back was to the wall and eased them to the ground. Laurel sat straddling his hips. She rested her head against the hard planes of his chest as his cheek rested on her crown.

"I could fall asleep as we are," Brodie whispered.

"So could I," Laurel admitted. Her eyes drooped closed, but a male throat clearing made her groan. "I don't want to get up."

"I know, *mo ghràidh*." My dear. "Neither do I. But it would be better if we waited together."

Laurel knew Brodie was right. If the enemy found their hiding place, which she supposed they could, the men needed to be prepared and alert. Clasping her hand, they stepped out of the shadows in time to see Monty and Donnan release theirs. Neither man looked in their direction, looking decidedly uneasy and regretful. Laurel lifted her skirts above her ankles and dashed to Monty. She threw herself into her brother's outstretched arms, while she waved in Donnan's direction. The men embraced her, and Brodie noticed how tiny she looked between the two towering Highlanders. She may have been tall, but she looked delicate in contrast. He noticed the care the men took as they returned her embrace, careful not to crush her. He witnessed the familial bond he shared with Dominic, and it gladdened him to see it between Laurel and Monty at last. They'd been at odds too many times over the past month.

"Thank you," Laurel whispered. "You led your men into battle, and it wasn't your fight."

"You will always be my wee sister. Any danger you face is my fight," Monty rasped. "Laurel, I haven't been the brother you deserved for years. I've taken the easy way-out time after time, but I will always protect you. Always. And not just because you're my sister. Because I care deeply for you."

"I love you, too," Laurel said, putting into words what her brother was too embarrassed to say in front of the other two men. "I've been a harridan for years, unidentifiable as the sister you once knew. I couldn't unleash my anger at Father to him, so you became the scapegoat. You look so much like him; at times, it was almost possible to forget you are not him. We've made many mistakes over the years, and we've both been cruel. I'm sorry for what I've done."

"I'm sorry too, Laurel. I don't want you to think you're no longer a Ross. I want you to know that maybe not today, but one day, you will receive the warmest of welcomes at Balnagown. Our story shall change as of today."

Laurel nodded and looked at Donnan. "Thank you for protecting me. I can't imagine the grief I would feel if I lost Brodie, and we have only been together a short time. I don't know that my brother would survive losing you. You have been a friend for as long as I can remember. There were times at court when I was certain you were my only friend. Thank you for loving me and my brother."

"Laurel," Donnan smiled. "You are as much my sister as you are Monty's. I've known you your entire life. You've kept our secret and protected us. It's my honor to return the loyalty. You're stronger and more loveable than you realize. And I think you've found someone who can finally show you that in a way I never could as your friend."

"I love you, too." Laurel embraced them both once more before she turned back to Brodie. She didn't know what to make of his contemplative expression. She realized that she'd spoken of love with ease to her brother and her friend. But, while the sentiment was even more powerful toward Brodie, the words didn't come as easily. Brodie stepped forward and caught her hands in his. They gazed at one another, understanding passing between them. They both knew it wasn't enough. "I'm too scared to say it," Laurel confessed.

"But I crave naught more than to hear it," Brodie responded. "I never want you to fear telling me aught. If I am to have your trust, I know I must show I am worthy of it. Laurie, I love you."

"Brodie," Laurel sobbed as tears streamed down her cheeks. "I love you. I didn't know I could. I never thought I would find a mon to love or who could bear to love me. But I have, and I do. I love you."

"Wheest, thistle." Brodie lifted her off the ground, cradling her in his arms. He glanced at Monty and Donnan, offering them a fraternal smile. He supposed he'd gained two brothers rather than just comrades in arms. He settled on the floor once more, and Laurel leaned against him. She dried her tears and relaxed. "Sleep, *mo ghoal*." My love.

"I ken I'm safe with you, *mo ghoal*." Laurel was soon asleep, her rhythmic breathing comforting to Brodie as he held her.

Brodie nodded at the two men. "We need to talk."

THIRTY

"We can wait out the night here," Brodie explained as he nodded to the stacked supplies. "There're oats for the horses and dried beef for us along with dried fruit. Once it's dark, I'll slip out to a stream near here to fill our waterskins and buckets for the horses. The Lamonts are likely still moving through the mountains searching for us. My men know caves and overhangs throughout the peaks and valleys where they will hide with your men. Just like I will at dawn, they'll send out scouts to see where the Lamonts are. They're too far up now, and likely too lost, to find their way down before night-fall. We'll need to remain until at least late tomorrow after-noon, if not the next morning."

"Do you think the Lamonts will push forward and go down the other side or turn back?" Monty asked.

"If they were smart, they would go back. As rough as today's going was, the descent is far worse. I worry more aboot that for Laurel than aught else. The slopes are nearly vertical in some parts. With her skirts, leading Teine, and not being used to hiking so long, I'm scared for her." Brodie felt no shame in admitting his fear. If anything, he felt better for it. He didn't worry that the two men sitting across from him would think him weak. He didn't worry that it made him weak.

"Laurel was surely part goat when she was a wean. She'd climb the crags along the Cromarty Firth and explore the caves. She would give our mother fits," Monty explained, laughing at the end. "Granted, she would do it in her chemise or steal a pair of my breeks. They'll be too long and too loose, but I'll give her a pair of mine in the morn. I brought them for court but blessedly never wore the damn things. She can belt them under her arisaid."

"I'd feel better with her in them. I have a spare leine for her. It may as well be a gown, but I ken she'll make do," Brodie nodded. "With the descent as it is, if we encounter Lamonts, there won't be any way to evade them. And we can't fight lest we die instead of them. There's also nowhere for Laurel to hide. We must be on the lookout for them. The best I can do is put distance between us and them. But I would prefer to avoid them altogether. They won't have planned for this detour, so the MacFarlanes may be at Kilchurn before we arrive. The MacDougalls won't know what to think when the Lamonts don't show at their meeting place tonight. The MacGregors and MacArthurs won't make a move without being sure they aren't facing my forces without the others."

"What aboot the dam?" Donnan asked.

"I'll send three of my men to relay the message. I need to see Laurel safely at Kilchurn, and I need to be there to coordinate the other branches I summon to the battle. The Lamonts and MacDougalls have declared war. I am not interested in a feud, where we raid one another and bicker. The moment they set their sights on Eliza, they set us on this path. Now that they've made Laurel their target, I won't settle until I grind them under my boot heel."

"You ken I sent a mon to Balnagown," Monty mentioned.

"Aye. Will your father come?"

"I didn't ask him to, and I don't think you need him or the Rosses. But will you accept his help if he does?"

"I'd be a fool not to. More sword arms on my side is for the better. And I don't wish to slight your family or your clan. I heard what you said earlier. I hope one day Laurel wants to visit Balnagown. I don't need the alliance any more than your clan does. But I want it for Laurel's sake. I want her to be at peace with your family."

"We want that too." Monty glanced at Donnan, who nodded. "Father and Laurel may not like one another, but neither does he wish her harm. He's been a fool to turn his back on her, to refuse to acknowledge what life at court is like. He'd rather assume she lives a life of luxury, swanning around the royal castle than accept that he erred in sending her there. His pride has been his downfall with my sister. But she's still his daughter."

"And she's still the Earl of Sutherland's niece," Donnan pointed out. "Laird Ross and Lady Sutherland aren't close, and neither are Laird Sutherland and Laird Ross. The cousins aren't friends like the Sutherlands are with their Sinclair relatives. But Laird Sutherland will raise all his forces in defense of his family, close or extended."

"In all likelihood, all will be said and done before my mon reaches home. We'll probably be back at Balnagown before Father can reach Kilchurn. But the MacGregors, MacArthurs, MacDougalls, and Lamonts have made powerful enemies by making this personal with Laurel. Every major clan in the northern Highlands is connected to the Sutherlands or Sinclairs."

Brodie considered what Monty said. He didn't exaggerate. The Sutherlands and Sinclairs, were bound, via marriage, to the Rosses, the Mackays, the MacLeods of Lewis, the Camerons, the Mackenzies, and the Frasers of Lovat. Now they were indirectly tied to the Campbells. Brodie chuckled but shook his head when Monty and Donnan stared at him.

"I was just thinking that it took the Bruce years to rally such a force, to convince the clans to stop the in-fighting and to band together against a common enemy. It's taken a few wee women with spirits fiercer than any mon, and they've accomplished more than the Bruce. He'd do well to remember who the real peacemakers in the Highlands have been, and who he owes a debt of thanks to."

"I hadn't thought of that, but you're right." Monty nodded at his sleeping sister. "I can think of several husbands and brothers who would disagree, but I say my sister is the fiercest of them all."

"I think so," Brodie agreed as he looked down at Laurel's peaceful visage. He looked back at the couple who sat across from him. "Rest now. When I go to scout, I need you awake in case you must defend Laurel."

"Aye. And I'll take the first watch tonight," Monty announced. He looked at Donnan and lowered his voice. "I'll check your arm again, but you need to sleep, *mo ghaol*."

Brodie looked away, giving the men as much privacy as he could. He supposed he would never understand it, but he reminded himself that it wasn't his to reason why. He just prayed the men didn't one day lose their lives for it.

***

"Laurie," Brodie whispered as he nudged Laurel awake. Her blue-hazel eyes fluttered open, a tired smile spreading across her face. She squeezed her arms around his waist and sighed. "I don't like disturbing you, but I need you to eat something. It's dusk. I'm going out to scout." Laurel jerked away and shook her head. "Wheest. Dinna fash. I need to fetch water for us and the horses, and I need to see if we can leave tomorrow. I'm the only one of us who knows where we are and what to look for."

Laurel looked doubtful, but she nodded her head. She knew he was right, but her chest burned with anxiety. She forced her smile back into place, but she knew it was hardly convincing. Drawing in a fortifying breath, she nodded again. "What do you need me to do?"

Brodie cupped her cheek. "I love you something fierce, Laurie."

"I love you." Laurel's smile was dazzling in the dim light. "But that doesn't answer my question."

"I ken. But I love you, nonetheless. This isn't the first time you've asked what you can do to help rather than asking for aught for yourself or avoiding a challenge. It makes me so proud to be your husband."

"I want you to be proud, Brodie. I'm so proud to be your wife."

"You don't have to try, Laurie. Being who you are is enough."

"You've told me that before. It feels odd and right all at the same time. I don't know how to describe it, but after so many years knowing I wasn't, it——" Laurel shrugged. "Thank you."

"You've always been just right, thistle. You just weren't around the right people."

"*Mo mathan.*" Laurel canted her head. "You looked angrier than a bear with a bee sting when you rode toward me. But you looked just as powerful."

"I was angry," Brodie frowned playfully, able to feel calmer about the morning's events now that they were past them. "You and your horse. By God, lass. I thought my heart would beat out of my chest watching you leaning along Teine's side. Then when he reared. By all the saints, I might have wet myself. I was certain Teine's hooves would kill you. I never imagined the beastie would put an end to David Lamont. I'm rather jealous of your horse! I wanted to mete out justice, but your loyal steed did it for me."

"He didn't appreciate David cutting his ear or the bastard's horse nipping his rump."

"Remind me to stay on the right side of your horse's temper."

"He's like his mistress," Laurel purred. "A few treats and a few rubs and pats in the right place. That's all it takes." Laurel winked at Brodie.

"You shall get all of that and more once I get us home in one piece."

"Aye." Laurel sighed and got up. She reached out a hand to Brodie, pretending to tug unsuccessfully. "Come on, auld mon."

Brodie was on his feet in one agile move, and Laurel stood blinking at her imposingly large husband. His muscles bunched and rippled as he moved, and she was hypnotized. "I'll never make it out of this cave if you keep looking at me like that."

Laurel nodded but didn't look away. Instead, her tongue darted out to swipe across her lips before she grazed her teeth over her bottom lip.

"Lass." The word came out as a strangled groan as Brodie gripped her hips and gave her a searing kiss. They pulled away, knowing that lingering would only lead to more. Brodie stepped away and opened a barrel of oats that he poured out for the horses. He showed Laurel the stash of dried beef and dried fruit before he woke Monty and Donnan. He took two buckets and the waterskins with him and slipped out of the cave.

"Did you sleep well?" Laurel looked at Monty and Donnan.

"Aye. And you?" Monty asked as he ran his hand over his hair, which stuck out in all directions.

"Better than I expected. I feel rested for the first time in days. I suppose it is the first time I really rested." Laurel pulled out strips of meat and offered them to the men, who eagerly thanked her. They sat in silence as they chewed. There was little to talk about as they waited for Brodie to return. As the minutes ticked away, and the sun sank below the horizon, Laurel grew uneasy. Monty and Donnan assured her that Brodie was fine, but she didn't believe them until she saw his hulking form enter the cave, a sloshing bucket in each hand. She hurried forward to take one to the horses, letting two drink at a time while Brodie handed back the waterskins.

Brodie took her hand when they finished their tasks and led her back to where Monty and Donnan waited. The four sat together as Brodie recounted what he saw.

"The closest band of Lamonts is aboot a mile and a half to the south of us. There's another group three miles west. But I have men near them, so they don't concern me as much as the ones to the south."

"How do you know that?" Laurel asked.

"I used a birdcall when I noticed the group. I got immediate responses, so I know where at least a dozen men are. I went further north and saw naught. But I called out and got responses there. Some men are already ahead of us. I hope to join them in the morning and work our way out of the mountains together sooner than I expected. But I'll scout again in the morning to make sure the way is still safe. If it is, we'll go. If aught has changed, we wait. My men will go on ahead if it's safe for them and your men."

"Then take the last watch," Donnan said. Brodie nodded, glad that he would stay beside Laurel for most of the night. He knew it was selfish, but he wanted to hold her. Once they ate, Monty slipped from the cave. Brodie explained where to position himself, so Monty would remain hidden but could hear anything that approached before it appeared. He could slip back to the cave and warn the others with no one seeing him. Donnan listened attentively, so he was prepared for his shift. Laurel felt useless as she watched the men discuss how to divide the night's hours among them.

"Laurie." Laurel nodded as Brodie waved her over and took her to the cave's entrance. "Do you see the bush just yonder? If you need privacy, you can go there."

"Thank you." She led him to where she'd laid out their bedrolls. Donnan was already snoring lightly, and Laurel marveled at how easily the man had always fallen asleep anywhere. He'd been like that since they were children. Smiling, she laid down with Brodie's chest against her back. But she rolled over to lay her head on his shoulder and drape her

261

arm over his waist. She needed to hold him as much as he longed to hold her. Brodie stroked her hair as her body relaxed, feeling boneless.

"What're you thinking aboot?" Brodie wondered aloud.

"Naught in particular. Just glad to be with you. You?"

"The same. I shall make this up to you."

Laurel lifted her head, her brow furrowed. "You say that as if any of this is your fault. There's naught to make up to me. You didn't do aught wrong."

"I trusted the wrong men with your care."

"They were your men. You shouldn't have needed to doubt them. That is their sin, not yours. Michael paid for it with each bump and hit as he fell down Ben More."

"But you're a target because of me."

"Mayhap. Or you're a target because of me. I ken the MacDougalls would rather put a rift between the Campbells and Rosses than allow an alliance. Mayhap they and the Lamonts continue this because you married me. Mayhap they would have let things go if you'd married someone else."

"Possibly. But it doesn't mean I don't feel guilty."

"I wish you didn't, but I ken you do because you take your duty seriously."

"This isn't just aboot duty as your husband and as a laird. This is aboot the woman I love being in danger, and I can't stop it. I can't protect you the way I want, the way I should."

"Brodie, cease." Laurel's voice was laced with authority, and Brodie's chin jerked back. "We can want everything under the sun, but we rarely get more than a taste. I've known since I was a wean that I would likely marry a laird one day. As I grew aulder, I understood the danger that comes with being a clan's lady. Whether I married you or some lesser chieftain, I could still be at risk. That isn't your fault. That is life among Highlanders, and the price we pay for our position. As for what you should or shouldn't do, cease your blathering. I'm alive and at your side, the only place I want to be. If you didn't make me feel the way I do, I wouldn't have been strong enough to survive. I would have given up. You've given me more than you realize, and that's kept me alive."

"Laurie..." Brodie didn't know what to say. His wife's philosophical perspective made simple work of what felt complicated.

"Hush, husband. I was exceedingly comfortable a moment ago. I'd like to go back to that."

"I am ever your servant, my lady."

"I shall remind you of that the first time you complain that I harp at you."

The couple smiled at one another before Laurel yawned. She sighed as she closed her eyes. They lay together in the now dark cave. Laurel wasn't certain when she fell asleep, but she was unprepared to be disturbed when Brodie shifted from beneath her for his turn at watch. She grumbled but settled back under the plaids they'd shared. Her hand rested where Brodie's heart had been. The heat he left behind was a slight comfort.

THIRTY-ONE

B rodie rubbed his dry eyes and leaned his head from one side to another, hearing the satisfying pop that released the tension that accumulated while standing guard. He'd had the ideal watch: nothing happened. The sky was lightening from midnight blue to the shade of sapphire. The sun hadn't risen, but it would soon. He slipped back into the cave and found Monty and Donnan awake and whispering. Laurel continued to slumber, but Brodie noticed her hand roamed over his spot as if she searched for him in her sleep.

"How's she been?" Brodie whispered.

"Mostly sleeping like the dead, but she grows restless from time to time," Donnan answered.

"I'm headed out to scout again. If the Lamonts are still nearby, then I want to know if they moved after my last patrol. If I don't return within two hours, remain here until at least tomorrow morning." Both men nodded as all three glanced at Laurel once more. "If I don't return, will you take her to Balnagown?"

With the sun rising rather than setting, Brodie and the other two men understood the risk of Brodie being spotted grew exponentially from the evening before. He needed reassurance that there was a plan for Laurel if he didn't make it back.

"Aye. At least until we know no danger follows her," Monty answered. "From there, I swear to take her wishes into consideration. I won't promise that I can or will grant them, but I won't ignore them. And I won't mock them." Monty's expression showed the remorse he felt for what he'd previously thought of Laurel's desires. Brodie's mouth drew into a thin line, but he nodded.

"I'll be back as soon as I can."

"Don't you dare leave without saying goodbye." Laurel rolled over as she looked at the three men. Brodie crossed the cave and knelt before Laurel stood. She wrapped her arms around his neck and held on. "I love you. I want to tell you that a hundred times a day for the next hundred years."

"I shall have a hard time hearing you if I'm already saying it. I love you, thistle." Brodie and Laurel shared a brief but tender kiss before Brodie rose and squeezed her hand. Laurel watched as he walked out of the cave. Then she turned her attention to her brother and friend.

"If he doesn't come back, you must take me to Kilchurn first. I'd like to inform his family. I pray we can return his body to them if it comes to that. But I pray harder that it doesn't. I may be Lady Campbell, but if Brodie isn't Laird Campbell, I will be a stranger in the way. I will go to Balnagown before I ever go to Stirling." Laurel was resolute, shooting each man an unwavering stare. "I will not marry unless it's my choice. If Uncle Hamish and Aunt Amelia agree, I'd like a cottage in one of their villages. I'll be a widow in truth."

"You've thought a great deal in such a short time," Monty mused.

"You assumed I slept the entire time. I didn't. It gave me plenty of time to think."

"And what are your thoughts aboot being at Balnagown, sister?"

"I'd rather not. But I can't arrive at Sutherland and assume I can make a home there. Father will never allow me to live in a cottage on Ross land. I don't want the king involved. I'd prefer he forget I existed, so he doesn't press me to marry again. I doubt I will be so fortunate twice. I also don't want to remain at Balnagown long enough for Mother and Father to bemoan my presence. A couple days at most."

"And if we can't arrange a cottage on Sutherland in a couple of days?" Monty sounded skeptical, and Laurel knew he was right to be.

"It may take sennights, even moons, to convince them. I said I'd like to have a cottage there. If I can't then I shall find somewhere else." Laurel shrugged. She knew her wishes were unrealistic and unlikely, but they were what she'd wanted for years. There would be no chance of having them if she didn't speak them.

"We'll do all that we can, Laurel. It's my preference that you stay on Ross land," Monty admitted. "Somewhere within a day's ride of Balnagown, so Donnan and I can check on you once in a while. Your hair will always announce from whom you hail, but you're still a Ross. You have a home on our land."

Laurel nodded, not wanting to argue with Monty. She believed he meant it, but it wouldn't be his decision to make. At least not likely for several more years. Their father was as fit as a mule—sturdy and ornery. Laurel busied herself by folding Brodie's and her bedrolls. Once the task was complete, Laurel accepted the breeks Monty offered her. She retrieved a leine from Brodie's satchel. She held it up before her. She would drown in it since it came nearly to her ankles. She had neither the height nor breadth to fill it out. She looked ruefully at the men and winced.

"I need a dirk."

Laurel set to work cutting down the leine, promising Brodie silently that her first task as Lady Campbell would be to make him a new one. Once it was a more manageable length, she took the clothes into the nook where she and Brodie coupled the day before. As she shed her kirtle, she wished she was doing it for an entirely different reason. She reminded herself that they would have plenty of opportunities once they were home. Rolling Monty's breeks over several times at the waist and ankles, she wrapped her arisaid around herself and belted the outfit into place. She could only imagine the sight she made, but she felt more confident that she could traverse whatever terrain they faced now that she wasn't likely to trip over her own clothes.

Laurel, Monty, and Donnan were surprised when Brodie returned within an hour. He chuckled when he saw Laurel's attire until she held up the remnants of the bottom half of his leine. She offered a semi-apologetic expression before laughing.

"I'll make you a new one."

"I may ruin all my leines if it means you'll make me new ones. They'll be the finest in all the land," Brodie proclaimed as he came to stand beside Laurel, wrapping his arm around her waist. "The group to our south is where I last saw them. But the ones to the west are on the move now. Our men are awake and ready to go. I got more responses than last night."

"Won't the Lamonts know it's you, if there's suddenly all these bird calls and no birds in sight?"

"I have my own call. My men have theirs too. Usually when one of us uses it, the actual birds respond. Those who don't know what to listen for don't hear the other responses. But we know what we sound like." Brodie knew most Highland clans used similar methods, but the meaning of the calls differed from clan to clan, ensuring they remained a secure way to communicate. Brodie watched as Laurel appeared to tuck the information away for later use. He could only imagine what she would come up with.

"Do we go now, bear?"

"Aye. While the sun is still low; otherwise, they're likely to spot us. Laurie, the path we're going to take is dangerous. It's not one I would usually traverse with horses. Do not attempt more than you can manage. Admit if you need help." Brodie gazed earnestly into Laurel's hazel eyes. She recognized the worry in his gray ones and wished she could ease it. But she knew neither of them would breathe easily until they were all away from the mountains and the Lamonts.

"I promise." With that, they left the cave.

While they could, Brodie led with Laurel behind him. Monty and Donnan followed Laurel, one on each side, slightly behind her. Between their hulking bodies and their horses, they shielded Laurel from the enemy to the south. They moved in silence, Brodie gesturing directions as he had the day before. As they moved along ledges and over crags and past steep drops into valleys hundreds of feet below them, Laurel couldn't imagine hiking through the mountains without Brodie as their guide. They stopped to rest the horses at the top of the sheep path down the mountain. Laurel steeled herself for the descent.

"Tie Teine's reins off and guide him by the bridle. If you feel yourself sliding, let go. If you pull him with you, he's likely to crush you. Trust that he's more sure-footed than you," Brodie instructed. "If you feel unsteady, grab my belt. Regardless, watch where I step, then step there too. We'll move slowly."

"Yes, Brodie." Laurel drew a deep breath and released it gradually. She followed Brodie's instructions and adjusted Teine's reins, whispering in the horse's ear about how proud she was of him. As though he understood, his massive head nodded. He nudged her shoulder, and she was certain he was telling her to get on with their journey down the mountain. She muttered, "I hear you."

With her first step, Laurel's foot almost slid out from beneath her. She righted herself, but her heart raced. She swallowed and locked her gaze onto Brodie's feet. It only took a moment to realize that he'd offered the best advice he could by telling her how to follow his lead. He moved with the ease of a mountain goat, giving Laurel confidence that they would survive.

Brodie listened to every sound around him. He listened for Laurel's breathing, her footsteps, the horses, birds overhead, and the sheep in the corrie they walked toward. His eyes darted from the trail to his left, then back to the trail before looking up, then down, and finally to the right. He repeated the pattern over and over. He spotted the first sign of trouble before their enemy spotted them. He held up a fist, and their group came to a stop. His only indicator of what he found was looking to his left. The other three members of their party gazed in the same direction. Shadows danced along the rock face, and they moved toward them.

Brodie signaled them to move on. He'd only stopped, so they were all aware of what they couldn't avoid. He was determined to reach flat ground before the group of ten Lamonts or before the enemy could reach them. He worried they would cut off the route Brodie planned. There was another way down nearby, but it led to a glen rather than off the mountains. They could hide there, but there was no trail. Not even an animal one. It would be pure luck to make it down, and he doubted all the horses would.

If he'd been alone, he would have risked jogging down the trail they took now. But he couldn't with the horses in tow and people unfamiliar with their location. He settled for reaching back for Laurel. When her hand met his, he wrapped it around his belt. With her connected to him, he increased their pace. While his gaze could survey their surroundings while he moved downward, he didn't dare look back while he moved. He had to trust that Monty and Donnan were progressing well too. They were a hundred yards from the base of the mountain when the cry went up. The shadows morphed into men who raced toward them.

Brodie predicted what would happen, but he wouldn't risk any of the Lamonts surviving their pell-mell descent. He spun around and hefted Laurel over his shoulder. She let go of Teine because she had no choice. Once more, her hand grasped Brodie's belt. She looked up to see Monty and Donnan had also released their horses. She glanced at the beasts and realized Brodie hadn't exaggerated that they would be more sure-footed. Monty and Donnan glanced over at their pursuers now and again, but their attention was following the feet in front of them.

Brodie slid over the shale, bending his knees to absorb the impact as he half-ran and half-slipped the last hundred yards. Trusting Monty and Donnan would follow his lead, he glanced back to see they were only steps behind him. He tossed Laurel into the saddle and helped her arrange the reins before vaulting onto Lann. Monty and Donnan followed suit as the first screams echoed through the pass. Laurel twisted to see and watched most of the men plummet down the mountain, their horses careening down with them. She only felt bad for the animals. But a few moved more cautiously and made progress in their pursuit.

They still had nearly a day's ride as they cut through foothills, careful not to exhaust their mounts. It wasn't long after they set off on horseback that Campbell and Ross men materialized, riding to catch up to them. Laurel kept count, praying that more would appear. They rode in silence for nearly two hours before Brodie signaled that they would stop to rest the horses. There was no water nearby, but the animals and riders needed a break. Brodie helped Laurel off her horse and nodded when Donnan offered to escort her to a private place. Brodie and Monty met with their men.

The two leaders nodded as they learned the fate of five men. Two Rosses lost their lives falling over a precipice. One Ross and one Campbell died from arrows to the throat. The Lamonts captured the last man, a Campbell, and ran him through. But he'd given his life so both Ross and Campbell warriors could find safety. Monty and Brodie exchanged a look, both knowing they had many families to inform that their loved one wouldn't return.

The mixture of Campbells and Rosses were an hour from Kilchurn when a Ross warrior spotted horses riding toward them. Laurel already rode in the center of the pack. She strained to see past the men to her left, but it was futile. She held her breath at the sound of swords being drawn from their scabbards. They rode until, inevitably, they had to stop and face the newest threat.

"Do not leave the center, Laurel. Trust that the men will remain around you, even if gaps form. They'll shift. They know what to do regardless of their clan," Brodie commanded. Laurel nodded, already knowing what to do but wanting to assure Brodie that she understood. She caught the concern in his eyes before he masked it. She reached out her hand before he steered his horse away. When she grasped his, she squeezed nodding again. She wanted him to know she wasn't Eliza. She wouldn't make the other woman's fatal error.

"MacFarlanes," Graham called out. The man's eyesight amazed her since the riders were still miles from them. The guardsmen lowered their weapons but didn't sheath them. Laurel squinted against the late morning sun as she tried to discern who led the clan's warriors.

"Wonderful," Brodie said, sarcasm lacing his voice. "Andrew Mòr and Andrew Óg." Mòr usually meant greater or larger, but when used with a name, it signified older or senior. Óg was the opposite. The laird rode with his son. Brodie wasn't certain if he was pleased to see either of them. Brodie drew away from the circle, Graham at his side. Monty and Donnan maneuvered their mounts a few feet behind the Campbell laird and his second.

"Fine weather we're having," Brodie called out once the MacFarlanes were within earshot. When they drew close enough to lock eyes, he added, "A fine day to come and kiss and be friends." Brodie laid his sword across his lap, looking as though he rested nonchalantly. But he fooled no one. He might not look like the aggressor, but he was prepared to fight.

"I understand my son will be kissing your boots several times," Andrew Mòr grumbled. He glanced at Laurel and scowled. "And Lady Campbell's." The older man sent his son a withering glare. Andrew Óg wisely remained silent, his expression justly chastised but his body held proudly.

"Now you've come to reconcile," Brodie surmised. "Are you prepared to fight?"

"Would I have ridden this far if I wasn't?"

"Are you planning to remain until it's done?"

"Will you feed us if we do?"

"No." Brodie grinned at the banter between the other laird and him. He liked Andrew Mòr, and he tolerated Andrew Óg, but he rarely enjoyed them together. His knuckles were white as he gripped his sword and reins, glad to have something in each hand lest he rip Andrew Óg apart with his bare hands.

Andrew Mòr glanced at his son and scowled again. He nodded his head in Laurel's direction. Andrew Óg nudged his horse forward, but Laurel didn't move. She wasn't sure if Brodie trusted them, and she most definitely didn't trust the younger Andrew. Her gaze was riveted on him, watching for any signal that he might attack.

"Lady Campbell, I did you grievous harm for which you have my humblest apologies."

"But are you sorry?" Laurel asked without hesitation.

"Your pardon?" Andrew blinked at her.

"Apologies are all fine and good. I suppose you'd like praise for admitting you did something wrong. What I wish to know is if you're actually remorseful. I doubt you are," Laurel's haughtiness harkened back to her days as the Shrew

273

of Stirling. For that she felt no contrition. He'd been a party to men willing to kill her. "You showed you were without honor. You did naught to convince the others not to murder me. Are you sorry for that? Or can you only admit you did something wrong because your da made you?"

Laurel watched Brodie's shoulders tense for a moment, but she still didn't feel contrite. He would negotiate with the laird, but Laurel would deal with the perpetrator. She knew accusing Andrew of being dishonorable would have wound her up in a fight to the death if she were a man. After what she endured, she couldn't resist taunting him. She trusted that Andrew Mòr was intelligent enough not to let his son take on Brodie in her stead.

"I never heard how much my death was worth. Twenty pounds? Thirty pounds? One hundred? How much did you lose because I'm still married?"

Andrew drew in a deep breath. "Two hundred and fifty pounds." He exhaled with a puff.

"Hmm." Laurel looked to contemplate what he said. "I'll admit, seeing me dead is worth more than I expected. Or you just really wanted to be right. We shall see whether your father thinks I'm worth that two hundred and fifty pounds by the end of the tomorrow, shalln't we?" Laurel turned her head away, dismissing Andrew as though he weren't heir to a lairdship.

"As sharp as a thorn, and as hard-hearted as a Scot from Scotland," Andrew Mòr said approvingly. "She might make a mon of you yet, Campbell."

"Aye. That's why I'm bent on keeping her at my side."

"You'd rather her with you than against you."

"Now you ken who to wager on. That's if you're daft enough to try."

"I'll leave that to my son."

Laurel thought for a moment that she would accept his apology aloud to ease his obvious discomfort, but she knew it was a lie. And she thought a dose of public shaming would serve him well. He would be a laird one day. He needed some humility. So Laurel sat quietly, having said her piece.

Brodie enjoyed Laurel's assertiveness and fought not to laugh. Not because the situation was humorous, but because Laurel was still one step ahead of most. But he was ready to end the chitchat and move the combined clans to Kilchurn. He needed to send riders to the other Campbell keeps and men to the River Orchy to scout the MacArthurs and MacGregors. He needed to know if his idea about the dam was feasible.

"Come. Your men can make camp outside my walls. I'm certain we can have chambers prepared for you both," Brodie announced. He glanced at Laurel as he turned his horse.

"I shall even make certain there are fires in both hearths," Laurel quipped before spurring her horse to follow the others. Brodie led the members from the three clans, Monty now riding to his right and Andrew Mòr on his left. Donnan rode alongside Laurel on one side while Graham rode on the other. She kept a lively conversation with both men when their pace allowed it. She found the last hour went quickly. But her stomach knotted when Kilchurn Castle came into view. Her new home and her new clan awaited.

THIRTY-TWO

Brodie signaled for the riders to rein in, pointing out to the MacFarlanes where they could pitch their camp. The Rosses were few enough that they would bunk in the barracks. Laurel wondered if she should remain where she was, even as the group largely dispersed. Brodie turned back to look at her.

"Laurie?"

Laurel nudged Teine on until she came to be side by side with Brodie. He wrapped his arm around her waist and hauled her into his lap with a squeak. She was unprepared for him to capture her mouth in a kiss, but she surrendered immediately, eager for it just like him. As the kiss drew on, she sensed impatient horses swaying around them, their owners not much more pleased to be kept waiting. But she cared not. They'd defied death countless times in the past two days. She would savor this moment of love and security.

"I've waited all bluidy day to do that, thistle," Brodie murmured against her lips.

"Mmm. I'm glad you didn't make me wait anymore."

"How do you wish to enter your new home? On your own horse or with me on mine?"

"What I wish and what I must do are, as usual, not the

same. I wish to remain as we are. But I must enter on my own. I'm your wife and lady of this clan. The first impression I make will be hard to undo if I appear too dependent on you."

"Sound reasoning. Or people will see I love my bride and can't go without her one more moment," Brodie countered.

"Compromise?"

"Such as?"

"Each on their own mount but holding hands."

"Agreed." Brodie proffered another kiss before setting Laurel back on her saddle. They rode through the village just beyond the wall, the bells tolling to signal the laird's return. As people came out of their homes to wave, Brodie laced his fingers with Laurel's. It wasn't the easiest position, but Brodie understood the powerful signal it sent. They entered as equals, as partners. That was exactly how he viewed Laurel.

They rode into the bailey to cheers but confused expressions. Laurel realized people expected Brodie to return with Eliza beside him, not her. He hadn't returned to Kilchurn before going to court. She glanced at Brodie and smiled at his sheepish expression.

"I shall have to explain," he murmured.

Laurel watched a couple standing together on the stairs. Laurel assumed they were Brodie's brother Dominic and his wife. The man resembled Brodie in most ways, but he didn't carry himself with the same certainty and confidence Brodie possessed. It was clear he was a powerful warrior, but Laurel supposed Brodie's demeanor came in part from being the laird, not the laird's tánaiste. The woman who stood beside Dominic was pretty, but she looked wan. Her expression and posture were unassuming. Laurel wondered if she might make friends with her new sister-by-marriage. She would try.

"Once we're inside, what would you have me do first?"

Brodie looked into Laurel's eyes as they came to a stop. She never ceased to move him when she thought of others first. If only people had been compassionate from the start.

They might have met the Laurel who always lurked behind the shield she wielded. She was unselfish and dutiful. Once more he counted his blessings.

"Brodie? Do you have a housekeeper who will see to our guests? Do I need to attend to their chambers and baths? Will your sister-by-marriage do it?"

"Sorry, *mo ghaol*. You distract me in the best ways. Aggie will see to our guests, so you needn't rush aboot a keep you don't know. Colina never took an interest in the household. I suppose she always knew one day my wife would arrive and be chatelaine," Brodie shrugged. He realized he'd barely thought of it in his brother's three-year marriage. Once it was obvious Colina didn't want the position, he ceased thinking about it, knowing he would have to marry to gain a lady to run his keep. The couple was too enamored with one another to pay attention to anyone else. They were a love-match.

"What would you have me do?" Laurel pressed.

"Stand beside me as we greet our people."

Laurel appeared uncertain, but she nodded. She would follow Brodie's lead. But she realized there was one thing more pressing than any other. "Do you have a healer?"

"Aye, Nora—or rather Honoria—is our healer. I'll send for her. She can see to the men who need her. Thank you for thinking of it. Come, Laurie. Let me show you your home." Brodie dismounted, then lifted Laurel from the saddle, easing her body along his until her feet were on the ground. "I regret I may be late to bed tonight. But I will be there."

"And I shall be ready. Wake me. Promise?"

"Do not fear, Laurie. There will be little sleep for either of us." Brodie pinched her backside before he took her hand. She reached across her arm and pinched him back. Brodie jumped, then laughed as he looked down at Laurel, who looked as innocent as a lamb. He walked them to the top of the steps outside the main door of the keep. They turned to look at those who'd assembled. "I am happy to be home."

People cheered, and Laurel saw the sincerity in people's excitement matched what she heard in Brodie's voice. He squeezed her hand in reassurance before he released it and wrapped his arm around Laurel. He whispered, "It's not just for show. Don't doubt that." Laurel had wondered that very thing.

"Stop reading my thoughts," she teased. Brodie drew her against his side and looked out at his people again.

"You know I left to settle the alliance with the MacMillans and to bring home a wife. God had a different plan for me and for our clan." Brodie paused as his gaze swept the assembled clan members. "Our party was attacked on our own land, and they killed Lady Eliza." He waited for the buzz to settle, purposely evasive about the aggressors. "I have been away longer than intended for several reasons. I returned to the MacMillans to allow Lady Eliza to rest in peace. I continued on and arrived in Stirling, needing to inform the king. While at court, the Lord blessed me ten times over. I met my wife, Lady Campbell. You may have recognized the plaids that aren't ours or the MacFarlanes. Lady Campbell was once Lady Laurel Ross. Our journey wasn't without incident. Those who wished to sever our alliances with the MacMillans are even more determined to sever our alliance with the Rosses."

Laurel wanted to squirm. She'd never been so uncomfortable in her life. She sounded like a replacement bride, which she knew in part she was, despite Brodie claiming their meeting was a blessing. It also sounded as though she made their clan troubles worse, which she knew was unintentionally true. Brodie looked down at her, and the love she saw eased her nerves. She smiled back up at him.

"I cannot offer Lady Campbell the feast and welcome I wish and that she deserves. We must postpone it until the threats to our clan are no longer. But I would have every member of this clan, be they members of our branch or a sept, understand that Lady Campbell is my partner in our marriage and in this clan's leadership. You will discover she is selfless and giving when you are fair and hard working. You will discover she is stern when you are not. This keep and all that happens within its walls, or pertains to it, is her domain. Her word is law. Do not come to me if you dislike it. I trust her choices and her advice as much as I do any member of the clan council. She doesn't have to explain herself to you, but I can promise there is a well thought out reason for each of her decisions."

Brodie looked at Laurel expectantly, and she realized he expected her to address the clan now. She still hadn't been introduced to Colina and Dominic, but she looked at them first. She was unprepared and unsure what to say, but she stumbled through. "Clan Campbell, I am proud to be your lady. In the time I've come to know and care for your laird, I've learned that he is wise and strong, a defender of his people above all else. I take my duties to you and my husband to heart. I cannot promise that you will always like what I say or agree with me, but as your laird said, I do it for a reason. I wish for the best for this clan, and I will fight alongside all of you to protect what is ours. God help those who test the might of Clan Campbell."

Laurel held her breath as awestruck faces gawked at her. She didn't know what to do. She slashed her gaze to Monty and Donnan, who stood two steps down from her. Neither of them looked reassuring. She was unprepared for Brodie to scoop her into his arms. She wrapped her arms around his neck, unsteady with surprise.

"And that is why I love my wife," Brodie announced before kissing her. As always, the world around them fell away, becoming a blissful land made for only two. Hoots and cheers eventually forced them apart as they grinned at one another. "I have a new home to show my wife."

Laurel entered the keep with the others and looked around the Great Hall. The crossbeams made an intricate pattern while serving their purpose: supporting the roof of one of the largest Great Halls Laurel had ever visited. Banners and tapestries hung from the walls. She wondered if Colina or Brodie's mother stitched any of them. Every surface her gaze landed upon was scrubbed clean. The floor had fresh rushes. There was no wax accumulating in the sconces, and the ash looked recently swept in the hearths. She assumed Colina was an excellent chatelaine, and Aggie clearly ran an efficient staff.

"Lady Campbell, welcome to our home," Dominic greeted as they stood near the dais. Laurel forced herself not to frown. Dominic's tone made it sound as if she were a guest. "Our" didn't feel as if it included her.

"Thank you, Dominic. I've been looking forward to meeting you." Laurel looked at Dominic and Colina, hoping to encourage the woman to join the conversation. When Colina said nothing, Laurel pressed on. "Lady Colina, you oversee a well-kept home. I'm very impressed by all that I see."

"That's Aggie," Colina sniffed. It took Laurel aback until she realized Colina wasn't being condescending. She had a genuine runny nose. Laurel wondered if the woman ailed. She still waited for her sister-by-marriage to say more, but nothing was forthcoming, so she turned back to Dominic.

"I didn't imagine you and your brother would look so similar," Laurel smiled.

"We are brothers."

Laurel swallowed. This wasn't the greeting she'd hoped to offer or receive. She used the opportunity to shift attention from her. She looked at Monty. "I'd like to introduce you to my brother Montgomery."

Monty reached out his arm, and Dominic offered a hearty handshake. Laurel wondered if Dominic merely didn't like women other than his wife. Monty turned to Donnan. "This is my second Donnan Ross."

"Welcome to Kilchurn," Dominic grinned. Laurel decided it was because she was a woman, not something else that earned her a chilly welcome. She looked at Colina once more, but the woman appeared disinterested in speaking to her. Colina's arms were folded, and Laurel noticed the hem of her sister's-by-marriage gown rippled. While Laurel couldn't see the appendage, she knew Colina was tapping her toes. Laurel was at a loss, so she looked at Brodie, who looked confused. But when he noticed she stared at him, he smiled down at her and linked their hands together.

"Come with me, Laurie," Brodie said. "Aggie will see to our guests, and you can become better acquainted with Dom and Colina later."

Brodie gave Laurel an abbreviated tour after he introduced her to Aggie, the housekeep, and Berta, the head cook. He pointed out his solar before taking her abovestairs. He opened the door to the chamber that was clearly intended for the laird's wife. Laurel grew nervous as she took in the bed that sat perpendicular to the right wall. There was a padded window seat where she thought she might enjoy sewing. But her attention returned to the bed, unsure whether Brodie had changed his mind.

"I intended to have it removed, but I suppose I should ask you what you want?" Brodie said softly.

"Take it out," Laurel blurted. Brodie chuckled and kissed her temple.

"I hoped you'd say that. Let me show you our chamber, *mo chridhe*." Brodie opened the adjacent door, and Laurel stepped into an enormous chamber. She supposed anything smaller would feel cramped considering Brodie's height and wide shoulders. She'd noticed that he had to turn sideways to pass through some doorways. Brodie sighed as they stood staring at the bed. "That is where I'd like to be, but I can't. I'll stay until you're in your bath, then I must join the other men in my solar. I'm certain Aggie will send a tray up for you. You must be starving."

"I am. You don't need to stay, Brodie. I can manage a bath, even in a new place." Laurel patted his chest. He captured her hand, pressing it against his heart as he encircled her waist with his other arm.

"And if my ulterior motive is to see my bonnie bride stripped with her flowing hair aboot her shoulders?"

"I'd guess you don't intend to meet with my brother and the others."

"You fear I will succumb to temptation?"

Laurel turned her lips down in a mock frown before playfully winking. "I might be the one who can't resist the temptation."

A knock at the door interrupted their banter. Their aggrieved sighs were timed perfectly before Brodie bid the servants enter. Laurel watched as a troop of servants hauled in the largest copper and wood tub she'd ever seen. She figured it made sense given her husband was a veritable Goliath at nearly six and a half feet tall. He needed space to fit his legs. Steam rose as the last bucket of water was dumped into the bath.

"Would ye care for help, ma lady?" a blonde asked, but her attention was on Brodie.

"Do you usually help with baths?" Laurel countered. The maid blinked several times before she shook her head. "Then I don't see why you'd start today."

"I could help ye undress then dress and fix yer hair, ma lady."

"Do you usually assist with undressing?" Laurel narrowed her eyes at the woman, who continued to stare at Brodie.

"Only maself, ma lady." The maid shook her head, confused.

"Then I don't see why you'd start today." Laurel leaned

forward, lowering her voice, but not so much that Brodie couldn't hear. "Find somewhere else to rest your eyes lest I pluck them out and feed them to the crows."

The blonde gasped, turning a stunned expression to Laurel before looking to Brodie for help. He stood with his arms crossed, his face set in stone. When she just kept blinking and shifting her weight, Brodie frowned. "You were in the courtyard not an hour ago. I know you heard what I said. Lady Campbell's word is law when it comes to everything in this keep. That includes me. It seems she isn't interested in sharing, nor do I intend to accept any offers."

"What's your name?" Laurel asked, softening her tone.

"Gara, ma lady."

"When you run belowstairs to tell everyone what a bitch I am, be sure not to forget to tell them I don't share."

"Aye, ma lady." Gara dipped into a wobbly curtsy before dashing from the room.

Laurel wasn't ready to face Brodie. She'd made an assumption that could have resulted in her humiliation instead of the maid's. She steeled herself for Brodie's disapproval. She was confident he wouldn't speak against her in front of anyone, but she knew he wouldn't hold back in private. She turned around, unprepared for the Cheshire-cat grin he sported.

"I do like it when you're fierce," Brodie said as he kissed the skin behind her ear and pulled at her belt. But Laurel stepped back.

"That wasn't my place," she whispered. At Brodie's confusion, she clarified. "It wasn't my place to turn down an offer made to you. I—We didn't talk aboot whether you'll—"

"Laurel." Brodie's tone warned her to stop. "Perhaps you don't recall, but we've had this conversation before. It bears repeating. I do not have a leman. While I dislike comparing you to Eliza, I would have you remember I was prepared to accept celibacy for at least two years."

Laurel nodded. She clearly remembered the conversation they had, but the maid's attentiveness to Brodie made her suspicious. "It felt like what she offered wasn't really intended for me."

"Gara and I have flirted from time to time, but naught more." He offered no more explanation, and she supposed there was no more to give.

Brodie guided Laurel to sit before he unlaced her boots and took them and her stockings off. With a light tug, he brought her back to her feet and pulled his cut down leine from the waist of her rolled over breeks and pulled the waist open. Laurel pushed them past her hips until they dropped to the floor. She bent to pick them up, but Brodie stopped her, reaching for them himself. He laid the breeks over the back of a chair before he lifted the leine over her head. She'd never been self-conscious in front of Brodie, but his silence was unnerving.

"Laurie, I love you. I love every bit of you. I am not telling tales when I say how blessed I am to be your husband. You make me happy in ways I never imagined. I won't do aught to jeopardize it. It's too precious to me. Our lives will demand much of us, and there will be sadness and frustration, even anger, as we serve our people. Happiness was all too fleeting until I met you."

"I love you, too. Despite everything that's happened since we left Stirling, I feel like the Laurel I once knew. I feel free. You've given me that. I imagined the only way I could have it was to be on my own. I'm so glad that isn't true. I want to be the one you turn to during those trying times. Not only the happy ones."

"You will be. We are partners. I wish for you to be by my side this evening when I meet with the others." Brodie looked past her shoulder at the wisps of steam still rising from the water. "I ken Aggie arranged baths for everyone else. I don't need to rush. Shall we discover if there's room for two?"

Laurel smiled as she helped Brodie undress. When they

stood naked, Brodie lifted Laurel, and she wrapped her legs around his waist. She cupped his jaw as they kissed before he stepped into the tub. As they settled into the soothing heat, their bodies joined. Brodie kneaded her breasts as they floated just above the surface. Laurel's head fell back with a moan. Brodie's tongue trailed along her throat as her hands skimmed his arms before moving to his shoulders, massaging the muscles that bunched beneath her hands. Their kisses grew more insistent as they moved together. Laurel closed her eyes, reveling in everything she felt inside and out.

"Oh, Brodie," she breathed as his love poured into her, and she knew she was finally home. But it wasn't the chamber or Kilchurn that made it home. It was Brodie.

"Laurie, I want to last, but I dinna think I can. I need ye too much. I'm struggling nae to finish without ye." With his guard completely lowered, Brodie gave no consideration to his speech. He wanted only to share how he felt, what Laurel made him feel.

"I'm close, bear. Dinna stop. Just a wee more."

Brodie grasped her hips, grinding her pubis against his. Laurel cried out as her belly tightened before pleasure spread through her body and into her limbs. Brodie moved her faster, with a determination that hardened his expression. Laurel watched as his muscles rippled. Need for her husband flared again. She moved with him, edging toward another wave of euphoria. They tumbled over the edge together.

"Laurie!" Brodie roared. Laurel collapsed against his chest, heaving to catch their breath. They filled the calm after the storm with affection as they soaked together. "Sleepy?"

"Aye. But this happens every time ye hold me. I canna keep ma eyes open. Ye're so comfortable."

Brodie's laughter rumbled through his chest, and Laurel felt her body absorb it. "I dinna ken that anyone else would describe me as such."

"Nay one else better be finding out. I claim all of this," Laurel waved her hand in his direction, "as mine."

"That it is, thistle."

"Brodie, I ken why ye're so comfortable." Laurel whispered as she played with the hair at his nape, then ran her fingers over his stubble. "Because ye've done what ye promised. Ye've given me freedom. Ye havenae tried to change me. Ye havenae turned away from me when ma tongue gets the better of me. I dinna fear what ye will say. I dinna feel like I have to protect maself from yer words, that I dinna have to always be on guard. I ken I'm nae alone anymore."

"Ye arenae alone." Brodie tickled her rib before reaching for the soap. "I suspect that ye shall be so nae alone that ye will tire of me trailing yer heels."

"I like it when we can talk like this," Laurel admitted shyly.

"So do I. I ken I can confide in ye, and I want to. I think when I realized that, I realized I would marry ye nay matter what."

Laurel smiled as Brodie ran the soap over her body before washing her hair. As he made her hair sudsy, she washed everywhere she could reach on his body. Brodie poured fresh water over Laurel's head before she returned the favor and scrubbed his. She was certain it was the best bath she'd ever taken, not only because she shared it with Brodie, but because it washed away the week's worth of dust and grime. She felt fresh and ready to begin her new life.

But temptation proved too great once again for the newlyweds as their hands ran over one another as they dried each other off. With a sudden and frantic need, Brodie pressed Laurel backwards until her back hit the bed poster. He lifted her leg until her foot rested on the bed frame. His fingers surged into her as her hips jolted forward. His fingers intensified her need, making her body ache with desire. She stroked him, alternating speed and pressure. She watched as a drop of creamy, viscous fluid leaked from the tip. But her concentration frayed when Brodie enticed the pearl that hid within its shell with his agonizingly slow movements. He rubbed over and over as Laurel grew more desperate, begging Brodie to ease the burning need for them to join. She gripped the poster over her head, barely able to remain on her feet as her legs trembled.

Brodie was in purgatory. It certainly wasn't hell because Laurel's body rubbing against him was hardly a punishment. But he was in limbo as he worked her flesh. Not yet in heaven but waiting for the torture to end and the glory to begin. When he feared Laurel was on the brink of frustration that ended her pleasure, he eased into her. He was certain he'd found the promised land. Laurel's hips undulated against his as her nails raked over his back. He spun them so he could climb onto the bed, still supporting Laurel's body. She pulled him down onto her as they rocked together. Bracketing his hips with her knees, she met each of his thrusts until she could no longer keep her eyes open. The intensity of her physical reactions and emotions were drugging her once more.

"I want to hear ye call out ma name, Laurie. I want to hear ma name on yer lips and ken I'm the one who brings ye the pleasure ye seek."

"Brodie," Laurel moaned. "How do ye do this to me? How is it always nearly more than I can handle, but always perfect?"

"Because our bodies were made to be together. We are a perfect pair."

"I'm so close again. I can feel it. So close," Laurel panted as she strained against Brodie, edging closer and closer to edge. "Brodie!"

Brodie felt Laurel's body contract around his, milking his cock as he thrust harder and faster, ringing another climax from her before he could no longer hold back. "Yes," he growled as he surged into her, uncaring if he was rough since she encouraged him, begging him to keep going. "Laurie!"

They collapsed together, rung dry once more. Brodie's arms shook as he rested on his forearms, trying not to crush Laurel. She pressed him down onto her, and he rocked his hips against her gently, sensing she still wanted more despite her breathlessness. When she moaned, and her back arched, he knew he rang the last drop of strength from her and left her blissful. They lay together in silence, content with one another's company as they basked in the afterglow.

THIRTY-THREE

The evening meal was a quiet affair. Both Andrews, along with Monty and Donnan, joined Brodie, Laurel, Dominic and Colina at the high table. The somber mood of looming battle spread through the clan. Brodie decided he wouldn't explain the situation until he discussed strategy with Laurel and the men. Annoyance nipped at him when Dominic excused himself along with Colina, claiming she wasn't feeling well, and he needed to tend to his wife. He'd always thought his brother doting on his wife was nice, and he better understood it now that he married Laurel. But Colina looked no different from she always did: pale and snooty. His brother missing the strategy meeting rankled. Brodie predicted the MacFarlane men would balk at Laurel's presence while Monty and Donnan would cross their arms and grin. He wasn't wrong.

"Campbell, I ken you're newly married, but can you let the lass go for a moment?" Andrew Mòr grumbled. Brodie glanced at Monty and Donnan. The men's arms were crossed, their expressions smug.

"Nay, I can't. Both because I don't want to, and because I ken my wife is a strategist. She's likely to win the war for us." Brodie rolled out a map of Kilchurn Castle and the surrounding area of Glenorchy. Laurel leaned forward and studied, finding the marks that represented the nearby keeps. She shifted her focus to Ben Lui, and the distance they'd traveled that day. She struggled to remember what she'd learned of where the Lamonts and MacDougalls intended to meet. She spotted the dam and where the MacArthurs and MacGregors likely camped. It surprised her how close their northern enemies dared come.

Laurel's mind ticked over, envisioning men on both sides moving from various directions. She pictured how the groups might move dependent on their enemy. She thought of at least five scenarios before anyone spoke. She listened attentively to Andrew Mòr when he was the first to make a suggestion.

"Rally your branches here. Send them across the Orchy to take on the MacArthurs and the MacGregors. We remain with you to fight what's left of the Lamont and MacDougall bastards who dare show their faces." Andrew nodded, pleased with his suggestion, sounding as though their battle plan was complete. Laurel looked at Brodie, who watched her. She said nothing, nor made any gesture, but her mouth thinned.

"How shall we place our men?" Brodie asked, looking at Monty. Laurel's brother jutted his chin at her.

"Ask Laurel. She already kens."

"Bah. Women are like weans. They're best seen and not heard," Andrew Mòr sniped.

"Father," Andrew Óg dared enter the conversation. It was clear he hadn't returned to his father's good graces. "Lady Lau—Lady Campbell earned her reputation at court because of her intelligence. People heard the barbs and sarcasm and thought her haughty or just mean-spirited. But a few of us realized they came easily to her and cut so deeply because she's more observant and astute than most. If Ross says you should consider her suggestions, then we should." Andrew shot another apologetic glance at Laurel. This time she believed it was genuine.

"Very well. The lass speaks," Andrew Mòr grumbled.

"I prefer Lady Campbell, but I'll accept Lady Laurel. I haven't been a lass in a decade," Laurel corrected. While people called women "lass" until their last days, she would demand the respect due to her. She didn't want the MacFarlane to think she played games. She looked around Brodie's solar before she collected a handful of quills, the inkwell, and a block of wax. She returned to the table and examined the map once more. She placed the inkwell where the mark for Ben Lui laid. She angled the quills over the other castles, and the wax was Kilchurn. "The Lamonts will follow the same route as we did. They're likely less than an hour's ride from here already. Since they cannot rendezvous with the MacDougalls like they planned, both clans will send scouts either to relay messages or to agree to a new stepping off point."

Laurel pointed to the inkwell. She made a triangle with her forefinger and middle finger upright against the tabletop. She spread the fingers of her other hand at the point she figured the MacDougalls would make camp. They were probably closer than originally planned, since they were unsure whether the Lamonts were still in the war. She walked her two fingers from the inkwell toward Kilchurn Castle. Her other hand slid toward Kilchurn at the same time.

"If they're smart, the Lamonts will wait until they see the MacDougalls regardless of what time they arrive. I would estimate they will meet here." Laurel nodded to where both hands rested. She lifted them and looked at the men, surprised to see even the MacFarlanes watched and listened. "The other keeps are well-positioned for Kilchurn's defenses. I assume that was the plan all along. But rather than using their proximity to summon them directly to Kilchurn, they move east from their homes. The MacDougalls will move past them undetected because they will assume one of two things. All the branches already rallied here, or that there wasn't time to rally them at all. Either way, they won't expect them along their route. Innes Chonnel stands the furthest south."

Laurel used the fingers of her left hand this time to represent the MacDougalls. She slid the quill furthest from her slowly toward her traveling fingers. She inched it along until it lay parallel to her fingers. As she moved her left hand forward, she slid the second quill directly toward them.

"This is Inishail, correct?" Laurel looked up at Brodie, who leaned over the map with rapt attention, his weight resting on his fists. He nodded. "When they reach this point, they'll be east of Fraoch Eileen. If these three forces merge into a wall that blocks the MacDougalls and Lamonts' retreat, they can press them to the river just south of the dam. If the Lord and the saints see it fit, the MacArthurs and MacGregors are already in the drink, or they'll launch their attack when they see the MacDougalls and Lamonts approach. The men here at Kilchurn join ranks with the Campbells to squeeze the MacDougalls and Lamonts into the river. If they attempt to stand their ground in hopes the other two clans will cross and join them, it will still leave them on their own. Block any path for them to escape. They wind up in the water, drowned or floating into the bay and at our doorsteps."

Laurel stood upright and looked at each man. All five of them continued to stare at the map. Slowly, one by one, they nodded their head. Laurel knew they were picturing for themselves the strategy she envisioned. She wouldn't rush them. When they finally all looked at her, she crossed her arms.

"There is one last thing you must consider." Laurel looked at Brodie, then Monty, and finally Andrew Mòr, the leaders of the three clans and the men who would bear the fall out. And she was certain it would happen. "As Brodie said before, this is no longer a feud. This is a war. This plan doesn't leave room to allow them to retreat. Its intention is to kill as many as we can."

Laurel looked Brodie in the eye. She drew in a breath before she continued, knowing she trod a fine line.

"Our clan has wronged the MacGregors since the Bruce granted you most of Glenorchy. They have nearly no land left.

Their clan shrinks each year. Depending on the force they send, this could destroy them. We must all prepare for this to be named a massacre. They may attack our home—" Laurel looked at Brodie once again, then to Monty and the Andrews. "—and your allies, but there will be no confusion aboot who the victors are. Are you prepared to be painted the villain for generations? Are you ready for people to say you led a massacre over a woman—two women?"

The somber group grew more sober as the men mulled over Laurel's predictions. Each man standing around the table knew two things: Laurel's strategy was the best, and she was right that they would shoulder the blame for what would be a massacre. Brodie looked at the MacFarlane first.

"Mòr, you've been our ally for a long time. We've fought together many times, but this isn't your fight for any other reason than our alliance. Are you willing to place your clan in jeopardy of King Robert's ire?"

"I am," the MacFarlane answered. "If they have the bollocks to take on the Campbells and think they stand a chance, then they will not think twice to overrun us. It ends before it starts."

"Ross?" Brodie asked.

"This cements our alliance."

"An alliance your father, the laird, hasn't confirmed," Brodie pointed out.

"If my father wasn't prepared to form a new alliance, he wouldn't have sent me to court to see my sister married. He knew it would be to someone. He couldn't ask for a better choice."

Brodie looked at Laurel and asked, "Are you prepared to weather this storm? I don't doubt that you're right. However, this may be more than the king can overlook."

"There will be consequences, but the king is no fool. He knew what he encouraged when he sanctioned our marriage. Besides the Gordons, there are no other powerful clans in the Highlands who aren't linked to us by marriage. He won't stand against you. He knows the Sutherlands and Sinclairs' loyalty is unwavering. But he also knows he won't live forever. He'll think aboot what he leaves behind for Prince David. Does he want the Highlands fractured again? Does he want his son to inherit a country where the most powerful clans turn their backs once he's dead? Nay. It's not the Bruce I worry aboot. It's everyone else. The Campbells have a long list of allies and just as long a list of rivals. Are you prepared to lose some of your allies and antagonize every rival?"

"We didn't become what we are by luck or happenstance," Brodie pointed out. He locked eyes with Laurel. "These four clans threaten our people, our home, our way of life. If I show any mercy, they will believe they can continue. This ends here and now. Whether people like it or not, the Campbells are Glenorchy, Glencoe, and Lorne. This is our land to defend. I am the mon tasked to lead. This isn't just aboot men attacking my wife. This is aboot my clan's future, one I intend to solidify as the most dominant clan for generations to come. What think you, Laurel?"

"You know I stand by you. I wouldn't have suggested this if I didn't think it was for the best, but each of you must decide what is best for your clan." Laurel looked at Monty. "Father will not be pleased. You and I both know that. There is no dancing around that point. But as you said, it cements our alliance and for at least two generations to come. Father would rather be friends than enemies with the Campbells." Laurel's lips twisted before she smirked. "He lends but a handful of men and can claim he was among the victorious. Sounds perfect for him."

"Everything you say is true. But understand this, Laurel: I accept Brodie's position because he's right. For him, this isn't aboot his wife. It's aboot your clan. But for me, for the Rosses, this is entirely aboot defending you. You carry the Campbell name now, but you are a Ross by blood. I will not turn my back on you—not ever again, little sister."

Laurel nodded. She didn't look away from Monty,

unwilling to let the MacFarlanes see how Monty's words moved her. Finally, Monty broke their gaze and looked at the two lairds. Laurel looked past him at Donnan, approval and pride in his eyes. She smiled, the reassurance worth more than she realized.

"We follow Lady Campbell's plan," Brodie announced. "I will send messengers by water now. They'll travel faster and be less obvious. I'll set my patrols to watch for either clan from the south, and Graham has gone to get reports from those along the river. This is Scotland, yet it hasn't rained in days. Pray for it tonight. It'll be miserable fighting in the mud, but it will make the river swell and surge."

The Andrews shook hands with Brodie, then Monty. The MacFarlanes left Brodie's solar, but Monty and Donnan lingered. Laurel stepped around the table to stand in front of Monty. "I wouldn't wish to repeat any of this. I wish I could return the men we've lost to their families. But I have my brother back. I am a Ross. I have been my entire life, and what name I bear now and what clan I live among can't change that. My loyalty is first and foremost to my husband and my new clan. But I no longer wish to sever my ties to my family or the clan of my birth."

"I no longer wish to let you do it. No matter what comes of tomorrow, you can come to Balnagown. I will stand before you and against Father if I must. You've earned the respect and that duty from me."

"I like it much better when we are like this than pissing vinegar," Laurel mused.

"Aye. It's a damn sight better to be on your side than your target. God bless, but you're terrifying. You may not wield a sword, but you're ruthless. I'm glad the others listened to you." Monty embraced Laurel before Donnan did the same. The couple left the newlyweds alone in Brodie's solar.

"What do you expect will happen?" Laurel asked as she leaned against Brodie while she sat in his lap before the fire. They sipped whisky from their cups.

"I expect a battle. I hope it goes as you planned. Your strategy keeps the fight from our people, but I will summon the villagers into the walls at dawn."

"Will you meet with Dominic this evening?"

Brodie shook his head and sighed. "I doubt it. It surprises me that he didn't join us at all this eve."

"It's clear they love one another."

"Aye, but he understands his duties as tánaiste. And Colina didn't appear any different than she usually does."

"Perhaps it's an ailment we can't see." Laurel cocked an eyebrow and gave Brodie a pointed look.

"Mayhap, but I'm still disappointed."

"I understand that." Laurel ran her fingers through Brodie's hair as his hand stroked her hip. It felt natural to sit before the fire with Brodie and discuss clan matters. "Once he's spoken to you, will he let Colina ken what's happening? Will she prepare the keep?"

Brodie snorted. "Not likely. Colina hasn't taken an interest in running the keep. I always assumed she figured I would marry, and my wife would assume the position. But it's been three years."

"Then I need to speak with Aggie and Berta before it grows too late. I need to be sure we have enough blankets for everyone in case this becomes a protracted fight. I have no idea what the stores are, so I need Berta to tell me how long we can survive if somehow they besiege us. Is it possible for me to meet Nora in the morn? I'd like to ken what medicinals she has on hand and if there is aught she needs foraged close to the keep. I need to ask what she expects me to do."

"She doesn't expect aught from you, Laurie. It's the other way around."

"Any other day, you're right. But once the wounded men pour in, Nora is in charge. I need to learn how I can help her and serve our clan."

"Neither of us shall seek our bed soon. I need to meet with Graham. He needs to know our battle plan and to know I've sent men along Loch Awe. He and I need to assign men to their stations. I might even rally Dominic." Brodie kissed Laurel's temple, and she sighed. "I'm so impressed with you. I wouldn't have accepted Andrew's plan, but neither am I sure I would have come up with yours. I wouldn't have thought to show it as you did. I love you more with each passing day."

"My home is where you are. I realized that the other night. It's not just the Highlands or this keep. It's you and the life we're already building together. But I couldn't be the woman I am right this moment if you hadn't taken me away from court. You've given me opportunity and purpose when you barely knew me. You risked a lot courting and marrying me." Laurel grinned and tickled Brodie's ribs, lightening the mood for a moment. "That makes you the bravest mon I ken."

"And the wisest."

"Aye, and the wisest. Wisdom comes with age, auld mon. We best be aboot our duties. I don't like admitting it, but we both need to sleep tonight."

"I ken. I dinna have to like it, lass." Brodie waggled his eyebrows at her, reminding her of Andrew's error. With a quick kiss, they parted ways. It relieved Laurel to find Aggie before the woman retired. They had a rapid conversation before the older woman set off to rouse some maids to help her. Laurel found Berta, who scrambled to show Laurel as many of the supplies as she could in the kitchens. Laurel would have to wait until morning to see the undercroft and storage buildings in the bailey. Two hours later, Laurel and Brodie fell into bed exhausted, but in one another's embrace.

THIRTY-FOUR

Dawn cruelly arrived far too soon for Laurel or Brodie. Laurel sat up in bed as she watched Brodie cross the chamber naked and bend over to stoke the fire. She would have been content with that view for the rest of the day. But once the chamber warmed, she slipped out of bed and padded to a chest that held her meager belongings. She and Ina packed everything in her chamber, but Brodie hadn't the horses to carry them. They were to be sent by wagon in a moon. The wrinkled kirtles and chemises she had stuffed in her satchel barely appeared presentable, but they were an improvement on the gown she'd worn for days or the breeks she arrived in. She hadn't considered her appearance when Brodie introduced her to the clan, but she'd groaned when she donned a gown for the evening meal. She'd wondered if that contributed to her brusque welcome from Dominic and Colina. But she cared little for her looks or sense of style when the more pressing issue was helping to keep as many people alive as she could.

Brodie pulled the laces tight on Laurel's gown. Wishing he could offer her the clothes she had to leave behind, especially the gown made from the fabric he gifted her. But he reminded himself that there would be time for that later. Laurel hadn't

301

indicated once since they left court that she cared a wit about her clothes or hair. He looked forward to spoiling his bride. He knew she would never ask, nor would she ever expect his generosity, which made lavishing her with it more appealing.

Once Laurel was dressed, she brushed her hair while Brodie pleated his plaid and donned a fresh leine. She giggled when she thought about the one she'd chopped down.

"I expect you to replace that," Brodie said jovially as he shook a finger at her. He finished dressing and went to a chest Laurel hadn't noticed. He opened it and lifted a gambeson from it. It surprised Laurel to see he had the padded doublet. Most Highlanders avoided them, arguing that it restricted their movement. Brodie brought it to the bed and laid it out, assessing it.

"Brodie?" Laurel came to stand beside him.

"I'm trying to decide whether I wear it."

"Do you usually?" Laurel sounded doubtful.

"Nay. Never."

"Then why would you today? Won't it be awkward and uncomfortable?"

"Aye. But I didn't use to have the same motivation that I do today." Brodie looked at Laurel. "This battle, this war is for our people. But when I swing my sword today, it is so I can come home to you."

Laurel swallowed. "I know this will help protect you against slashes, but it can't stop a sword from going through you. There's no mail in it. If it's awkward, if it could keep you from fighting your best, then don't wear it. I ken the danger of you not, but I fear the danger of you not being able to defend yourself is far greater."

"That is what I'm considering." Brodie stared at the protective doublet before he shook his head and returned it to his chest.

"Mayhap I could make you a sleeveless cotun instead," Laurel suggested. A cotun and a gambeson were similar and served the same purpose. But Laurel could make it from leather rather than cloth. The leather would be harder to slice through, so Brodie wouldn't require as much padding. If it weren't so bulky, and his arms were free, he could fight more naturally.

"You ken how?"

"Nay." Laurel grinned and shrugged. "But it's sewing. I can figure it out. Tell me where the padding goes, and I'll stitch it. The tanner is bound to have leather I can use."

"You're a good wife, Laurie. I didn't think I needed taking of, but mayhap I do." Brodie winked and squeezed her bottom.

"None of that, or you'll be late to your war." Laurel attempted to keep their conversation lighthearted, but they grew serious as they approached their chamber door. "I ken you can't promise me, so I won't ask. Just try. I love you, bear."

"I will do everything in my power to return to you, thistle. I love you."

What their kiss lacked in passion, they made up for in tenderness. Hope and devotion poured forth. They walked belowstairs hand-in-hand. They knew there would likely be hours before the first wave of attackers arrived, but they both had plenty of duties to tend. Laurel watched as the first groups of villagers arrived. She smiled and greeted them, offering them a chance to break their fast in the Great Hall. When she could hand that duty off, she found Berta and went on a brief tour of the storage buildings. She was impressed and relieved to see they were overflowing. If forced to, they could survive months.

Laurel had looked for Colina as she broke her fast, but the woman was nowhere in sight and didn't appear throughout the early morning. She noticed Dominic joined Brodie as her husband left the Great Hall for the bailey. She supposed Brodie was informing Dominic of their strategy. Laurel wondered if Brodie would mention she'd devised it. She sensed Dominic would be less accepting than the MacFarlane had been. With Colina not volunteering, she bustled around the keep and bailey, rattling off a mental checklist, pleased that everyone helped. Everyone but one. There was one wrinkle in the otherwise smooth operation. Gara.

The woman stared at Laurel, even when Laurel offered a pleasant smile. She refused to make it sugary when she'd made her displeasure clear the day before. But she wished to move on. Gara wasn't of the same opinion. More than once, Laurel discreetly asked Aggie to set Gara back to work. After the fifth time, Laurel finally asked the burning question that plagued her.

"Aggie, is Gara the laird's leman?"

"What, ma lady? Good God, nay. She might wish it, but the laird's never done more than smile a few times. He's practically a monk. And when he does—pardon me, did—seek—ah—well anyway," Aggie grew flustered, but Laurel wanted the answer. "He never sought it with the women in the keep. He never intended to take a mistress, so he never played favorites."

A monk? I suppose two years wouldnae be such a sacrifice if he didna that often. But he does now. All the time. Nae that I'm complaining. Mayhap making up for lost time?

Laurel knew she would gain no answers from thinking about it, so she pushed it to the back of her mind. But she kept an eye on Gara. The woman made her uneasy.

Brodie ran along the battlements to meet the scouts, who galloped back to the keep. He met Graham and Dominic in the bailey. He spotted Laurel and called her over. It would save him searching for her and relaying the story. Breathless, the scouts warned that the MacDougalls and Lamonts united and were half a mile from the point where the combined forces would attack. Laurel and Brodie exchanged a look before Brodie called for his men to mount the horses that stomped and shifted restlessly. He watched as the men settled on their horses before he kissed Laurel one last time. Her stoicism would give their clan strength, but he knew it came at a cost. He looked back once before he led the men through the gates.

Conserving their horses' stamina, the Campbells, Rosses, and MacFarlanes rode toward the planned meeting place. Brodie, Monty, and Andrew Mòr drew forward from the line of warriors at their backs. Brodie watched as Martin MacDougall rode forward. James Lamont reined in beside Martin and glowered at Brodie, who observed them. Neither man seemed any the wiser that there was an army at their backs, nor did they appear curious about the angle at which the Campbells and their allies sat.

"Did you find your father?" Brodie called out to James, now Laird Lamont. The rage that swept over the new laird's face told Brodie they had. "My wife and her horse send their regards." Brodie was certain James had already heard the tale, but he twisted the knife another notch as he spoke loud enough for everyone to hear that an unarmed woman and her mount felled the great David Lamont.

"You smug bastard," James called out.

"Smug, yes. Bastard—well between the two of us, we all ken which one of us is certain aboot both his parents. Tell me, could you ken it was your—*laird* because his body was the only unaccounted for mon? It certainly wasn't from his good looks."

"If only you swung your sword as well as you talk," Martin cut in. The men behind Brodie laughed. Brodie earned his reputation fighting alongside Robert the Bruce as he battled for his throne. While he didn't have the moniker his father did —the Black Campbell—he was certain he caused many a man's nightmares.

"My swords—both of them—swing just fine. In fact, I'd like to hurry and swing this one, so I can return to my bonnie bride and swing the other one." Brodie knew Laurel would have his bollocks if she heard him speak about her like that.

But he also knew the preamble to most battles was a cockerel fight, and he intended to be the victor of that before the battle began in earnest. It had the power to set the tone for the entire encounter.

"They're here," Monty muttered, just loud enough for Brodie to hear. "Center left."

Brodie swept his eyes over the opposing forces, who gathered more tightly as they waited. It was just what Brodie wished for as he stalled by tossing insults at the Lamonts and their lapdogs, the MacDougalls. Brodie spotted Matthew and Nelson.

"Edgar?" Brodie said under his breath, his lips not moving.

"Nay," Monty replied.

"Clyth." Brodie hoped the man had gone home and cut ties with the MacDougalls. If he hadn't, the war would shift to the northern Highlands. The Gunns would be the first clan to face the full force of the strongest pact across the country. And they had nowhere to run unless they wished to fall into the North Sea or cross onto Mackay, Sutherland, or Sinclair land. He scanned the opposing forces, but he didn't spy Liam Oliphant either.

"Where is that new bride of yours?" Martin sneered.

"Tucked away, waiting to scrub my back and minster to whatever aches." Brodie's wolfish grin spoke to which aches he meant. None that came from fighting. He noticed Danny eased into the formation, signaling that the sept forces were in place. It was what he waited for. With a piercing whistle, the battle commenced.

Taken off guard, James and Martin bellowed out commands, yelling over one another. The Lamonts led the opposing force, so they hadn't discovered the horde of warriors approaching from the rear. But as screams rang out, Martin and James looked behind them. Martin swung back to look at Brodie. He'd set his first target. But Martin had no chance to act before his men surged forward, both attempting to flee the army behind them and to engage the one in front of them. Brodie whistled once more, and the formation shifted. It opened to allow the Lamonts to surge past them. Brodie and the men from Kilchurn joined the fight as the Campbell, MacFarlane, and Ross ranks squeezed the herd of attackers like they were shepherds corralling sheep. The MacDougalls and Lamonts followed one another, just like the animals did. The fighting was vicious as Brodie and his counterparts worked to keep the Lamonts and MacDougalls from breaking free. But the Lamonts and MacDougalls stood little chance, outnumbered at least two to one. Pushed toward the river, the riders in front tried to retreat, but there was no place to move. Over the cacophony of clanging metal, war whoops, and screams of pain, those not closest to the river didn't witness the first tidal wave surge down river.

Brodie watched for Matthew and Nelson. He and Monty already agreed Nelson was Brodie's target, leaving Matthew to Monty. Brodie waited until Nelson rode past where he fought. He ran the man through who'd engaged him before he spurred his horse after Nelson. He would end it without delay, or he would wind up in the crush and unable to extract himself before being driven into the river.

Sensing him, Nelson turned to look at Brodie, shocked to find him so close. Brodie raised his sword, and with no preface, swung. "For my wife," Brodie called out before cleaving Nelson's head from his shoulders. Brodie watched the skull bounce before hooves kicked it. He supposed the retribution was for either wife, even if he'd intended it for Laurel.

"For my sister!" Monty howled as he stood in his stirrups and barreled toward Matthew. The force that came with the speed from his horse made Monty's sword spear Matthew clean threw. Monty twisted the blade before yanking it out. He spat at the dead man as he fell from his horse. With Donnan at Monty's back and Graham at his, Brodie led them out of the fray as the Lamonts arrived at the riverbank. The momentum of their charge carried one man after another over the berm. There was little the defenders had to do but watch.

"Waste of bluidy good horseflesh," Donnan quipped with feigned regret.

The first wave of battle was brief but intense. Brodie looked down at his side to find blood soaking through his leine. He'd barely felt the wound but realized it was more than a nick. It would have to wait until he was certain that any enemy who survived and came ashore wasn't long for the living. He discovered more opponents than he would have liked ended up in the bay alive. But his archers picked them off, firing from the shore and the battlements. They cut down the handful who climbed the banks as they stood up. Used to daylong campaigns, Brodie found it unnerving to secure his victory in a matter of hours. He rode the battlefield as his men searched for survivors, both friend and foe. They helped the wounded to the keep and gathered the bodies for those who would mourn. When none of his men or his comrades remained, he looked at the destruction left in their wake.

Laurel hadn't been wrong to name it a massacre. But no regret tugged at him. No doubt niggled at the back of his mind. He knew he would ride into his bailey to find his wife, sure that she and his people were safe for yet another night. He'd done his duty as best he could, and he would never regret serving his clan.

THIRTY-FIVE

Laurel's patience expired. While she and the staff rushed to feed the villagers, find places for them to sit and sleep, and shuttled food out to the men, Colina remained absent. Laurel eventually ceased asking Aggie to tell Gara to work. The woman found excuses to stand in Laurel's way or force Laurel to go in a different direction. After the fourth time, Laurel called the woman's bluff, and Gara came out the loser. Instead of taking a detour, Laurel barreled past Gara, knocking the maid onto her backside. Rather than help Gara up, Laurel glared at the woman.

"Be glad I only carried blankets. You wouldn't have been so fortunate if I carried something scalding. You move for me, not the other way around." Laurel tried to keep the peace, but she wouldn't let Gara or any servant believe Laurel demurred to them. She didn't wait to see if Gara stood. She already knew the hateful things the woman likely thought about her, but Laurel didn't have the time to care. Between Colina not assisting as a member of the laird's family should, and Gara being awkward, Laurel would accept no more nonsense.

Laurel heard a piercing whistle, the whinny of several horses, then the clash of steel on steel. She didn't hesitate to make her way across the bailey and up to the battlements. The

Lamonts and MacDougalls weren't attacking the keep, instead meeting Brodie's forces head-to-head. Laurel didn't fear arrows flying toward her like she would had it been an attack on the castle. She ran along the battlements until she could see Brodie atop his horse. She watched with morbid fascination as he swept one man after another off their mount, their corpse left in his wake. The last time Brodie fought was the only time she'd seen Brodie fight, and she'd been more focused on defeating David Lamont.

Laurel watched in awe as Brodie wielded his claymore with one hand when he had to steer Lann and defend himself. Other times, he swung his sword with the power that came from both arms while Lann moved with commands from Brodie's legs. She'd been proud of Teine's fearlessness, but she knew her horse wasn't trained to do nearly half of what Lann did. He and Brodie were a single entity, relying on one another but fighting as one. Brodie had aptly named his steed Blade.

When the battle shifted toward the river, and Laurel could no longer spy Brodie, she descended the steps and moved throughout the bailey, checking on people. She watched as the fletcher scooped a massive load of arrows into his arms and sprinted to the battlements. Maids dashed to storerooms, gathering more sacks of grains for Berta to bake countless more loaves of bread. The villagers wouldn't be able to return to their homes until at least the next day. The carnage from the battle had to be cleared away before it would be safe for anyone to return. She visited the herders, who brought cows, sheep, and goats to a crowded corral since they couldn't risk leaving the livestock in the pastures. The danger that their enemy would reive some heads of cattle or kill them meant the animals came within the castle walls along with the people.

Once her tour satisfied Laurel that everyone was well taken care of, she made her way toward the undercroft. She hadn't checked their stores as closely as she wanted that morning. With no imminent threat to the keep or the people within, Laurel kept herself distracted by remaining busy. She shivered at the dampness in the space hollowed out beneath the keep. She prayed Berta stored their dried goods in the undercroft like she did in the kitchens and storage buildings, or the dampness would ruin everything. Sunlight poured through archways that would allow workers to bring large quantities of sacks and barrels into the undercroft and keep them there until the laborers could place them in the correct storeroom. Taking the ring of chatelaine keys Aggie gave her that morning from her girdle, Laurel tried various ones until she unlocked the first portion of the cavernous cellar.

Light filtered along the corridor, but Laurel was glad to have a torch. She let herself into a smaller storeroom and pried the lid off a barrel. It was filled with grains. She looked closer, scooping a handful and letting it sift between her fingers before doing it again, pushing her arm deeper with each pass. She nodded to herself when she didn't discover any weevils. She'd placed the torch into a sconce, so she could use both arms and all her body weight to press the lid back into place and seal it. Satisfied with other barrels in the storeroom, she locked the door behind her and moved on to the next room. She discovered it was the buttery.

The storeroom smelled of grain and yeast. The first barrel she pressed against gurgled with ale that the laird's family provided their servants and warriors. Laurel looked around, counting the dozens of barrels. She'd sampled some the night before, and it impressed her. She'd asked Brodie to introduce her to the brewer at another time. Shelves built against the walls held miniature casks of wine. The smaller casks were used to make it easier for maids to bring wine into the keep without asking for someone stronger to carry a large barrel.

Laurel sniffed at a few and recoiled each time. They smelled more like vinegar that wine. She doubted the vintner intended to store wine and vinegar together. The drink had gone off. She hadn't been nearly as taken with the wine at the evening meal as she had been with the ale. Brodie sensed her evasiveness when he asked what she thought of the wine. When she'd relented and admitted it disappointed her, he'd confessed to sharing her feelings. He promised they would speak to the wine maker together.

Laurel descended a flight of stairs and shivered once more, this time from the cold air. She suspected the only door on that subterranean level was the larder. Berta told her there were several shanks of preserved beef hanging in the storeroom, but Laurel wanted to see their size to better understand how much meat they had stored for the winter months. She needed to visualize what they would cook and what would need to dry for the guardsmen to eat when they were away from the keep. As she entered the final storeroom, she pulled her arisaid tighter around her shoulders and placed the torch in a sconce. She wished she had a second plaid. The keep's builders perfectly positioned the larder to remain cold throughout the year to preserve the meat, but it was unpleasant to visit.

Laurel walked among the hanging flanks of beef and sheep, noticing the meat was lean. She felt a burgeoning sense of pride for her new clan as she kept a mental inventory of all she'd seen. There were abundant supplies, and the quality of everything—except for the wine—was superior. The Campbells hadn't grown powerful by muscle alone. Their leaders ensured their people thrived by keeping them fed well. She hoped Brodie would show her the pasturelands soon. She hadn't paid close attention to the animals herded into the bailey, and she had paid no attention to the sheep in the glens of Ben Lui, more focused on remaining alive.

Just as Laurel reached the back wall of the spacious larder, the door she'd purposely left open slammed shut. She hadn't felt a wind that would push closed the portal that opened into the larder. It would have only shut if someone pulled it closed. With a torch in the sconce, it was clear someone was inside. Laurel hurried to the door and pulled on the handle, already suspecting what she would find. It was locked.

"Bluidy bitch," Laurel muttered. She was nearly positive Gara meant to punish her. Laurel recognized the jealousy Gara showed, but she didn't understand the possessiveness if she'd never had a relationship with Brodie. As Laurel drew the yards of wool tighter around her shoulders, she wondered if Brodie chose not to tell her the truth. She considered what Aggie told her, but the housekeeper would be loyal to Brodie before she would be loyal to Laurel. Perhaps she kept Brodie's secret. If Brodie had lied, Laurel wondered if that meant he'd lied about his plans to remain faithful. She held no interest in learning about Brodie's past, but it scared her that Brodie might not value fidelity as much as he said.

With no windows to look through or climb through, Laurel sank along the wall beside the door until her bottom rested on the freezing stone floor. Gara, or whoever locked her in, wouldn't answer if she banged on the door. With a huff, she resigned herself to waiting for hours before anyone would think to look for her. She had told no one that she was going to the undercroft, so they wouldn't know to look there. She was certain it wouldn't be until Brodie, Monty, and Donnan returned that anyone would notice she was missing. They would be concerned enough to search for her. But until then, she could only draw her legs close to her chest and huddle to remain warm.

A freezing larder to match a freezing reception.

Brodie rode into the bailey with Monty, Donnan, and Graham. He was exhausted but livid. His brother rode out with the other men, and Brodie spotted him a few times throughout the battle. However, he could find Dominic nowhere once the battle shifted to the river, and his archers launched their attack. He hadn't been there to see the few survivors leave the river only to be sent to their maker. He hadn't been searching among the bodies like the rest of his men. Growing scared, Brodie gave the order to search specifically for Dominic. Fear washed over him and guilt that he hadn't protected his younger brother threatened to choke him. They'd always found one another at the end of a fight, battered and the worse for wear, but together. Not a moment after he put out the cry, one of his men said he'd witnessed Dominic ride back to the keep. Brodie blinked at the man, even more fearful that his brother was hurt if he returned home. But when his warrior informed Brodie that there was nothing wrong with Dominic, Brodie nearly exploded.

Duty demanded Brodie remain with his men, despite wanting to kiss Laurel and murder Dominic. He was relieved when he passed beneath the portcullis. He looked around as women and children gathered, searching for their husbands, sons, fathers, and brothers. He'd expected Laurel to rush out and greet him. But she was nowhere to be seen either. While anger manifested as he thought about Dominic returning to the keep, panic edged at the corners of his mind. Laurel wouldn't miss their return. If it weren't to see to him, it would be to find Monty and Donnan, or to see how she could help. He'd caught sight of her hair on the battlements twice when the battle began, but he had to pay more attention to who he fought if he wanted to remain alive.

Brodie leapt from his horse and charged toward Dominic, who stepped out of the keep with Colina. He ran up the steps and grabbed Dominic's leine. He demanded, "Where's Laurel?"

"I don't know where you wife is," Dominic said as he tried to push Brodie away.

"You've been here for hours. Laurel wouldn't avoid being here when the men returned. She kens her duties. Where is she?"

"Where's Laurel?" Monty asked as he joined the two brothers. He looked between the men, his eyes narrowing at

Dominic. He felt uneasy around the man. Then he noticed Brodie was trembling with rage. Monty gritted his teeth and hissed, "Where's my sister?"

"The hell I should know. She wandered off hours ago. No one's seen her. Probably taking a nap," Dominic snapped.

"Don't confuse my wife for yours. Mine isn't lazy," Brodie barked before he turned his ire on Colina. "Have you done a single bluidy thing today or left my wife to run herself ragged? Where is she? Have you left your chamber long enough to notice?"

As he fired one question after another at Colina, he realized he'd harbored more anger and resentment toward the woman than he imagined. Her ambivalence to her clan, and now her blasé attitude when Brodie asked about Laurel, made him want to rip her apart. He supposed bloodlust still pounded through him, but he'd only felt exhausted and calm when he rode in.

"Leave my wife alone, Brodie. Speak to yours however you wish." Dominic stepped in front of Colina.

"Aye. Be the doting husband. Protect her from everything. Don't even let her speak for herself. It might be too taxing." Brodie opened his mouth to say more, but he caught sight of Aggie running toward him.

"Ma laird! Ma laird!" Aggie waved to him as she beckoned him to her. "I canna find Lady Campbell. It's been hours since I've seen her."

Brodie's heart pounded. Had someone sneaked in and taken Laurel? Had she been injured somewhere while watching the battle? Did she fall ill? Questions buzzed in Brodie's mind as he looked at Monty and Donnan. He shook his head.

"She wouldn't rest," Monty stated.

"She wouldn't be able to," Donnan added. "She'd have to keep herself busy."

"Where was she last seen?" Brodie tried to calm his voice as he spoke to Aggie, who was visibly distressed. Aggie had been a second mother to him and Dominic, even before their own mother died.

"Here in the bailey, ma laird. People saw her checking the storage buildings and visiting the shepherds by the corral. A few noticed she'd gone up to the battlements when the battle started, but that was before she worked her way around the bailey."

"Could she have gone into the village?" Monty asked.

"I dinna think so," Aggie replied as she shook her head. "I asked the guards at the gate, but none saw her."

"She'd likely cover her head with her arisaid to make her hair less visible to the Lamonts and MacDougalls. She might have gone to make sure no one lingered there," Brodie reasoned. He spun on his heel, wincing at the pain in his side. Now that the fight was won, and the fatigue set in, he noticed the pain. He was certain he needed stitches, but he needed to find his wife more. He'd looked earlier, and the bleeding had stopped. It could wait until he knew Laurel was safe.

He passed Graham as he moved toward the gate. "Can't find Lady Campbell," was all he said before his second fell into step. Brodie didn't have to look back to know his brother wasn't with him. But Monty and Donnan were. They fanned out as they reached the village, having walked since it lay just beyond the barmekin. He didn't have to issue any instructions, the others knowing what to do without asking. Brodie knocked on doors. He was grateful no one answered, assured that the residents were at the keep. But it frustrated him that he didn't find Laurel. It took the men an hour to work their way through the village and to no avail. The four men wore matching fearful expressions as they returned to the keep.

When a blonde woman walked toward the well in the center of the bailey, a thought permeated the others churning and whirling through Brodie's mind. "Where's Gara?"

Brodie spoke to any and everyone. The woman had shot daggers from her eyes at Laurel throughout the morning meal. She'd bumped into Laurel's chair several times the night before. He didn't understand the woman's hostility since he'd done nothing more than tease her a few times. There was no relationship beyond laird and servant. He looked around, but the woman didn't appear. Furious and frightened, Brodie stormed into the Great Hall.

"Gara!" Brodie bellowed, and he was certain the rafters shook. He waited, but she still didn't appear. "Gara!"

"Ma laird, nay one's seen her either," Berta said, wiping her hands on a linen towel as she rushed from the kitchens.

"Search every chamber and the attic," Brodie commanded.

"We already did, ma laird," Aggie said.

"Do it again. Lady Campbell is the priority. If you find Gara, bring her to the Great Hall and don't let her move." Brodie didn't look to see where Monty and Donnan went. He suspected out to search the bailey. Graham helped give orders alongside Aggie and Berta. Brodie took the stairs to their chamber two and three at a time. He burst into the room and went to Laurel's satchel. The same clothes she arrived with were still there. The only things missing were the clothes and boots he'd seen her don that morning. He rushed to his solar, but nothing looked out of place. The map remained on the table with the objects positioned how Laurel left them. He crossed the room and pulled the drawers to his desk open, riffling through papers, but nothing was amiss.

Brodie left his solar and ran through the Great Hall to the main doors. He sprinted across the bailey to the postern gate. Before he could ask, the guard assured him that he hadn't seen Laurel except for when she was near his section of the wall and met with the shepherds. Brodie called up to the men on the battlements, but none saw anything.

"Laird!"

Brodie spun around and spotted James, a guard he'd planned to assign to Laurel's personal detail. "Lady Campbell?"

"Nay, but ye need to see something."

"It waits until I find Lady Campbell."

"This canna wait, Laird."

Brodie looked at James's expression before he nodded. The man was shaken. He'd known James their entire lives. The guard was a year older than Brodie. A reason he wanted James to help protect Laurel was because it was nearly impossible to rattle the man. Brodie grabbed James's shoulder as the guard spun around.

"Tell me now. Is it my wife?" Brodie whispered.

"Nay, Laird. But it's vera bad." James led Brodie toward the back of a storage building. Brodie squinted at a shape on the ground in the shadows. As he drew closer, he noticed blonde hair. His stomach sank, suspecting who he would see. But he was unprepared for what he found. He glanced at James, who shook his head. Brodie squatted beside Gara's dead body. Whoever killed her had been vicious. Someone had stabbed her twice in the throat and several times in the belly.

"Get Ross and Graham," Brodie ordered. He rolled Gara's body onto its side, looking for any wounds to her back. But he found none. He rose when Monty, Graham, and Donnan joined him.

"What the bluidy hell?" Donnan hissed.

"I don't ken." Brodie looked at the men and shook his head before he squatted again. "This one on her throat killed her. It hit her jugular. It would have geysered blood, so why continue stabbing her? Or why not stab her there first?"

Donnan squeezed past Monty and Graham to kneel on one knee across from Brodie. He glanced around before he pulled the dead woman's blouse up to her neck. "Look at how shallow these are. One of two things happened. Whoever killed her wanted to torture her before killing her, or they killed her but were furious enough to keep going even as she lay dying."

Brodie nodded. He picked up each of Gara's hands and

looked at her fingers, turning them over. "No blood or hair. No more dirt than you'd expect. She didn't fight back."

"She knew whoever led her back here. She trusted them," Monty mused. "Does she have a lover? Why else would she be back here during the day?"

"I don't ken." Brodie shrugged. Beyond her being a servant in the keep, he didn't know the specifics of Gara's personal life. He knew a couple men showed an interest in her, but he didn't think she was involved with anyone.

"I'm thinking aboot what Donnan said. Other than the lethal strike, the other stabs are shallow. Would a mon do that? Wouldn't you expect them to be deeper?" Graham asked. He pulled a dirk from his boot and one from his waist. "And look at the size of the holes. A mon's blade isn't that narrow. Even a *sgian dubh* would create a wider cut. These look like they came from an eating knife."

"You think it was a woman," Brodie said to Graham, who nodded. "But why would a woman lead her back here? Or rather, what could a woman say to lead her back here? A mon I could understand. He could lure her back here for a tryst or force her."

Donnan pushed up Gara's sleeves, twisting her arms side to side, but there were no marks to show someone pulling her. Graham shifted uncomfortably, and it caught Brodie's attention. He narrowed his eyes at his second.

"Speak."

"Laird, we assume it's someone she trusted. What if it was someone who ordered her?"

Brodie rose in one fluid motion as he turned to look at Graham, a man he trusted with his life. A man, who just that day he thought he could trust more than his brother, now stood before him, implying Laurel killed the woman at his feet. Graham took a step back, unnerved by an expression he'd never seen on Brodie's face before.

"Laird, there's more than one woman with that authority," Graham rushed to say. Brodie's expression didn't change.

"It's not Laurel," Monty stated matter-of-factly. "I saw Gara's rudeness to Laurel last night, so I asked her aboot it when you stepped off the dais this morn to speak to Dominic. She told me what happened yesterday over the bath. She may have been unimpressed by Gara, or even disliked her, but she wouldn't kill over such a slight. If she would, there wouldn't be a lady-in-waiting still alive. And aye, I ken, she's never had a mon she'd fight for, but that isnae Laurel. She'd tear the woman apart with her words and leave her a shell of her old self, devastated for days. That is how Laurel punishes."

"And she wouldn't have used an eating knife," Donnan chimed in as he rose. With a shrug, he explained. "After what happened with the wager and being left among strangers today, I didn't like kenning she only had her eating knife. I left her with a dirk this morning. Monty and I ken she knows how to use it. We taught her."

"True. And she would have gone for a clean, swift kill like we showed her. She would have gotten this right with the first strike and not waited around to do more. This isn't Laurel," Monty repeated.

"Then who?" James chimed in. He'd remained still and silent while the other men spoke.

"Who's left in a position to order her to do aught? Aggie, Berta, and Colina," Brodie answered.

"None of them would do this," Graham stated. Brodie's eyebrows twitched, and he sighed before nodding.

"Graham, James, tend to Gara. Don't let anyone ken aboot this until we find Lady Campbell. I don't think these are unrelated." Brodie fought against the returning panic. If Gara's death and Laurel's absence were connected—and Gara was dead—he feared how he would find Laurel. He, Monty, and Donnan left Graham and James to move Gara's body and cover it. He scanned the bailey as he tried to imagine where Laurel could be. He spotted Aggie speaking with the laundresses, clearly still agitated. He called out, "Aggie."

320

The woman met him halfway. She still trembled and appeared distraught. But she greeted him with a steady voice. "Did you give Lady Campbell the chatelaine's keys?"

"Aye, ma laird. Berta gave her a wee tour of the undercroft, then she came to me and asked for them. She wanted to look in the barrels and crates in the storage buildings."

"The undercroft? How brief was the tour?" Brodie asked.

"I dinna ken. Nae long. I think Berta only took her down and pointed out the doors and what we use each room for," Aggie answered.

"Take me down there," Brodie ordered. He knew where his wife was. A brief tour wouldn't have satisfied her. She would want to count every barrel and cask, check all of them herself. Aggie nodded and picked up her skirts to keep up with the three men and their long legs.

THIRTY-SIX

B rodie swung open one door after another, waving the torch in front of him, but he didn't find Laurel. He began to doubt he'd figured out where she'd gone. Monty, Aggie, and Donnan remained in the corridor as he stepped into each room. When he entered the smallest room, he paused and sniffed. "She's been here. I smell lavender," Brodie announced.

"The only place ye havenae checked yet is the larder," Aggie pointed out. "Merciful Lord, if she's been down there for hours—well, I dinna want to imagine." The woman fumbled to find the right key before she handed the ring to Brodie, who stared impatiently at the flight of descending stairs. He practically snatched the keyring from Aggie's hand when she held it up.

Laurel heard heavy boot steps outside the door. She drew a deep breath and twisted toward the door. It took the last dregs of her strength to lift her hand and slap it against the door. Her fingers were too inflexible to make a fist, and she didn't have the energy to pound on anything. She tried to call out, but the only sound she produced was a cracked whisper. "Brodie," she rasped.

She fell back against the wall when she heard a key in the door. She was certain it was Brodie, but she would be happy with anyone at that point. The torch had guttered hours ago, so she sat in the dark. When the door flew open and torch flight flashed before her, her sensitive eyes made her moan.

"Dear God, Laurie!"

She opened her eyes to see Brodie thrust the torch behind him before he swooped down and lifted her into his arms. Her head lolled onto his shoulder as she looked at him. She had no strength left to smile or nod. Even the notion of keeping her eyes open was daunting. She'd stopped shivering hours ago, too weak to continue. She'd never imagined she could be so cold and yet still be alive. She knew if Brodie hadn't found her, she likely wouldn't be for this world in another hour.

"Get a bath to our chamber," Brodie commanded. Laurel tried to see who he was ordering around.

"M—" Laurel only produced the sound when she recognized her brother and Donnan. Brodie's warmth, and the security she felt now that he'd found her, made her want to sleep. She hadn't let herself, fearful that if she fell asleep, she would never wake.

"Thistle, nae yet. *Mo ghaol*, ye canna sleep yet. I ken ye're so tired, but I must get ye warmer before ye sleep. Stay with me, Laurie."

Laurel heard the desperation in Brodie's voice, and her heart ached for how her husband must feel. She mustered energy she didn't think she held and nodded. She pushed forth the sound, "Bro—"

"Aye, *mo ghaol*, I'm here." Brodie bounded up the steps as though he carried nothing at all. He rolled Laurel, so her face nestled against his chest, protecting her eyes from the sunlight. Clan members stopped in their tracks as they watched their laird running toward the keep's main doors with their lady in his arms. The guards at the top of the steps pulled the double doors open for Brodie. He didn't slow as he ran the entire way up to their second-floor chamber. Monty and Donnan were behind him, but Monty sprinted forward to reach the door and open it for Brodie.

Without a word, Monty went to the fireplace, adding bricks of peat and poking the embers alive. Brodie laid Laurel on the bed and stripped off boots and stockings. Donnan went to the chest Brodie silently pointed to and pulled out two extra plaids. He went to the bed and unfolded them halfway before stacking them. Looking at one another, all three men reached for the brooches at their shoulders, unpinning the extra yards of wool. They dropped their scabbards and belts to the floor as they unwound their *breacan feiles*. Standing in just their leines, they added their plaids to the two already laid out on the bed. Monty and Donnan looked at Laurel, then Brodie before they left the chamber.

Alone with Laurel, Brodie stripped her of all her clothes, alarmed by how cold the material was. He ripped off his leine and climbed onto the bed beside Laurel. He covered them both with the five plaids before he pulled Laurel's body flush with his.

"Laurie, dinna sleep. Nae yet. Ye can sleep the night and the day away, but nae until I ken ye're warm enough to—" Brodie couldn't finish. What would he say? Survive. Live. Not die. He didn't want to say any of those aloud. When Laurel's moans grew more pain-filled, he knew it meant sensation was returning to her extremities. He knew it would be excruciating, but it meant she would regain feeling. He prayed that without a biting wind and truly frigid temperatures, she wouldn't suffer frostbite and risk losing fingers and toes. But try as he might, Laurel gave in to her body's demand to sleep. Less frightened as her body started to warm, Brodie didn't force her awake.

When Nora the healer knocked, Laurel didn't stir. The old woman had helped deliver Brodie and Dominic. She'd stitched up Brodie's wounds since the first time he got hurt

325

and needed tending. He'd positioned Laurel, so he didn't lie on his wound. Not moving and panic subsiding left Brodie in his own pain. He winced as he drew back the covers and revealed the slash to the back of his ribs.

"Och, nae more than a wee scratch, lad," Nora reassured as she peered at Brodie's wound while she fished around in her basket. "That willna take me more than five minutes." The wizened healer hadn't exaggerated. She finished stitching the gash before Brodie registered the additional pain. The gash was at least six inches long, but Nora's experienced fingers were deft and efficient. She rubbed an ointment on it and told him to let it breathe for a bit. She looked at Laurel, frowned, but nodded her head and slipped out of the chamber. Until Laurel joined his clan, Nora was his favorite woman on Campbell land.

Brodie wrapped his arm around Laurel's middle and slung his leg over her hip. He clung to her so tightly he feared he might crush her, but it made him grow warm faster. His heat poured into Laurel as she moaned. She stirred, and her eyes fluttered open.

"Brodie?"

"Wheest, thistle. I'm here. I swear I am tying us together, and I am nae letting ye out of ma reach again."

"Too hot."

"What?"

"Too hot, too soon. Hurts."

Brodie eased his hold and drew back his leg, but he kept his wife pressed against him. When she sighed rather than moaned, he counted it as progress. A knock at the door kept Brodie from asking Laurel how she felt. He called out, and a troop of servants entered with the tub and buckets of hot water that they poured into the tub. Aggie ordered additional buckets placed before the fire to remain warm. The empty buckets remained for when Brodie needed to change out chilled water for more heated water. His brow furrowed when he glanced at the passageway. He was certain Colina stood watching just beyond where Monty and Donnan stood staring at Laurel. He leaned for a better look, but whoever it was, turned away. He didn't understand his sister-by-marriage.

I understand why Dom wouldnae come, I suppose. But why wouldnae Colina? They're nae friends, but it would be decent and right. How did I nae notice just how off-putting Colina is? Because she makes Dom happy, and that's all ye wanted. Mayhap she feels out of place and doesnae want to intrude. I'm judging her without reason.

Aggie lingered after the other servants left. She offered to help Brodie, and he admitted he needed it. While Laurel was regaining feeling, she was still too worn out to support her own weight. And he knew the pins and needles she faced would likely make her thrash. Preparing the items around the tub, Aggie looked away while Brodie retrieved his leine. Once he was covered, he carried Laurel to the bath and eased her in. When the bathwater touched her skin, she screamed. Brodie knew that against her freezing body it would feel scalding.

"Thistle, it'll ease in a moment. Then it will feel much better."

"Dinna lie, bear. Going to hurt more soon." Laurel rasped. "Water. Drink." She added the second word to clarify. Aggie held a waterskin to her lips, but Laurel's eyes darted to Brodie. The last time someone she didn't know offered her a drink, they drugged her. Brodie reached for it and took a long draw before he placed it to her mouth and nodded. The water was more restorative than it had ever been before. Laurel squirmed but positioned herself, so she could hold her body up on her own if she leaned against the tub.

Laurel knew Brodie wanted to pepper her with questions, but she was grateful that he left her in peace. Soaking in the tub was all she could manage at the moment. She squeezed her eyes shut, flexing her fingers open and closed when the pins and needles started. She didn't say a word, didn't even make a sound. But Brodie knew she suffered. As he watched his plucky little bride struggle in silence, he was certain he would kill whoever caused her a moment of discomfort. He cared not who it was. A member of his clan, a stranger, whoever.

Laurel winced several times as her feet twitched and moved on their own accord. She remained silent lest she started screaming and never ceased. She rubbed her thumb over her palm before switching sides. She squeezed her fingers and rubbed them. Anything that would make the sensation end faster, but she knew it would go away when it was ready, not when she wanted it. Inhaling deeply and releasing it slowly, Laurel forced her eyes open as some of the initial pain eased. She glanced at Aggie and knew the woman suffered from guilt. It was clearly etched in her face, but Laurel knew it wasn't guilt from committing a crime. It was guilt from not having prevented it. Struggling against the pain and the leaden weight of the water on her arm, she reached her hand for Aggie's, which rested on the lip of the tub.

"Nae yer fault," Laurel whispered. "I'm certain ye didna do it, and I'm certain ye wouldnae have let someone if ye'd kenned."

"But ma lady, all that happens under this roof is ma responsibility."

"It may have been the last few years, but that ended yester-day. This wasna yer doing, or lack of doing really. Aggie, I never blamed ye." Laurel scowled and muttered, "I blame that tart Gara."

"She's dead," Brodie stated. Both women looked at him in shock. "A guard found her behind a storage building while he helped search for ye. She'd been stabbed several times."

"How long before ye found me did ye find her? Who kens?"

"Half an hour, mayhap. Monty, Donnan, Graham, and I went with James when he fetched me."

"Graham and James wonder if it was me?"

Brodie's mouth thinned. His wife's perceptiveness wasn't always convenient. He supposed that was part of what caused

Laurel's problems when she arrived at Stirling. She'd figured out people, and either didn't care for them or didn't care for their reaction to her. He nodded.

"Even if I hadnae been locked in the larder, I wouldnae have done it that way. One clean wound, and I wouldnae have lingered for more."

"That's what Monty and Donnan said," Brodie frowned. He glanced at the door but pushed aside a hint of a thought.

"They'd ken. They taught me." Laurel shifted as some pain eased, allowing her to sink lower in the water until it rippled on her chin.

"They said that too." Brodie ran his hand over Laurel's head, wanting to touch her, to show his concern and affection. But there was little more he could do while she was in the tub and with Aggie present. He also worried that he'd hurt her if he touched anything but her hair.

"Ma laird, ma lady. I think it's best I take maself off to some other task or whatnot." Aggie rose from the side of the tub and the stool she'd sat upon. She patted Laurel's hand that still rested over hers. "Ye're a good lass, ma lady. It's been clear since ye rode in holding hands that ye love the laird, and if anyone doubted it before, they canna wonder now. He loves ye too. Ye'll be good for our clan, ma lady. I'm glad ye've come."

"Thank ye, Aggie. That means a great deal to me. I'm happy to be home."

Aggie beamed at Laurel and glanced at Brodie before taking her leave. When the door clicked shut, the couple looked at one another. Brodie's mouth descended to Laurel's, as her neck strained to lift her chin to meet him. The kiss was hungry and frantic. It was as if none of the time lying in bed or while Laurel soaked had been enough to reassure one another that they were safe and together. Laurel's dripping hands pulled at Brodie's leine.

"Off," she demanded, her voice growing stronger. As though their first kiss was the succor Laurel needed, she found strength she'd believed had been sapped. "I want to see you, touch you."

Brodie obliged before his hands plunged beneath the surface. They skimmed along her legs, over her belly, up her ribs. He squeezed her shoulders and massaged her neck. Laurel's hands prowled over her husband's chest and back, covering every inch she could reach. But when she found his stitches, she gasped and jerked away.

"It's naught but a wee scratch," Brodie claimed, repeating what Nora said. She'd always downplayed his injuries except for the few that nearly killed him. She'd done it since he was a child, and he knew that while he didn't need her to make him brave, he found it endearing.

"A wee scratch ma arse. Let me see," Laurel demanded. She tried to sit up further to look, but she hadn't the strength. She didn't touch the wound, but she ran her fingers next to each side. "Did Nora do this?"

"Aye."

"She's vera good. She's likely a better seamstress than me," Laurel grinned. Seeing the clean sutures and recognizing the scent of the ointment relieved her initial fear. The wound was long, but she could tell it wasn't deep. She didn't forget that it could get infected, but she didn't hold any immediate fears for Brodie's life like she did when her fingers touched the stitches. With a nod, she motioned for Brodie to come closer. He leaned across her, bringing his mouth back to hers. When his kisses didn't meet her demands, she cupped his jaw and deepened them. Brodie groaned as he gave in to her. He'd been cautious not to overwhelm her, fearing she was still too weak. When they were both breathless, they rested their foreheads together.

"I still feel weak as a day-old foal, but yer kisses certainly have restorative powers," Laurel grinned.

"I can think of one thing yer kisses have brought back to life," Brodie chuckled. When Laurel glanced down at his groin with interest, Brodie tsked. "Mayhap in the morn. I need to get ye back into bed and some food in ye."

"That isnae what I want in me," Laurel grumbled, but she knew he was right. She didn't have the strength for anything. Her mind was willing, but her body wasn't able. As she watched Brodie's hardened length move as he stood to help her out of the bath, she considered what Aggie told her that morning. She remembered how flatly he'd told her Gara was dead. It didn't strike her as though he harbored any sentiment for her. But she struggled to reconcile all of that with the lusty man she knew. "Brodie?"

"Aye, Laurel," Brodie rarely used her full name when they were alone together, but her tone made him feel his response warranted it.

Laurel waited until they were both under the covers once more. She struggled but managed to roll onto her side to look at him. She observed him for a moment, trying to tell what he was thinking, how he might answer her questions. But she knew she could read nothing into his expression until she asked.

"Gara seemed far too jealous and possessive for a woman ye never bedded. I dinna ken if I believe ye anymore." Laurel watched his reaction. There wasn't a moment of guilt for past actions or for being caught.

"I told ye the truth, Laurel. But I also ken what I saw too. It didna make sense to me either. I dinna have a reason why Gara acted as she did. But I didna lie to ye." Brodie didn't like Laurel doubting him, even thinking for a moment that he would lie to her. But he'd left her alone with strangers while he went to fight a battle from which he might not have returned. He couldn't blame his bride for being on edge and worrying.

"I admit I asked Aggie. I just couldnae understand why Gara was so hostile. She spent most of the day glaring at me. When she stepped in ma way one too many times, I didna change course. I walked right into her and knocked her on her arse. I thought she'd locked me in the larder as revenge."

"I canna say she wasna who did that, but she isnae alive to do ye any more harm if she was. What did ye ask Aggie?"

"I asked her if Gara was yer leman." Laurel looked at Brodie once more. She believed him, but there were still too many things to reconcile for her to feel at ease. "She laughed and denied it. But then I wondered if she was just being loyal to ye and hiding yer secret."

"Aggie kens I dinna bed servants. The way Gara acted was just what I've always wanted to prevent. I didna want a moody woman or a boastful one upsetting the other maids."

"That's what Aggie said."

"Because I've made it clear for years, well before I became laird."

Laurel's brow furrowed as she came to the part that left her in the most doubt and was most confusing. "Aggie said that ye go to the village when ye wish to couple."

"Wished, Laurel. Wished. Went, nae go. As in the past. Nae present, and nae the future."

Laurel nodded at the sternness in Brodie's voice, appreciating the conviction. "She said ye're practically a monk. I ken ye swore ye would have waited for Eliza. But I canna make heads nor tails of how the lusty mon I ken is the same mon who isnae that interested in coupling."

Brodie smiled down at Laurel, seeing her genuine confusion and discomfiture. He saw the logic in her thoughts, and he reminded himself that she didn't know him as a young man. She only knew him as the staider leader, the one who didn't chase women.

"Laurie," Brodie's voice softened. "Ye tease me that I'm auld, and I am. I'm auld enough to nay longer let ma cock lead me aboot. I dinna need a woman in ma bed to feel content with life or to feel like a mon. Those days came and went before ye met me. I felt that way once, but nay anymore. Mayhap I outgrew it. It's nae that I dinna enjoy coupling, and ye ken that I dinna have any issue being able to. It just wasna as important as other things." Brodie grinned. "As for now? Well, I have this bonnie and lusty wife, who's younger than I am. I have to keep up with her, so she doesnae run off with a younger mon. And I canna help it if I find ma bride to be the finest lass I've ever seen with or without clothes. It's nae ma fault that she tempts me and distracts me. I say it's her fault that I canna keep ma hands off her—or ma cock out of her."

"Is that so?" Laurel giggled. "This wife sound vera demanding."

"Aye, and I love it," Brodie's grin widened before he grew serious. "Laurie, I love ye. I want to be a mon ye trust and respect."

"Ye are," Laurie asserted.

"Wheest a moment. I want to be a mon ye trust and respect because I dinna want ye to live in yet another place where ye dinna feel welcome, where ye feel out of place. And more than aught, I want ye to keep loving me. Ma life is so much richer for having ye in it. I dinna want to give that up."

"Ye ken I felt like a pauper for so many years. I ken the Rosses are hardly anyone's poor country cousin, but ye ken how things stood. I ken ye can provide me with whatever cloth and jewelry I wish. But I feel richer now than I ever did at Balnagown when I had everything given to me, richer than I ever did eating in the king's home. I feel richer because I have a mon I love and who loves me, and I have a life that gives me hope. I've never felt so rich."

"Laurie, I know this wasna a comfortable conversation for ye, and I canna claim it was lovely for me either, but I want ye to always come to me if ye have questions or aught is troubling ye."

"Ye may regret making that offer," Laurel grinned once more. "I have kept to maself for so long that now that I have someone I trust, whose opinions I value, and whose advice I trust, I may nae leave ye alone."

Brodie grew quiet for a moment, a speculative look entering his eyes. Laurel felt equal parts curious and hesitant, unsure how to interpret the expression. Seeing her reaction, he smiled and pressed a quick kiss to her lips.

"Ye know that I'll spend ma mornings in the lists, sometimes even the entire day. There are two mornings a month when I adjudicate issues among clan members. Oh, as an aside, ye shall adjudicate any conflicts between women. Some afternoons I ride out to villages or to inspect fields. I meet with the council once a week."

Laurel wondered what Brodie was getting at. She knew the responsibilities of a laird. She might not know which day of the week he did some things, but he wasn't telling her anything new.

"I ken that your duties will often keep you tied to the keep all day." Brodie watched Laurel. She nodded, encouraging him to get to his point. "On days when I ride out, if ye can join me, I'd like ye to come. Nae only because I want ye to ken yer new clan. I want to spend the time with ye. And I had another thought." Brodie wondered if it was a mistake to make his next suggestion, but he continued. "There are also times when I must tend to correspondence and accounts, things that keep me at ma desk. I was wondering if ye'd share yer solar with me."

Laurel's brow furrowed as she looked in the adjoining chamber's direction. She canted her head and nodded. She didn't understand what Brodie meant, but she was happy to share any space with him.

"Ye dinna have to say yes if ye would like to have somewhere that is just for ye. But I thought mayhap, once the bed is removed, that I could bring ma work up here, and I could keep ye company if ye're doing the household ledgers, or mayhap ye're sewing me a new leine." Brodie tried to add some levity, nervous that he was being foolish. Laurel's warm smile made him relax.

"I canna think of aught I'd like more, Brodie. I ken there will be some days when people will pull us in every direction, when there's so much to do that we canna sit down until the evening meal. I dinna need yer company to help me be a chatelaine, but I wish for it because I enjoy it. If I can snatch even an extra hour with ye alone, even if we're both working, then I canna wait."

Laurel tried to smile again, but a yawn escaped. She no longer feared she would freeze to death, and she was even comfortably warm. But as much as she wished it had, neither the bath nor resting in bed with Brodie gave her back her strength. She needed sleep.

"Can ye stay awake long enough to eat, thistle?" Laurel heard the immediate concern in Brodie's voice, and she sensed he felt guilty for pushing her to remain awake and to talk.

"Brodie, I'm glad ye let us talk. At the time, I needed answers more than I needed sleep." Laurel stretched to kiss his cheek. "And aye, I can stay awake just that long. I'm starving."

Brodie left their bed and called out to a servant, requesting a tray for them both. It was past the evening meal, but Brodie knew Berta would have something set aside for them. As he climbed into bed again, he realized he was running out of steam too. He reminded himself that he fought a battle that morning, sustaining an injury that he ignored for hours while he searched among the dead. Then he'd raced around the keep and bailey, searching for his wife, despite the untended wound. He'd found strength from a reserve he didn't know he had to carry Laurel to their chamber. The stitches still stung like the devil, but he was more concerned with Laurel's well-being. But as he took a moment to breathe, he realized he had reason to be tired.

"Did Nora leave a tisane for ye, or mayhap something stronger?" Laurel looked at the bedside table behind Brodie's shoulder, but she didn't spy any cups. "Yer wound must feel like ye're going up in flames."

"It smarts," Brodie said nonchalantly.

"I ken what a good liar ye can be, Brodie. I can only imagine what ye told the Lamonts and MacDougalls this morn before ye fought. But ye dinna lie to me vera well. Or at least nae right now. Yer side pains ye."

"Naught a few drams of whisky canna cure."

"A few drams of whisky with medicinals stirred in. A tincture wouldnae go amiss. Dinna suffer when ye dinna need to." Laurel frowned and shook her head. "Brodie, I dinna ken how to find Nora if ye develop a fever in the middle of the night. I dinna ken where any medicinals are stored in the keep. I didna find aught besides what Berta uses to cook with too. Can ye please ask for some willow bark and yarrow to be brought here, mayhap some angelica too? I would sleep better kenning it's here."

Brodie knew Laurel was right, and he could see how her eyes pleaded with him. He rolled over to get out of bed once more, but another knock sounded. He pulled two clean leines from his chest, donning one and giving the other to Laurel. Once she wore it and was covered to mid-calf, he opened the door. He wanted to groan when he saw how many people waited outside their door. He just wanted food and Laurel. But he knew Aggie and Berta worried about them both, Nora was there to check on them both, Graham wanted to be certain he was fine, and he could tell Monty and Donnan were anxious to see Laurel. He let everyone in, and his spacious chamber felt overcrowded with anyone but Laurel and him. Once the Rosses spoke to Laurel and Graham spoke with him, Aggie and Berta dropped off the tray, and Nora examined them both, Brodie locked the door to the outside world.

THIRTY-SEVEN

Laurel woke warm and comfortable against Brodie's side. He laid on his back, his wound away from her. Her head rested on his chest, and one of her legs had found its way between his. The bed beneath them was more comfortable than hers at Balnagown or Stirling. The sun already filtered in around the window hangings, and Laurel knew it must be close to midmorning. She had a moment's panic when she realized Brodie still slept next to her, but when she tilted her head to look up at him, she found gray eyes watching her.

"I'm keeping ye," Laurel mumbled as she tried to pull away and sit up. A brawny arm pulled her back down.

"I'm nae ready for ye to leave me."

"Me to leave ye? Ye're the one who must have a hundred things to do today. I have at least half that."

"There are things I canna leave until tomorrow, but there are none that must be done this vera minute. Ye needed sleep, and I didna feel comfortable leaving ye alone." Brodie saw the fear flash in Laurel's eyes, and he realized his wording didn't convey his thoughts. "I meant, I wasna comfortable leaving ye when I wasna sure how ye'd feel today. This is yer second morn here, and I havenae even introduced ye to most of the people ye had to work with yesterday. This isnae at all how I thought I would welcome ye here and help ye become Lady Campbell."

"Mayhap, but it's what the Lord gave us. Thank ye for being here when I woke. I admit I would have been vera sad to wake alone."

"Laurie, I had to leave ye yesterday even though I didna want to. There will many more times in our life together when I must do the same thing for the same reason. But I dinna want to abandon ye to figure out life here. I will make the time to show ye around, to help ye get to know yer new home and yer new clan. Ye have yer brother and friend here for now, but I dinna want ye to be lonely when they leave. I ken Colina isnae a likely new friend, but there are women I think ye'd get along with. I'd introduce ye rather than leaving ye to find them on yer own."

"Och, I love ye. Ye are a good husband. I canna think of another mon who would think aboot such things for his wife."

"Laurie, that isnae true. Think of the ladies ye ken who married. Their husbands adore them just as I adore ye. I'm sure they all did things to help their wives. All but mayhap Padraig."

Laurel's face turned into a thundercloud, and Brodie wished to bite his tongue. "I'm nae angry at ye for mentioning Padraig. I just havenae moved past how much I loathe Myrna. I'm nae too keen on Padraig either. I ken he and Cairren are happy now, but I dinna like how things started between them. Probably because I feel guilty for nae telling Cairren more before she left court. Anyway, that isnae the point ye were trying to make. I dinna ken how their husbands treat them, but I can imagine it, and ye're right."

"If ye feel up to it, would ye go for a walk with me this afternoon?"

"I'd like that, bear. But will ye promise me something?"

"What do ye wish, Laurie?"

"Dinna go into the lists for at least two more days. I dinna want ye to rip yer stitches." Laurel glanced down, embarrassed by her request. It seemed silly once she said it aloud. Brodie had been swinging a sword for at least thirty years— longer than she'd been alive—and likely riding out to fight for more than twenty. He didn't need her telling him what to do.

"I admit I'm tempted to, but yer request speaks of common sense nae just concern. I willna train for a couple days. Besides, there will be plenty to deal with over the next few days."

"How soon do ye think the king will demand ye return?"

"Och, that summons will be here in less than a sennight. Someone is already hying off to tell him what wickedness we did to them. He'll dispatch a messenger the same day."

Laurel nodded. She'd assumed the same thing. She didn't revel in the idea of being left at Kilchurn so soon after she arrived, but she'd survived harder introductions to new ways of life. She worried about what would happen to Brodie while he was in Stirling. She jumped when Brodie's hand slipped down to her bottom and gave it a quick squeeze.

"Unless ye dinna want to, I assumed ye'd be coming with me."

"After the mess I caused on the way here? I didna think ye would want to travel with me again so soon."

"That ye caused? Laurel, I wasna fighting ye on the battle-field yesterday. I fought the bluidy causes of this nightmare. Ye didna do aught but get stuck in the middle. Nelson and Matthew were looking for ways to cause trouble with me. They realized ye would be the best way to draw me into a fight. They did it because we were already feuding with the MacDougalls, and they allied with the Lamonts because we were feuding with them, too."

"All the more reason I shouldnae travel. If I stay here, then I canna be used against ye."

"Laurie, there are two reasons I wish ye to come. One is completely selfish, and one is unfortunate. I dinna want to miss ye. If ye come with me, then I can see ye, touch ye, talk to ye the whole time. But I'm also nae comfortable leaving ye here without kenning who caused yesterday's incident. Even if I asked yer kin to remain, they dinna ken who to watch for. They dinna ken who is or isnae trustworthy. I dinna feel it's safe. I hate admitting that when I want this to feel like yer home and yer clan. It angers and embarrasses me. I willna leave here if I canna be certain ye're safe. But neither can I ignore a summons."

"I feel the same way. If ye dinna mind me coming, I would rather be with ye, even if it means returning to Stirling so bluidy soon."

"Then expect to leave here within a sennight."

The hairs on Laurel's nape rose again as she walked alongside Aggie as they made their way to the buttery. Three Campbell guards accompanied them. Laurel had already grown used to the men being her second shadow. Brodie tasked them as her personal guard the morning after he found her in the larder. That was three days earlier, and the men were polite and dutiful. They'd even fought not to laugh at some of Laurel's more choice comments about gaining three wet nurses when she wasn't even pregnant.

But even with the men in tow everywhere she went, she still had moments of inexplicable unease. She couldn't pinpoint if she felt like someone watched her, or if she feared something was about to happen, or if it was something else entirely. It was unnerving and tiring. She hadn't shared her feelings with anyone. She couldn't articulate them clearly to her guards, she didn't want to worry Brodie, and she didn't want to accept that they might be accurate.

She found she felt safer outside the castle walls than inside. The afternoon following the battle, Laurel accompanied Brodie when he met with his dead warriors' families. She'd begun her role as Lady Campbell by helping the clan through a crisis. She didn't relish such tasks as Brodie's, but she knew her presence served a purpose, that she could help people. She consoled women and children, then helped the widows and mothers work through what they would need now that at least one man in their life was gone. Brodie praised her in public and in private, impressed with her compassion and level-headedness. She relished the praise, even though she wished she could have earned it some other way. She looked forward to her daily visits to the village and the opportunity to meet more clan members. But she was happiest when she went riding with Brodie. They raced as they left the keep, but they returned with Brodie's arms wrapped around Laurel as they shared a mount.

However, a sense of doom—or at least trepidation—returned to Laurel each time she rode back into the bailey. She felt it even more strongly as she opened the door to the buttery and entered with Aggie. One of her guards entered with the women while the other two remained in the corridor.

"These are the casks I mentioned," Laurel said to Aggie as she lifted down ones that smelled like vinegar. "Are they meant to be fermented like this?"

Aggie leaned forward, then jerked away as her lips puckered. "Nay, ma lady. That's foul."

"How old are they?"

"Last year's fruit. Even if the batch went off, they shouldnae smell that horrendous so soon."

"The ale seems fine. Do the brewer and vintner work together?"

Aggie chuckled and shook her head. She glanced at the man who stood at the door. Laurel looked back and found the guard struggled not to laugh. She raised her eyebrows in question. Aggie laughed again. "Too competitive, they are."

"So they don't get along?"

"Worse than that," Aggie chuckled. "They're brothers!" Aggie and the guard both gave up trying not to laugh.

"Ye'll see, ma lady," the guard chimed in. "Bernard—the

brewer, ma lady—willna let his brother live this down. Cal will be stuck listening to Bernard crowing for sennights."

"But the other wine isn't spoiled. It seems quite fine, even if I didn't care for it. If Cal makes decent wine, then what happened to this newest batch?" Laurel lifted another cask from the shelf and sniffed. It was putrid too. However, when she pulled three casks from the shelf below, they smelled delicious. Laurel handed Aggie a rotten cask, and she picked up another two. When they entered the corridor, the guards tried to take the casks from Laurel, but she refused. She insisted that their laird didn't assign them to her as her servants. He assigned them to swing a sword if need be. They couldn't do that if they were carrying things for her. She noted their displeasure and carried on without relenting.

Laurel led them to a patch of grass outside the undercroft. She and Aggie set the wine down on the ground. Laurel stared at it as she wracked her memory for what she'd learned while her mother trained her. She'd spent time with the Ross brewer and vintner to learn the process and to distinguish quality. She pulled the stopper out of one offending container and poured out the contents. The color looked as it should, but the smell nearly overpowered all five of them. Laurel shook the empty container, certain something remained in the bottom, even though she couldn't see anything.

"Smash it, please," Laurel asked her largest guard. The man stomped on the small wooden barrel, and the wood splinted apart. Laurel lifted the bottom of the barrel and pulled apart a few slats of wood. She'd been right. There was something stuck to the bottom of the barrel.

"What is that?" a guard asked.

"Tar," Laurel and Aggie answered together.

Laurel looked at Aggie, certain she already knew the answer. "Would Cal do this?"

"Never, ma lady," Aggie said while shaking her head. She looked distraught.

"I'm not going to do aught to Cal. Someone else is

involved." If only Laurel knew who. But she still struggled to put names with faces. Now she needed to determine who intended to poison the laird's family and senior warriors. The wine was only intended for those who sat at the dais. She looked back at the evidence before speaking to the guards. "I need your help after all. I want to put these on the top shelves in the grain storeroom. Well above most people's reach. I don't want anyone accidentally or intentionally serving this wine. Will you help me, please?"

The guards were still unaccustomed to Laurel's requests. They all knew they were rhetorical, but the courtesy she included was foreign. She supposed she hadn't been very polite until the last few years. She was making the most of a fresh start and trying to set the tone for her life at Kilchurn as one with courtesy—most of the time. A guard took both remaining casks that had been rather cumbersome for Laurel and Aggie but were dwarfed by the imposing arms that carried them. Laurel opened the storeroom and pointed to where she wished the man to place them. He didn't need to stretch to place them above his head on the top shelf. She thanked all her guards, then dismissed Aggie before going in search of Brodie.

THIRTY-EIGHT

Laurel hurried up the stairs to her solar, assuming Brodie was already there since she hadn't found him anywhere else. She turned on the landing and ran into Colina.

"I'm sorry. I wasn't looking where I was going." Laurel smiled, but it fizzled at Colina's look of disgust. It raised Laurel's hackles.

"You should be," Colina snapped. Laurel narrowed her eyes.

"I should be what? Which part?"

"Both, I suppose." Colina sniffed. Laurel was accustomed to the habit now, and she knew it had nothing to do with illness and everything to do with demeanor.

"I ken I'm still new to your clan, so mayhap I must learn that the laird's family isn't held to the same high standards as the clans I'm accustomed to." Laurel looked down her nose at Colina. Then sniffed. "Because I'm certain the wife of the laird's little brother doesn't issue commands to the clan's lady."

Colina's back went rigid, and Laurel was certain the woman bared her teeth for a heartbeat. "You'd do well to remember how new you are."

"And if I should forget?" Laurel taunted. She'd seen

345

Brodie step into the passageway from the corner of her eye. He crept along the wall until he could hide within arm's reach of the women.

"You seem accident prone, my lady," Colina mused.

"It cannot be both accidental and intentional."

"So you say."

Laurel narrowed her eyes and looked questioningly at Colina, as though she tried to figure her out. "You do understand why something can't be both, correct?"

Colina sneered, "I'm not stupid."

"Just lazy."

"Too good for the likes of you or this clan."

"But you chose to marry into it."

"Aye, well, I didn't get everything I chose."

"Didn't you know you were getting the baby brother?"

"I chose a mon determined to lead. I got a milksop."

"You chose Brodie but got Dominic?" Laurel pretended to sound confused. She was intrigued by what she might learn.

"Nay, you eejit.

Laurel furrowed her brow and looked up at the ceiling as though she was trying to work through what Colina said. "You thought Brodie was a choice. You thought he might marry you."

"If that's what I wanted."

Laurel struggled not to laugh. "You knew Dominic is the younger brother. You believed you could have had the aulder brother. You were certain Dominic was the better leader of the two. Even if he were, what would it matter? You passed up the heir for the spare."

"There's a spare for a reason."

Laurel kept her expression light, but she grew deadly serious. "One person's accidental is another person's intentional."

"Now you understand." Colina glared at Laurel before offering a sugary smile. "And you do seem accident prone." Colina tried to step around Laurel, but Laurel shifted to block her.

"And if I'd like to stop being accident prone?"

"It's not aboot what you'd like."

"Who is it aboot?"

"Me. Are you daft? Can you not keep up?"

"It's aboot you wanting to be Lady Campbell and not picking the right brother. You've had a chance to be the lady of the keep for three years, but you didn't take it."

"I didn't take the job of being a servant."

"What do you do all day?"

"What a genuine lady does." At Laurel's studiously blank expression, Colina huffed, "Sew."

"Sew? Like a seamstress?" Laurel grinned.

"Hardly. I embroider."

"Seamstresses do that too."

"I'm through with you." Colina tried to move again, but Laurel remained in the way.

"For today or for forever?" Laurel narrowed her eyes. "Just to be clear, since I'm such an eejit, you wish for me and the laird to die, so your husband the tánaiste becomes laird. That makes you the lady of the clan. But you didn't want to actually be the lady while you had a three-year chance because that involved work. You merely want the title."

"I ken you tell your husband everything. Speak of this to him, and your next accident will be sooner than you expect."

"Like Gara's?" Laurel tossed out. She suspected who encouraged Gara to be so hostile. The maid was a perfect scapegoat.

"Exactly," Colina snapped.

Laurel wasn't going to press for more. She'd learned an intriguing—or rather disturbing—number of things about her sister-by-marriage. The woman's scorn was too genuine for her to just be testing Laurel by saying outlandish things. What concerned Laurel more than Colina's thinly veiled threats was Dominic's role in all of this. She decided she had one more question.

"Dominic must look forward to elevating his status. Is he as eager as you?"

"Bah. He's content as the tánaiste. I told you, I thought I chose the better one. He's a follower, not a leader. I was duped, but never again."

Laurel couldn't resist. "Why tell me this if you think I might tell the laird?"

"Because you're not so simple that you won't understand your role now that you know."

Laurel moved out of Colina's way, letting the woman descend the stairs to the main floor before nodding to Brodie. Her husband slipped from the shadows and drew her into his arms. He didn't know what to make of what he saw and heard. He'd feared several times that Colina would shove Laurel down the stairs. But Laurel's skill for ferreting out information impressed him. Grateful that she'd survived the conversation without harm, he held her close.

"I was on my way to our solar," Laurel explained.

"I ken. I heard your voice, then Colina's. I was worried."

The couple walked to their shared solar, and Laurel locked the door. Brodie joined Laurel on the window seat, and she recalled when he'd sat beside her on the window seat in her chamber at court. Brodie's smile told Laurel he remembered too. They laced their fingers together, and Laurel leaned her head on Brodie's shoulder.

"Could you hear everything?" she asked

"Aye. The woman is addlepated. There was never a choice. I never considered her as aught but my younger brother's intended. She could have chosen me, but I never would have chosen her."

"She basically admitted she's responsible for me being locked in the larder. And it sounded an awful lot like she indirectly admitted killing Gara." Laurel froze. Her heart leapt into her throat, and her mouth went dry. Slowly, she raised her head and leaned away. "Brodie, you said they've been married for three years. Hasn't your mother been gone that long too?"

Laurel wished she could pull back and swallow her words when she witnessed Brodie's stricken expression. He nodded as he stared into space. "They'd been married a fortnight when mother fell ill. Colina gave everyone the impression that she would one day be an excellent chatelaine until I married. She cared for Mother and seemed so concerned for her. But once Mother faded away, Colina no longer seemed interested in running the keep. Dominic and I thought it was grief. We thought she and Mother had grown close." Brodie sprang to his feet. "Fuck."

"Brodie?"

Brodie tipped his head back, an anguished groan seeming to pour out from his soul. When he looked at Laurel, the pain in his eyes made tears come to hers. "When Dom and I visited Mother, Colina would step out. Mother would become agitated. Dom and I thought she missed Colina, so we didn't linger. She couldn't speak much the last couple of months. Do you think she grew upset because she couldn't tell us what Colina was doing to her?"

"Oh, Brodie." Laurel's heart ached. She had little doubt that Colina caused the previous Lady Campbell's death. While Colina appeared sallow and mousy, the woman Laurel encountered today was menacing. If she'd been Brodie's mother's frequent caregiver, then it was likely she played a role. "I don't know."

"You do, Laurie. You just don't want to say it." Brodie sank back onto the window seat, and just as she had in her old chamber, she wrapped her arms around Brodie as he leaned his head against her middle. They remained silent, each lost in thought, but comforted by the other's presence. When Brodie could no longer keep his thoughts to himself without going mad, he asked Laurel, "Do I tell Dominic?"

"Not yet, Brodie. He loves her. He won't believe you." Laurel ran her hand over Brodie's back. "Would you believe him if he accused me of such things?"

"No," Brodie admitted. "Do you think he's aware?"

"I don't know. He hasn't been warm to me, but I don't get the impression that he'd hurt his own mother."

"Nay. He wouldn't. We were both close to Mother, especially once Father died. We adored her. Her death devastated him."

"And Colina was right there to comfort him."

"Aye. We thought she shared our grief. I admit I was even jealous that Dom had someone to turn to, and I didn't."

"Then, you can't say aught until it's irrefutable."

A thought struck Laurel as she considered why she'd sought Brodie out. "Has Colina taken an interest in aught at all aboot the running the keep?"

"Only the wine. She's very particular aboot it. Dom calls it that, anyway. I call it pretentious."

"Is she just interested, or is she involved with the wine?"

"She selects what's served, but I don't think she speaks to Cal aboot it."

"Fuck."

"Laurel," Brodie gasped.

"You're not the only one who kens the word," Laurel said with a shrug. "I was coming up here to tell you, Aggie and I found tampered with wine. At least three casks. When I was looking around the other day, I noticed a funny smell from a few. Aggie told me they were newer vintages, so there wasn't a reason for them to be putrid already. I poured one out, and Declan smashed it open for me. There was tar at the bottom of the barrel. The casks we found them in were small. The kind that fit on a shelf and would last a night or two. Awkward, but Aggie carried one, and I carried two. Colina could have managed at least one. Brodie, if she mixed the poisoned wine with pure wine, it would mask the taste enough for people to drink it. It wouldn't taste right, but no one would complain at the table. A couple nights of that, and we'd all be dead."

"Dominic doesn't drink wine. Ever." Brodie shook his

head. "We drank ourselves sick when we were younger. Ever since then, Dominic heaves at even the taste of it."

"So Colina wouldn't have to worry aboot explaining to Dominic why he shouldn't drink the wine."

"Where are the casks now?"

"In the undercroft's grain storeroom. I had Declan place them on the top shelf. Just aboot any mon could reach them, but no woman could. I couldn't, and I'm taller than most."

"Do you think there are others?" Brodie was growing more and more concerned by what he heard.

"Possibly. But three of those would be enough to poison everyone at the high table over the course of a few days."

"Show me."

Laurel led Brodie to the undercroft, showing him the hidden casks first before taking him to the buttery. They inspected each barrel and cask, but found nothing obviously tampered with. But Brodie voiced Laurel's concern. They might need to dump all their wine in case Colina had sabotaged more, and they just couldn't smell it. They walked into the Great Hall together, both somber and deep in thought. Laurel shook herself from her stupor, knowing it was Monty and Donnan's last night at Kilchurn. They'd stayed on to ensure Laurel was safe, and Brodie gratefully added the partners to Laurel's guard rotation. Now Laurel realized how much she would miss her brother and her friend. She could only truly trust Brodie, and she'd made no friends yet. The days grew infinitely longer.

THIRTY-NINE

L aurel and Brodie left the stables after their morning ride. Just as Laurel requested, he forewent training for two days after he sustained his wound. She could only shake her head the morning he returned to training. He'd bounded out of the keep like a young lad. But he'd delayed his entry the past four morning since Monty and Donnan departed. She'd stood beside Brodie as she waved to her brother and his lover until they faded from sight. Brodie understood Laurel was lonely, so he tried to start her days with a smile. They reached the steps to the keep when the cry went out that a rider approached. The man who entered the bailey wore King Robert's livery.

Laurel and Brodie sighed in unison. Their summons had arrived. Precisely a sennight after the battle. Brodie hadn't exaggerated. Whether it was the Lamonts or MacDougalls who raced to inform the king, the Bruce hadn't dallied before sending a messenger. Brodie accepted the missive before he and Laurel went to their solar. Brodie knew it was less likely someone would interrupt them there than in his own solar. They shared the window seat, their favorite place in the chamber. Brodie opened the parchment, and they read the missive together.

"You predicted it, Laurie. The king understands, but the court is rallying for my head on a pike. Everyone is calling it a massacre."

"We knew it would happen. What do you expect the king will do once we're there?"

"Levy a fine against me for fighting an unsanctioned war with four other clans. He'll likely demand I pay restitution to them. We'll ride with four times the guards because I will not only have you to protect but several chests of coin."

"You're going to pay?" Laurel was aghast.

"Aye. I have little choice. But no amount of coin is going to give any of those clans their men back. None of them will harry us again for years. Not if they wish to survive. The money will feed and clothe the innocent, so I feel no resentment making restitution. But neither do I feel guilty for decimating their armies. They knew what they faced when they took on the Campbells. They met the fate they created."

Laurel sat back, nodding her head. She understood Brodie's logic, and she admitted she hadn't really considered those who'd been left behind. She'd worried about the widows among her clan, but she hadn't thought about the widows in the other clans. They were not in positions to dictate whether their men went to battle. She slipped his hand into Brodie's.

"I admire you, husband. Most lairds would refuse to pay those who attacked them. They wouldn't care what happened to those left behind. You are gracious in your victory."

"Thank you, thistle. It feels good to hear you say that. Are you ready to leave in the morn?"

"I am, but do you feel comfortable leaving Dominic behind? We still don't know if Colina's done aught else."

"She needs Dominic if she's to become Lady Campbell, so I believe he's safe. Neither of us thinks he's colluding with her. I trust him, and I ken he's a good tánaiste. Our people are safe with him in charge. If we're away, who is there to harm? She only wants us dead." Brodie said with a shrug.

"But she wouldn't have been able to taint only our wine. She was willing to kill members of your senior guard."

"Aye, but they'll be with us."

Laurel drew her lips in and frowned. She wasn't so readily convinced. It didn't sit well with her to leave while matters were unresolved. But she knew they couldn't ignore the Bruce's demand that they attend court. They had found no evidence to connect Colina with Gara's death, so they'd named it an accident. Her parents were dead, so there was no one to insist upon seeing the body. They arranged her funeral for the next day and tried to minimize the gossip. Laurel had found no more contaminated wine. It made her wonder when Colina intended to strike. Laurel figured Colina hadn't discovered her weapon of choice wasn't in the buttery anymore. She and Brodie discussed the situation daily, but they didn't know how to learn more.

"Brodie, what if I remain here?"

"Absolutely not. No, Laurel." Brodie's voice was unwavering.

"You trust Dominic, but he doesn't ken what his wife is up to. We can't be sure she won't try to harm people."

"She hasn't done aught when I've been away in the past."

"That you ken. If you hadn't overheard us talking, would you have imagined Colina capable of aught nefarious?"

"No. But I'm still not relenting. You are not remaining here without me. I will not accept that risk. You nearly died the last time I left the walls without you. And I was less than a bluidy mile away!" Brodie rose and paced.

Laurel watched Brodie's face grow red as his frustration rose. She'd never seen him react this way. Even when he'd been angry in the time she'd known him, he'd never gone red in the face. As the flush deepened, she grew alarmed.

"Brodie, sit down." Laurel tugged at his hand, but he didn't budge. "You're scaring me."

Brodie immediately looked contrite. "I'm not upset with you, Laurie."

"I ken that. It's your face. You're so red I fear you'll keel over." She retrieved her embroidery and used the scroll frame that held the fabric in place as a fan. "Do you feel well?"

"Nay." Brodie shook his head. He felt overheated and lightheaded. "I've never felt this way just from being angry."

"Who filled your waterskin this morn?" Laurel's chest tightened. They'd broken their fast together, sharing a trencher. They'd had watered ale in the same chalice. The only difference was Brodie drank from a waterskin while they were on their ride, and Laurel hadn't.

"Graham. Why?"

"Does your tongue tingle?"

"Aye."

"Don't move." Laurel ran to the door and flung it open. She went to the railing and looked down over the Great Hall. "Aggie! Get me all the gool we have and hot water. Now. Just do it."

Laurel dashed back to Brodie, whose face was turning purple. She prayed Aggie hurried with the oxeye daisy. She knew Berta would have water heating for one thing or another, but she didn't know whether Aggie would have to find Nora for the medicinal. She doubted Brodie had that much time.

"Laurie," Brodie choked.

"Aye. Dinna leave me," Laurel begged. "Dinna talk. Just breathe, Brodie."

Laurel didn't notice the tears that streamed down her cheeks until Brodie tried to wipe them away. She squeezed his hand and ran next door to retrieve the chamber pot. Grateful that it was clean, she shoved it under Brodie's chin.

"Brodie, ye need to throw up. Ye've been poisoned."

Brodie turned horrified eyes at Laurel, but he bent over the bowl and stuck his fingers down his throat. He gagged, but nothing came up. As he kept trying, Aggie arrived with Graham behind her. Laurel turned a thunderous glare at him. "Get out. Come near my husband, I will kill you," she threat-

356

ened Graham. She watched one eye twitch. It was all the confession she needed. She hissed, "I will kill you. Run before I find you."

Laurel snatched the medicinal from Aggie, nearly spilling the mug of hot water the housekeeper poured. Laurel sniffed it and sipped. When she was convinced it was pure, she dumped the plant into the mug and used her eating knife to stir it. She was relieved Aggie brought so much. Normally, the plant made a weak tea to reduce fevers, but excessive amounts caused vomiting. She held the mug while Brodie choked down the brew. His throat felt as though it was swelling shut. He feared he would suffocate.

"Stand up, Brodie," Laurel begged as sweat poured from Brodie's forehead. She looked at the stunned Aggie and begged, "Get Dominic."

Laurel watched Aggie leave, but if she hadn't been unwilling to leave Brodie's side again, she would have butchered Graham, who stood watching in the passageway. She helped Brodie to his feet, but he was unsteady on them. He was too large for Laurel to support on her own. She needed Dominic's help. Her husband's younger brother stormed into the room, having heard a commotion as he entered the Great Hall and learned something was happening abovestairs.

"Help me," Laurel pleaded. "I need him to stand up. I need the tea to get to his belly faster. Please, help me."

Dominic was at Brodie's side without hesitation. He wrapped his arm around his older brother's waist and bore much of Brodie's weight. Laurel fought against the need to sob, praying Graham hadn't added enough poison to kill someone Brodie's size. When he groaned, Laurel lifted the chamber pot. With Dominic holding him up, and Laurel holding the chamber pot, Brodie emptied his stomach.

When there was nothing left, Brodie sagged onto the window seat, his previously scarlet face now deathly pale. Laurel patted his forehead with her skirt as she watched

Brodie. She didn't know what else to do. If his body had already absorbed too much of the poison, throwing up wouldn't be enough.

"Brodie?" she whispered.

"Aye, Laurie," Brodie wheezed. "A wee better."

"What happened?" Dominic demanded, speaking for the first time.

"The only thing Brodie ate or drank that I didn't was water while we were out riding. He said Graham filled his waterskin." Laurel turned her head to investigate the passageway, but Graham was no longer there. "Brodie was poisoned. And now his second is no longer in sight."

"Brother?" Dominic's voice held uncertainty.

"Go. Find him." Brodie nodded. Dominic gave a jerky nod, his expression still uncertain. But he hurried out of the chamber. Brodie leaned against Laurel, still too weak to sit up on his own. He felt his wife trembling as she held his hand and rubbed his back once she sat beside him. "Wheest."

Laurel squeezed Brodie's hand, unable to speak now that she had no orders to issue. She looked at Aggie, who'd remained silent and out of the way. She saw the raw pain in the woman's eyes as she watched a man she'd helped raise struggle to remain alive. Laurel waved her over and stood. Without releasing Brodie's hand, she moved to stand on his other side, giving Aggie her seat.

"Och, lad. I dinna ken if ma heart is beating again yet," Aggie whispered as she took Brodie's other hand. "I love ye like ye're ma own wean. I canna imagine losing ye."

Brodie looked at Aggie and knew she spoke the truth. Despite being nearly forty, he didn't resist when the older woman embraced him. He found the comfort she'd given him his entire life, but it didn't last as it had when he was a child. The person he needed most was Laurel. She hadn't released his hand since she'd taken it once more. But he eased it from hers, watching her pained expression grow worse until he wrapped his arm around her waist.

"Thank ye," Brodie whispered. "Real water?"

Aggie rinsed and filled his mug with water that had cooled since she brought it. Brodie sipped it until his throat no longer burned, and the lightheadedness faded. He had never felt so drained as he did that moment. Not after any battle, not after his parents died, not even once he found Laurel after her abduction and finding her in the larder. He'd been confident that he would find her, refused to believe he wouldn't. But as he gasped for each breath, growing more certain that he would die, he feared leaving Laurel alone. He feared never seeing her or listening to her again. So now that the crisis was averted, and he knew he wasn't leaving her a widow, his energy was sapped.

"Do ye wish to lie down, bear?" Laurel asked softly. Laurel noticed Aggie smiled at them, then slipped from the chamber to give them privacy.

"Aye. Will ye stay?"

"I'm nae going anywhere," Laurel spluttered, aghast that he thought she might leave his side.

"Dominic? Graham?"

"I dinna ken," Laurel shrugged as she helped Brodie struggle to his feet once more. He staggered his first couple steps, but he grew steadier as he approached the door. As they left the solar and turned toward their chamber, an unholy roar rose from the Great Hall below. Brodie and Laurel went to peer down over the railing, stunned to find Colina in Graham's arms as Dominic surged forward with his sword drawn.

FORTY

"Cease!" Brodie bellowed, uncertain how he summoned the strength to speak, let alone yell. He looked at Laurel, who stood wide-eyed as she watched the scene below. Brodie gritted his teeth as he took Laurel's hand. He muttered, "We have to go down."

"I ken." Laurel sounded as eager as Brodie felt. When they reached the bottom of the stairs, Brodie moving slower than usual, he approached the trio. Colina remained in Graham's embrace while Dominic held them at sword point. Graham appeared unrepentant, and Colina's expression was pure arrogance.

"Shite," Laurel hissed. "They're having an affair."

Brodie gawked at Laurel, disbelieving what he heard. His second barely tolerated Colina and was more open about his disdain than Brodie ever had been. And he was certain that despite Colina's standoffishness, she loved Dominic. Though he'd begun to doubt that of late. What he overhead on the landing and then deducing what Colina likely did to his mother, made Brodie second guess his sister's-by-marriage intentions.

Laurel stepped beside Dominic and pressed down on his

361

blade. She looked at the devastated man and knew her suspicions were correct. Graham wasn't protecting Colina merely because she was a woman. "Dom, not until we know everything," Laurel whispered.

"I already ken all I need to know," Dominic snapped. "They're lovers and tried to kill my brother."

"But why? What motivated them? It's not love. Not really," Laurel countered. She pressed harder on Dominic's sword, and he relented. She stared at Graham, thinking about how loyal he'd always seemed to Brodie, how he'd protected her. She struggled to reason why he would betray Brodie in such a hideous way. She couldn't fathom why he'd tried to kill Brodie.

"Laurie, he's our brother," Brodie rasped as he watched Laurel. He guessed her mind was alive with various explanations, but he already knew. "He's our aulder brother."

Laurel looked at Brodie and understood what he meant. She closed her eyes before turning back to Graham and Colina. "You were talking aboot Graham that day."

"Finally figured it out," Colina sneered.

"Why poison, Graham? That's a woman's weapon?" Laurel asked, but her mouth fell open as she looked back at Colina. "You found out I discovered the wine. You assumed I would be the one who needed a drink. You meant the water for me. Did you know, Graham? Did you know the water was poisoned, and you let your brother drink it, anyway?"

"Nay, I didn't ken."

"So, despite protecting me while we traveled, you want me dead." Laurel's mind jumped from idea to idea as she tried to piece together what was said and left unsaid.

"Is that true?" Brodie demanded. Graham looked at Brodie, anger simmering beneath the surface.

"I didn't ken the water was poisoned, but I wasn't sorry you drank it. He loved my mother. I should have been the one to inherit. Not the son of a woman he despised. A son he thought was weak."

Brodie inhaled, his chest expanding to its full breadth as his hands fisted beside him. It was only the restraining hand Laurel placed on his arm that kept him from launching himself at his former best friend and older—albeit illegitimate —brother. Laurel stepped in front of him, shaking her head.

"You both assumed the love Brodie and Dominic feel toward Graham, and Dominic's love for Colina would keep them blind. You didn't anticipate me. You must have been terribly upset, Colina, when Brodie rode into the bailey with a wife, when you worked so hard to ensure his bride died," Laurel gloated. "Does no one recall Colina's clan? She was a MacLean. Brodie told me how Dominic and Colina fell in love at a gathering, and their marriage brokered a truce. But do you ken who else is a MacLean?"

Laurel turned to look at Brodie, hoping that he followed her train of thought. He closed his eyes for a moment as he fought to control his temper. "David Lamont's wife." Brodie wracked his memory as he thought about the marriage contract he'd signed allowing Dominic to marry Colina. "Bluidy hell. The woman is Colina's aunt."

"Aye. It wasn't Michael, Brodie. At least it wasn't Michael acting alone. He fed information to the MacDougalls, but Graham gave it to the Lamonts."

"It was your idea to take the horses to the farrier, claiming your mount needed his shoes checked. You took me there to distract me while Michael and Wallace took Laurel to the docks."

"Aye," Graham admitted. "I thought she'd be as easy to kill as the MacMillan chit. I respect her tenacity."

"But you don't respect my life," Laurel cut in. "You were in on the wager, weren't you?"

"Lost a bluidy fortune when Brodie married you. I hoped to get it back by ending your marriage."

"Did you tell the MacDougall brothers and their partners which route we were travelling?" Brodie demanded.

"They asked, I answered."

Laurel rubbed her forehead, growing confused as she tried to sort through everything she heard. She tried to line up all the events and people in her mind before she moved them into their places.

"You and Colina have been lovers since she arrived, haven't you?" Neither person denied it, so Laurel assumed she was right. "Colina believed you would become laird one day. She counted on it. She killed Brodie and Dominic's mother because she was the first woman in her way to being Lady Campbell. She convinced Graham that he should be laird." Laurel's brow furrowed as she continued to think out loud. "Colina used Graham to get information to her aunt, who gave it to David. That's how the Lamonts knew to attack your party and to target Eliza. But no one expected you to find a new bride at court. Graham, you entered the wagers to encourage the others to keep Brodie and me apart. It wasn't aboot the money, was it?"

"Nay. Though I'm still angry that I lost it all," Graham muttered.

Brodie followed Laurel's line of thinking and realized just how nefarious Graham's perfidy had been. It shocked him to the core. "Once Laurel and I married, you knew our clan gained a powerful ally. One that would guarantee the Lamonts and MacDougalls didn't win. You made certain the Lamonts knew where to attack us. But how?"

"Liam Oliphant," Graham stated. "When the MacDougalls gave Laurel to Monty, they assumed she would go to Balnagown. She'd be out of the way long enough for the Lamonts and them to attack with the MacGregors and MacArthurs on their side. MacFarlane and MacBain broke it off with the MacDougalls in truth, and Gunn eventually went home, too. But Oliphant was Nelson's lackey, even though it seemed like Liam was the leader and Nelson was the follower. Nelson was canny and made it appear that way. Liam went to tell the Lamonts where to wait for us."

"You counted on a lot of different things playing out just as you needed them." Laurel shook her head, going back to her list once more. "You needed the MacMillans to end the alliance with the Campbells, thinking the Lamonts and MacDougalls would stand a chance when they attacked in full force. You needed to keep Brodie from marrying again, and when that didn't work, you needed to be rid of his new wife. You needed Nelson and his friends to take care of that part, and you likely encouraged the wagers to trick them into doing your bidding. Not that it would have been hard since the MacDougalls already wanted to weaken Brodie—personally and politically."

"When none of that worked, and you returned to an angry mistress, Colina decided she would take back control and kill the current Lady Campbell just as she did the previous one," Brodie remarked. "Assuming you succeeded and had killed Laurel, when did you plan to kill me and Dominic?"

"We'd hoped you'd have the courtesy to die in battle," Colina hissed. "But your wife got in the way again. Her bluidy strategy worked. You killed my uncle."

"All of it—every minute of our marriage—has been a lie," Dominic whispered. Laurel watched as Dominic retreated into a shell, visibly shaken by what they all learned.

"With no wife, Brodie had no heir. If he and Dominic were dead—the laird and his tánaiste, it was likely the council would elect Graham as the new laird. He was Brodie's second, and it seems like no secret that Graham is Brodie and Dominic's brother," Laurel surmised.

"You really want to be laird that much?" Brodie asked, still unable to believe the depth of Graham's betrayal.

"Nay, but it still should have been my position," Graham shook his head.

Laurel had been watching Colina and Graham's body language throughout the showdown. Graham hadn't relaxed his protective posture for a moment. But there was also a gentleness to how he held her. Colina, however, had done nothing to show even a moment's interest in Graham. There was no affection from her. It was almost as though he didn't stand behind her.

"You did it for her," Laurel stated matter-of-factly. "You might believe you deserved it, but you wouldn't have tried to take it if she didn't want to be Lady Campbell." Laurel canted her head as she tried to meet Colina's gaze. When their eyes locked, Colina's disinterested mien fell away, and the hatred returned. "You want to be Lady Campbell because of what comes with the title. The prestige and power you believe the position holds. That's why you never took on the duties of chatelaine. You really do think they are below you. You want the glory without any of the work. You believe you are entitled to be Lady Campbell."

Brodie shook his head, the effects of the poison still lingering as he fought to appear confident and in control as his clan surrounded him, his duplicitous sister-by-marriage, and his best friend—former best friend. But he needed to sit down before he fell down. He needed to speak to Laurel to untangle everything they learned. It was too confusing for his still fuzzy mind.

"Lock them below. Separately," Brodie commanded.

"Brodie," Dominic turned to his brother. "She's still my wife. Put her under house arrest in a chamber."

"No, Dom. She's a danger to everyone, especially Laurel and you. I can't risk her wheedling her way out and coming after either of you. She goes to the dungeon but to a cell separate from Graham." Brodie's heart ached for his younger brother. The man's devastation was clear for everyone to see. He'd been besotted with his wife since the day they met, and she'd manipulated him every moment that they knew one another. "Come to my solar with Laurel and me."

Laurel walked beside Brodie as the three went to Brodie's solar. She signaled for Berta to send food. She would have preferred Brodie went straight to their bed, but he couldn't. She settled for pouring several drams of whisky, praying they would be fortifying and not soporific. Brodie eased himself into his chair before the fire, tugging Laurel onto his lap after she handed a mug of whisky to Dominic and poured a healthy portion for herself. Dominic sat in the other chair. No one spoke for a quarter of an hour, all lost in thought while sipping their drinks. Finally, Brodie reached out and placed his hand on Dominic's shoulder.

"Thank you," Dominic whispered. He turned a rueful look at Laurel. "I owe you an apology. I sensed Colina's dislike of you immediately. I thought she knew you from court or somewhere else. I trusted my wife's judgment, so when she didn't offer a warm welcome, neither did I. I'm sorry."

Laurel nodded. "I don't think there's really aught I can say to make this easier for you. But your apology is appreciated and accepted."

"What would you have me do?" Brodie asked Dominic.

"She doesn't deserve to retire to a convent. She killed our mother. That alone warrants her death, never mind how she's plotted against us."

"But you asked for her to go to a chamber," Brodie noted.

"She was going to have an accident or take her own life," Laurel whispered. She shot Brodie a pointed expression.

"Your wife is far too astute. Thank God you married her. We'd be dead by now if she were our enemy," Dominic mused. "You know what must be done, Brodie."

"Doesn't mean I have to like it if it pains you."

"I think it would pain me far more knowing she lived. I don't know what to say aboot Graham. He and I were close, but not as you were."

Laurel looked between the two brothers, their resemblance undeniable. A smile flickered at the corner of her lips. When Brodie asked what prompted it, she confessed, "I hope one day that we have two sons who look as much alike as you two do. And I hope they love and respect one another as much as you two do. If we're blessed with sons, they will have two fine men to look up to."

Brodie kissed Laurel's cheek warmed by her sentiments. He wondered if they were already on the path to that, but he knew it was too soon to tell. He turned his attention back to Dominic. "The stalks will go up this afternoon. They'll spend the night there. I would make it longer if Laurel and I didn't need to leave so soon. Tomorrow, Graham will go to the gallows, and Colina will go to the drowning-pool."

A shiver ran along Laurel's spine. She'd assumed that would be their fate, but to hear it aloud—especially Colina's fate—made her shudder. She understood they often drowned women for such crimes as Colina committed—adultery and treason—but she wasn't convinced it was a more humane or lenient death, like men argued. She thought the gallows were, assuming the person's neck snapped.

"We leave the day after tomorrow." Brodie's announcement jolted Laurel back to their conversation. They'd decided when to leave during their ride that morning, but they had told no one yet. "Will you be all right here?"

"Aye. It'll keep me occupied and give me purpose," Dominic nodded. "Brodie—"

"Aye?" Brodie waited for Dominic to continue.

"I'm sorry I didn't stay, that I came back here. Colina begged that I return, saying she feared she'd be unwell with worry. Now, I think she wanted to learn if I lived or died, so she could adjust her plans if I survived. I knew it was wrong to leave, but she'd been so adamant. I hadn't wanted to upset her."

Brodie nodded. He'd suspected as much, but he hadn't confronted Dominic. Returning to find Laurel missing had been a higher priority. With a night's sleep, his anger subsided. He'd opted to overlook it for the time being, intending to address it before they rode out the next time. He thought it would be better to be fresh in Dominic's mind before the next battle rather than long forgotten.

"It's forgiven."

The trio left the solar soon after. Dominic organized the raising of the stalks and the gallows, while Brodie and Laurel went to their chamber, so Brodie could rest.

FORTY-ONE

Laurel grimaced as Teine's hooves clattered on the stones within Stirling Castle's bailey. She dreaded returning, even if she was relieved their four days of soggy travel finally ended. With her head bowed against the wind and driving rain, she'd had plenty of time to contemplate how her life changed since the last time she was at court. She'd struggled the first day of the journey to rid her mind of the sight of Colina floundering as Dominic held her head below the water. Brodie offered to carry out her sentence, but Dominic said he'd brought the viper into Eden, so he would be the one to remove it. Brodie forced Graham to watch before he hanged from the gallows for his part in the treasonous plot.

"We will leave the moment the king allows it," Brodie pledged as he lifted Laurel from the saddle. He held the extra length of plaid over Laurel's head, but she was already soaked. They hurried inside, and Laurel led Brodie to his former chamber, using servants' stairs and passageways to avoid being recognized. They slipped into the chamber and shed their sopping wet clothes, huddling together in their spare plaids once Brodie built up the fire. They'd had little chance for intimacy while on the road. Between their guards' presence and Brodie's constant vigilance, there hadn't been a chance to slip away. They traveled with three score of warriors, so Laurel felt well protected, but she was glad for the privacy and the time alone with Brodie.

"Do you recall the last time we sat before this fire?" Brodie whispered against Laurel's ear before he trailed kisses along her neck and nipped at her bare shoulder.

"As I recall, we were lying, not sitting," Laurel corrected. She opened her plaid and leaned back, Brodie supporting her head as she laid down. His body hovered over her as she reached for him. Brodie's hand skimmed over her silky skin, his lips following its lead. His kisses scorched the inside of her thighs as his fingers peeled back the petals before his tongue lapped up her dew. She moaned as her hands clenched the plaid that laid around her. As Brodie's teeth raked over her sensitive nub, she raised her hips to him. When he slid two fingers into her sheath, she was certain she would float away.

"Thistle," Brodie murmured as he continued to lavish his attention on her core. She writhed as her belly tightened. "You're close."

"Yes," Laurel whispered. Increased pressure and speed from Brodie's fingers and a long draw on her nub between his lips pushed her over the edge. She willingly surrendered to the sensations Brodie created. She clawed at his back, silently begging him to shift so she could embrace him. When his length was within reach, she stroked with deliberate slowness. She brushed the tip against her entrance, smiling when Brodie growled. "I didn't want to wait, but you made me. I shall do the same."

Brodie nipped at her ear as she guided the head of his cock into her sheath. The moment her hand released him, Brodie surged forward, seating himself to the hilt. As their bodies moved together, they locked eyes and gazed at one another as the passion and need enveloped them. Nothing existed to them beyond their embrace. They rocked together in a rhythm they learned the first time they made love before the very fireplace that crackled beside them.

"Brodie," Laurel pleaded. She clung to him as their lips fused together, and they both increased the pace and force of their thrusts until they cried out together. Laurel's entire body tingled as pleasure coursed through her. Brodie's cock twitched as his seed emptied into Laurel. He rolled them so he rested on his back, his stitches reminding him that he shouldn't move with such disregard. But he'd gladly accepted the twinges of pain for the powerful release that came from making love to his wife. Laurel sighed, "I ken it's only been four days, but it feels like forever."

"Aye. I wish there were a way we could soar like a bird and fly as the crow does. We could be home without days of travel, days of hideous abstinence."

"To have such magic," Laurel smiled wistfully. "I don't want to be in Stirling, and I don't want to be at court. But I am happy to be before this fire with you. It reminds me of the first time. I'd never imagined a body could feel the way you make mine feel. I didn't know then the happiness you bring me now."

"I loved you then, Laurie. But I feared you didn't feel the same. I wanted to tell you, but I was too cowardly to face the possible rejection."

"I felt the same. I desperately wanted to tell you, but I feared making a fool of myself. But I knew even then what I know now: I love you and marrying you was the richest blessing I've ever received."

The couple laid before the fire, talking about everything and nothing as they held one another until they drifted off to sleep. The world outside their chamber door long forgotten.

Laurel gritted her teeth as Margaret Hay glared at her. Her courtship ended when Nelson died on the battlefield. But the woman whose eyes shot daggers at Laurel seemed to have forgotten that Liam Oliphant now courted her. Unimpressed with Margaret's attempt to intimidate her, Laurel rolled her eyes so everyone could see and turned her back on Margaret. But she came face to face with Catherine MacFarlane. The lady-in-waiting before her wore the same angry expression as Margaret. Her uncle, Andrew Mòr, refused to sign the betrothal agreement with Edgar Gunn once Andrew Óg explained Edgar's role in Laurel's abduction. From what Andrew Óg admitted when Laurel and Brodie found him at the evening meal the night following their arrival, his father had nearly torn him to shreds for suggesting the betrothal move forward. The irate laird asked how his son could be so daft as to think he'd create an alliance with a man who tried to harm the clan they'd just fought a battle alongside.

Sarah Anne came to stand beside Catherine and folded her arms, as though her posturing would intimidate Laurel. Rather than cower at the matching glares, Laurel laughed. Loudly. She folded her own arms and used her height to tilt her head forward and look down at the two women.

"Sulk and hiss as you please. I survived abduction, a battle, a night lost among the mountain peaks, and an attempt to kill me. Your pathetic attempt to intimidate me is just that: pathetic. Find someone else to bully. It didn't work on me when I was stuck with you before, and it won't work now."

"You're awfully full of yourself for someone whose husband was forced to accept her without a dowry," Sarah Anne snapped.

"Think what you will, but either way, I married Laird Campbell, and you're still a spinster."

"Penniless pauper. You seduced Laird Campbell, so he had no choice but to marry you," Sarah Anne pressed on.

"I wasn't penniless after you spent one hundred and sixty pounds on that gown and two others," Laurel said smugly. She no longer felt she needed to keep her secret. "Och, aye. I ken all aboot that. Do you want to ken how I do?"

Laurel's expression was patronizing, and she knew it would antagonize Sarah Anne.

"Probably because you wanted the gown for yourself and couldn't afford it," Margaret chimed in as she came to stand beside her sister.

Laurel cast her gaze around the queen's solar, grateful Queen Elizabeth was yet to join them. She pointed to the three women before her and to five more ladies-in-waiting. "Look at the bottom left of the embroidery on your bodice, tell me what you find."

Laurel waited, amusement tempting her to laugh again. But she lost the battle and laughed so hard she nearly wet herself as one stunned face after another looked in her direction. All except Sarah Anne. She'd long suspected the woman couldn't read or write. As the younger sister, it was clear her father hadn't given her the minimal tutelage Margaret received. She looked blankly at Laurel before her eyes darted from side to side, trying to read the cues to how she should react.

"It's an L and an R, Sarah Anne. I might have been the fourth daughter, but I'm still the daughter of an earl. He bothered to educate me. In case you truly don't know, Laurel begins with an L, and Ross begins with an R. I made the gowns each of you is wearing. The others already figured that out."

"You were a seamstress?" Margaret asked in disgust.

"Aye. And I've had the pleasure of watching ladies flounce around in my creations for years. You've looked down on me, thinking me a pauper, kenning my father wouldn't provide for me. But I kenned you'd have naught to show off, no way to preen, if it weren't for me. Tell me, have you found any gowns that compare to these since I left?" Laurel watched as eyes lowered and a few heads shook. "The best seamstress in Stirling suddenly disappears at the same time that Laurel Ross marries one of the most powerful lairds in the Scotland. An almighty coincidence. Look down on me all you wish, but I held the power to your social status while I was here. And I took it with me. You have naught to compete with. You're all as plain as you were the day you arrived. I gave you status, and now I've taken it away. Do you ken what you can do?" Laurel watched as the women looked at her questioningly. "You can sod off."

"Lady Campbell, I've missed your unique perspective on life at court." Laurel froze as Queen Elizabeth's words floated to her. When the woman said no more, she turned and dipped into a low curtsy that matched all the other women in the chamber. When they all rose, Laurel found the queen gazing at her, a suspiciously knowing expression in her eyes. "I long suspected you were the talented dressmaker, but none of my guards could ever catch you. I suspect it was your husband who deduced what you got up to. He is likely the only mon with the wits to keep up with you."

"We met when I was returning from purchasing fabric, Your Majesty," Laurel admitted.

"Well met, indeed." Queen Elizabeth opened her mouth to say more, but a page entered with three missives. He handed one to Laurel and gave the other two to Margaret and Catherine. Laurel broke the seal to hers, recognizing Brodie's penmanship immediately. She tore her gaze from the missive to look at the queen. Laurel didn't understand the missive, but she would oblige Brodie's request.

"Your Majesty, my husband requests my attendance in the Privy Council chamber," Laurel explained.

"And you wish permission to leave," Queen Elizabeth surmised, and Laurel nodded. The queen looked at Margaret and Catherine before she responded to Laurel. "What say yours, Lady Catherine and Lady Margaret?"

"Liam Oliphant requests I go to the Privy Council chamber as well, but why would I do that? There is naught there I wish to see or hear," Margaret sniffed. "I do not run to any mon. He may run to me."

"My cousin asks that I attend to him too," Lady Catherine replied. "Why would I wish to be stuck in a chamber full of men looking at maps and discussing things that don't interest me? If my cousin wishes to speak to me, he can find me at the evening meal."

Queen Elizabeth turned her attention back to Laurel. The royal raised her eyebrows at her former lady-in-waiting.

"If my husband asks me to attend him, there is a reason. May I go, Your Majesty?" Laurel prayed the woman didn't refuse her. She didn't sense it was anything urgent, but it was an excuse to leave the solar. She even wondered if that was Brodie's intention.

"You may go, Lady Campbell."

Laurel dipped a low curtsy, then swept out of the chamber before anyone could call her back.

FORTY-TWO

B rodie gritted his teeth as he glared at Liam Oliphant and noticed Andrew MacFarlane shifting nervously in his peripheral vision. He struggled not to reach out and wrap his hands around Liam's neck and squeeze until there was no air left in the man's body. It had displeased him to find Liam in the Privy Council chamber, but he thought the man would have the sense to keep his distance. To Brodie's annoyance, Liam approached him while Brodie waited for King Robert to acknowledge him.

"Seeking refuge after sennights with the shrew?" Liam grinned. "At least she didn't talk while she was with me."

Brodie fisted his hands at his side, keeping a fine leash on his temper lest he murder the man before the king's eyes. Andrew shifted to stand between him and Liam, his discomfort obvious. Brodie felt no sympathy for Andrew. He had shown his prowess on the battlefield and had fought valiantly, but that didn't mean Brodie had to enjoy his company.

"How is your bonnie bride, Campbell?" Robert the Bruce sauntered over, looking between Brodie and Liam.

"Not with me," Brodie grumbled before he bowed to the monarch. "She is well, Your Majesty. Despite what she endured at his hand," Brodie glared at Liam.

Robert the Bruce grimaced as he turned his own glare toward Liam. Brodie wished to resolve the matter that brought Laurel and him to court and then be on their way. He recognized Liam Oliphant was an unfortunate part of the events, but that didn't mean he intended to suffer the man's company.

"Is Lady Campbell with the queen?" King Robert asked Brodie.

"Aye, Your Majesty."

"I suppose she is happy to see familiar faces," King Robert offered. Brodie knew it for the test that it was.

"There are certain to be many familiar faces," Brodie responded.

"Right, then," King Robert turned to Liam, abandoning his attempt to goad Brodie. "Oliphant, I understand you originated the wager that Lady Campbell would remain unwed."

"Not exactly, Your Majesty," Liam clarified before grinning at Brodie. "I wagered that no mon could tame the harridan."

Brodie was certain his teeth would crack from how he clenched his jaw. He fought the urge to turn around and walk out, leaving the king and his advisors to stare at his back. He would not take Liam's bait.

"Is the Shrew of Stirling tamed?" King Robert asked Brodie. Brodie's nostrils flared as he turned his gaze to a man he'd considered a friend for many years. Their positions put distance between them, but Brodie never imagined the man he'd fought beside, slept beside, ate beside, and nearly died beside would insult his wife to his face. "What say you, Campbell?"

"There is naught to say that won't put me in your dungeon." Brodie crossed his arms, uncaring if he appeared surly. It kept him from lashing out.

"Come now, Campbell, it can't be that bad," King Robert smiled. "She'll come around. There are plenty of years ahead of you to bring her to heel."

Andrew coughed, but it sounded like a croak. He glanced

at Brodie before shooting King Robert a warning stare with a minor shake of his head. Only Andrew knew the dangerous ground the other two men trod; he didn't doubt for a moment that Brodie would defend Laurel's honor against anyone, including the Bruce. When he feared King Robert would say more, he turned the attention to the king.

"Your Majesty, I've seen Lady Campbell and Laird Campbell together. They are a couple clearly in love," Andrew declared.

"That doesn't mean she's obedient," Liam snarked.

"She doesn't have to be. She's my wife, not my dog," Brodie stated.

"You're being evasive because she has you by the bollocks, Campbell."

"*Laird Campbell,* Oliphant." Brodie's tone was calm, but the steel rang throughout the chamber as they gathered an audience.

"Perhaps a wager to see who speaks the truth," King Robert suggested.

"That wouldn't be wise," Brodie warned.

"So you admit you know you won't win," Liam gloated.

"You'd already run away to tattle, Oliphant." Brodie grimaced, remembering that he discovered Liam evaded the battle to travel to Sterling and convince King Robert that Brodie was the aggressor. "But MacFarlane will tell you what happened to the last two men to place a wager on my wife."

"Liam, Campbell took Nelson's head from his shoulders a moment before Montgomery skewered Matthew." Andrew opened his mouth to proclaim Laurel was the mastermind behind their victorious battle plan, but he swallowed his thought, lest he endanger her again.

"No coin will exchange hands," King Robert declared. "The winner will have the satisfaction of kenning he was right."

Brodie glared mutinously at the king. The Bruce shrugged before looking at Liam and Andrew. Liam practically bobbed on his toes like a child at Epiphany, while Andrew appeared to fight the urge to vomit. Brodie knew no matter what the king proposed, it would end with either Laurel or himself humiliated. He didn't understand why his friend would do this. As he watched Robert, he knew any friendship they'd once shared no longer existed. They'd gone in separate directions, and they had nothing in common now that they no longer fought a common enemy. He didn't mourn the loss of a friend, but he regretted he lost respect for a man he'd admired.

"Oliphant, you claim Lady Campbell will never be an obedient and obliging woman. Would you say Lady Margaret is such a woman?"

Liam's brow furrowed, confusion on his face. "That's why I believe she'd make a fitting wife."

"And MacFarlane, now that the deal is off with the Gunn, you shall need to find another groom for your cousin. Do you believe she shall be a modest wife to her husband?"

"Lady Catherine is demure by nature, Your Majesty," Andrew replied.

"Then we shall see which mon kens the woman in his life best." King Robert signaled his scribe to bring three sheets of parchment and three quills. "Jot a missive and request the women in question join you here. Give no reason for their attendance, merely say you require her presence. We shall see who comes first, and who comes most willingly."

Brodie scrawled his note to Laurel and sealed it. When all three missives were ready, the men handed them to a page, who ran off to deliver their messages. Brodie crossed his arms once more. He was confident Laurel would come, regardless of whether the other two did. He was eager to see her because he despised wasting time with the king that he could spend with his wife, but he was nervous about the reception she would receive. If anyone humiliated Laurel, Brodie would take her and leave without a glance over their shoulder. When the smile fell from the Bruce's face, Brodie was certain the man understood his silent warning.

Laurel hurried along the passageways until she reached the corridor that held the Privy Council chamber. She smoothed out her skirts and ran her hand over her hair. Taking a calming breath, she gracefully approached the door, making her way past petitioners who stared at her. She hadn't seen Brodie since that morning, when he'd kissed her goodbye before he left for the lists at sunrise. She hoped he appreciated her surprise. She'd donned the gown she wore to their wedding, made from the fabric Brodie gave her as a betrothal gift.

The doors opened to her, and she dipped her head in thanks to the royal guards. She spotted Brodie immediately. His posture made her apprehensive as she passed her gaze over the chamber's other occupants. She struggled to hide her loathing when she noticed Liam standing near the king and Brodie. She supposed the pugnacious man was the reason for Brodie's scowl. She approached but missed a step when the king howled with laughter.

"Enough," Brodie snapped. "You've seen what you wanted. I'm taking my wife to our chamber."

"No," King Robert stated, suddenly serious. "I shall speak to your wife. Approach, Lady Campbell."

Laurel drew closer, her eyes locked with Brodie's but unable to interpret his expression. He looked furious, but she couldn't understand why this was so if the king appeared jovial. Liam and Andrew looked annoyed, but nothing appeared out of sorts enough to warrant Brodie's ire. When she was within arm's reach, Brodie held out his hand. She slid hers into his, and King Robert laughed again.

"Bruce," Brodie warned under his breath. Laurel's knees shook at Brodie's affront. Robert turned a warning glare at Brodie, but he no longer laughed.

"Thank you for coming, Lady Campbell. I'm certain it surprised you when your husband summoned you here. Before

I explain why, are Lady Margaret and Lady Catherine not with you?"

"Nay, Your Majesty," Laurel said softly.

"And why not?" The king pressed.

"They didn't wish to come here."

"Why not?"

Laurel blinked as the Bruce continued to push for more details. She looked up at Brodie, who nodded. She met Robert's gaze. "They weren't interested in coming here because they said it was boring. They believe Oliphant and MacFarlane will go to them, but they will not come here."

"And why are you here, Lady Campbell?"

"Because my husband asked me."

King Robert crossed his arms, a satisfied expression on his face as he stared at Liam and Andrew. Brodie had realized Robert's motive when the king asked about Margaret and Catherine's disposition. But he still resented Robert using Laurel for his amusement.

"My wife and I are retiring," Brodie announced.

Laurel frowned, not understanding why she came only for them to leave. "Brodie?" His expression told her not to ask anything more. She nodded and took the arm he offered.

"Not yet, Campbell." Robert said. Laurel felt the tension in Brodie's arm, and it made her more anxious.

"Lady Campbell, I instructed the men to write missives to each of you to see who would come when beckoned. Oliphant and MacFarlane were certain Lady Margaret and Lady Catherine wouldn't hesitate since they are so demure."

Laurel nearly swallowed her tongue to keep herself from laughing.

"I take it that is not how you would describe the ladies in question," the Bruce observed. "Oliphant was certain you would be the one to refuse. He doesn't believe that your husband has tamed you. You should know that MacFarlane spoke on your behalf."

Laurel looked at Andrew, and he wanted to melt into the

floor. He had no idea what she would say, but he was certain he would have nothing on par to say in return. "You spoke on my behalf to inform the king and Liam that I'm now tamed?"

"Nay, Lady Campbell. I said that you and Laird Campbell love one another," Andrew clarified. It stunned him when Laurel said nothing more.

"It would seem Campbell was up to the challenge to tame the Shrew of Stirling," King Robert crowed. Laurel flinched, knowing the humiliation would come, but still not prepared for how it stung. "If only there had been money on the wager."

"Wager?" Laurel whispered as she turned her face up to Brodie. His heart ached to see the pain in his wife's eyes. She believed the worst, and he didn't blame her for how the king made it sound.

"Don't carp at your husband, Lady Campbell. He's the reason there was no coin involved. He insisted we not wager on you. But it seems he won nonetheless."

"How is watching you humiliate my wife winning?" Brodie snapped. "You made your point. You even think you took my side, but all you've done is hurt Laurie. Call on me when you need my army or my coin, but do not call on me as your friend." Brodie wrapped his arm around Laurel and turned them toward the door. He didn't stop when the king called out to him. The guards barred their way at the door. Neither of them looked back at King Robert or anyone else in the chamber. They stood together, their backs straight, and their heads held high.

"If anyone has been tamed, it's the Lion of Lorne. Well done, Lady Campbell." Neither Brodie nor Laurel acknowledged King Robert's proclamation, instead walking through the doors when they opened. When they heard the doors close, Brodie swept Laurel into his arms and carried her to their chamber, where he explained the entire farce. Laurel remained quiet, nodding from time to time. It was only early afternoon, but they climbed into bed, where they found solace in one another's arms as their bodies became one. Neither felt tamed as they moved together, their passion combustible. But Laurel no longer felt like a pauper or a hellion. She was richer for having found love with a man who'd now be known as the Lion of Lorne. Just like a phoenix, Brodie's moniker rose from the ashes of her own.

EPILOGUE

"Bear?" Laurel walked to the entrance of the Balnagown lists. She shaded her eyes as she watched Brodie approach, his gray hair swept his ever-expansive shoulders. Two steps behind him, fanned out like the five peaks of Ben Lui, their sons followed their father. Brodie wrapped his arm around Laurel's waist and lifted her off her feet for a passionate kiss that still made her toes curl in her slippers.

"Good morn, thistle." Brodie nuzzled her ear as he whispered. "I thought you might sleep till midday."

"I wasn't the one complaining aboot being too auld to chase me around that bed," Laurel giggled, her peal of laughter making her sound more like a young girl than a matron in her fifth decade. Brodie claimed that Laurel looked no different at fifty-six than she did at twenty-six. She accepted the compliment graciously, even if she didn't agree. While Brodie's hair was now gray, her sixty-eight-year-old husband was more handsome than any man she knew—that is, besides their five sons. He didn't swing his sword like he once did, but he still went to the lists and trained their men.

"Have you seen Monty and Donnan?"

"Aye," Brodie nodded before he looked over his shoulder at Montgomery, Donnan, Broderick, Aidan, and Niall.

"Not those two. The auld bodachs who complain aboot their aching bones just so they can have another dram of whisky in the morn."

"Your brother and Donnan are still in the lists." Brodie put Laurel back on her feet and pointed past their sons to the far end of the lists.

Laurel shielded her eyes once more and squinted. She made out the figures in the distance, her brother holding up a sword, and Donnan pointing as he explained something to a young warrior. She scowled, knowing the two men weren't nearly as aged as they claimed; in fact, they were a few years younger than Brodie. Her husband whistled, making Monty and Donnan look in their direction. If the men hadn't recognized Laurel's family, they would have recognized her hair. She and Monty's heads still sported shades of red, even if they both had white hairs interspersed. The men made their way to where Laurel and Brodie stood with their sons.

"Aches and pains, my arse," Laurel greeted them.

"Good morn to you, sister," Monty said as he dropped a kiss on Laurel's cheek.

"Will you be ready for the ceremony at sunset?"

"Laurel, stop fretting. Everything is already in place," Monty assured her.

"If you say so," Laurel nodded.

"Mama, you ken it's because you've been buzzing aboot the bailey like a bee bent on finding every bit of honey," the younger Monty grinned.

Laurel cast her second-oldest son a withering glare only a mother could manage. With a snort, her son wrapped his arms around Laurel and pulled her against his massive chest, nearly suffocating her. Though all her children were adults, it still surprised her when her wee bairns felt as sturdy as Brodie always had.

"The better question is whether you'll be ready," Laurel said as she tapped her son's chest, nearly suffocating.

"Aye, Mama. I'm ready. You and Da, and Uncle Monty

have prepared me for this for years. It feels odd that it's finally time, but I am ready." Young Monty straightened as he looked at his uncle, Laird Montgomery Ross. He'd admired the older man as both an uncle and a laird since he was big enough to toddle over to him and attach himself to his uncle's leg, begging him to walk as he clung on. For his part, Monty always had a special bond with his namesake, and that day he would officially bestow the title of laird on the youth.

Laurel glanced at the older Monty and Donnan and smiled. The couple stood shoulder-to-shoulder, appearing as always to be a brotherly pair. The only people on Ross land that day who knew differently were Laurel, Brodie, and the younger Monty. A riding accident five years after Laurel and Brodie married offered her brother the opportunity to alter the course of his life. The former Laird Ross was pressuring Monty to marry, but Laurel's brother had evaded the matrimonial noose year after year. When he was injured while on patrol, he seized the chance to claim his injuries kept him from siring any children. It freed Monty and Donnan to remain together, neither having to forsake the other or live a lie with a wife.

Laurel and Monty's two older sisters had only borne daughters. Laurel's five sons became the closest living males to Montgomery Mòr. Broderick, named for his father, was Brodie's own heir. As the second oldest, Montgomery Óg, became his uncle's heir two years after the accident. Neither clan received the initial announcement well, but the alliance between the Campbells and Rosses had only grown stronger when the elder Montgomery assumed the lairdship. More than twenty years after being named the heir apparent to Clan Ross, the day had come where Montgomery Óg would be named Laird Ross. Laurel and Brodie agreed their son needed to know and understand the truth about his uncle and Donnan if he was to lead in Montgomery Mòr's stead. They'd feared their son's reaction, but he'd only shrugged and admitted he already knew. History had repeated itself, and at much the same age as Laurel was when she discovered Monty and Donnan in the woods, the younger Monty had found the lovers in an embrace when he burst into the elder Monty's solar. He'd kept the secret for more than a decade.

"Nephew, it isn't easy to hand over the privilege to lead our clan, but I can no longer ride into battle alongside you. I can no longer make the long journeys to court, nor do I have the patience for negotiations anymore. I know how much it pained your mother to allow you and Aidan to foster here, but I will always be grateful that she did. I retire as laird today, and Donnan retires as my second. You shall rise from tánaiste to laird, and Aidan shall take your place as tánaiste until you have a son. Our clans are one, just as they have been since your parents married. Now it shall be official. The new laird shall be Montgomery Campbell."

"But for the love of God, find a Ross woman to marry," Donnan Mòr quipped. "Your aunts will never cease harping at you if you don't."

"Who knew ma wee hellion would be the lamb to yer two aulder sisters' lions," Brodie chuckled as Laurel pursed her lips. Life with Brodie filled her with more love and happiness than she imagined one person could possess. They still went for rides almost daily, stopping to enjoy the Highland air and the expansive landscape that surrounded them. Laurel rarely looked back at her days at court. Her life among the hills and lochs was too fulfilling to linger over memories of her stifling life as a lady-in-waiting.

Laurel fought against the tears that threatened as she stood beside Brodie in the Balnagown Great Hall. With his arm wrapped around her waist like it so often was, and her head resting against his shoulder, Laurel couldn't imagine a prouder moment. She watched her son swear his fealty to the clan of her birth. Her brother pinned the Clan Ross brooch onto his nephew's Ross plaid, naming Montgomery Óg Campbell the new Laird Ross.

She lost the fight to control her tears of happiness when Broderick stepped forward and thrust out his arm for a warrior's handshake with his brother. The gesture signified the renewal of the Campbell-Ross alliance. Their oldest son had assumed Brodie's duties and position as laird a year earlier. Brodie's vision wasn't what it once was, and swollen knuckles made it difficult for him to write and grip his sword. Despite retiring as Brodie's tánaiste, Dominic remained at Kilchurn while they traveled.

"Wheest, Laurie," Brodie whispered. "You shall soak my leine." Brodie kissed the top of Laurel's head, closing his eyes as he inhaled his wife's lavender scent. When he opened them and gazed at his two sons—now lairds—and the three who stood behind in support, he couldn't imagine a life without Laurel beside him. A few carelessly tossed words over too many drams of whisky had brought him immeasurable happiness. Laurel was no tamer than she'd been on the day he met her. She was still as wild as a thistle, with roots that wound deep into the Highland soil. He'd promised her freedom, and she'd trusted him when she'd trusted no other. He never took for granted the faith his wife placed in him. Brodie and Laurel found peace and love together. The bear and the thistle. They were as much a part of the Highlands as the Highlands were a part of them.

"Then I shall just have to help you find a new one, Brodie," Laurel whispered in return, her hand sliding precariously close to his backside before Brodie felt a small pinch. She may have appeared the staid Lady Campbell, wife to the mighty Brodie Campbell—the Lion of Lorne—and mother to five sons, but she still had the heart of a hellion.

"Promise, thistle?"

Laurel's answer was a grin and a wink. Brodie sighed as he held Laurel tighter. Laurel claimed that he'd taken her from rags to riches by offering her his love. But Brodie was certain there was no richer person in the Highlands than he as his wife beamed up at him, love shining in her hazel eyes.

"I love you, Brodie."

"I love you, Laurie. Now and forever."

The couple watched as the next generation of Rosses and Campbells forged their future together.

THANK YOU FOR READING A HELLION AT THE HIGHLAND COURT

Celeste Barclay, a nom de plume, lives near the Southern California coast with her husband and sons. Growing up in the Midwest, Celeste enjoyed spending as much time in and on the water as she could. Now she lives near the beach. She's an avid swimmer, a hopeful future surfer, and a former rower. When she's not writing, she's being a wife and mom.

Subscribe to Celeste's bimonthly newsletter to receive exclusive insider perks.
Subscribe Now
Have you chatted with Celeste's hunky heroes? Are you new to Celeste's books or want insider exclusives before anyone else? Subscribe for free to chat with the men of Celeste's *The Highland Ladies* series.

Chat Now

www.celestebarclay.com

Join the fun and get exclusive insider giveaways, sneak peeks,
and new release announcements in
Celeste Barclay's Facebook Ladies of Yore Group

THE HIGHLAND LADIES

THE CLAN SINCLAIR

His Highland Lass **BOOK 1 SNEAK PEEK**

She entered the great hall like a strong spring storm in the northern most Highlands. Tristan Mackay felt like he had been blown hither and yon. As the storm settled, she left him with the sweet scents of heather and lavender wafting towards him as she approached. She was not a classic beauty, tall and willowy like the women at court. Her face and form were not what legends were made of. But she held a unique appeal unlike any he had seen before. He could not take his eyes off of her long chestnut hair that had strands of fire and burnt copper running through them. Unlike the waves or curls he was used to, her hair was unusually straight and fine. It looked like a waterfall cascading down her back. While she was not tall, neither was she short. She had a figure that was meant for a man to grasp and hold onto, whether from the front or from behind. She had an aura of confidence and charm, but not arrogance or conceit like many good looking women he had met. She did not seem to know her own appeal. He could tell that she was many things, but one thing she was not was his.

His Bonnie Highland Temptation **BOOK 2**

His Highland Prize **BOOK 3**

His Highland Pledge **BOOK 4**

His Highland Surprise **BOOK 5**

Their Highland Beginning **BOOK 6**

PIRATES OF THE ISLES

The Blond Devil of the Sea **BOOK 1 SNEAK PEEK**

Caragh lifted her torch into the air as she made her way down the precarious Cornish cliffside. She made out the hulking shape of a ship, but the dead of night made it impossible to see who was there. She and the fishermen of Bedruthan Steps weren't expecting any shipments that night. But her younger brother Eddie, who stood watch at the entrance to their hiding place, had spotted the ship and signaled up to the village watchman, who alerted Caragh.

As her boot slid along the dirt and sand, she cursed having to carry the torch and wished she could have sunlight to guide her. She knew these cliffs well, and it was for that reason it was better that she moved slowly than stop moving once and for all. Caragh feared the light from her torch would carry out to the boat. Despite her efforts to keep the flame small, the solitary light would be a beacon.

When Caragh came to the final twist in the path before the sand, she snuffed out her torch and started to run to the cave where the main source of the village's income lay in hiding. She heard movement along the trail above her head and knew the local fishermen would soon join her on the beach. These men, both young and old, were strong from days spent pulling in the full trawling nets and hoisting the larger catches onto their boats. However, these men weren't well-trained swordsmen, and the fear of pirate raids was ever-present. Caragh feared that was who the villagers would face that night.

The Dark Heart of the Sea **BOOK 2**

The Red Drifter of the Sea **BOOK3**

The Scarlet Blade of the Sea **BOOK 4 Coming March 2021**

VIKING GLORY

Leif **BOOK 1 SNEAK PEEK**

Leif looked around his chambers within his father's longhouse and breathed a sigh of relief. He noticed the large fur rugs spread throughout the chamber. His two favorites placed strategically before the fire and the bedside he preferred. He looked at his shield that hung on the wall near the door in a symbolic position but waiting at the ready. The chests that held his clothes and some of his finer acquisitions from voyages near and far sat beside his bed and along the far wall. And in the center was his most favorite possession. His oversized bed was one of the few that could accommodate his long and broad frame. He shook his head at his longing to climb under the pile of furs and on the stuffed mattress that beckoned him. He took in the chair placed before the fire where he longed to sit now with a cup of warm mead. It had been two months since he slept in his own bed, and he looked forward to nothing more than pulling the furs over his head and sleeping until he could no longer ignore his hunger. Alas, he would not be crawling into his bed again for several more hours. A feast awaited him to celebrate his and his crew's return from their latest expedition to explore the isle of Britannia. He bathed and wore fresh clothes, so he had no excuse for lingering other than a bone weariness that set in during the last storm at sea. He was eager to spend time at home no matter how much he loved sailing. Their last expedition had been profitable with several raids of monasteries that yielded jewels and both silver and gold, but he was ready for respite.

Leif left his chambers and knocked on the door next to his. He heard movement on the other side, but it was only moments before his sister, Freya, opened her door.

"That armband suits you well. It compliments your muscles," Leif smirked and dodged a strike from one of those muscular arms.

"At least one of us inherited our father's prowess. Such a shame it wasn't you."

Made in the USA
Coppell, TX
26 August 2021